Salthill

ST. MARTIN'S PRESS
NEW YORK

JUDITH BARNES

Salthill

Grateful acknowledgment is made for permission to reprint the following:

"Sunday Morning Prophecy" from *The Collected Poems of Langston Hughes* by Langston Hughes. Copyright © 1994 by The Estate of Langston Hughes. Used by permission of Alfred A. Knopf, a division of Random House, Incorporated, 1993.

"Long Distance Call" by Muddy Waters. Copyright © renewed 1959, Watertoons Music (BMI)/ Administered by BUG. All Rights Reserved. Used by Permission.

"(I'm Your) Hoochie Coochie Man" by Willie Dixon. Copyright © 1957, 1964 (renewed) HOOCHIE COOCHIE MUSIC (BMI)/Administered by BUG. All Rights Reserved. Used by Permission.

Book design by Michelle McMillian

Library of Congress Cataloging-in-Publication Data
Barnes, Judith.
    Salthill : a novel / Judith Barnes.—1st ed.
      p. cm.
    ISBN 0-312-29018-7
    1. African American horsemen and horsewomen—Fiction. 2. African American men— Fiction. 3. British Columbia—Fiction. 4. Rural families—Fiction. 5. Horse trainers— Fiction. 6. Race relations—Fiction. 7. Family farms—Fiction. 8. Horse farms—Fiction. 9. Ranch life—Fiction. I. Title.

PS3602.A834 S25 2002
813'.6—dc21
    2002068360

First Edition: October 2002

10 9 8 7 6 5 4 3 2 1

For Bereneice

Acknowledgments

I would like to express my gratitude to the people who helped me write this book:

Sands Hall, author, playwright, actor and editor, under whose guidance I wrote and rewrote, for her generous support and insight from the beginning; my agents, Michael Carlisle and Michelle Tessler of Carlisle & Company; Kelley Ragland, my editor at St. Martin's, for her enthusiasm and vision; Susan Taylor McMurray; Anne Wade; Alison Leslie Gold, author; Bonnie Ross; Consilia Geraghty; Rita Teves; Oakley Hall and the staff of Squaw Valley Community of Writers; the James Jones Literary Society; and my guiding spirit, Sebastian Bermudes.

The Skillihawk Region
British Columbia, Canada, 1946

I may be pensive said
the king, for I have seen
the marvellest sight
that ever I saw.
—*Le Morte d'Arthur*

Chapter One

THAT WEEK GREY WENT into Four Queens, and took Harris with him.

They left the valley and drove the switchback road over the mountains. As they labored uphill, the Enid rushed downhill beside them in its gorge of rough yellow shale. They crossed a bridge with red trusses like upside-down tulips; the tires shuddered and bounced over the railroad ties that floored it. Harris looked down through the railing into dark blue water creaming around logs and boulders.

It was a cold late spring day, with cloud shadows lying over grassland hatched with Russel fencing, snake and buck fencing. Cattle and horses dotted the redgrass or stood in bunches, their heads together as if in conference.

The two men did not speak. As always, Grey made a point of ignoring his hired man's hostility, which seemed to follow a law of nature, like an untreated illness or the conduction of heat along copper wire. Harris rebuffed every attempt at friendship; to be alone with him was presently to give up speech. Other men moved gingerly around him, base errors as yet uncommitted clanging and pitching in their ears. He was a quick, resourceful worker. For the three weeks he had been at Salthill, it had had to be enough.

He had lost his gaunt look and filled out. The hands that could persuade a horse to do anything and enjoy doing it rested one on a thigh; the other was cupped gently over the crown of the Stetson Grey had lent him to supplement the cloth cap. His profile was smooth basalt; the gloss of the eye, old-leaf green in its luminous hollow, turned to fix out the window. The hooded lid and tarry lashes gave him a feral, sequestered look.

A seam of water showed through scattered woods bordering the fields. As it widened, Harris, studying the landscape intently, saw that it was the long end of a lake standing among the trees. Homesteads with fenced-in gardens appeared by the road. The white hull of a boat went by, a dock, some buildings. A church steeple rose above silver and canoe birches. They were in Four Queens.

Instead of driving into town, they turned down a side road and bumped over a set of tracks. Above rows of shunted boxcars and slag-roofed metal sheds, the Canadian Pacific Railroad station appeared, its roof and gables checkered with soot.

The stockyard pens were packed with cattle, their moony lowing sounding on the air like the magnified grizzling of bees. Piwonka rode over to meet them on his palomino. He was a man of about sixty, chunky and short in the leg, in tooled boots and jeans, a vest with the wool side in under a long-skirted corduroy coat. His Resistol was pushed back on his head, the hair under it the shade of ground pepper.

"I don't need your help, you old fool," he barked while the palomino shifted and rolled his polished hips. "You're just here to get a side of beef."

"Hah. You're too cheap to hire help so you get your neighbors to do your work for you," retorted Grey. "Marv, this is Harris. He'll teach that outfit of yours how to ride without busting a leg. Harris, Marv Piwonka."

Harris flicked Grey a contemptuous look. Piwonka examined him briefly, taking in the eyes under the hat brim, the scar from the temple to the mouth, repugnantly shiny and grape-colored. Whoever had done that had laid his face wide open.

"What he means," said Piwonka, "is a bronco broke my foreman's leg for him last week and this one here's giving me a bad time because I had to ask for some manpower. Glad to meet you."

Harris nodded distantly.

"Anyhow this lot's off to Quesnel," went on Piwonka cheerfully. "Twelve-twenty on the live freight hauler. I got two thousand head of cattle below the pass and five hundred on the upper range. I got stock scattered all over the place. Ain't you lucky you just raise horses?"

"I don't know, Marv," said Grey, with a grimace at the cattle milling and bumping. "Horses don't smell as good as cows."

"Can't eat a horse, either. Not if you want to keep your friends anyway. Let's have Nevill get you mounted up. We'll cakewalk this stuff in and go for a beer after. Nevill!" he shouted. "Get these boys a couple horses, with a nice gentle nag for St. Oegger here."

Nevill hailed them from beyond the pens, where a few cowponies clustered at a rail with their tails tucked in like whippets. The shout was faint and spent itself like dying brass, because they were on the plain.

As they came to the end of the lane where it debouched into the inner yard, two men, one dark, the other blond, with chaps over his jeans, moved away from the fence they had been leaning against and blocked the way. Their smiles should have been warning enough. But by then it was too late. By then, Grey thought later, there was nothing he could have done to stop them. They were men, after all, he and Harris. Men did not walk away from the threat in a smile.

They all stopped in the narrow passage.

"Well, gawd *damn*," said the man in chaps, in a loud, jovial voice. "Look what the day done brought us."

"Guess the boss hired him to dance a jig while we work," said the other. "You know them jigaboos just *luv* to dance!"

Americans, thought Grey, dismayed. The flattened vowels, the drawl more authentic than Piwonka's, who could drop his anytime he liked. The faces, boyish though they were no longer young, were at odds with the glinting old eyes. The grins were a chirpy parody of humor.

He cast a glance at the man beside him. Harris was standing bare-headed in the lane. His hat dangled from his hand, between two fingers; his expression was a hardening and settling of his habitual remote look.

"I hadn't realized how noticeable he is," Grey said later to his friend Tom Pushkin. "He's as hard to ignore as a lynx sitting on a rock."

"They would've noticed him anyway," said Tom.

Grey felt no apprehension for himself, only that dread that greets the sensitive man when he knows another is about to be laid bare by insult in his presence. "Please let us by," he said firmly.

"Don't matter what he's here for," drawled Chaps, ignoring him, grinning broadly at Harris. "I ain't loadin' cattle with no nigger."

From the corner of his eye, Grey saw the hat drop to the ground.

"Harris." He put out his hand palm down, like a crossing guard. Harris pushed past it.

"Ah, pardon; are you addressing me?" he asked in a friendly tone.

Chaps goggled. "Shit, I guess so. You the only nigger *I* see here. What-all you going to do about it, boy?"

Harris spoke in a voice so hushed, almost a whisper, that from five feet away Grey heard only fragments of words.

Chaps drew his head back sharply. The grin switched to an incredulous gape. "Why you fuckin' sonofa—" He threw a wild punch. Harris side-stepped swiftly and kicked him in the crotch. All the weight and heft of his body went into it. The man dropped with a scream. Harris kicked him in the face. His head snapped back and scarlet bloomed around his mouth.

Grey grasped at Harris and was knocked back, staggering.

"Marvin! Nevill!" he shouted.

He seized Harris by the shoulders with both hands and hauled back. In spite of his superior weight, it was like trying to pull a bough from a tree. As he struggled against the frantic strength, losing ground, Grey felt a blow in his face. He staggered back again, swearing. Blood spurted from over one eyebrow. He groped hurriedly in his jacket for a kerchief but the blood was pouring into his eye socket now, blinding him. He found the kerchief and applied pressure to his brow, seeing with his good eye Chap's buddy jump in and lurch away, then the hatless booted figure kicking, releasing a strangled grunt with every blow.

Nevill ran up, moaning with haste, and dove in. Cursing scalp wounds, sponging furiously, Grey watched them all go down. They rolled over Chaps; the inert legs jiggled violently under their weight. Then Nevill lay on his back with the wind knocked out of him.

Harris leaped to his feet, looking pensive. The dark man was upright but weaving, his hair varnished to his skull in patches with bright blood. He closed on Harris. They exchanged blows, clutched, slid full-length to the ground. Harris got his opponent in a headlock. The dark man thrashed feebly, then flipped on his side. They lay on the path like spooning lovers. With the soaked wad to his eye, Grey moved forward, seeking a scruff or crook. He heard a hiss, saw the gleam of a blade travel along the heaving belly, in the brown hand.

"You're dead, motherfucker," said Harris to the head straining in the vise of his arm.

There was a rush of hooves as Piwonka rode over them on the palomino, lashing left and right with his quirt. The lash knocked Harris flying. He rolled and bounded back to his feet as if made of india rubber. The palomino reared, eyes bulging, and tried to skew around on his haunches. Piwonka kicked him forward. As the horse shot past, he leaned over with a creak and pop of saddle leather and grabbed Harris by the jacket, lifting him nearly off the ground. Nevill closed in on the other side. Harris shucked out of the jacket in one swift movement and punched Nevill in the mouth. The knife flashed and skidded along the path.

Piwonka shook out his rope, tossed the loop over the wild dark head and shoulders, and flipped the rope around the horn. The palomino backed swiftly, snapping the rope taut. Harris's feet left the ground. They backed up the lane and into the yard.

The air was ripe with shaky curses and cattle bawling. The whistle shrieked, drowning all of it, as the twelve-twenty from Winnipeg streamed in over the tracks, on time.

Chapter Two

SUMMONED FROM FOUR QUEENS by the yard office, the sheriff looked Chaps over. "Jesus. Who started this?"

"Th' one that's out cold," mumbled Nevill painfully. "He threw the first punch. But that black's a dirty-fighting son of a bitch."

The sheriff approached Harris. "You all right, son?"

"You touch me, I'll fucking kill you," said Harris. His arms were still pinned back, his face bleached under streaks of blood and dirt.

"Here here, that's no way to talk. Brewie, give me a hand with him."

Grey came over with the yard officer. "Harris. Steady on, man."

"Go fuck yourself."

"He's nuts," said the yard officer, looking scandalized.

"Come on, son, this isn't doing you any good," said the sheriff. "You'll have your say."

They urged him forward, one on either side. Grey had a look at his eyes, bleak with their load of hate, then Harris lunged. The yard officer landed on his back and lay swearing. The sheriff pulled out a cosh and cuffed Harris behind the ear. Harris grunted and looked stunned, but stayed on his feet. They snapped manacles on and hoisted him into the sedan with their hands under his armpits.

They drove into Four Queens for their beer. The hotel and livery stable had burned to the ground in 1902 after the Gold Rush, but the saloon that had given the town its name still stood halfway along the main street, a tin-roofed cedar building between the bootmaker and the local newspaper.

The upstairs had been a brothel. The vacant rooms, with unboarded windows gaping like mouths to expose palates of ribbed ceiling, bore to the last degree the air peculiar to such places of being haunted. Grey's daughters, teenage Flavia and eleven-year-old Elsa, knew about the brothel; imagined ghost parties, a piano tinkling, the powder of yellow lamplight at mysterious and lively midnight. The men would wear Prince Albert coats and the women rustling gowns, or the pantaloons such women wore to entertain. Their garments left an almost visible essence of violet on the dust. You could smell it, if you sat on the stairs without speaking.

The railroad party found a table near the bar.

"He really meant to kill 'em," said Piwonka. "They get that blind look when they're playing for keeps. And could he move? Shoot, he was regular greased lightning."

"Didn't last more'n a couple minutes," said the yard officer. "Worst fight I ever saw."

Nevill sucked cautiously at a beer, nursing his mouth. "Didn't care what he did."

"He didn't like being called a nigger," said Grey. There was a plaster on his forehead. "Where the hell do you get your help, Marv? That's not the way a man's measure is taken here. Nevill or Blaise would never speak that way to anyone."

"I know it," said Piwonka gloomily. "They'd have more sense, for one thing. I get my casual labor the way you did; they drift into my yard. Are you going to keep him on after he belted you in the face?"

Grey thought of the ambulance arriving for the injured, one on a gurney, the other, drunken and red-streaked, having to be held up to walk. The nearest hospital was at Darmstadt.

"I don't think he even knew I was there," he said. He added, "He has a gift with horses."

Piwonka grunted. "He's got eyes like an old whore."

"A colorful analogy, Marv. When did you last see one?"

There was a shower of laughter. Piwonka grinned.

"Just don't send him to do any work for me," he said. "Dai or Gordon can help out if need be. Keep that knife-toting black out of my sight and we'll stay friends."

"Wish we'd found it," said Brewer. "The knife."

"Dagos carry 'em," said Nevill.

"I don't know about that," said Piwonka, relenting. "I got good eyes and I didn't see one, so maybe there wasn't one."

"I saw it," said Nevill darkly. "I know what I saw."

When Grey got back to Salthill, Gordon and Daithi had the news already through the country grapevine, an instrument more efficient than any newspaper or radio.

"Is he going to stay in gaol?" asked Gordon, looking rather pleased. Not that he smiled or appeared gratified, but there was a softening of the planes of his face, as though some tension had gone out of it. Grey was so accustomed to his son's harboring of self that he paid no attention to it.

"Ah, he's a mutt, gettin' worked up fur bein' called a name," said Daithi with cheerful scorn. "What d'ye think he said to get t'other to send off a blow like that? Must've been something dreatful, aye?"

"I don't think I want to know," said Grey.

Grey rose early and dressed in a white shirt and tie, an Eisenhower jacket and gray slacks. He got into the truck and drove to Darmstadt, stopping at Dee's General Store outside Four Queens to buy petrol. Darmstadt, the provincial seat, was 116 miles distant. When he pulled out of Dee's it was still dark, the dark of very early morning when the sky is chilled to a starred brilliance and the earth appears as a pale horizon along its shore.

At the junction to the CPR station he picked up the Skillihawk Trail and drove northeast. The forests of aspen, ponderosa and yellow pine flattened into open plain, much of it bog. Spectral trees grew like shipwrecks out of the shallow lakes glimmering in the twilight before dawn. Occasionally, on higher ground, were the remains of a defunct homestead: crushed-in barn roofs, cabins with black gaps for windows, fences smashed and buried under creeper. He passed the highway to the sea channels, which he had last seen from an RAF flyer on the flight that had decided him on settling in Canada. There had been neither time nor funds since then to explore the coast with its isolated settlements, the oceans filled with drowned mountains he had read of.

The sky brightened, and he remembered to turn off his headlights.

The mossed and sedged lowlands gave way to wooded summits. The McKenna curved toward him, its great scythe awaiting the sheen of daylight. He drove through an Indian reserve. A circlet of bungalows stood well back on either side of the road, smoke from their chimneys pluming on the dull air. On the way out he passed a miniature piazza fenced in wrought iron, with a cluster of tombstones within. One stone was capped with an infantry helmet. He slowed, curious. There was a fist-sized hole through the crown. The dolmens were whitewashed and decorated with dried statice and sweet william, Brownie snapshots with deckled borders, obsidian and colored beads. A long-braided native man trudged over a field behind the bungalows, following the line of the trees.

He reached the plain, sparsely wooded except around the infrequent settlements. The road ran alongside the river now, as so many roads in Canada did. On the far side of a newly macadamed bridge, beyond a lumberyard and mill straddling long scars of demolished shingle, the city of Darmstadt came in view.

In spite of its postwar attempts at vivification, Grey had always found Darmstadt bleak. Odd for an Englishman—insulated by breeding from the dampening of the spirits caused by cold (or hot) depressing climes, insulation often fortified in those cursed (or blessed) with the Celtic miasma by over-imbibing of fermented grains—to dislike a place merely because it was cheerless; but he disliked Darmstadt. The surrounding plain and lackluster northern sky gave the town an air of wreckage washed ashore. The modern spires, spindles and glass-walled cubes erected for some royal visitation vexed him, standing about as they did like pieces of farm machinery left in a field. Everything reeked of displacement. There was a large Indian population, no employment and much alcoholism.

He drove slowly through the streets to the civic center, parked and went into a restaurant. While he drank a cup of coffee, he looked out the window at a graceful Federal period building in yellow brick with a portico and cupola, too imposing to be torn down and replaced with a cube.

What a shame, Grey thought, that his grasp of the past brutalities of Harris's life was so instinctive. It had gotten him out of bed even earlier than usual. For that livid, scarred face with its peculiar attentiveness, whether focused on the trail or on the distance, in the mirror of a polished saddle or on horse clods at the end of a shovel; for that look alight with the vividness of assumption, he was spending a tank of gas today.

When in Harris's company, Grey was aware of an unconciliatory other presence that seemed to govern his hired man's—or was it his horseman's? surely his horseman's—daily meditation on work. Grey sometimes thought of the gnomonic shadow on a sundial, signifying the diffuse and enormously meaningful planet also extant. He did not question whether Harris knew he sensed this *éminence grise,* which seemed also to be a source, in some manner, of light. Of course Harris did not know it, for Harris disliked him intensely, on principle. He on the other hand failed to dislike Harris, accepted Harris rather grandly on his own principle. He could not help it. And he felt that this acceptance somehow pierced the young black man, perhaps in sleep while his armor lay on the floor in unhinged halves, the presence extinguished without his consciousness to feed upon.

The whole affair made for a singular alertness between them that it would have been gratifying to find expressed in some form of friendship, however reluctant. Grey wondered if this mission would earn him some trust. *I am sowing seed on earth like iron,* he thought.

Chapter Three

HE PAID HIS BILL and crossed the scruff of frost-eaten lawn. The vaulted rotunda reminded him of his college at Cambridge, where he had read history for some reason now sunk in the past. The mural of fur-hatted explorers, mounted police and rail trains, however, was pure Canadian. They were mad for murals here. He followed brass rails alongside a ribbon of paint emblazoned with A MARI USQUE AD MARE, and signed in at the sergeant's desk.

Presently a male secretary came and fetched him to the chief officer of the district. The man was just sitting at his desk; he rose again and shook hands with Grey. The two men knew each other socially, though not well.

"You've come about your man, Colonel?" asked Inspector Woodhough.

"I'd like to do what I can on his behalf," said Grey.

He took a seat in one of the armchairs provided for visitors. The inspector found a file among others on his desk and removed it from its casing.

"If one of those men had been killed, the charges would have been quite serious," he said perfunctorily, turning pages. "Fortunately, they're both on the mend."

"I'm glad of it," said Grey.

"From the statements taken, it appears the conflict was provoked by one of them. That may be of some help. Though given the injuries he inflicted it's hard to say how far a plea of self-defense would serve. What did you have in mind?"

"Have him released into my custody until the matter's settled," said Grey. "I've reason to believe it won't happen again."

Woodhough looked wary. "Really. How do you propose to control him?"

"I don't think he needs to be controlled," said Grey. "I'll arrange for his good behavior in future."

Woodhough drummed his fingers on the file, then sat back and sized up his visitor. He saw a man in his early fifties, perhaps not that much, with a look of intelligent forbearance. Tall and well set up, with the unusual combination of fair hair and dark brows. The gaze that returned his bore a simplicity that was perhaps deceiving. Woodhough was politically astute, and made it his business to know the landowners of his district. Grey St. Oegger had been in this country for five years, having emigrated from Galway in 1941. He had bought the Venola estate in the Skillihawk Valley after old man Venola died. St. Oegger was a man of means, from an old Anglo-Irish family; had been in British Intelligence in the war before a jeep accident put him on the sidelines. He was no queer or screwball, two expressions Woodhough sometimes used privately for visitors. The credentials of the man seated before him, however, with one trousered leg crossed over the other, completely at ease in this office and in his presence, did not automatically confer acceptance of conventional wisdom. In Woodhough's experience, quite the opposite. He proceeded with caution.

"We wired Toronto for information and had a file made up," he said. "When you called to say you were coming I had it brought in."

"His papers are in order, I suppose," said Grey.

"They're fine. Didn't you see them when he came to work for you?"

"I've never asked for them," he said lightly.

"Good lord, why not?"

"They didn't interest me. I saw he could be useful to me and I hired him." He paused. Woodhough sensed a reserve. "He came up my drive about three weeks ago, on foot, near nightfall. Half starved, wanted work. I said I didn't have any but he could eat with us and stay the night. So he did. During the meal he said he could ride any horse I had. He correctly identified my Irish Thoroughbreds and the two Connemaras I keep.

"So I put him on my worst horse. Ex-steeplechaser who scrubs his riders off on rails and the undersides of trees. Jobbers, I call them. I buy them cheap, train them over and teach them manners, then sell them for a good price. The horse wasn't safe for an amateur to ride. I felt any man who knew an Irish Thoroughbred when he saw one could handle this horse or any other. He did beautifully. Jumped him over the fence in the dark and vanished for an hour." He smiled wryly. "When a man dines at your table, then steals your horse, you must look as well as possible."

"Humph! Well, don't mention it outside this room, please. What about his benefits and enrollment in the Health Insurance?"

"I was prepared to take care of any needs he might have."

Woodhough stroked his nose thoughtfully, then opened the file and removed two typed sheets of quarto. "Perhaps you'd like to look at his docket. To clarify your thoughts."

Grey smiled. It was a smile of uncommon charm. "You mean change my mind? Thank you, no."

"Wouldn't it be better to know what you're up against?"

"I know what I'm up against. He's a murderer, isn't he?"

The room became quiet. Woodhough laid the two sheets of quarto aside.

"I believe he had been in jail," Grey mused. "His clothes didn't fit. I think they just have things stored and pick out a set for whoever's being discharged. Don't they?"

Woodhough moved his head from side to side, in wonder.

"He's not a common crook," said Grey. "So it had to be that. He had lost quite a bit of weight, drifting around, but even so I sensed the clothes weren't his. And of course he came from America."

"The United States," corrected Woodhough absently. "What makes you think that?"

"He sounds West Indian a little, but West Indians carry themselves differently. They take more pride in their African heritage, I think. Not that he is ashamed . . . I'm putting it badly. He's been shocked."

"You lost your calling when Intelligence let you out," said Woodhough, amused. "You sound like our best detective. Quarter Haida named Reese that I'd hate to have on my tail. A minor can't be tried as a felon under the law; otherwise I assure you Mr. Harris wouldn't have crossed our border, regardless of his citizenship. Canada doesn't welcome the type represented by Mr. Harris, Colonel."

"A minor?" For the first time, Grey looked surprised. "How old is he?"

"Nineteen. Nearly twenty."

As though by prearranged signal, the phone on the desk burred. Woodhough picked up the receiver and spoke into it.

Grey rose and walked to the window. The view gave onto the spire of the clock tower, rising before a bald hill the shape of a man's head. A poor sun labored low in the sky; it was going to be a dull day.

Woodhough hung up. "Sorry. I've been waiting for that call."

"Never mind." He remained standing.

"I gather you mean to keep him on."

"I think so."

"It was in Buffalo, New York. A witness spoke on his behalf. The woman companion of the victim. Not a good witness of course. A poor reputation, not reliable, but she swore under oath it was self defense. There was no reason for her to lie; she'd never seen him in her life. Point was, the dead man was . . . not colored. They hunted for him for a month before they found him. You know how they are down there, about that."

"I've heard of it," said Grey with interest.

"We have our own troubles with color," said Woodhough, a smug note creeping into his voice. "But very little comparatively. Our West Indians are a high-minded population. Then of course there's the present weapon—the knife Mr. Nevill and one of his opponents state Mr. Harris was carrying. Had it been found, there would be nothing I could do for you."

"So I understand," said Grey.

"I appreciate his usefulness to you. But given his past use of such a weapon, the possibility that he had one in his possession as recently as yesterday is disturbing."

"Of course it is. But as you've pointed out, nothing was found." Grey smiled again. "I'll take his papers in anticipation of his being delivered to my care, if you'll allow it. No point driving back to fetch them. Shall I consult an attorney?"

"No need to if you're willing to vouch for him," said Woodhough. "The court clerk can help you post bond. He'll have to appear in court, but he can be remanded to your custody until then. You'll be notified of the date by marshal's service."

Grey took the papers. He had retrieved these artifacts from the dresser in the turret room and given them without a glance to the deputy. Why had he not looked at them, the creased sheets and the passport with the navy cover? He glanced over them now.

"Isn't dual Canadian–United States citizenship rare?" he murmured.

"Relatively. A freak of parentage makes it possible," said Woodhough rather irritably. "He's a British subject however, not Canadian, as you see."

Grey folded the papers and put them in his jacket with the passport.

"Please be careful," Woodhough added on impulse as he offered his hand.

"I shall be," said Grey distantly. "Nineteen years old."

"Every time I look he's in the same place," said the deputy in Four Queens, working a key from an ancient set in the cell lock. "Won't eat, won't sleep, just lies there staring like a damned cat."

Harris lay with his arms behind his head and his legs crossed, stockinged feet propped on the bed rail. He did look feline, with his light eyes and lean, graceful body. He was grubby but his cuts had been cleaned and were starting to heal. There was a saffron bruise on one temple. He watched Grey while the deputy explained what was going to happen to him.

Grey signed him out. They collected jacket, stained crushed hat, boots and belt from the storage locker and walked across the road to the pickup.

"You attacked a man and injured him badly," said Grey coldly. "You would have killed him if you hadn't been stopped."

Harris stared ahead at distant mountains. "No one calls me that."

"You tricked him into assaulting you in order to indemnify yourself," said Grey, his voice flicking like the lash of a whip. "I don't give a damn what he said or what you won't stand for being called. You can't get into fights if you're going to work for me. Life is filled with injustice. Learn to live with it."

"What the fuck do you know about it?" asked Harris conversationally.

"If you mean the hardships you must bear as a member of your race, nothing at all. But there are other hardships, equally unpleasant, that must be borne by all men. Either control yourself or get out. I don't expect to have to spring you from gaol again."

He swung into the truck and slammed the door. Harris got in the passenger side.

"You'll have to pay for Frank Nevill's tooth," said Grey as they pulled away. "He's carrying it around in his handkerchief."

"Fine." Harris glanced at the plaster on Grey's brow. "Sorry about your face."

"Apology accepted," said Grey. "Have you eaten?"

"Not lately."

"We'd better get something in town. Sno-Bird refuses to come to the house since you were flung in gaol, and I don't cook. The place is a bloody mess. I hope you don't mind being seen with me at the Cattleman's."

Harris was startled. "Not if you don't mind being seen with me." And they both suddenly laughed. And Grey smiled at him. It jolted him, that smile. Harris looked away, struck dumb.

Chapter Four

THEY GAVE HIM THE ROOM they called the turret room. It had a bed, a lamp with a cowhide shade, a Turkish carpet, a dresser with a mirror scattered with silver shot. The walls were papered with roses whose twigs and nettles he traced with troubled eyes, staring at the sun-pressed walls on Sunday afternoons. The connecting room was fitted with a toilet and pine washstand. He bathed in the bathroom down the hall, sharing it with the family.

A large window faced the garden, its low sill framed with dogwood. He soon got used to opening the curtains on a vista of rambling roses and clematis with yellow-hearted flowers. Verbena, sweet clover and hellebore were tucked around the paths that lay all over like dropped threads. Lavender grew in tufts in the sun, and he sometimes saw the grown daughter out there gathering it in a newspaper horn.

Among the woodland of fruit trees that hid the brickworked wall was a Jonagold that filled the air on hot days with the winey smell of apples. A persimmon tree left windfalls in the grass and foxes slunk over the wall at night to eat the red-gold fruit.

During the warm dusky evenings he could see in the distance, where the highway ended in a pearl of light, the mountain rearing straight up out of the floor of the valley, cold and blue with approaching nightfall. That first evening he had hesitated between keeping on up the highway and turning into the drive. There was a sign by the frontage ditch with a single name woodburned into it. SALTHILL. He didn't know if it was a house or a ranch. A ranch or farm was what he needed. His belly told him to pick the drive. Then he saw the Thoroughbreds in the lower pasture, and his head told him to stay.

Now here he was, living in this queer place like a man in a dream.

The dogs, who weren't allowed upstairs, slept in his room when he let them, the way dogs always did. The barn cats slunk in when he left the window open and slept on the bed, the way cats always did.

The house was like nothing he had ever lived in. It was made for a race that used softness, fabrics and polished woods as protection, as much as guns and war. A race that hid menace with roses, in plaster and on wallpapers, on chair legs, in gardens, to show how nice they could be. Even his room had a musty grace that breathed a history without peace. It weighed on him like an anvil.

He did not know how to express his awareness of this imperial violence. He only knew that it made him angry. When he opened a door on a clutter of neglected furniture, cabinets full of unmatched china, framed watercolors of Turkish minarets and Heywood Hardy hunt scenes, he was filled with a dull rage. Bruised silk lampshades sprouting like mushrooms in a cellar, fireplaces with pitches and scuttles green with neglect, old flower-patterned rugs with holes that he caught his foot in before he knew they were there; this was what he had come to live with. This careless ownership of centuries, this dusk before the nightfall of rule, which he sensed was part of his own ignorant history.

As far as he knew, the house was empty. The door to the study down the hall was closed. He knocked, waited long enough, then went in, leaving the door casually open.

The closest window was open on the yew grove outside. He could fall out of that if he heard anyone coming. The desk was striped oak, the brass pulls smoky with age. He went swiftly through it, moving things aside delicately. In the front drawer was a .22 automatic. There was a box of .38 hollow-point specials, so there was another gun somewhere. He checked the action on the .22. It was empty. Pushed in the back of the drawer was an eight-shot clip and some folded Canadian currency.

He exhaled slowly. So the means were there. If things went sour he had the means. He could be dead in the end, maybe after a siege, but so what? He could wait until the Indian woman had gone for the day and it was just him and the three men.

His hatred of white men sometimes came on him like an ague. His hands jerked and his heart slapped in helpless response to whatever squeezing and prodding inside his cranium set off the reflexes. It was a malarial attack that left him yellow and sweaty. Once he even hit himself in the face to stop the images that flew at his eyes and beat him with tense black wingstrokes. The fits didn't come on when he was plotting revenge. Revenge soothed him like quinine.

He heard no sound from the doorway and that was why he nearly fell over her going out. The little daughter, Elsa. She melted back into the hall shadows, scrawny in a dress that bared her legs. The papery skin and white knees repelled him.

"Are you leaving?" she whispered hoarsely.

"No," he said.

"Don't leave."

He stared at her, then brushed past her.

He stood outside on the veranda with the sunshine beating on his head, wondering if she'd seen. He could strangle her first. All she did was goggle at him.

The yard stretched out below with the fields all around it, slow and golden, the windbreak a lush stripe along the backside. Beyond the tamaracks the valley spread in layers, a continuous hollow of green and blond and brown ripples widening under the sky. He waited patiently for quiet. The rage receded to a place behind his eyes, where it continued to burn like the dull red bars of an electric fire.

Chapter Five

HE WENT DOWN the hall and stood inside the study door with his cloth cap in his hand.

The oak-paneled walls were lined with bookcases crammed with registries and breeders' publications, veterinary manuals and textbooks. The windows opened with a crank and had little diamond-shaped panes but were wider than the gunwale windows in the dining room. He smelled the must of paper and wood stain. A lemon left untouched on the desk had withered into a brown nut. On shelves over the desk were shot glasses and a decanter of whiskey, a pair of decoys, an old wind-up clock with a green face.

Framed photographs of horses and riders hung between the shelves. Harris stepped forward to examine them. Anything about horses was irresistible, even old photographs. There was a shot of a group of mounted men and women in hunt dress with their chins propped on their stocks. A stone lodge rose out of a grove of chestnuts behind them, under a sky mottled with storm clouds. The dogs at their stirrups had the same jittery look as the hounds that ran with men through the Cumberland nights, hunting the coon with lanterns and guns.

He edged over to a photo of some teenage boys on a field, all in striped shirts, shorts and knee socks. A signature inked with a flourish and a few words were scrawled on the bottom, both faded. They were laughing and dirty, their shirttails pulled out, arms draped over each other's shoulders. They looked privileged and carefree, sure of themselves and their road in life. It was easy to identify the rancher in the middle of the circle of faces. He hadn't changed enough over the years not to be easily recognized.

He studied the boy who had become the man. The face was Gordon's and Elsa's who hadn't been born yet. But while theirs was a closed look, a look of intense reservation, Grey's had an openness that seemed to create its own sun.

He heard a tread down the hall, and straightened as Grey walked into the room.

"Sorry I'm late," said Grey, taking his seat. "No, don't stand; sit over there."

Harris sat down on one of the chairs. He laid his cap on his knee and let it rest there. The yews grew thinly outside the window, and the sun came in through the panes and fell on the rancher's arms, muscular and covered with gold hair. The chair creaked when it turned. It was a big chair, sprung like a carriage with a heavy oak frame and base, the leather cushions worn to a soft caramel color.

Harris knew the interview was about the court date. He'd made up his mind what to do, lying on the bed staring at the railed gallery around the ceiling, with molding featuring naked men hunting and stags on their knees, with arrows through their hearts. Take what he needed to travel on and get out before they brought him in front of the judge. He believed fervently and wildly that judgment would be against him. Shoot the old man with the gun in the drawer if he tried to stop him. If he tried one fucking thing. It was a pleasure just thinking about putting a bullet through that white heart. It would jerk and quiver like he had, flapping on the ground and peeing in his pants. He'd leave it there with the blood draining out, like he'd been left in the night. Waiting for them to come back. Waiting for Chauncey. *Chauncey's on the way, nigger. He's gonna cut your dick off, nigger.* Eye for eye, tooth for tooth: why hadn't he seen before that this was the way to end the pain? In this wilderness it would be easy. He'd be over the border and hiding in some ghetto before they knew he was gone.

"I want you to know the charges against you have been dropped," said Grey.

He didn't believe it. "Why?"

"Because your plaintiffs 'skipped town,' as you say on this side of the ocean. A very expressive phrase, I've always thought. Signed themselves out of the hospital and vanished." Grey leaned back in the chair and studied Harris. His eyes were the blue of stones washed by a cold sea. "I suppose they had something to hide," he added. "Or they were frightened."

Harris struggled with a sudden desire to laugh. The picture of the sons of bitches catching the first boxcar out of town was amusing. Relief tore through him like a wind, washing his mind clean.

"Thanks," he said.

"For what?" said Grey dryly. The eyes held his. There was no gold in the irises. There was no fear in them, either. And Harris saw that there would not be fear or surprise at any time where he was concerned. He saw that he was already known. He was known not only as what he was here, in this house, but as something he had been when he was nine. It was the innocent, uninjured self, distilled and waiting to be a hero. The gun in the drawer, the money, the violent way out, had never been, because for this man, with him, they had never yet existed.

He rose to his feet in slow puzzlement. As he stood there among all those books, with the dust of paper in his nostrils, his image of Grey changed swiftly and completely, forever. It was like a kaleidoscope turning, the pieces tumbling into a new pattern, an arrangement of shapes and colors he had never seen, and wondered at never having seen. When he spoke, what came out was what he had never intended to say.

"Thanks for sticking up for me."

"You're welcome," said Grey. "How's the sorrel colt doing?"

"All right on the ground rails, but he needs to pick up his feet. I'll take him over them tomorrow."

He retrieved his cap and went blindly out the door, his heart a cramped bud unfurling in the dark.

As was customary on alternate Thursdays, Grey and Gordon were in Four Queens to take care of whatever business occupied them in the town. While his father was at the bank, Gordon picked up the mail for Salthill and Piwonka's ranch, Mountain Inn. For Salthill there was a periodical, a few bills and two letters. One was from the aunts in Vancouver, for the girls. Gordon slit the other open with his penknife and read breathlessly. He put the mail pouch in the back of the sedan with the groceries and slid into the passenger seat beside his father.

"Grey," he said. "How d'you think I'm doing here?"

"You mean with the business. Fine, just fine. If you stick with it there's no reason it can't be a success. Frankly, I'm relieved you came instead of staying in Galway."

"I had to come," said Gordon, vaguely irritated, as well as nervous at the prospect of this talk. "Someone had to bring the girls."

"You needn't have stayed," said his father cheerfully.

They were driving through town. Again Gordon was surprised, as at his first view, by the beauty of this land: its vastness, the dry majesty of the mountains, the sun lying across canyons like wrinkled cloth of gold. Everything was on such a grand scale, he wondered why he failed so utterly to respond to it. The trees were in full leaf, making green tunnels of the small side streets: these he liked better; they reminded him of England. As they idled at the light that had been installed at the intersection, Gordon struggled with words.

"I'm glad I came, too. But I'm not sure about the horses."

"What do you mean?"

Gordon stared at a gaggle of blue-jeaned children hopping their bicycles across the street. The light turned green and the sedan started forward. He drew a breath.

"I don't think I want to go into ranching."

Grey made a left and drove down a side street. A park appeared, planted with evergreens, a statue of a grizzly bear carved from redwood in the center. Grey pulled to the curb, lifted the hand brake and regarded him bleakly.

"Why not?"

"It's not what I want to do," said Gordon.

He thought of saying, *I'm sorry.* He was able now, at times, to stand away from himself and see who he was, how he was. He was like his mother, who had never said she was sorry in her life. His self-containment was ele-mental. How odd that in memory his loyalty had always lain toward that inflexible woman who had never kissed him, instead of his father. He di-vined, in a wily fashion not customary to his temperament, that his father was capable of loving him. Only not usefully. He drew another breath.

"I applied to medical school before leaving Galway. I just had the notice today. From the school. I've been accepted."

His father got out and walked into the park. Gordon watched his passage up one of the gravel walkways. Well, he'd said it. He tightened his lips.

He left the sedan and joined his father. The two men sat on the base of the statue and spoke beneath the ursine snarl.

"Are you telling me you want to become a doctor?"

"Yes. I want to study medicine."

"Good god." Grey studied him frankly. None of that looking away that would have given him some relief. There had never been anything com-fortable about his father. "A doctor. How long have you wanted to be a doctor, for god's sake."

"Quite a while," said Gordon, riveting his eyes to an infant evergreen. "I didn't want to say before."

"Well," said his father, and gave a short laugh. "What school?"

"McGill University. In Montreal. I'd like to stay in Canada." Even that admission was hard for him. Yes, he had wanted to stay here. He wasn't quite sure why.

"First you didn't want to finish at Cambridge, which I went to and my father and his father before him. Now you want to become a doctor. Carrying a bag about."

"It's a fine thing to do," said Gordon, hearing the waspishness in his voice, yearning to express his love of beakers and blood and titers. "I liked my science courses. They were my favorites. Are you going to let me go?"

"How can I not?" said Grey. "I can't deny you your vocation, whatever it may be. You might have discussed this with me earlier. I thought you'd back me up at Salthill—been given no reason *not* to expect it since you got off the train."

"There's always Harris," said Gordon bitterly.

His father studied him again. "You have a problem with him, don't you? Of course Harris is not what I had in mind. You're my son and heir and I don't expect anyone else to fill that role."

"He would if he could."

"I disagree with you," said Grey in a reasonable voice, contrary to what Gordon expected. Learning his father had always been a Sisyphean struggle. And that scar-faced black had no trouble reading him at all—a man who got thrown in gaol for brawling. A man not of their race or class. Everything in Gordon reached fervently toward the rock-security and tranquillity that blood and class defined.

"You feel sorry for him," he said.

"I never feel sorry for any man," said Grey.

He felt the impossibility of getting past this iron will to support Harris for no reason.

"I'll be leaving after the summer, then," he said.

"You'll be badly missed," said Grey. "We won't tell the girls yet. I've no idea why you should feel Harris is anything more here than a *lusus naturae* on horseback."

Chapter Six

LANKY, WHITE-HAIRED TOM PUSHKIN was Grey's attorney and a friend of the family. He had been ill that winter and Grey had invited him to recuperate at Salthill during the summer weeks.

"The steelhead are thick," he wrote. "And fishing is good for a man's health. Don't consider yourself an imposition, we'll carry on around you."

An avid fisherman, Tom accepted.

"You're not *driving*," said Daisy, when he mentioned it in a visit to the aunts at Lisnasheoga, their house in English Bay. "It's nearly two hundred fifty miles north, on not the very best roads."

"I shall take the train," he said. "By the way, you're much too young to have a nephew with nearly grown children."

"I know I should be older," said Daisy, who was handsome and not old at all. "Grey's father and I are brother and sister, but we're nearly forty years apart. My father remarried very late in life and had another family."

"And Iseult?"

"Was married to one of our uncles. She's our Irish addition."

"A good thing, too," said Iseult in the doorway, massive in a floury apron. "Unleavened English is a dry morsel to swallow. Come, everything's ready in the parlor. I've a wonderful Darjeeling, Tom, from that shop in Chinatown you mentioned that has teas from all over."

He was met at the station two weeks later by the girls, Flavia having driven the sedan from Salthill. They were dressed for the occasion in skirts of that unattractive length that falls far enough below the knee to make the calf look shapeless and truncated. Flavia's hair was in a loose bell and her shoes had a heel that compensated somewhat, displaying a pair of shapely ankles, while the little one sported mary janes. Crisp blouses with Peter Pan collars and box-pleat bodices completed the ensembles.

Grey's children had joined him in Canada earlier in the spring. Gordon had gone north to Salthill after leaving the girls in Vancouver to spend three weeks with the aunts, having their wardrobes smartened. At Lisnasheoga a certain mode of dress was considered suitable for well-brought-up girls; "jazzy" styles were eschewed. The effect was droll on Flavia. Her body lifted and poured in womanly curves that defied suitability.

"Hullo, Tommy," she said with face alight, offering her hand. "We've come to take you to Salthill."

He gave them lunch in a tearoom on the ground floor of one of the old Edwardian buildings. The table was laid with a cloth and embellished with a luster jug of flowering orange and flame hummingbird's trumpet. The silverware wasn't silver but looked like it, and the napkins were real linen. Pretty spiffy for Four Queens, said Tom. The girls spread their napkins carefully on their laps. The little one tugged her gloves off and tossed them on the table, flexing her fingers with relief.

Elsa had somewhat of a simpleton's affect, a little skewed, a little wild. On first meeting them Tom had wondered whether she was of normal intelligence. But in time it appeared that the problem was not one of intellect. Elsa was "strange"; she was "not completely right." It was, he was given to understand, unfortunate, but he was given to understand no more. A secret drama seemed to surround Elsa to which he was not to be privy. The St. Oeggers were mum on the subject, as he guessed they would be mum on the caperings of an alcoholic uncle, a divorce, a lapse from Roman Catholicism to Church of England. From the viewpoint of his own unguarded, emotionally strewn family, Tom did not think silence was always such a very bad thing. Regarding Elsa he sensed the revving up of a convoy of effort, which would march inexorably over the landscape of resistance to aid the distressed other, a sort of spiritual Red Cross; everything was going to be twitched and drilled and belatedly smoothed into place.

This impression had been reinforced during visits to Lisnasheoga while the girls were there. He really came to see Daisy, who intrigued him, but the girls were in view, and must be spoken to. Elsa gaped at his kindly worded queries with a feral apprehension that stung Tom alternately with pity and exasperation. She was a fierce child who never sucked her thumb, twiddled her hair or indulged in any other of the solaces children seek when *in extremis*. She seemed never to have learned the power of tears to command attention or relief for an overburdened spirit. She was maddeningly wily and coarse. Her large mouth seemed incapable of forming words properly, of making of language a vehicle for the expression of thought. She spoke a rough English, as well as the Irish of the West of Ireland. He somehow gathered that she could not yet read. This had piqued him to fiery curiosity, since she was then eleven years of age, but he dared not broach it even to Daisy.

Of Grey's children she resembled him most, having his strongly marked brows and rather doggy eyes, and the kind of aquiline nose that looks well on a male. She had been chalky-looking in the spring; now masses of freckles clustered on her arms and face like the soft, spilling shadows of tree leaves. The fawn cast of her skin went pleasantly with her hair, streaked nearly white in places by the Skillihawk sun. She favored him with a brief but friendly smile that augured well for the luncheon party.

In contrast, Flavia was a girl of the type Tom thought was still referred to as "finished." Her manners were elegant and unpretentious. She presided over the table, passed sandwiches and plied the teapot with a sweet air, unleavened by humor, that would have been cloying had it not reflected real goodness. Like her brother Gordon she was dark, rosy and handsome, with lapis lazuli eyes that were at first look nearly black.

She had had her eighteenth birthday at Salthill, he was informed. She seemed to have arrived at maturity as polished as an apple, and like a sweet, gleaming apple, he felt, was as ready to be plucked from the branch by some happy man.

They filled him in on the goings-on at Salthill. Gordon was gone for a week to Montreal on some business he had declined to mention. Gordon's mare had a new foal, who was to be named Zanzibar. A new goat had replaced the one that had died of a mysterious ailment in the spring.

"Eating poison toadstools, I expect," said Elsa in clear English. "She was stupid, for a goat."

Flavia gazed fondly on her sister. "Elsa has a talent for drawing. You ought to see her pictures, Tommy."

"Is this true, Elsa? Are you going to show me any?"

"Course not." Elsa's lower lip slid forward; she glared from beneath a hedge of brow.

"She doesn't like my mentioning it, do you, love," said Flavia. "But I don't care; I wish I could draw half as well."

"How about reading? Do you like to read, Elsa?"

"Rather, now I've caught on."

"Father expects us to continue our education at home," said Flavia. "Gordie taught her to write and do sums. Writing exercises and history in the morning, sums after tea. Music from me, but we have to sing a cappella because of not having any instrument. I read to her every day for a long time, then one day I saw she had got on to the page ahead by herself. She's read *Jane Eyre*."

"It's about a madwoman," said Elsa, restored to cheer. "Can we have ice cream for dessert?"

"I think it's in order, if you are reading Brontë," Tom replied.

Harris and Sno-Bird were in Four Queens, too. They had driven to town in Sno-Bird's Chevrolet. On the way in she started talking. He had never heard her speak more than a word or two.

"The guy made that house, him from Eu-rope," she said. "They make farm, big stone little wood in Eu-rope. Grey he buy it when he with RAF, come over in big war bimeby. No woman, him woman dead. Dai, he work for Grey father in old country, him come too. Dai no like be in house with family, so you get the room. Him be here first."

"He can have the frigging room," he said.

"Frigging," she repeated thoughtfully.

She went on. These people surely did love to talk, when they talked. "Five year Grey be here. The kids they stay Ire-land till Grey make come them now. They okay nice kids, good looks too, 'cept the little one. Her look like one them lizards suns-um on rocks by river."

Her voice was touched with pity, for she herself was a handsome woman. Her skin had a red cast, like the skin of a fire cherry tree. She wore her hair in braids or the way it was this afternoon, in a dusty coil at the nape of her neck. She hummed popular tunes on laundry day, cranking denim out of the wringer in thick blue tongues after soaking it in the boiler and scrubbing it with yellow soap. There was no electricity in the valley. One of Piwonka's men stopped by with a block of ice for the pantry box on his way back from town with ice for the big ranch.

"My people, they be the Klaxta," she said. "Next to Haida we most strong tribe this land. Once great numbers, many gone now. You African mens lucky, they say you brought here. Better than found here. You found here, you guy get run off your land, make live on reserves like us. Like deer."

She helped herself to a cigarette from the pack on the dashboard. Smoke shot from her nostrils. With the cigarette in her mouth, she spread a hand on the wheel and examined her nails, work-polished to the pink of conch shells. "Know my true name?"

"Nope," he said.

"Helen Louise," she said. The smoke flipped up and down. "Helen Louise Travers."

"I thought it was Williams," he said.

"That my husband name. Now. When I'm seven, go one year to white man's school, 'cause my father work for guv'ment people Vancouver, mens say I have to go-um school. Me only native in school. Bimeby we study Indian lore. Make up Indian names us kids, make headdress with beads and fedders, collect pictures people painted faces, that shit. Nothing my clan do, but so it goes. I pick name Sno-Bird. Make all up, spelling, too. Bimeby bin call that ever since, me."

She darted a grin at him, showing strong teeth. "Had to go white mens school to get Indian name. Go in Helen Louise, come out Sno-Bird. You beat that?"

"Nope." He smiled slightly back. "You know what? If you went to school, you must be able to speak real English."

"Certainly I can," she said with dignity. "But I prefer to keep some distance between me and my conquerors."

"Don't bother with that pidgin crap around me," he said after a while. "It won't do you any good with them, either."

> "O Danny boy, the pipes, the pipes are callin'
> From glen to glen and down the mountainside . . .

"Like that one?" she asked. "Kind of pretty, huh?"

"Not bad," he said. "No time, though."

"Time?"

He thought. "Time. The tempo. The way it moves. You sing white."

She dumped him out of the car and drove off.

He stood at the corner of Main and Leaf, grinning. He knew her by now. She would go to the grocery store, stop by her cousin Myrtle Strongbowl's to pick up a sack of homemade donuts, then come back to get him.

There was a little library on a plot of grass, with the Maple Leaf drooping on a pole over the door. He went inside and looked around. It was dim and dusty and the windows over the stacks showed no sign of ever having been opened. Heat poured from a furnace grate in the floor even though it was the middle of summer, giving off the odor of old varnish that he had always associated with school. The librarian studied him through her glasses, probably never having seen anybody like him before. Not in Four Queens.

He looked through the shelves. The few readers, including two children cross-legged on a rug with picture books, seemed to assess him only briefly. He had never run into people more unaggressively polite and nice than Canadians. Still, he smelled their whiteness, floury and chapped, the smell of clean babies' butts. His own blackness coursed like nicotine in his bloodstream, a created separation. The thought came: What in hell was he doing here, anyway?

Near the foyer was a box of books and a coffee can with a sign taped to the front: SALE, 25 CENTS EACH. He went through the box, stacking the books on a chair so he could replace them in order, and picked up a book of poems with a picture of a man on the cover. A black man, in a collar. He could see the edge of a pinstriped suit. They stared at each other, him and this warm-faced man.

He opened the book. Poetry, by Langston Hughes.

> *. . . and now*
> *When the rumble of death*
> *Rushes down the drain*
> *Pipe of eternity,*
> *And hell breaks out*
> *Into a thousand smiles,*
> *And the devil licks his chops*
> *Preparing to feast on life,*
> *And all the little devils*
> *Get out their bibs*
> *To devour the corrupt bones*
> *Of this world—*
> *Oh-ooo-oo-o!*
> *Then my friends!*
> *Oh, then! Oh, then!*
> *What will you do?*

He left a quarter in the coffee can and stood on the curb turning pages.

Chapter Seven

THE LUNCHEON PARTY DROVE DOWN the main street with its turn-of-century buildings of wood and ocher brick, its platform sidewalks like rows of teeth. Saddled horses dozed at the hitching rails between cars. In the distance the steamer was putting out from the wharf, bound for Wanda Creek. It looked as fragile as a leaf on the water, but they knew it had four cabins and an engine room you could stand up in. It had a shallow draft so it could run out a gangway and take aboard cargo from places where there were no wharves. They had been on it when they first came, and a disappointing tour it had been for these children of Ireland, accustomed to the big fishboats that plied from Clew to Dingle Bay, with the water flashing over the gunnels like sword points in the storms.

"She goes twice a week around the lake, stops at Lockerby on the east, then at Wanda Creek at the north end," said Flavia. "There are some *huge* ranches up there. From Wanda Creek she goes west, stopping at the fish camps tucked away in the inlets."

The house appeared on its promontory.

"Good god," said Tom faintly at the sight of the rectangular fortress of dark gray stone, the crenellated battlements broken every few yards by lookouts. What he had mistaken for chimneys above the brow of the hill as the sedan toiled up the drive was a pair of square towers, one at each end of the house. Two turrets with hats of red tile bracketed the wall facing the yard, their foundations sunk deep into the incline. A retaining wall of the same dark stone extended down the hill facing the drive, ending in a thin, many-pathed wood. One or two lime trees nodded against the gray flints.

"It was built in 1898 by a Norwegian immigrant who admired a Gothic ruin in his homeland," said Flavia serenely. "But we're not to call it a castle, though I'm afraid people do, when Grey isn't there. He says if it weren't for the veranda and side porch we'd be walled up alive."

Grey was in the ring below, schooling a colt in the flat English saddle. The colt moved sideways, crossing one foreleg gracefully over the other in the *pas de côté*, without an apparent signal from his rider. As they went through this maneuver, he switched his tail restlessly. Horses always reminded Tom of cats, independent and clever-minded. Flavia sounded the horn. The colt stopped in the center of the ring and jingled his bits.

Because it was Tom's first day at Salthill, tea was in the dining room. "Bless us, O Lord, and these Thy gifts which through Thy bounty we are about to receive through Christ Our Lord Amen," Dai intoned swiftly, his Irish inflection rising and falling. They blessed themselves.

There was a smoke-ring on the mahogany finish where a hot dish had been mislaid. Two apple pies breathed under a cloth on the sideboard. Color from the leaded windows, pressed from behind by the sun, lay in loose scraps on the table. A flag of mallard green unfurled across Grey's shirt; bronze dust swam in the hollow of his throat. He sat gracefully in his chair. When he moved to lift his glass a marigold bloomed, the gold of a great seal, in his hair.

"What am I to do tomorrow?" asked Elsa. Her hair had come out of its clamp and hung about her face in silvery sheets. Her young forehead was stamped with a violet band. It moved when she did, in a jiggling pattern.

"Halter break the colts," said her father. "Did you leave the Winchester out last night? I found it propped against the water pipe."

"Are ye daft?" said Elsa, working her jaw.

"Elsa!" said Flavia in a low distressed voice. "Remember."

"It's all right, Fi," said Grey.

"I did it," muttered Dai. "Fergot it was left. There, I'm sorry."

Flavia shook out her napkin briskly and studied her plate; a curve of dark hair hid her expression. But Elsa faced her father with her head high. With a deep breath, she began over.

"Am I all right with the riding?"

"You're doing well," said Grey thoughtfully. "If you continue on with it you can start exercising the horses."

Elsa poked distractedly at the butter with her knife. Flavia cut a pat from the dish and transferred it to her plate, speaking to her father over the blond head.

"She rode in Ireland a lot, Gem Connor let her."

"So she says. If Gemmy taught her, she was all right. I see no wrong with her seat at this point."

Flavia plowed on, cheeks flushed. "Gem said she has nice hands."

Her father grunted, a sound of agreement or dissent. "Needs to stop dreaming."

Tom was amused. Apparently Grey paid little attention to his children, assuming their happiness and well-being to be provided, along with their education, by each other and whatever resources his library offered.

Dai sat hunched over his food, absorbed as a horse at its evening flake. Harris was leaning back in a rather thuggish way, arms locked behind the chair so his body musculature stood out in hard relief under the T-shirt. He was directly across from Elsa and the violet band lay quietly on his mouth, unmoving as the stripe on the wall. He was the type of man who made no unnecessary movements. In the smoky crook of his arm were marks no larger than pinpricks, faint with age but still darker than the skin. Tom had taken note of these earlier, as he had the hesitation marks on the wrists. They contradicted the sullen assurance being radiated. He wondered whether the pose was deliberate, an attempt to proclaim manhood by making the body one provoking, rippling line toward the phallus. Tom was accustomed to the pose, having been reared in predatory urban poverty. Did Harris really belong in that class? He doubted it. Harris was an enigma, possibly the product of a superior orphanage; the clearest thing about him was that he could not be placed. Was Tom mistaken or was there a gleam of amusement under those half-closed lids? He concentrated on the iris until it surged toward him, drawn by the sensation of being observed. Their gazes caught and held. The glint was replaced by a bleak stare. It was as though the cover had snapped shut over the eye of a periscope. But what Tom thought he had surprised in that moment was a lucid awareness.

Elsa had developed a fierce crush on Harris. Harris magnetized her like the Arctic pole. She followed him about and sat with him on the porch while he whittled or smoked. She examined his palm, which he held flat on request so that she could trace the threadlike brown lines carved into it. She hurried through her less interesting chores in order to hang on the fence and watch him ride. Although her father gave her a half-hour lesson in the morning, of a remarkable compression and succinctness, it was Harris she followed keenly around the track and emulated, first on the Connemara pony she was given to ride, a sturdy thing with a coat as shaggy as a fisherman's beard, then on the larger horses.

If he cleaned tack, she sat between his knees and wiped the bits. She sometimes chattered to him in a rough brogue, peppering gossip and sharp asides with swear words. When he refused to answer, she gave him the rough edge of her tongue. The things she said made him smile, though if her father had heard them, he thought, she would surely have been in trouble. Like Sno-Bird, she pushed past his barriers simply by ignoring them. Sometimes, when they had been sitting together and he had accepted her as he accepted the dogs who flopped down and lay unmoving at his feet, she would stroke and even kiss the dark muscular arm in the rolled-up shirtsleeve, her egret's face grave with attention.

She and Flavia had to help in the kitchen.

"Your father doesn't like Canadian cooking. He stood me at the stove with a book and taught me how to cook English," Sno-Bird told them. "For many months I made curries and puddings and toads in the hole."

"What's this?" asked Flavia doubtfully of some squares of meat wrapped in newspaper.

"The moose Javier and his friend killed," said Sno-Bird. "Nice, huh?"

They stared in disappointment at the slices of beeflike flesh skirted with yellow tallow.

"Where are its antlers?" asked Elsa.

"Gone to the bone shop."

Elsa began to weep. "I don't like it."

At breakfast Grey took his place at the head of the table and handed out the day's work evenly. Gordon and Harris passed dishes, their eyes glazed with mutual dislike. They were close in age, but that was the only thing close about them. Sno-Bird breathed heavily at Tom's shoulder because she resented him frying the trout at her stove that he caught every morning.

Elsa served with a tea towel around her waist, pouring coffee from the willow pitcher with the mended lip. In an openmouthed reverie she watched Harris peel an apple with a paring knife. The skin swayed over the saucer in a delicate helix. You felt he was challenging himself to get it off in one piece, and that at the same time it was ridiculous; in this way his humor showed through, tough and iconic. There was a peculiar look on his face, brows raised over the taut eyelids, nostrils spread a little, that reminded Elsa of Peruvian burial masks she had seen in a book in the library. The flesh of the apple had not one speck of red left, so perfectly had it been removed. Sno-Bird saved the skin to give to the chickens.

"After the dishes, put fresh sheets on the beds," Sno-Bird ordered. "They're in the upstairs cupboard."

. . .

After a half hour of copying script in her roundest hand, and an hour of reading history (or *Chi-Wee, an Indian Girl* or *Daughter of Thunder,* when Hudson became boring), Elsa pulled on jodhpurs and riding boots and descended to the yard. She lost her awkwardness on horseback and rode with elfin grace, the plait of fair hair tapping between her shoulder blades. At the far end of the ring Flavia rode in a polo shirt and breeches, gloved hands on the reins, a whip sprouting like a lily stalk from beneath her wrist. The hair under her cap shone with the violet luster of health; the ends bounced tamely on her shoulders. She changed gaits and leads smoothly, leaning easily into the turns. Her horses minded her.

"Let's trade for a while," Elsa suggested.

"All right," said Flavia. She dismounted and gave Elsa her mare.

The mare instantly turned fractious. Elsa rode her several times around the track, struggling to maintain control. The mare finally tossed her off and galloped away, kicking up her heels.

Elsa climbed to her feet, red in the face. "Bleeding bitch."

"Elsa! Just fetch her and get back on."

Elsa chased the mare around the ring and cornered her by the gate. She was furious at getting dumped, but remained grimly mum throughout the capture. It was a rule of horsemanship that if you fell off, you got on and rode again. The knowledge of this was bred in her bones. You had to master the horse and not show it defeat. And you couldn't be angry; that was childish and temperamental, and hindered your mastery of it. To ride was instantly to assume the role of an adult, omniscient, protective and assured, even if you were four years old yourself and on your first pony.

She clambered into the saddle and sternly retraced her steps around the track, keeping the mare well gathered. The mare champed the bit and rolled her eyes, but moved through the gaits with docile step.

"Well done," said Flavia, coming up alongside. "Heavens, Elsa, don't let Grey hear you talk like one of the stable hands at home. He'll send you to *convent* school."

They both giggled.

Chapter Eight

IN THE EVENINGS THEY WENT to hear Daithi play the concertina.

The bunkhouse stood in the center of the meadow, with lupine and goldenstars floating like winnowing insects around it. There was one room where all the living was done. It smelled of bacon grease and porridge, a glutinous pot of which stood perpetually on the hob, and spirits. There was a pungent fragrance of ash from the Swedish stove with its pipe twisting into the rafters. The window let onto an evening sky speeding from blue to slate, the clouds edged with rose and the first stars emerging from the shelter of the firs.

Dai sat on a stool and tapped time with one foot. The red concertina with its corrugated belly swayed between his hands, giving out a sour wild sound.

> " 'Tis no wonder they say of your father the heart
> Inside him has turned to lead,
> And likewise your white-haired mother on
> whose white milk you once were fed,
> Not to mention the girl you married, who never
> managed to share your bed,
> For when my arms should have been around
> you, ohhh . . . you were drowned and lying dead."

He played "Star of the County Down," "The Duke of Leinster's Wife," "The Hen's March O'er the Middin." After a swig from a tumbler of tinted water, he played mazurkas. On the three-eight time they danced arms aloft and adroop, smirking like postcard angels, blond and blackstrap horsetails swaying against their backs.

Dai broke into a jig. He shuffled toward them, tiny and gnarled, hands working the bellows. The black hair, artifact of some Iberian warrior, sat on his head in a lump, too lush for the wizened face. They leaped around him in silence with skirts hitched and lashing out behind, arms akimbo. Out the door they flew and into the meadow where they jigged until they fell sputtering in the lupine, with Dai in the doorway with his arms opening and closing, opening and closing, like a woman spreading her skirts in a never-ending curtsy.

He would sit on the stoop after and play the ancient air *"T aimise 'im Chodladh"*: "I am Asleep and Don't Waken Me."

Flavia, who had a lovely voice, sang "Silver Dagger." The concertina gulped and faded; she sang alone. The other two sat in the dark, or in the white arc of the gas lamp with dark hollows for eyes, generously silent. For it was the music, the music, aye, that counted. Her contralto took the room, flowed rafterward with steely femininity:

> *"Don't sing love songs, you'll wake my mother*
> *She's sleeping here right by my side*
> *And in her hand a silver dagger*
> *She says that I won't be your bride.*
> *O once I had a fair young lover . . ."*

Elsa halter-broke eight colts with her pockets full of broken carrot, snubbed them at a post until they could stand to it quietly, led them until they bobbed along at her right hand. She sacked out the yearlings.

Her father handed her a worn potato sack. "Pass this down her back and around her withers and belly," he said. "Don't make sudden movements. Don't move the sack where she can't see it without showing it to her first. Good girl. Let her sniff it now. When she gets used to the feel of it, run it down her legs. Pick up her legs one by one and stroke them with it."

At first it was interesting. Elsa held the sack under the filly's nostrils and let her smell it. The filly fidgeted and snorted, but calmed as Elsa stroked her here and there with the sacking.

It was so quiet she could hear the bees sizzling in their box hive on the slope below the garden wall. She went into a pleasant trance. A beach stretched before her. She stood bare-legged, with spent waves creaming around her toes. Seawrack surged among the rocks, lifted by the swell of the tide; olive-gold weed and Neptune's girdle lay in long strands on the shingle.

She had found a doll's head once, washed up from Iceland or Connemara, blind-eyed and creamy, with green hair.

Ah, but she was here now at Salthill, in the morning sun with one of her father's horses; this she was more alive to. Elsa let the sacking drop and laid her face against the filly's flat, satiny neck. Sloughing hairs flew up her nose, fine as vegetable silk. The odor of the filly was powerful, as memorable as the sea, a hot, blood-filled smell that expanded in her head and lungs and filled her with a mysterious ardor.

One day they all rode into the valley, where white-faced cattle grazed and the lodgepole fencing vanished in thin air. Before them, in the long hollow between the mountains, lay open range bounded by rivers and stands of trees.

"The tall blue peak to the west is Mount Endeavour," Grey pointed out to Tom. "A volcano of the Coast Range, of which there are hundreds. Dormant of course, but when it overflowed thousands of years ago it left a rich silt that was gradually deposited on the valley floor, brought down by rivers and through natural erosion. That's why the land here is so fertile. The surrounding mountains are lush and green to the west, fed by coastal rains, and arid and rocky on the east. That dry peak above the Bluffs is Mount Skillihawk."

"Magnificent," said Tom, meaning it.

They were taking the brood herd to swim in Lake Lavender. The mares were being driven by Grey's stallion, a chestnut with liverish brindling on his flanks and shoulders. The stud plunged back and forth at the mares' heels with his tail up like a flag and his muscular neck curved. He bared his teeth at a laggard, who bolted with flattened ears to catch up.

"I bred him and brought him with me from Galway," said Grey as the herd poured through the gate onto open land. The foals ran at their mothers' sides, their long legs folding and unfolding in flight. "A good Irish strain, by Curragh King out of a Kelsaway mare. He stays with the herd as a rule. If I want to breed him to a visiting mare, I bring him to the pen, where he's very anxious to go once he gets wind of her."

The herd moved along the edge of the woods to an unpaved road. Bluffs of yellow clay towered over it, with long crumbling slides in places, and in others anchoring vine, dense and with a succulent texture, draped like tattered purple carpet over the shale. Where the road petered out, the lake lay on the broad pelt of the range, its water bright and smoky, with a wood along the east border.

Harris and Gordon rode behind the mares, crowding them into the water while the stud urged them forward. Horses were like cats, Elsa told Tom; not crazy over water. As soon as they were all well out and the silk of their wake had once more smoothed into a quiet plane, one of the mares broke from the herd and made for the nearest point. She swam back and forth along the rocks, her neck a brown stem above the water, then found footing on a smaller beach strewn with driftwood.

Harris instantly turned his Appaloosa out of the water. Tom had seen the horse in the paddock, asleep on three legs. With a single leap he was in flight down the shoreline, stretched out like a greyhound with Harris over his withers. The Appy's tail made a feathered streak and his legs flashed in that streaming rotation that mesmerizes racegoers. They skirted the debris in a few floating bounds. The mare was running hard, swerving from side to side to elude them. Tom watched the Appy close on her. They merged with bitter squeals flung back like gull cries. With the negligent grace of a dancer Harris curved and caught her by the mane. The two horses galloped in a circle, bounding against each other, panicked by their own muscular proximity. Harris floated suspended between them. They began to slow, to rise and fall like carousel horses. The circle caught the gully in its loop; they came charging through in a hail of chowder and grit, nearly rocking, and flashed past Tom.

Harris let the mare loose on the beach. The stallion had left the water and was waiting. In a flash he was after her, head snaking along the ground, ears screwed into knots. The mare squealed as his teeth closed on her flank. He chased her zigzagging until she pounded into the water, headed toward the safety of the herd, then galloped off, shaking his head and snorting.

The Appy scudded sideways under Harris like a blown leaf. Harris glided with him, glued to the little saddle with its stirrups like iron toys, insolently supple.

"Someone gave me that creature," said Grey, watching the paint-spattered rump bound away. "I don't like their conformation but he's smart and fast."

"What's his name?" asked Tom. All the horses at Salthill had interesting names.

"Frederic Remington," said Grey.

Gordon taught Elsa how to clean, load and shoot the guns at Salthill: the .22 automatic their father kept in his study, the .380 British Service revolver in his room upstairs, the Winchester rifle. Elsa practiced target shooting with the automatic, drawing and firing until she could shoot eight tin cans at thirty feet with an eight-shot clip every time. She was a naturally good marksman. Gordon took her out to find small game, taught her the rules of hunting sportsmanship as they had been handed down by his race from century to century. He liked having her along. She wasn't squeamish or sentimental, and her habitual silence suited his taciturn nature.

Flavia and Elsa made more formal excursions into the valley. With their saddlebags packed with sandwiches, they rode beside the streams and through meadows bright with moving grass, looking for the perfect place to have lunch.

"Dreadful, we'll be eaten alive by mosquitoes," said Flavia, turning up her nose at a lily-laden stretch of water and riding on.

They found a silky mound on which to eat, and drink cold tea from the canteen they had found in one of the hoary cupboards in the storeroom. Elsa had come upon a book on native flora in the library. In a desultory fashion they studied trees and plants: lodgepole pine, hemlock, grand fir, red cedar. *Saccato gordo* and deerhorn. Waterside forget-me-nots, named after a legend about a lover tragically lost. They lay in the sun with their hats tilted over their faces like old men, scratching fresh insect bites. Upside down, rugged carpets of lupine, gentian, red larkspur and Indian paintbrush swam into the azure sky.

"D'you think I'm doing all right?" asked Elsa.

"You're doing quite well," murmured Flavia.

"I wish I were like you, Fi, happy and kind all the time. I wish we could stay here together and never ever leave."

Flavia set her straw hat aside with a frown. Elsa was flopped on her stomach, sampling the smorgasbord of grasses and small cover offered by the mound. Her pinched, homely face was solemn beneath the knot of hair that opened loosely and rather gloriously around it.

"I'm not going on to college, you know," said Flavia.

"What're you going to do, then?"

Flavia stretched her arms to the sun, then added her legs and scissored them back and forth. Her hair spilled on the grass, berry-dark and berry-sweet. The half-closed lids were tinged with violet like the sepals of an orchid. She sat up abruptly and gazed across the meadow.

"I think I'll stay with Daisy and Iseult. They've invited me. But I'll come home often."

"Make sure you do," said Elsa severely. "I still get confused by things, and I'm not sure I deserve to have them go right."

"Golly, that's a clever thing to say. You *are* getting on."

"I'm serious. Things get mixed up when you're away."

"Nonsense," said Flavia warmly. "They always go right if you're sensible. Look how fast you've learned to read. Just follow your heart and head over things; that's what Gem Connor says when you're trying to get a difficult horse over a jump. Throw them both over the hurdle and the horse will follow."

Elsa watched her choose a field-oat stem to work between her teeth. She said, turning her attention to a beetle bumbling over a lot of other stems, "Fi, if things ever get bad, you know. Truly bad? Will you come and fetch me?"

"Of course I will," said Flavia. "I promise, darling."

Chapter Nine

IT WAS SO HOT AND THE WEATHER so fine that in midsummer the timothy they grew for winter came ready to be hayed.

Grey fired up the old Harvester and drove in his shirtsleeves. The grass was tossed and spread and left to dry. When it had cured, it was baled and loaded onto a wagon drawn by George Torenose's team of white mules. The team stood in the traces on the long stops, slapping their lips at the flies, waggling their ears, working up a green-tinted lather around their bits. The hay was hauled into the stable loft by rope and pulley, the bales stacked on both sides of the walkway.

Grey worked alongside the other men. As the day wore on his arms and the back of his neck turned pink, then brightened to the shade of boiled lobster. He could feel his face flaming as though he were leaning over a stove. The heat seemed to suck the breath from his lungs. He stopped beneath one of the larches, feeling dizzy.

The men moved away from him down the rows, dark, fair and red men, arms rising and falling, digging, lifting and tossing. The last thing he saw was one of the roving Irishmen he had hired standing on the wagon bed, a blue-shirted figure balancing on bowed legs as the wheels rolled slowly over the uneven ground. He must have fallen asleep after that. He woke to a semi-circle of faces: the tomahawk blade of George Torenose, spread cavernous nostrils and soft mouth of Harris, George's cousin Roger with braids hanging over his shoulders, Gordon.

"The tea," said Gordon in a deep, decided voice, as though his coming alive had forced them to action.

Someone emptied the tea jug over him.

He shouted and swore. "For god's sake!"

He heard Flavia's voice, high with concern. They helped him to his feet.

He was chilled, not from the tea running down his neck but from within, his blood sluggish and torpid. Gordon's fingers pressed burned mats on his arm; he felt himself steered toward the cool stable passageway. Grey put his head under the spigot until the pounding in his head stopped.

"Please go upstairs and rest, Father," pleaded Flavia tremulously. "You should see yourself! You can't work in this heat."

"Christ, I'm not that delicate," he moaned.

"She's right, it's too hot," said Gordon. "You haven't enough pigment in your skin to work out there. You've given yourself sunstroke."

He removed his arm and said with reserve, "I appreciate your concern, son, but I can't leave them to do all the work. It's not my way."

"It will be if you end up in hospital."

They were arguing, standing by the dripping tap.

"I've no intent of ending anywhere!" he shouted. "Get upstairs, girl, and fetch another jug of tea. And put plenty of sugar in it!"

Flavia fled.

"Suit yourself. I'm going out," said Gordon coldly. He stalked into the tack room and came out with the Winchester. "Nothing I say seems to be worth your consideration," he said, looking bleached under his tan.

"It's not true I don't consider your opinion," said Grey. "But the time to say what you have to say is not when I have a headache."

Gordon rode off toward the benchland. Grey drank the tea when it was brought and wet his head again under the tap. He put on a long-sleeved shirt and straw hat and stepped cautiously back into the field. Gordon was as pigheaded as his mother, always had been. He had a sudden rather woozy vision of Alice lying crushed in the leaves, surrounded with scarlet coats, the horses blowing. He hadn't been there, that morning. His head throbbed dully.

"You all right?" asked Harris, squinting at him.

"I'm fine, goddamn it. Leave me be."

Harris grinned and turned away.

Gordon came back with a brace of rabbits. Sno-Bird skinned them with a knife, peeling the hides away like the skins of grapes to reveal the veined pink fruit beneath.

They ate the evening meal in silence, the energy drummed out of them by the heat. The two Irishmen sat together, a matching set the size of half-grown boys, with muscular bodies and spongy pink faces. The rancher was English, likely a bloody Protestant, and they from Ulster and Catholic. They had come in late, and were ignorant of the blessing. Ah well, this was the New World, a blank page on their race-book, and they held no grudge against him for the now. Anyway and with luck, the truck would hold out till they got to Bella Coola, and who knew what they might find in that fine place?

Their eyes, fringed with coarse white lashes like Piwonka's heifers', slid warily over the Negro man as he sat silently mopping his plate with a wad of bread. They had never seen such a creature, proud and bold as he was, and all black in the skin. What a fellow! And next to him a slew of Injuns digging silently into the food, with the dust on their cheekbones and the lean hard mouths on them.

The Indians felt at ease with Harris. All the Klaxta knew of the fight in the shipping yard at Four Queens. They approved of his laconic, cool toughness, his willingness to kill for being called a name, for their sense of honor was different from the white man's. Harris drank no whiskey, but neither did many of the Klaxta. They sneered at the weakness for alcohol that had consumed other tribes. It was good to be in this kitchen, sharing food with the dark warrior and the English chief whose skin was burned the scarlet of a blustering sunset. They felt a mild spiritual contempt for the two little foreign men who spoke such bad English. And always, always they were filled with sadness at the small part they now played in the drama of the land. They had done their best to adapt. They obeyed the white man's laws. They were superior horsemen; were they not prized as cowboys? They were enterprising; did they not work as guides, fishermen, trappers, farmers? And yet, and yet it often seemed they were like the salmon who swam upstream to meet violent nets at the river bend, wide, entrapping and final.

Sno-Bird was going around with the coffeepot and rhubarb pie. Harris watched George Torenose light a ready-made. George looked self-possessed, even stately, holding the cigarette like a reefer between his thumb and index finger. He was only about thirty, but his profile seemed hewn out of ancient granite. Under the dignity, Harris sensed resignation and loss.

He looked down the long kitchen, at the walls hung with willowware, the old pine hutch with a piece of tile under the chipped leg. The rows of faces, absent and dreaming, following separate thoughts of sleep or adventure or defeat. The windows were open and flies were dive-bombing the screens, some of them big deerflies. It was hot and they were furious because there was no water. Water had been brought down to the hives below the garden for the bees, with leaves left floating in the pail for them to stand on while they sipped, but any bee could keep a fly away from water. Maybe it was the brutal droning, like the whine of a saw biting into wood, that did it. Rage came on him suddenly.

It was the fit, the malarial attack. He went rigid, trying to block it. It coursed through his body like a drug, hot and poisonous, flooding his blood: rage. He sat petrified, unable to lift his foot; it was made of lead and so were his hands. There was a steady buzzing in his ears of the thousands of sounds his autonomic body made—the ticking and booming and gurgling, the bristle and spark of nerve endings, arteries throbbing as the blood shot through, whirring and crashing and drawing back, whirring and crashing again, while his brain leaped in his brain pan, and his heart seemed to jump out of his chest. The sensation of violent, involuntary movement when he was sitting still made him dizzy. He put down his fork, hearing it click through the roar and drag of sound. The room fell away. He was going under, being pulled down. Dragged

They drag him to his feet. The white barns, paddocks and tracks scrubbed out in the dark, under a stormfringe of darker trees. Even the moon is down. The moon. Is down. The air smells like the lilacs by the stable doors, sweet in the night. He smells the blood that will spill, the stink of his own fear.

They aren't going to say why, while they hold him up swaying. They don't need to. It's been all over for two days. How they found her blond and dead in the back of the car, by a side road in the old hickory grove. By word of mouth that flies around the black community when this kind of thing happens, he knows. Raped, strangled, left. Black or white man, it'll never be found out. She liked both. They won't say this out loud.

Now he knows that he is it.

Those remarks he heard in passing. The old Negroes warning him, the old stableman's mouth moving, thick with age.

You watch out, boy. Jus' 'cause you can ride anything in this heah stable, don' mean you can ride anything you want.

No laugh. It isn't a joke.

His auntie: Son, you going to get yohsef in trouble . . . why can't you be good like your cousin Luther? Goin' 'round acting like you was the same as white folks! Now you know they can't stand that. I'm a-scared what's going to happen if you keep on with this no-'count girl. Why can't she stay with her own kind and leave my family be? Chile, they are plenty nice gals right here when you get ready to settle down. . . . There's that Marvelle, Dede Tucker's oldest. Why, she can make a sweet potato pie that make you never want to leave her! And she's brown as sugar, and just as pretty as she can be! O chile, why can't you be good!

O husbands, brothers, sons, uncles, lovers. Women weeping and weeping with broken eyes, over rivers and rivers of blood.

Now in the drowned night he hears other voices:

Let's do it, Delmarr.

Can't. Chauncey's on the way. Says he's goin' do it hisself. We're waitin' for Chauncey. HEAR THAT, NIGGER? He's goin' cut that black dick of yours clean off. Then we're going to hang you up in that tree down by the water tank, nigger.

The nigger kilt her! Now, you know he kilt her, Del! Let us at 'im!

Delmarr, a whippin' won't spoil nothin' for Chauncey!

Shut up and get a ladder. Go do what you want, the rest of you. Just don't kill him.

He doesn't say a word, doesn't plead. He's black. He just hears it.

They pin him down. He fights then. Murderous hands tear at his pants. He twists on the ground, spittled, eating Georgia clay, a boot chunked on his belly. Hears the whistle of the whip. It's not the rage flaring after the blows, like gunfire barking from a distant hill, that changes him forever. It's the pain. The pain amazes him. It makes him sad, like he's already dead and gone, grieving down at his lost self. Like he's God. Asking who has done this. Why.

Fear, it was fear, sweeping through him in a flood. He fought it frantically, tried to put it behind the rage, make the rage supreme. Coldly he replaced fear with rage, fighting with the only weapon he had, all trust gone. A willow plate swam in front of him, the picture of the boy and girl in love on it, turned into two birds, flying into the sky away from the parents, the ones in the poor house and the ones in the rich house. Slice of pie plunked down on the temple and the blue cherry tree. He saw this dimly, he clawed toward it. Then gave up and sank back, almost panting. Around him St. Oeggers filled the spaces between red people. He could force that evil out in the open, but how? Kill the son, openly or while he slept? *Right up front, a sword through the eye.* Kill son and father, set the stable on fire? Rape the black-haired daughter? Leave her laying in a pool of blood with her skirt up and that happy smile wiped off her face, in some sweet field under the August sun? Slice the white throats and run? *Heads in one place, bodies in the other.* He pondered them like a fat woman in front of a box of chocolates, overwhelmed with choice, all things possible in this vertigo of fury.

He felt other eyes pulling him into their orbit, his gaze being dragged stumbling from visions into focus. Blue picture plates swam on the wall.

Beneath them, blue unmoving, blue laced with goldless light in the burned face, held his. He turned to it like a blind animal. The eyes searched, unblinking, and the man sat with calm strong stillness. He stared back, knowing he was being read.

A breeze was coming in through the windows. He felt its faint wick on his face. It was strange how knowing he was being ferreted out brought him relief. Around him the kitchen slowly returned to life and the walls were golden with sun. The girls were clearing the last dishes, moving innocent and quick. He heard the slap of dishwater, a distant pond. They looked at each other, him and Grey. The soul in the eyes moved like a second iris, speaking to his. There was no explanation, or apology, just the look that held him and the sense behind it, stirring faintly, that he was known. He flushed, hot again, because no explanation, no apology, made him feel naked. He kept looking, to deny the nakedness, to say he was a man. And around him, he didn't know why, the present returned in its full color, form and life. He let his breath out slowly.

And then rose with a mutter of excuse, filling the room, majestic in temperament and meaning, so that everybody looked; and pushing the chair away casually with the backs of his legs, made for the door.

After the washing-up, Elsa went looking for Harris. She searched the grounds, counted the saddle horses to make sure he hadn't taken one out riding. The lanes were empty. She climbed the ladder to the loft where he sometimes went.

The rolled-back doorway yawned on a terrific view. Forgetting her mission, she stood perilously close to the opening with her bare toes scrunched on the planks where the hay had been fed in. Two stories down, the fields looked burnished and soft, unfolding in thick curves like dough, or the pie crusts Sno-Bird lifted from the board, which hung elastically. The earth really did undulate, just not when you were on the ground. On the ground everything looked flat. This was grand!

She felt a rush of hunger to re-create what she saw, an itch to unearth and possess, make over and over with joy. She tried to find the words. But words were useless, in the end you rushed past them still longing. Suddenly there came a vision, familiar but newly clear: the priest folding the cloth over the cup. Then he shuts the tabernacle door on the host and leaves, having captured heaven and put it in a box.

She turned dizzily from the door and wandered between towers of hay until she found Harris sitting against the wall on a bale. The day's heat was sealed under the roof. He had stripped off his shirt and the darkness of body and hard-skulled head was part of the dusk into which the stacks sank like pylons upholding a building. The loft smelled of sweet hay and his sharp human odor.

"You didn't finish the pie," she announced, flopping down beside him. She seldom addressed him by name.

He didn't answer. She heard him breathing in the dark.

She gave a faint derisive snort and picked up a straw. Gordie could whistle down a straw by shaving the tip off with his Swiss army knife. She tried biting open the stem, but mushed it instead. Harris's arm hung over her like a shadow, dangling on a cocked knee. She reached up thoughtfully and scratched two furrows on his skin. They looked like the marks you could make by running your nails down the velvet love seat in the parlor.

"What the hell are you doing." He pulled his arm away.

"Did you leave because you felt funny?" she asked.

"Yep," he said after a minute.

"That's silly," she said. She licked her finger and wet one of the furrows, to make it vanish. "If anything was wrong, all you'd have to do is tell my father. He'd fix it for you."

"I don't need your daddy to fix anything for me," he said.

Chapter Ten

HARRIS WENT TO A DANCE at the Klaxta reserve the Saturday after the haying. He wanted to stay in his room and read, the way he usually did in the evenings, but he had agreed to go. Basically, he agreed because he liked George Torenose and didn't mind pleasing him.

Elsa had a fit because she couldn't go too. Howling and flinging her leggy self around, huh. If he had behaved like that at her age, his auntie would have given him what-for. Of course by then he'd been man-grown and working for pay, his childhood behind him.

"Certainly not," said her father while she lay at his feet groaning. "Harris doesn't need a child with him on his social outings."

"I won't be a trouble to him," she sobbed, tears running into her mouth. "Pul-eeze."

Sometimes she said and did wild things that stirred him with a kind of envy. Sometimes she aroused a strange longing in him, what he might feel for a place more dreamed of than remembered, a country or odor or unknown sense that for some reason he resisted examining, filled with unease at the power it had to arrest him. He was relieved when Grey lifted her into another room and shut the door.

Tom Pushkin witnessed it too. He and Harris glanced at each other, then quickly away.

"She's really been doing very well," said Tom as if to himself.

While the last junco of the day chipped in the alders outside the bathroom, he dressed in the white shirt and twill pants, fitted at the waist and loose in the hips, that he had bought at the dry goods store. He had put on hard flesh in the last months; his eyes seemed to jump out of the sun-darkened face in the glass. He felt his first flicker of vanity in some time.

George's convoy truck was parked by the gate. The bed was covered with camouflage tarping, stretched over a metal framework that towered high above the cab. During the war it had carried soldiers with arms. In its current role it hauled farm equipment, schoolchildren, vegetables, hay and wood.

"There's two cases of beer in back," said George, turning the key in the ignition.

"You know you guys can't handle booze," said Harris with a grin.

"Go to hell."

The truck roared, belched, lurched into gear. They swayed out of the yard.

The long twilight had started and shadows were lengthening over the fields. Harris rolled the window down. The air streamed like warm water past his hand. Mountain Inn came up on the north side of the road, the long dusky hollow leading to the yards. Piwonka's sign with his brand, an M straddling a horizontal I, hung on chains over the entrance.

The sun broke as it sank behind Mount Endeavour, flooding the summit with red light. The mountain seemed to move back as they approached, but it was really lowering its vast, dignified bulk to accommodate the truck laboring up its flank. Below lay the the valley, its stands of pine and sweet rolls of grassland already in dusk. Harris felt a unexpected expansion of his heart. Well-being, surprising and sweet, throbbed in his chest. He was filled suddenly with the uncomplicated pleasure of a man released from prison for an hour.

He had never studied his pain to see what it was made of, just lashed out at it, escaped any way he could. Now, from the distance given to him by this summer, when he seemed to be re-creating himself, when something was being created in him, he saw that sorrow was one of its shapes.

Then as he rode, with George beside him in his own dream and the evening still ahead, it came to him that the sorrow was not just for himself, but for all of them. They had all failed in some mission that he could not name. *Even those gone to get the ladder, those waiting for Chauncey. Drinking bourbon in the tack room with the windows open on magnolias and blood. Even those assholes.* The sorrow was a spell, like the ruby light leaving the cedars as evening gathered behind them. There were no more shades etched brutally on the Southern night, no more evil. They were just assholes. It was a start.

His sorrow lifted. It rose like his rage at the table the other evening, then sank, then lifted again. He felt somehow not part of this mindless drifting and returning, saved from it by his newfound inspiration. It was a relief to just watch, and not burn. For the first time in his life, he understood the healing power of insight. For the first time, he saw that if he was careful, rage would not destroy him. He would not become an old black man with ashes where his heart and guts had been.

They turned onto a side trail. The truck ground to a stop on a gravel turnout.

"Welcome to our place," said George.

The arrowhead of meadow, wooded on three sides, gleamed like an opal under the midmonth moon. Light poured out the doors and windows of a big cedar shoebox onto the roofs of trucks and cars in a dirt parking lot. A few saddle horses and a mule were turned out on the grass.

They brought a case of beer into the kitchen. The room was hot and close with the smell of venison, berry pie and coffee percolating on a stove that dwarfed the one at Salthill. Fiddle music drifted in from the main room.

"Ever hear of the potlatch?" asked George. "All the members of a tribe used to get together and hold a big feast. Each clan would bring food and gifts to show their wealth. There was so much wealth in those days, we competed with each other to see who had the best stuff. The great artists would bring their art. Everyone dressed up, and there was dancing and singing and eating for days. We only have potlatches now when an important chief dies and his family wants to pay for one."

Harris moved to the doorway. A cowboy band was sawing away at "Red Wing," their faces sweaty and jovial with concentration. Oil lamps were set in caged perches along the walls, the mantles hooded in orange paper, casting wrinkled grannies, couples, little children, men in cowboy outfits and silver jewelry, the few solitary women, all in a harvest glow. Their cheekbones were sharp and ancient in the ruddy light. Men and women had black hair, black as oil or a crow's wing. Their faces floated disembodied and strangely beautiful, freed from the commonplace, against the sharp-shadowed walls. Two men edged past Harris politely, giving him plenty of space. Their hair hung down their backs in knotted clubs that sponged up the light. Occasionally a white face was seen, ghoulishly backlit, moving through the crowd with tense purpose. Next to Harris a woman nursed an infant under a shawl, swaying gently as she stretched to see the dancers. The Klaxta were a quiet, flint-humored people. An occasional shout of "Ahhhh-hah!" or "Hey-a!" sprang randomly from the crowd, like corn popping out of a fry pan. He heard giggling from a little gang of schoolgirls nearby, their calico and flower-sprigged dresses pumpkin scraps as they bumped against each other, too shy to dance. But it was quiet when the music stopped, and voices stayed low.

Looking on, he suddenly saw the faces of his own people,

sweet-sour with dreams that had died young. O they were dark, but not hard and stupid as stones, as they seemed to be when they answered the white man with cast-down eyes, speaking incorrect English. Now they were bright and sturdy, at home with their own. Intelligence rose out of them like little steam clouds. They spoke their own ideas in their own words. They fed the children with dark hands, fed them with songs. He listened to the language forged in bondage. Home. Home.

"Come on, man," said George. "Let's eat."

They got in line at a trestle table laid out with food. A woman scooped beans, biscuits and venison on a paper plate and handed it to him with a smile, revealing shriveled brown gums in front instead of teeth. They made their way to the wall and leaned against it to eat. The food was good. There was constant traffic in and out the door. Some of those returning bore the hallmark of alcohol, a fuddled look and heavy, uncertain tread.

"It's just beer," said George. "Only the men drink and some older women, their kids grown up and they don't care what anyone thinks."

The fiddles stopped, leaving the crowd buzzing like an overturned beetle. Two braying notes split the air so loud Harris nearly jumped. A young Klaxta lowered his bugle, wet his bottom lip with his teeth, made the gesture that signifies tapping spit out of the bell, raised it and brayed again.

"Polka!" came a shout. A line formed quickly. The shy schoolgirls spilled past him with hands linked, legs flashing under their skirts, and were taken into the crowd that surged onto the floor.

Harris watched with alarm as the line swayed toward him to the *oom-pah-pah* of the bugle and the long-bowed screed of the fiddles. Damn, what was this anyway? He tried to ease away but was pulled into the serpent, his hands grasped by a woman and a teenage boy with wet palms. Bodies shoved and swayed. He struggled against them, looking wildly around, every fiber in revolt against the thumping and the weird *oom-pah.* Boots clopped on the floorboards, sounding like ponies being driven over a bridge. Women and girls shot dusky arms into the air. Harris pulled his hands free and ducked out around three men wagging booted feet.

Chapter Eleven

HE GOT A COKE FROM THE KITCHEN and wandered outside. A summer moon green as lichen pierced the crowns of the pines edging the slope of the field. A gang of local teenagers was holding up the wall, brooding. Occasionally one would dart into the night like a deer. He heard their flung shouts in the distance.

A woman was standing alone in the dusty light cast by the kitchen lamp. She wore a fringed cowgirl skirt and boots. Her cowboy hat was pushed back to show a high-bridged nose and bangs cut straight across. He looked at her without looking at her.

"Nice night," she said to the moon. Her arms were crossed tight over her breasts, as if he had broken her feminine solitude.

"Very nice." He smiled.

She studied him all over. "Why don't we sit down?" she suggested, smiling back.

"I don't think that would be a good idea," said Harris.

"Pooh. No one'll care," she said. Her hair smelled sweet and grassy, like the wildflowers drunk with sun on the mountains. "And if they did, *I* wouldn't care. All right?"

He gave up. They sat on the running board of the truck and lit cigarettes. She blew smoke rings and told him she taught at the government school in Four Queens. She was a fine-looking woman, with a fine ass and nice brown legs. She had a cute little oriental face.

"I've heard about you," she said. "You're the *genash* from St. Oeggers'."

"*Genash*. What's that?"

"Black man." She gave him another, wider smile.

"It's refreshing to hear a spade get called a spade." He took a swig of

Coke. "I'm really an English pirate. Or a Spanish pirate. They both made it
to the place I come from."

She looked solemn. "Does that mean you're really white or that you're a
thief?"

"Both. I'm a white man and a *genash*. Naturally that makes me a thief.
It's a curse that strikes all colored people, like the evil eye. Black boys are
born with it."

"And Indians are savages, but really children at heart."

They grinned at each other.

"If I kiss you and take the curse away," she asked slyly, "will that get you
back your soul?"

"*Soul?* Who said anything about soul?" He felt lighthearted, ready to be
amused. It was an innocence he had never experienced, sitting with a woman
at a country dance, moving toward something in a casual way. He felt himself
growing dangerous. "Look, why don't we go in and dance?"

She wasn't worried about him trying to take advantage. Of course he
would. She decided, as they bumped around the floor being studiously ignored by a platoon of her relations, that she was a grown woman and she'd
be with him if she felt like it. She told him he didn't know a thing about
dancing. He admitted it, smiling.

Two dances later they climbed into the bull-nosed cab of the truck. The
seat was covered with a trading blanket. They sat and smoked and spoke,
and spoke less often.

He leaned into the job of getting her ready for love. He talked to her
quietly while his eyes, alight with sympathy, held hers. He made no sudden
moves, but with remarkable economy filled her with interest and desire. She
let him hold her hand and for a long while he was content to hold it, gently
rubbing her fingers, releasing them from time to time as though touching
wasn't what mattered. She knew she was being talked into bed, charmed
and gentled into it, but she didn't care. She was amused and astonished at
his skill, the trouble he took. When he finally lifted her chin to kiss her, she
said *yes* silently to the soft drag of his lips.

"Girl," he whispered, "you're so sweet I think I must be dreaming. Sweet
as cherry pie." He kissed. "Right here. And right here."

She giggled. How strange it was, being coaxed along in that droll tongue!
She didn't even mind being called *girl*. It was a word with invisible quote
marks around it, implying a virginal innocence and gaiety. This wasn't how
Klaxta men courted their women. Their lovemaking was silent and obstinate,

with something in it that reminded her of her uncle's dogs waiting at the door while the family ate dinner; something, too, of triumph, as though they watched her make her way down a corridor with a single door at the end, only one way out. It was the fate of most women. The idea of having to be *charmed,* diverted from other pleasures to join a man in pleasure, was novel and compelling.

"C'mon now, are you real?"

"Maybe, maybe not," she said saucily. "I could be a bad dream."

"Well, bad or good, let me know. Uh-um . . . this is *nice,*" in a honeyed whisper.

When he undid the snaps on her blouse, she didn't try to stop him. She didn't stop him when he popped her bra and caressed her bare back. Would she, O would she? Or would he retire all obedience, conquered either way? With a sigh she turned to him, for the space of a juicy kiss. Love . . . O my god . . . where would they go? Fifty miles back to her place, or a bed in the woods? His beard was moist, recently subdued by razor and lather. The scar's gristle made her shiver. . . . She clasped his neck inside his collar, feeling the taut warm muscle shift.

From behind them came a faint but deep groan.

They froze, startled. She rolled an eye over his shoulder at the glassined rear window.

"Someone's *in* there," she hissed.

They listened. It came again, a gargling moan. "*Uhhh . . . Aw.*"

"Hell," said Harris, releasing her. She sank back, his palm still warm on her tingling flesh.

"*Uh . . . Ugh.*"

She fumbled with her bra hooks. He turned her around and did her up.

"Can you wait?" he murmured to her back.

"All night if I have to," she answered.

Harris jumped down out of the cab, unfastened the tarp in back and hooked it to the ring. He stared for a moment into a deep cave, then returned to the cab. There had to be a flashlight in there somewhere.

"I'm sorry," he muttered, groping around the seat and her legs. She smelled so good it nearly made him dizzy.

"It's all right," she whispered.

He found the flashlight. The beam swung around the back, sending shadows leaping from the floor up the arc of the vault. The other case of beer was pushed in front of the cab window, next to some folded army blankets. A hank of fair hair covered part of the stenciling on the side.

He crawled in the back on hands and knees, following a stale, not-so-good smell, and found a socked ankle. He shifted the case and rolled the limp thing onto one of the blankets, then dropped to the ground and tugged the blanket toward him. Its burden slithered over the slats to the gate.

A few men had gathered, attracted to the flashlight like moths.

"Holy smoke, it's that daffy Sanegger kid," came a voice.

"Shut up," said George, retrieving the flash. "You didn't see this." The light snapped off. Shadows worked silently away between cars.

Harris sat Elsa on the tailgate and held her upright by the shoulders. She wore jeans and a sweater with reindeers marching across the yoke. She was dead drunk. She weaved in his grip and stared at him with glazed, senseless eyes.

"Hawish," she muttered.

George found one of the quart bottles in the case, emptied and put back in its honeycombed section. The cap had even been screwed back on.

"Poor thing," said the cowgirl, joining them. "You'd better let me help." But when they tried to pry the child loose from Harris, she stiffened and struck out blindly.

"Get yer sodding hands off me."

"Hold her over, she's gonna throw up."

Elsa retched while the cowgirl stroked the hair back from her face. They tossed earth over the vomitus and mopped her mouth with water. Elsa wept, choked, crowed. Harris wrapped her in the blanket and lifted her in his arms. She fell asleep at once with her face against his shoulder, an arm hooked around his neck.

"You can take her home on Roger's mule," said George good-humoredly.

"The hell I will," said Harris. "I'll bring your truck back in the morning."

He loaded his burden into the passenger side. He straightened up.

"Look," he said. "About her."

George shrugged. "Sandrine? She's a free woman. She lives in town. I don't give a damn."

"That's all I want to hear," said Harris.

The cowgirl was waiting, looking entertained.

"I'm sorry, cherry pie," he whispered. "Another time soon?"

"I might be around," she said dryly. "And I might not."

He kissed her farewell. Her lips were cool and distant. Damn that fool kid, anyway.

The lamps were all lit on the ground floor of the castle. Grey watched Harris emerge from the truck and climb the path into the light with his daughter in his arms. Her sneakered feet dangled from one end of the blanket, her head bobbled at the other. She snored, her shoulders trembling with each snore like paper wings in a draft.

"Stowed away in back and drank a quart of beer," said Harris. The two men inspected the face with its sealed lids and slack mouth. "She's going to feel like hell in the morning."

"Thank god you found her before I lost my mind," said Grey.

Harris carried her upstairs and put her in bed. While Grey went through the chest of drawers for a nightgown he stood at the window, scratching his neck and yawning with lust. From up here he could see a light from the Klaxta reserve, shining through the firs on the mountain.

Chapter Twelve

SOMETIMES HE WANTED HIS OWN PEOPLE, like he sometimes wanted greens made the way they were down South, boiled good with bacon, then some peanuts sprinkled on top, and nothing else would do. He wanted to touch a woman of his race. He was living in the land of the blond people—that was what he called it, in his best mood. The Land of the Blond, Blue-eyed People. Red beards, green eyes, dishwater hair, strawberry blond, slate and agate eyes, freckles, orange-peel noses, blue noses in the winter. Watery little red eyes. Pink boiled necks. White bodies, hairy and burly or lean and hairy and laddered with ribs. Because of Grey he couldn't hate the way he wanted to anymore. He couldn't blame them for him being so far from home, either. It was just the way things had worked out. So he plunged into them, dove into the whiteness because that was all there was to do. It was either jump in or lose his mind. In some way that jumping in turned into being a chronic reader.

He read in the evenings when chores were over. He borrowed the turf registry and plowed through it, undeterred by his ignorance of bloodstock terminology. Then he set about reading everything else in the house. There was a diligence in his nature that opposed whatever made him do crazy things like giving himself up to the police so he could sit in the street with a dead woman. Maybe it was the same diligence. He worked his way methodically through the bookshelves. When he didn't know a word he consulted the dictionary. Sometimes he just read the dictionary, drawn on to the next word by the previous one. The words opened up like cocoons, and the mysteries of their meanings burst on him like butterflies and took soft, powdery wing in his heart. Grey said once that his reading was voracious and indiscriminate. He looked up *voracious* and *indiscriminate* in the Webster's Sixth.

He read books on Canadian history and biographies of settlers in the

Northwest Territories. He read classic fiction and mysteries Grey had brought from Ireland. He read books about people and experiences and places as remote from his own life as the moon, as remote as another century. He honed his skills during hours lying on the bed in his stockinged feet, eyes screwed up under the light of the lamp he had confiscated from the parlor, turning pages.

In a collection of stories by Somerset Maugham he found one about an Englishman living in the tropics whose native wife put a curse on him when he left her to return to England. The curse was that he would die before he reached sight of land. The Englishman laughed it off, said it was all super-stitious nonsense. But as soon as he was on board ship, he developed a mysterious case of hiccups that he couldn't get rid of. Unable to eat or sleep, he began to sink in health and fell ill. The ship put about for the nearest port to seek help, but the Englishman died at dawn of the day they sighted land.

Harris finished that story with an ironic smile on his lips.

There were the racing stories of John Taintor Foote, the word *nigger* scat-tered through them like ground seed. A remorseless code of honor seemed to bind white folk, their chicanery and wrongheadedness, to black folk and their comic sensibility. He studied the stories carefully the way a scholar studies voodoo, as though he could through sufficient concentration come to an understanding of the bizarre, mysterious beliefs they reported. He thought them over without internal conflict, lying in the summer twilight with the curtains open and the strong lamp of the moon reflected on the walls. It seemed to him that land and possessions lay behind it all: land, wealth and possessions, including women, the most prized possessions of all, more worth fighting over than anything else. He thought of bullet-headed young black boys, fine crops that had to be plowed under any way they could. When he wasn't reading and this was on his mind, he thought how good it would be to fuck a white woman, not because she was better than a black woman or a superior fuck, either, but because it would be like robbery, fertilizing another man's rows with a smile and a grunt, stealing his history away.

He read Twain and Hemingway, books about Galway and Scotland. He read about the savage Celts who roamed the steppes and forests of primitive Europe, who dyed their blond hair purple, blue and pink with nut dyes and berry juice. Who preserved their enemies' heads in boxes of cedar oil or hung the skulls like Christmas bells from their horses' bridles. How they worked themselves into hypnotic frenzies with war dances and wild piping, and stormed into battle naked with their hair greased into towering poles. How they were cunning and mixed the truth with magic and prophecy until it was all the same to them.

When he was tired of reading, he would put the books aside and reflect on how good it felt to be around Grey. Grey was real.

Gordon left for Montreal at the end of August. The girls were grief-stricken. They genuinely loved and admired him, as brothers deserve; they hung over him and gave him intimations of the pleasures of female company. Sno-Bird packed a basket with chicken, a blackberry tart and a slice of Stilton from the aunts, unobtainable in the Skillihawk. He accepted basket, embraces, farewells, with solemn grace. They were his womenfolk.

"Mind your manners," he cautioned Elsa. She clung to him like a monkey, wordless. "I'll be back. We'll have some good times again."

"I'm so happy for you," whispered Flavia, with her arms around his neck. "Why didn't you tell me this was what you wanted?"

"He's going to be a doctor," said Elsa importantly to Harris.

"I bet he'll be real good at cutting people open," said Harris.

"I wish you had let me go with you," said Grey on the way to the CPR station. "We could as easily have driven."

"It's too long to be away," said Gordon happily. They were coming down from the pass. The world lay ahead, his world: beside him was his father, that mercurial being who had somehow managed to be there for what mattered, wanting to drive him across the country, helping fund him for this thing that confounded his own sense of what St. Oeggers did. He was going to study medicine and his father didn't dislike him for it. There wasn't much more to wish for than that.

The golds and greens of summer faded. The country fell under the spell of an autumn pallet, a haze of squash, rust, sage and silver, of animal-pelt fawns and browns. The aspens turned scarlet and a tremulous, veined yellow. These are our shades for autumn, said Grey, the turning aspens and the night sky. They went out on the porch in the evening to look, to be sure it was still there; a panorama of darkness, but not of stillness or nothingness. A violet sheen around the moon, a liquid thickening of color at the margins of that heavenly body, drew them irresistibly. The thick, strokable nap of the sky was scattered with milky skeins glimmering in margarite nets. They came out separately, stood without speaking, gazed, moved back in, as evening chores called or were finished. They went, men and women and children, dark, fair and red, not to be amazed but to look and be comforted, to be sure of it: that the night, like the ceiling of a vast and necessary house, still held them firm to earth.

At the foot of the stairs, after one of these evenings, Grey offered Harris the money to buy a horse.

"Why?"

"I imagine you've begun saving for one," said Grey.

"I have," he said warily.

"Then it stands to reason I might want to contribute. Come in, please."

Harris followed him into the office. The ghosts of the photographs gleamed in the lamplight.

"Find one," said Grey, handing him the current Thoroughbred registry. "One you think will suit. I'll make up the difference between the price and what you have to spend."

Still Harris couldn't believe it. He stared at the registry, feeling everything in him, what he had endured, what he hated and feared, revolt against belief.

"Why do you want to do this?" he asked.

Grey hesitated. A look of craft glided over his face, like sun shooting through a cloud. It was Elsa's expression when she wanted to hide something. "I suppose because in Ireland, a man with a gift such as you have with horses can name his terms. Your own horse should come with this job."

"This isn't Ireland."

"I would feel more comfortable." The look was gone, he had imagined it.

"I'd rather pay you back," he said.

"If you insist," said Grey. "If your manhood requires it."

He got exasperated. It was the first time he had ever been plain exasperated with a white man. "I can't give you anything back except money," he said. And knew as he said it that it was not true, and that Grey knew it, too.

"Suppose I don't stay here," he added, to throw them both off the track.

"The offer's firm," said Grey, putting out the lamp.

Tom Pushkin left for Vancouver, taking Flavia with him. She was to stay with the aunts and be "brought out" by Daisy. A stream of bills from dress shops made their way from the city to her father's desk; during the season that followed, a flow of checks for luncheons, dances and other affairs was dispatched to Lisnasheoga, accompanied by some grumbling.

The remnants of a herd of Lapp reindeer, with brown shawls and dewy, flapping proboscises, migrated from Mount Endeavour and settled in the east meadow for the winter. Snow could be counted upon to fall within a week of their arrival. A series of light storms passed through the valley. Bales of timothy somersaulted out of the loft. The roads turned glossy and treacherous; Dai and Harris spread rock salt on the drive to keep the truck from skidding on the long turn down into the yard.

From the first snow through March the house was closed off except for the ground-floor offices. Elsa slept, read and studied in the parlor next to the dining room, where a fire was kept; her father slept on the veranda in a truckle bed before the hearth. The fires and kitchen range brooded day and night, fed from the slowly sinking monument of wood on the porch. Woolen underwear hung like headless men in the upstairs hall, crotches unsnapped, inching dry at glacial speed. The hens set in canned-goods boxes filled with straw in the pantry. On mild days the rooster stepped jerkily in through the back door, his comb bright as three holly berries. The peeping of chicks in early spring accompanied the groans and twitchings of the dogs under the table, the slanging of pans as one of the men cooked for the rest. The men shook chicks out of their boots in the mornings and sometimes trod on them by accident. The fragile corpses were tossed in the fire to keep the dogs from getting used to their taste.

Sno-Bird came to air out the rooms and bake bread. She would wave a hand to clear away the "man smell," fire up the range and drop certain leaves in the kettle to drown the smell in boiling amber. Their own smell comforted them. Her female odor they liked too, of a woman no longer in youth, worldly with children grown: a powder puff left on a shelf, a knot of mature sweet sage.

There was tack and harness to clean. They cleaned and oiled the guns. They patched jeans and mended horse blankets on the industrial Singer, pushing the treadle with broad foot, guiding the stuff through with fingers and swear words. Grey did accounts and thought about prospects for the coming year. He placed, as was his custom, advertisements for the stud in carefully chosen American and Canadian bloodstock publications. In the evenings he and Elsa read before the fire companionably, sometimes to each other. She sang in a wavering soprano, "My Heart Is Offered Still to Thee" and "He Moved Through the Fair," while the fire reddened her legs. In home pasture, the mares waited out the final weeks of their eleven-month gestations. Those who looked ready to go were kept in the stable in one or another of the boxes set aside for foaling.

After the first snow, Harris took the train to Chicago. He had a little money to spend, carefully put by. He got a cheap room in the Negro district, dressed up at night and went out to see what trouble he could get in. In a shop that catered to Negroes he bought a sports jacket and slacks in a pale cocoa to wear with a baby blue shirt. He also bought a cream snap-brim hat with a coffee ribbon.

"Now you *know* I'm clean, man," he said with a big white smile, checking himself out in the mirror.

Three times he went to a restaurant run by West Indians to eat beans and rice, curry with mango chutney, saffron chicken smothered in a fiery red sauce with fried bananas on the side. He went to the clubs. He ordered ginger ale and listened to jazz in tiny, blue-lit holes. One time he heard Billie Holiday, lush as a lily, swaying a little but in command of the mike, in a place so small you had to go outside to change your mind.

He didn't have to pay for love. He found a sweet thing in the bar to spend some time with. He'd always been lucky that way.

He took the train back and got off at the station in Four Queens. The air was cold and tranquil, the yards silent except for the grating of a tractor scooping fresh snow to the side of the road. He carried his suitcase to the highway and got a lift from a farmer who hung out at Dee's and knew Harris because he bought gas for the truck there. The old man drove him clear home. Harris had a feeling the man was glad of his company, though neither of them said much. He had leisure to notice that in winter the mountains looked taller and bluer above the plains.

Grey and Elsa went to Lisnasheoga to spend Christmas with Flavia and the aunts. He took Dai with them and left Harris in charge of the ranch.

"You're invited," he told Harris. "George and Javier can look after things here."

He said no. He had never met these women, but he thought he knew what they were like, how they would feel about people like him.

On Christmas Day he did the morning chores, then sat down with a bowl of heated-up soup and opened his gifts. It was snowing, a screen of white falling endlessly past the windows, layers of screens of white. Snowflakes clung to the glass like soft patterned kisses before melting. There were two packages carelessly wrapped in red and green Santa Claus paper. The first was a steel Ronco lighter engraved with the letter *H.* Just *H,* in strong curlicues. He flipped it on and a torch of flame shot out.

The second gift was a dictionary in a red and blue cover. He turned it over in his hands.

Chapter Thirteen

GREY RODE NORTH along the eastern edge of the valley as far as Mount Skillihawk. Ice was loosening in the streams. In a few weeks the spring freshets would be fully under way, snowcaps melting at four thousand feet, everything breaking down into the great drainage systems of the Enid and the McKenna. He picked up the road beneath the Bluffs and rode toward the lake between columns of lodgepole ranked in cold shadow.

He heard a sound, measured and heavy as the tread of giants. It shook the needles of the trees and sent a few quivering loose on its current. The earth, still slumbering in its dream of spring, stirred as though something were rising beneath it; sound undulated in a wave toward him. The wave tightened until the stretch of road became its locus, though its reverberation still stirred the trees. Whatever it was came from the lake not a half mile away. He heard men shouting, then their voices were lost in the thunder of hooves. A herd of horses swung around the bend. Their packed bodies spanned the road, a wall of chestnut, bay, black, sorrel and dun horseflesh with tossing manes and tails; sixty or seventy horses in flight with eyes rolling, half wild after a winter on the plateau. The remuda was coming in.

Grey pulled up beside the road and let the ponderous mass foam and eddy around him. One of the men loped toward him from the rear, moving along the shoulder past the herd.

"MacRae!" Grey shouted above the din. "Have you seen any of my two-year-olds?"

"Nope! Saw a bear bring down a deer about five miles back, though. Dragged it off still twitching. Nearly lost the whole bunch right then and there—they spooked like mad."

"I didn't know bears killed game. There's so much fish in the river—"

"They don't, usually. Eat berries, grubs, fish and stuff. But they sometimes hunt after hibernating. This one must've got up early."

Grey swung his big buckskin mare around. "Could your men keep an eye out for two of my colts? Chestnuts with flaxen points. One has a white sock on his off hind. They're inseparable. They didn't come in last fall with the rest. . . . I thought they might have joined your remuda."

"Nope." MacRae pinched the butt of his cigarette dead and dropped it in his breast pocket out of habit. He had the flinty, roving eye of a man who has spent his life scanning distance. "Wasn't anything that didn't belong there but an old cow pretending to be a horse. I'll keep a watch out for them, though. They could be wandering around in the low meadows. There's new grass poking up there."

They saluted each other. He watched MacRae's gray scud back along the gully in full sail. The remuda trailed around the turn and was lost to sight. In the distance a few aspens bent toward the tarnished oval of the lake like women studying themselves in mirrors.

Flavia and the aunts were at Salthill for Grey's birthday. Gordon was back, too, making a flying visit, literally; Grey had met him at the airport in Darmstadt. The entire family was together except for Harris, who had asked for a fortnight off and was gone on some mysterious journey.

"He's back," said Dai, coming in from the kitchen. "An' he's pullin' a horse trailer."

They threw on their coats and went down to the yard, leaving behind the poached salmon, the corn pudding, the sherry in the Waterford glasses. No meal at Salthill was more important than a new horse.

The Chevrolet was parked in front of the stable passageway with the trailer hitched behind. The horse's tail, clubbed like a hunter's, hung over the gate. Harris got out, natty in a turtleneck, sports jacket and new dark jeans.

"I knew you'd come back with something," said Grey. "Take him out, son."

Harris unbolted the door and lowered it to make the ramp, then went into the trailer. After a short delay a pair of enormous hindquarters emerged, followed by a long body under a horse rug. Harris snapped the lead to a fence rail, unfastened the rug and pulled it away.

The horse was of heroic height and build. His coat was solid red, the highlights like shot silk, following the contours of his body in blazes and swirls. There was no black on his legs as was common in horses with red coats. Mane and tail were the same shade, slightly duller in tone, like unfinished cedar. He had no marking, either sock or star or stripe. The head turned toward them with an eagle's glare in the eye. He sucked the cold mountain air into his nostrils, tossed his head and snorted. The snort sounded like the boom of a cannon.

Harris detached the lead from the rail. The horse revolved around him, stepping with great deliberation in the mud.

Iseult gave an unladylike hoot. "What a grand creature! He must be over seventeen hands. Wherever did you find him?"

Harris eyed her. It was the first time he had seen the aunts. "California. He's Canadian-registered, though."

They stared at him in disbelief. California was as far away as the moon, a distant planet of palms and winterless sunny desert.

"I'm going to let him out," said Harris. "He needs to stretch."

"A good idea," murmured Grey. So California was where Harris had spent his fortnight. Harris was resilient; that was the form his vitality took. He looked thin and etiolated now, as though the journey into America had made inroads on his health.

The dinner party trooped behind him down the lane to the paddock next to the training ring. Dai trotted ahead to open the gate. Harris led the horse in and unsnapped the lead. Everybody lined up along the fence.

The chestnut wheeled and trotted swiftly around the paddock, making a wide swing when he passed the gate. His stride was smooth, powerful and reaching. His mane, trimmed to racing length, rippled away from his crest and the clubbed tail sprang stiffly from his croup.

"He's beautiful," said Flavia, shivering with cold under Gordon's anorak.

Gordon watched the horse sweep past with rage in his heart. What a brute! A bloody enormous thing the size of a draft horse! How dare Harris bring a horse like that to his father's place, to eat expensive fodder and require hours to be taken care of! He could feel the color climbing up his face. He set his teeth, as close as he had ever been to being outside of himself. How had Harris paid for the animal? Good horses weren't cheap, and this was a good horse.

Elsa said nothing, crammed between her brother and sister with shining eyes. She had grown nearly as tall as Flavia.

"Gelded a bit late, wasn't he?" said Grey dryly. The arched neck was as fully developed as a stallion's, a sign that the horse had been neutered in maturity, not as a colt as was generally done.

The red horse shifted to a gallop and floated around the paddock.

"He's goin' awful fast," muttered Dai.

Harris opened the gate and went in. The horse seemed to sense his intent and circled to the far end of the paddock. He wore what looked like light-weight racing plates, Grey noted. Probably Harris would have him shod more suitably for this terrain after he had settled in. For a horse of his size, this one was amazingly swift and light in movement, in the way large men some-times are light on their feet. His attention seemed directed not toward his near surroundings but to what lay beyond the windbreak. His ears pricked forward until they nearly touched and his stare was fixed on Mount En-deavour, lying cold and pied with snow in the distance.

To Grey the horse seemed out of place in the setting of Salthill, its neat paddocks and stable, its air of domestic containment. Wilderness was surely the rightful frame for such equine majesty, wilderness or the realm of the fantastic. He felt some apprehension as of the mysterious, as in his father's library with its collections in glassed and beeswaxed cases, the sour odor of woodcuts under parchment. Those ocherous prints had always brought their musk to him, as the sight of a lilac brings to mind its singular fragrance. Heraldic images arose, and the forests of medieval Europe where such splen-dor roamed unhindered, to be tamed like the unicorn by magic or a virgin's touch, but not by any ordinary means. It was for creatures like this that such legends had been made. But at what price, by what treachery had the unicorn been taken!

Harris walked forward, clinking the chain lead against his thigh. The horse doubled back and bounded away from him across the paddock. The explo-sion of speed and energy was instantaneous. They stood silent, marveling.

"Oh god," breathed Flavia suddenly into cupped hands. The paddock fence was six feet high, the footing mushy and treacherous.

The red horse rose to the fence and cleared it with ease. The bound tail flopped over the muscular rump.

Harris ran to the far end, the tail of his jacket whipping behind, and ducked between the rails. But the horse was already halfway across the field.

"It's no good, it's no good," trilled Daisy, until now forgotten. Daisy had never done much with horses.

Alive with pain at sight of the laboring, hopeless figure, Elsa slogged awk-wardly after him in her galoshes, around the paddock, through the icy pud-dles that everywhere lay, out into the meadow. The horse was running at amazing speed, floating really, past the tamaracks. As Elsa watched, he cleared the boundary fence and became a speck on the range, then not even a speck. She put her hand to her mouth.

Harris ran past her, headed for the stable. His face was an ashen mask, frightening, only she was not frightened; she blazed with ardor and fear for him.

Grey's voice rose on the air.

"Everyone who can, saddle up, please. We'll have to try and catch him."

The horse had a registered name, as all purebred Thoroughbreds did, but they never used it. The Red, they called him. It would have been, as Flavia pronounced, "totally superfluous, really gilding the lily," to call a horse that glorious anything more fanciful.

Wherever they went, they kept an eye out for the Red. He was not in the valley or on the range below the pass. Harris posted a reward for him on the board at Dee's, where the rigs pulled out onto the highway after tanking up. Piwonka's outfit looked; the Klaxta looked when they went into the mountains to scout their hunting lays. Inquiries were posted at the ranger's station in the provincial park at the foot of the pass.

Grey sent a note to Wanda Creek, asking his friend George Georgewood, who had his ranch there, to watch for an unmarked red gelding between seventeen and eighteen hands high, wearing a halter but no lead. "He's quite noticeable," he scrawled at the end. There would be no sign of the horse in Wanda Creek, of course. Already he believed in its mythology; he embraced it with a hundred generations of superstition. Such a beast would never be found grazing in a pasture, or roaming with the remuda like an ordinary mortal. His two colts finally straggled into the yard, one of them lamed from a fall in a ditch, but the red horse had vanished.

Chapter Fourteen

A WEEK AFTER THE RED'S DISAPPEARANCE, Harris packed a bed-roll and saddled Petronel, the former steeplechaser he used most often as a saddle horse.

With its doorway letting into the stable passage and its one window shuttered, the tack room lay in perpetual twilight. Leather seemed to thrive there, its earthy masculine odor fulminating in the gloom. A desk was shoved against the wall, its drawers full of dried-up pens and tins of petrified saddle soap. No one had used the scarred surface to write on within memory. Like the furnishings of the adjacent small room, which had a bed and ancient cooker and must have been lived in by a farmhand, the desk had been there when Grey bought the ranch.

Harris added a couple of hobbles to the kit, one for the chestnut to keep him from straying, the other for the Red.

Grey came in, ducking his head in the low doorway. "You'd better take the rifle," he said, nodding at the Winchester on its rack.

"I'm not big on guns," said Harris.

"A knife, then," said Grey calmly.

"I don't have one."

Grey reached into his coat pocket and produced an ivory-handled object. The ivory was yellow like old piano keys, with brown striations along the grain. It was strange to see that familiar shape in Grey's hand with the fingers half curled around it, their joints dusted with blond hair.

Grey pressed the catch under the hilt. The blade shot out with a warning hiss. Harris didn't move.

"You can defend yourself with this," said Grey. "And pick a stone out of a hoof if need be."

He stared at the gleaming blade. "I knew you had it."

"You did not," said Grey, folding it back into the shaft. "Here, take it. Though what you want with a dago's tool like that when you can shoot a gun like a decent Englishman I don't know."

Harris grinned. "I'm a dago." He put the knife in his jacket.

It looked like rain. Harris mounted the chestnut and shrugged into a slicker. "I appreciate getting time to look," he said.

"No matter; we'll carry on," said Grey. He added lightly, "Don't take this thing too damned hard."

"I just want him back," said Harris, surprised.

"Of course. He's valuable and I hope you find him, though he looks like a hell-raiser to me, frankly. Good luck."

After he had gone over the surveyor's map, instinct drove Harris onto the trail to Mount Endeavour. The Red would have been seen by now if he was still in the valley, and the plateau where the remuda wintered was pretty much grazed out. It had to be the mountains, and he could starve there. The upper meadows hadn't thawed and any grass he got would have to be pawed out of the ice, something stable-bred horses weren't used to. And coming from California, the horse had no winter coat.

By late afternoon Harris had gained the passage into high country and it was raining. Ice water dripped off his slicker and curly-brimmed Stetson; the trail was a string of ponds. He rode off-trail where the footing was better, moving west from the Klaxta reserve. Instead of melting in the downpour, the snow stiffened into frozen buttresses coated with skins of yellow ice. Barren slides provided the only relief from monotonous miles of forest climbing upward into the mist.

Alone and physically miserable, he began to grieve. He strained for a sight of the red-coated horse, stumbling ahead of him in devil's flight. A thing had been removed from him, something that had given him hope . . . his own horse. He would have viewed with a like pride his own house, as an extension of his blood and sinew and his own hammering and sawing. To run the brush over that heavy coat that was paid for, breathing in its red richness—the idea had come to him in a gush whenever he stopped the van to let the horse out. There had been a youthful pride in passing other horse vans, even station wagons full of families, with the hot great thing stirring behind him. He had an uncanny idea that if he looked back into the window of the van, he would see not a horse, but instead as if in stained glass, a miniature landscape of grasses flowing like currents in a river, brown and gold and tawny ash, and of plantations of fir thrusting long fingers onto a valley floor.

The depression deepened as he traveled through fog and past looming granite without a sighting, until hopelessness turned him to lead. He did what he always did when the black mood came, wanted to kill something, even a rabbit. Shrouded figures hung tar-black from the trees, tattered limbs and swinging feet dripping when he passed under them.

He felt under the slicker for the familiar knot of the switchblade.

He stole the first knife off a dead man in an alley. He didn't know why the man was dead. There was no mark on him, no slash or bullet hole; he was just slumped against the wall, legs flopped out. Even though Harris had never seen death, when he saw the bloodless face he knew. He pawed through the clothing. He needed a fix and there could be money, a wallet, anything. His nose was dripping and his hands shook. He found a roll of bills and a knife in the inside pocket of the jacket. He stuffed them in his pants and left. He didn't know about the knife until after he had dozed through the fix. Sometime the next day, or the next, he took it out and discovered the switch that made the blade shoot out of the shaft. After that he always had it on him. Sometimes he thought of snapping it out and driving the blade into his own neck. He could do that, if he had to.

The rain stopped on a cold, lightless dusk. Harris pitched camp for the night in a clearing with a rain-swollen stream gushing through it around rocks and ridges. The dead monument of a cedar, probably hit by lightning, lay in charred slabs against a boulder, forming a shelter against the elements. The niche of ground where tree crossed rock looked dry enough to sleep on.

He unsaddled Petronel and spread some oats for him on a piece of tarp. After cleaning up the oats, the chestnut found a dry patch under the nearby pines and hemlocks and lowered himself to the ground. Harris smoked a cigarette and watched the horse roll, scratch and grunt, his shoes flashing in foliage the color of rusty nails. The horse got to his feet and shook himself like a damp dog, then shambled back to camp for his dessert apple.

Harris gathered all the dry kindling he could find, built a little pyre and lit it with the Ronco. The flames grew to a blaze that consumed itself with crackling noises and sparked when he prodded it.

He had never camped before, but he'd always been good at figuring out how to do things. He scrambled two eggs in the skillet he had packed and ate them by the fire, wiping the skillet clean with a hunk of Sno-Bird's sourdough. He boiled water in an aluminum pan by balancing it over the coals on rocks carefully placed earlier, then added a scoop of coffee and one of the eggshells. The nutty smell of the coffee brewing drifted through frigid air perfumed with pine and dank earth. Harris poured some into a mug, pushing the broken shell and grounds behind the thin stream with a spoon. The sky had cleared and the stars were out. He drank with gloved hands wrapped around the mug. The chestnut stood as close to the fire as a horse will comfortably go, dozing on three legs while the light cast a round sheen on his belly.

His bedroll was a sack made out of blankets sewn together and ribbed with heavy stitching to make them lie flat. Harris urinated at the root end of the tree, then climbed into the bag with everything on except his hat, belt and boots.

The sky was pierced with stars and hazy clusters of more distant stars, all suspended in the indigo night. He studied them, lying on his back with the wool scarf that went under the Stetson pulled down around his ears, listening to the occasional cough of the horse. He had read a little about the stars. These were the closest bodies, part of earth's own galaxy. Another galaxy lay beyond it, in a night like the one surrounding him: galaxies without number filled the unbelievable reaches of eternity. Dizzy with staring, he became a loose star passing through universes of blue shot with the pathways of billions of stars. He shook his head a little, to stop himself as the flight.

The sky was a canopy of black or navy or sunny cloth covering a void. The void was God, the unseeable and unknowable. He shivered suddenly in his deep center. Why did he see God in that void? It was an image that tied him to other men, other minds. He wasn't sure he liked that. He was just starting to understand what it meant to be original. Was he incapable of believing outside the framework of what he'd been taught? In Indian cultures the framework of the spirit was strong, the mysterious revealed, everything laid out in clear historic patterns. There was a story for the sun and rain, the animals, crops, childbirth, rivers, the differences between the sexes. The mysterious was revealed while it remained a mystery. He thought of church, the pews and colored paper on the glass, the Good Book version of genesis. No sun story, no rain story after genesis, just the void like a prophecy, with little figures running around beneath it living and dying and procreating.

His forehead ached from the cold. He pulled the blankets up, turned on his side, and summoned sleep. But the night bore down on him with smothering force. He opened his eyes and stared into the blackness that pressed all around. He had slept outside before, in the fields by the highway, but never with this suspenseful waiting for something awful to happen. Suddenly he felt himself rise toward the roof of night, parting company with earth—torso a slab, toes stretched apart, cords popping in his neck, brain pan whirling. Terror elevated him. He lay rigid with the hollows of his back and legs cupped, fighting being absorbed into the night, being turned into nothing.

Then he dropped suddenly into a deep peace. One minute he was frightened because this primeval night was stronger he was, stronger than God. The next, the sky was a friendly, hovering cape. He felt its rich dark folds drop around him, and fear was gone. He lay in quiet wonderment that it no longer mattered what became of him. And knew that what might become of him was what he had feared. The fire's coals flowered and blackened at his side, the ash feathered up in gray heaps. He breathed in wood smoke and ozone, then was absorbed into the earth.

The next morning was dry and clear. After breaking his fast with dried fruit and hardtack, Harris rode on into the wilderness. A Steller's jay shot past, swooping through a grove in blue flight to where its nest was hidden. That was his color in a world waking from death, blue and the split-up trees lying like chunks of soft yellow flesh on the snow. Winter cushioned everything. The snap of a branch, rustle of reeds in the few pools, hollow silence running down the hollows between ridges, sent no echo back. After an hour the plod of hooves and creak of saddle leather were stilled by the din of a river. Coming on it, he reined in and watched the water roar downhill throwing chunks of itself over the rocks, bounding snow-laced into swarming pools shot with brown foam.

He reached the high country. A herd of wild sheep with horns that curled backward sprang out of nowhere and up a mountainside as if on coils. It was unlikely that the Red would be found at this altitude, so he traveled laterally north toward the winter plateau, lost on the other side of flights of mountains, in the smoke of ridges. At night he lay in his bedroll and watched the moon tread through the clouds and the shooting stars jet and stutter. Boreal light hundreds of miles north sent up mares' tails of pink and violet vapors.

On the second afternoon, as he sat on a ridge overlooking one of the valleys that dropped suddenly between the mountains, a cougar padded over a ledge less than ten yards in front of him. He must have been upwind of it, because it ignored his presence. Harris sat very still. The size of it was amazing. It was a giant version of a housecat, with a lion's head and long tail that flicked nervously at the tip. Its coat was dun-colored, with dark stippling around the loins and muzzle.

He had never seen anything so proud, so unselfconscious, concentrated and alert. He watched it prowl the ridge, then drop down onto a lower ledge and vanish. All while the chestnut nipped peacefully at the new plants growing around the rocks, as unaware of the cat as the cat had been of them.

He saw no big, red-coated Thoroughbred, and after three days of looking knew he had run out of time. His store of oats, coffee and food was nearly gone. He had to get back to Salthill.

He made his way down the mountains, riding through the Klaxta reserve in case the red horse had moved on there. The shotgun houses of weathered clapboard faced each other across the road, their back gardens starting to bud with vegetables. Flowers the size of cabbages were growing by the road where the snow had melted.

Harris cruised the darkened streets of Four Queens some nights later, past the Catholic church, the kerchief-sized park, the wharf where the steamer slept wrapped in oilcloth and canvas. The stars were sprinkled like salt over the lake. He parked on a side street in front of a bungalow. The roof and porch were matted with yellowed virgina creeper and its rootstock. No one would know who the truck belonged to, because Grey disliked advertising and had never had the ranch name painted on it. It was a beige Ford truck like any other beige Ford truck.

"Welcome," she said, closing the door gently behind him. The house was warm and smelled like baked salmon.

"Smells good." He sniffed and smiled, looking around.

She cast him an amused glance. "Tastes good, too."

He followed her into the kitchen.

She sat with him while he ate. From time to time he caressed her with his friendly, expectant, impertinent smile. The smile said they were in this together, and there would be no backing out. By the time he had finished, in his crisp white shirt with his good table manners, jumping up to take his plate to the sink, she felt heavy, locked into a congressional agreement, bound and made over to the sensual.

They undressed by lamplight. He let his slacks rest courteously on his hips. His body was a sooty brown with old-penny highlights, like the kettle on her fireplace mantel. There were lighter marks like scratches, long and short ones, straight and broken, on his abdomen and below. He had the lean, flat horseman's musculature, with its air of springy capability.

As for him, he sensed her shyness, which wasn't virginal, but the shyness of a woman who is spending her first time with a new man. He understood in a rough way that she guarded her body, afraid of how it would look as she came out of the dress, whether it was pleasing enough. His job was to make her not give a damn what she looked like, only what she felt like.

"Did you bring what I said?" she asked.

He felt in the pocket of the jacket looped over a chair and put three small foil-wrapped packets on the nightstand.

They lay in a hushed embrace under the lamp. After a while she sat up and threw her pink slip over the shade. Now their bodies glowed, his terracotta, hers apricot, without shadows or indentations to mar their planetary luster. The tufts at their groins were russet shrubs, the nipple he nuzzled a tiny plum, those purple ones that were sweet and so juicy.

She watched him peel the foil off one of the packets. He looked at the thing in the palm of his hand.

"Do we need this?" he asked.

"Of course." She smiled. "I'm not going to get in any trouble. Haven't you ever used one?"

"No."

"Oh my god," she said. "I'll help you. Come here."

Chapter Fifteen

ELSA WAS RIDING THROUGH THE FIELDS above the Bluffs, hunting game and not having much luck.

It was mid-June, but the earth was still dappled and streaked with snow. A blanket of new alkali stirred in the thaw, beneath a faint breeze that probably carried her scent before her. Elsa pondered riding on to the lake. She and Gordie often came back from Lake Lavender with ruffled grouse, ptarmigan or rabbit dangling behind their saddles. Hunting was a necessary duty shared by family members. There was a side of beef every year from Piwonka and a lamb from a farmer in Lockerby, but game made up much of the table meat at Salthill.

She skirted the ridge, looking for the wash everyone traveled to get to the road below. It had been created by a landslide, then further widened and deepened by seasons of rain and drought. Piwonka's men kept the path down the middle cleared of brush with machetes. The cliffs rose gradually on either side as the path descended, until it emptied into the road between two looming columns of rock-striped clay.

She found the trailhead and started down. The mare planted each hoof cautiously before putting her weight on it, like a cat negotiating a tree limb. The ground was sprinkled with a lichenous cover like sea heather that would be gone before it thrived, pulverized by tramping boots and hooves. Gorse stuck out of the banks and dragged at the legs of her jeans.

She was looking at the ground, as one did automatically riding down a steep trail, when she heard the report of a rifle. Elsa plucked at the reins. The pony gathered her hindquarters under her and halted.

The ridge rose on their right in a broad upward sweep. A man stood on the summit. A few more steps and the rising walls would have hidden him from view. The wash was filled with sun, bathing the crest, brimming down the path into the shadows. As Elsa screwed her eyes against the glare of stone and light, the figure appeared again, sharply black against the sky. A gleam cast itself before him like the spark from a flint.

He was aiming down at the road, legs braced, buttocks squeezed a little under black trousers. A scrim of brush blocked her view of his feet. The butt of the rifle was tucked under the arm, which flared to accommodate it. It was the classic shooting stance, trim and attentive, rock-firm. He wore a leather jacket with a fur collar, the leather dark brown with the gloss worn off, and a hat like the ranger's hats worn by Mounties. As Elsa watched, sitting bolt upright in the saddle, he lowered the rifle and wiped a hand deliberately down one leg.

Some feral instinct held her frozen on the path. He turned his head. She saw his profile, the part not shaded by the hat. Fear leaped in her because he was smiling, and because of the way he smiled.

He raised the rifle again. Automatically she gauged the distance from the barrel to the ponderosa growing out of the road below, where the trail let out. The rifle crept counterclockwise past the old pine. A scope sight winked above the barrel, its nozzle flashing liquidly in the blue air.

She wanted to call out, turn and scramble up or stumble down the cul-vert—anything to show him she was there. As she struggled with this idea, she knew it was mad. If she moved, he would see her. The ancient inner self that senses as a wolf does, that sees in water the reflection of its lupine smile, knew what she would read on his face if he saw her. She felt cold all over except for her feet, which were perspiring in her socks. The rifle inched toward her as she waited in the little draw, a clear target in the sunshine.

She reached behind her into the saddlebag and her fingers found the butt of the .380 British Service. She eased it out by the nubbed grip. The blood was starting to pound in her body, driving the chill away, but her hand was steady. Without thought or reflection, she cocked the hammer to bring a cartridge to the bore, holding it pressed to the mare's neck to muffle the soft snick.

She dropped the reins and raised the revolver with both hands.

The sights wobbled over a line of brush, thick and woven tight as sea sponge, wavered upward, found a jaw and nose and a sliver of barrel. Not being able to see the eyes, their expression, made the creeping passage toward her more ominous. Her arms trembled a little with the effort of holding the gun up. She steadied them and looked coldly down the sights. The figure became a ghost of itself, dark moving crookedly against silver grass and earth.

It turned oblong, then wedge-shaped. The hat brim faced her, turned down. The barrel of the rifle foreshortened, then snubbed to a point above the sights.

She applied pressure to the trigger as the sights lined up, then relaxed it as they swung slightly off. There was a sudden tensing of the target—not movement but full of the intent to move, like a bird in a thicket. The sights were aligned.

She squeezed the trigger.

The mare leaped in the air and dropped like a stone.

Elsa struck the earth with loose shoulders and slid downhill, slowly at first, then with gathering speed, ricocheting around in the wash. In midflight she changed direction and slid upside down with her legs pointing uphill at one o'clock. Horse pats of wet earth splattered her in clumsy showers. Brush whipped at her face and hands. She could hear the mare crashing downhill somewhere nearby, grunting and cracking her shoes against the wild stones. She scissored desperately away from the racket with her legs. As though obeying some gravity-defying command from an outer force, her body flipped and skidded belly first the rest of the way down the slope, where a sturdy mesquite halted her flight.

She sat up gagging, the wind knocked out of her, then scrambled to her knees, spitting and wiping soil from her mouth with a shaking hand. An uneasy new slide lay between her and the road. Except for the mutter of settling gravel, there was no sound. Silence echoed like thunder down the ravine, over the ridge, into the sky.

The mare was standing in the road, trembling and filthy but on all four legs. The saddle was still on. The reins had flipped over her head and were trailing on the ground.

"Wait. Wait, please," called Elsa. But no sound came from her mouth.

She scooted down the slide on her bottom, dropped to the road, and rushed to the mare on legs that wobbled helplessly. Her hands fluttered without her will; she watched them fly about as she tried to gather the reins. She scrambled into the saddle and cast a single look upward to the ridge. A raven shot suddenly over it with strong wing thrusts, its tail fanned in a wedge. A breeze caught and blew it twisting and flickering like a bit of burned paper released from a fire, until it was gone.

Chapter Sixteen

AN ELDERLY, GRIZZLED MAN in the chaps and mackinaw of a range rider rode into the yard at Salthill and stopped at the stable door. Harris was squatting beside a colt tethered in the doorway, unwinding a plaster from its leg. He glanced up, but did not rise.

"Afternoon," said the rider. His voice crackled like a defective loud-speaker. "Colonel St. Oegger about?"

"He's at Wanda Creek."

"When'll he be back?"

"Tonight sometime." Harris laid the plaster aside and touched the colt's leg. The colt snorted but stood without moving. He reached for a sponge floating in a bucket of water, squeezed it dry and blotted a welted area on the leg. An odor of antiseptic rose from the bucket.

"You alone?" asked the rider patiently.

Harris dropped the sponge back in the pail and swirled it around. The rider, who had heard of Harris but never seen him, noted the strange color of his eyes, pale green like those olives that came in a tin. The lashes were short, black and curly.

"Why don't you stop fucking around and tell me what you want," said Harris.

"I'm Blaise, foreman at Mountain Inn. His daughter's there. Been in an accident. Mr. Piwonka wants someone over. And if you talk like that to me again, I'll knock your block off."

Harris got to his feet. "Is she hurt?"

Blaise shook his head. "Says she shot someone."

"You need his son," said Harris. "He's up at the house."

Blaise rolled a cigarette while Harris stabled the colt and went upstairs.

His brown gelding fell into a splay-footed doze. When Harris returned, young Mr. St. Oegger was with him.

"I'll drive over," said Gordon hurriedly. His dark blue eyes looked almost black.

The foreman jerked his head at Harris. "He said any able-bodied man."

Gordon pulled the sedan out of the garage. Harris got in the passenger side. As they roared out of the yard, Blaise gave a mental salute of gratitude for the ending of their communication. These long verbal exchanges were hard to get through, and he was always happy when they were over.

The first thing they saw at Mountain Inn was Elsa's blue roan mare, her coat curly with dried lather, moving stiffly around one of the corrals in the sprawling yard. Piwonka's palomino was tied to the fence. There was a rifle in a holster behind the saddle.

Piwonka came striding down the walkway with a grim look on his face.

"Where's St. Oegger?" he asked Blaise, who in spite of being on horseback had beaten the sedan to the ranch.

"At Wanda Creek. Supposed to be back tonight. Brought them instead."

Piwonka greeted Gordon and glared at Harris. The two men hadn't spoken since the fight at the CPR yard.

"We'd better ride now and talk later," he said. "I'll explain on the way."

"Where's Elsa?" asked Gordon.

"Upstairs with my housekeeper. She's fine, just a little shook up. Look, time's important. You'll see her later."

"As long as she's being looked after."

"This would be looking after her, son. We've got a problem to solve."

Before they left, Piwonka took Blaise aside. "Send Steve to Wanda Creek to pick up her father. He can take Seventeen to the park, then cut down that service road before the first campground. It hooks up to Miller Road and Miller runs straight east to Wanda. It's the Georgewood Ranch, about three miles north of there. We might miss him coming back, but we'll have to try. And Ned?"

"Yes, boss."

"Keep this quiet. I don't want anyone getting downwind of it. Not until we know what we're looking at."

Gordon and Harris were waiting at the gate on two of his horses.

"I forgot to tell you to bring a gun," said Piwonka, offering a Luger from his coat pocket.

Gordon checked the action absently and slid it into his jacket.

"She came flying in the yard, hair sticking out and covered with dirt and scrapes," said Piwonka as they headed out. "Says she shot a man by the Bluffs. That's where we're going."

They spent ten minutes picking their way through the woods around the Bluffs. When the tip of the ponderosa appeared above the ridge, Piwonka reined in. They gazed across the field separating them from the ridge.

Piwonka pitched his gruff, naturally loud voice low. "She was riding down the big gully, the one I keep cleared out. You both know it. Says he was on that ridge just right of it with a rifle. That's where he is if she got him, where that pine sticks up. If he was even there." He looked at Gordon. "Does she make stuff up?"

"Never," said Gordon.

The field offered no real cover. In summer it would be deep in grass, lavender brush and wormwood. Now it was patchy with snow the shade of old shellac, the alkali a tender sheen a foot or two high.

"I think one man should scout," said Piwonka. "That's what'd be done in a combat situation. You two wait here."

"You can't go. That wouldn't be right," said Gordon. His face was wooden, his eyes bright. "Did she tell you he had a rifle?"

"She sure did."

"She definitely shot him."

"So she says. But if she did it was from an awful angle."

"Yes, there is that." Gordon looked across the field at the ponderosa. He seemed to have left them abruptly, wriggled out of his clothes and left them standing with no meat in them.

"I'll go," said Harris from behind.

They stared at him. He was already sliding off his horse.

"Don't be a fool," said Gordon sharply, gathering his reins. "Elsa is my sister."

"You're not used to this shit," said Harris matter-of-factly. "I don't want to have to tell him you got shot."

"You could get shot yourself," broke in Piwonka, bewildered by the animosity that suddenly made the air heavy. Harris took off his hat, looking contemptuous and indifferent, and hooked it over the saddle horn. Piwonka felt a chill come over him that he hadn't experienced in years. Harris was used to this shit.

"He's got a point," he said to Gordon. "Let's cut the cackle and let him get on with it."

"No," said Gordon.

"You can't get around like I can," said Harris.

There was a silence broken by the snuffing of the horses.

"Let him go then," said Gordon, in a voice Piwonka had never heard him use. "He knows all about murder."

Piwonka shrugged. "Take the Luger," he said to Harris.

Harris shook his head and dropped the reins. The horse stood like a carving with one leg furled, arrested in the act of stepping. Harris walked bareheaded into the field.

Piwonka glanced at Gordon, who sat his horse with his face turned away. The boy was in an agony, of rage or sorrow or what he could not tell.

"Look," he said. "It was better for him to go, son. You'd do it if you had to, I know you're not a coward. But I've seen him in action. I don't know where he was before, but he knows how to deal with this."

Gordon moved his horse a few feet from the palomino, blinking rapidly. With a shrug, Piwonka left him to whatever he was feeling.

Harris crunched through saucers and platters of snow, stepping occasionally into soupy pools. He was calculating. It was fifty yards, maybe a little less, to the ridge and the pine tree. Fifty yards of being an exposed target, easy to pick off as a buck. It wouldn't be so bad to die here, surrounded by mountains and sky. He thought of the mountain lion who'd crossed his path when he was looking for the Red. The great game cats deigned to live and die on this turf. It would be a good place for his bones to dry, his skin to crisp and turn to earth as he dissolved. There were a hell of a lot worse places. Alleys, toilets, cold hotel rooms.

He felt no fear, only the watchful vigor of the hunter. Energy pumped through him and his muscles felt springy and warm. He palmed the knife from inside his jacket. The blade snapped out with the familiar sound of spit hitting a hot pan. He walked with it close to his leg, feeling the weight of the sun on his hand, its warmth on his back.

He came up on the wash on the opposite side from where the rifleman was supposed to be. Was, or had been. That bigot brother of hers was right, she never messed with the truth. About ten feet down the trail he could see brush yanked out, then the skid-marked earth and scattered rocks, darker on their underbellies, of a recent slide. The earth in front of the slide was cut with sharp hoofprints.

He scanned the ridge. There was no point squatting or creeping. Without cover, he was in full view of anyone who might be waiting there. He zigzagged up the slope toward the brush as silently as he could, stopping to listen for a cough or rustle, the click of a bolt, scrape of a boot. He heard nothing. Even the small creatures seemed to have deserted the ridge, taking their noises and scufflings along.

When, knife in hand, he stared into a clearing the size a man's body would fit into, he heard at last the hootle of an owl. He listened to the call fade, looking down at the stained tramped ground.

Waiting in the trees with the rifle across his saddle, Piwonka saw Harris leave the brush and start back across the field. He had been wanting a cigarette badly but hadn't dared risk one. It annoyed him that Harris had failed to signal and wait for him. Like most men of his type, Piwonka respected independence but preferred men who worked well in teams. Harris tended to play a lone hand. He understood the tendency but would have liked to ride forward to look.

"He's found something, by god." He reached in his coat for his smokes. "He's found it, Gordon."

Chapter Seventeen

IT WAS CLOSE ON DUSK when Grey arrived at Mountain Inn in the car driven by Piwonka's messenger. All the lights were on in the ranch house, and the yard was filled with trucks and men and dogs. They were bringing the body in.

Grey had been briefed roughly during the drive. He was out of the car before it stopped, striding forward to meet Piwonka and the investigating officer, a big, balding man with the soulful eyes of a beagle.

"A dirty shame you were gone," said Piwonka. "This is Sergeant Carradine, Grey. I hated to call them, but it's illegal to hold off."

"You did what was necessary," said Grey. He did not shake hands with Carradine. "What happened?"

"Your daughter apparently shot a man on what Mr. Piwonka calls the lake road, on his land," said Carradine in a surprisingly high voice. "The man is dead. We found her revolver on the path near where her horse fell. A British Service. He was carrying a rifle. We have that, too."

"British Service? I have one," said Grey. "She must have taken it hunting."

Carradine looked at him closely. His beagle eyes were sad and luminous. "Is your daughter a good shot, Colonel?"

"Yes, of course. We all are. There are guns at my place and everyone knows how to use them. I want to see her."

"I'd appreciate it if you'd have a look at the body first, then we'll go up, if you don't mind. Tell us if you recognize him."

A pickup truck with a shell over the bed was parked nearby. As they approached, Grey saw two packhorses hitched to the fence, a travoislike conveyance of shafts and netting propped against the rails with the straps unbuckled and the leathers hanging loose.

"Four-wheel drive's in for repairs," said Carradine. "It took all afternoon to get him in. Two of my men had to carry the back end of the travois. You should have heard them swear."

The body was in the truck bed. At Carradine's request the sheet was drawn back and a policeman in a field jacket and billed cap played a torch over it. The front of the body looked clean except for a stained tear in the shirt where the bullet had entered, and a trail of dark fluid at the corner of the mouth. But the backs of the torso and limbs, already beginning their process of rigor, were coated with congealed blood, as though the body had lain in a pool of red lacquer that had subsequently hardened around it, and from which it had been removed with difficulty.

The face bore the anonymity conferred by death. Grey studied the features, the waxen fingers, the cochineal stain.

"I've never seen him in my life," he said, withdrawing.

The rifle lay on a cloth on the passenger seat, next to his revolver. He looked at the rifle without touching it. It was a sleek weapon, adroit and murderous-looking. The barrel had been fancifully blued.

"A .99-T Savage with a Noske 2.5-X scope," Carradine said. "There were two spent cartridges in his pocket. We found another one in the roadbed along with a couple of footprints, his as far as we know. No other shells, either on the road or up on the cliff. He must have climbed down and retrieved the two earlier."

"A lot of work," said Grey mildly. "Slogging back and forth."

"The Savage is a good deer-hunting rifle," said Piwonka. "Why shoot into the road at nothing? If he wasn't hunting, why not snap-shoot at bushes or plink rocks in the field where he was?"

"He could be some jackass who didn't know any better," said Carradine, not jokingly.

"The mount looks specially made for the scope," said Grey. "Maybe he did."

"Your son stopped upstairs before he left and told her to wait until you were here before she said anything. We wouldn't have expected her to, of course," said Carradine. He drew in his breath, then said with an air of plunging in, "Colonel, your daughter is pretty nerveless for a girl her age. She shot this man under his raised arm at about a forty-five-degree angle. A tough, risky shot. It looks as if the slug struck the large aorta into the heart. He must have collapsed and bled to death in a short time. It was an incredibly lucky shot with a one-in-a-hundred chance of going where it did. The slug's still in there; the angle slowed the trajectory and it didn't exit. We'll get it out at the autopsy."

"My god," said Grey.

They eyed each other. At the far end of the yard the hounds brought to sniff out death milled, their tails swinging like scythes, their voices sad horns over the neighing of the horses and the banging of truck doors.

"Let's get out of here," said Grey suddenly, sick of the smell of blood.

They climbed the steps to the house.

"Gordon and Harris rode out with me to look," said Piwonka. "I thought it might be her imagination. It wasn't."

Her father grimaced. "Elsa never wastes her imagination on reality. Where *is* Gordon?"

"He left to find you. Said he was going to Wanda Creek."

"Your man cut through the park and down some road, driving like blue blazes," said Grey. "He must have missed us. And Harris?"

"Gone to feed the stock. He insisted on playing scout. Harris. The dead man was clear across the field. Harris had to cover open ground to get there, and none of us was sure she'd killed him. She could've just winged him and he could've been lying doggo, waiting to pick off the first man who came to look. Nothing wrong with Harris's guts, is there?"

"I don't think so," said Grey.

"Gordon thought he should've been the one."

"Nonsense," said Grey. "It would have been insane for anyone else to try it."

Gordon stopped at Dee's for gas on the way back from Wanda Creek. The sedan was a Buick, hulking, ceremonious and ornately chromed. Without thinking he had followed George Georgewood's suggestion and cut across the provincial park via the service road, then down a farm road to Seventeen. The farm road was paved but rutted, and no salt had been laid down on it that winter. He had had to creep along frequently, slithering in muck, until he reached the main road.

He paid for the gas and pulled onto the highway. It was nearing dusk, as dusk appeared here, a sky the color of turned maple leaves, with a black band on the horizon that seemed to unfold like a storm front over the huddled buildings. He had always been less conscious of the shape of the earth here than in Ireland, more aware of the vastness of the sky, that dry arena that failed to move him. He felt in a rush that had nothing to do with Elsa's need for protection or succor; Grey would be there by now to provide those things. Still he pushed the accelerator to the floor, something he rarely did. The Buick gathered itself and poured forth more power, and he had to remember to slow for the sharp turns and the bridge with its girders riding the evening light.

At the entrance to Mountain Inn he waited while a Mounted Police truck with a camper shell pulled out, jouncing deliberately over the pipes straddling the drainage ditch. There was no sign of his father or Piwonka in the yard, just a few of Piwonka's men whom he knew by sight. The porch lamp was on over the door of the ranch house. He parked the Buick quickly and climbed the steps.

Chapter Eighteen

ELSA WAS WAITING IN THE DINING ROOM with the housekeeper. The room was large, beamed and wainscoted in dark timber, papered in green floral vines, cold though a fire had been kindled, with an air of being seldom used. A tray with sugar and cream and a carafe of coffee had been set on the polished table, for Mrs. Leopold had a sense of propriety. A one third-empty pint bottle of brandy stood next to Elsa's mug. The brandy had restored a little color to her face. Her arms and neck were crossed with scratches; a large scrape on her forehead had been bathed and tinted with mercurochrome. Her thick plait was brushed out. In lamp- and firelight the hair flamed around her face in a rude yellow mass that made her look even younger than she was, a child of ten or eleven; Carradine could be excused his air of disbelief. Her Levi jacket, stretched over a chair to dry, had withstood the test and was grubby but untorn.

She gave Grey her intense, black-browed look. "Dad."

He took a seat at her side, looking squarely into her eyes. Carradine pulled up the chair opposite. A deputy sat at the end of the table, pausing first to turn down the lamp at his elbow.

"Tell us what happened," said Grey quietly.

"I was taking the shortcut to the road," said Elsa, glancing at the deputy. Her hazel eyes looked liquid and frozen at once, like a startled deer's. "That trail, you know, the one down the wash. I heard a shot. He was standing on the ridge beside the wash, aiming down at the road. It was a rifle but I couldn't see well, I was behind and too low. He started to move it in a circle. Like a sentry. There was a scope on the rifle, I saw that. . . . I waited until the muzzle came around to my sights. Then I shot him."

They waited for her to go on. She sat with her hands in her lap, not fidgeting.

"What made you think he was dangerous, Miss St. Oegger?" Carradine asked finally. "Did he make a threatening gesture or movement?"

"No. He never saw me. Or if he did, it was at the last moment. Just before." She stopped.

O my god, thought Grey. *Condemned out of her own mouth.*

"He *was* dangerous," she added after a brief meditation. "It was an ambush. He was going to shoot whoever came down the road."

Grey asked Carradine without taking his eyes from her, "Had he any identification on him?"

"Actually, no," said Carradine. "Nothing. A five-dollar bill, the two shells and a box of matches. No wallet. He was wearing a gun belt with seventeen rounds left. We found a canteen of water a few feet away. He could have filled it at the river."

Piwonka spoke from the doorway. "And he was on my land. That's private land, miles from any public road."

Her father's voice came again, gentle but insistent. "Elsa, what made you think he was going to harm you? Were you frightened?"

She stirred uneasily. "Not very. I just knew."

There was another silence, which felt menacing and perturbed. Elsa glanced around the room. Beside her sat Mrs. Leopold in a print coverall, large, placid and childless, her features heavy with concern but empty of wisdom. Mr. Piwonka stood near the door, his face shrewd and blank at once. It was the look he wore when he played poker with her father and the Georgewoods and Dee Lachlan in the dining room at Salthill. And there was Gordon, whom she thought had come in after the rest. He looked oddly breathless. Her father's expression was neutral, hiding, she knew, a rising impatience to get on with the facts. But she had already marshaled and offered her facts, had in fact emptied her small store of reality. And Gordon seemed so strained; she stared at him; he stared back blankly as though uncomprehending; he looked dusty and throttled. The room seemed filled with strangers, even her father, even her brother, all staring at her as though she were some sort of outsider, a person who did things they didn't do, an unnatural person. She was exhausted, and the emotions stirring fitfully under the brandy like some grotesque marine life were morbid and frightening. She raised her hand to her mouth to stem a rising tide of panic.

Then she saw Harris. He had taken a seat in one of the chairs near the door. She wondered how long he had been sitting there, listening and watching. She was familiar with his short range of expressions and she knew she had done something to surprise him. His narrowed eyes regarded her intently and with interest. As her eyes met his in desperation, his mouth turned up on the unscarred side in a dry, minimal smile. It was not a greeting. It was not a smile of encouragement or reassurance. It was a salute.

She turned back to the images of authority crowding the room, her father and the sergeant, the deputy with the notepad he was trying to not let show.

"I don't *have* to explain how I knew," she said. "He was going to kill me. That's all I'm going to say."

Elsa would not leave Harris.

"I'll walk home," she said tearfully, when Grey told her to get in the sedan with Gordon. "I'm going with *him*."

"The Buick's more comfortable," said her father. "I'll ride with you if you like."

"I'm going with Harris." There were circles under her eyes; her large mouth quivered.

So Gordon followed in the sedan and Elsa rode in the truck, wedged between Grey and Harris. Within moments she had succumbed to exhaustion and brandy and was asleep, covered with Grey's jacket, sneakered feet splayed on the floorboard.

"You put your life in jeopardy this afternoon," said Grey. "I'm in your debt."

"It was no big deal," said Harris.

"I think it might have been," said Grey. "He had nothing on him but a rifle. A poacher would have carried more."

Harris lit a cigarette and rolled the window down. The winter had been mild, according to them, but spring seemed to be a long time coming. Moonlight turned a grove of deciduous trees into a jeweled haze. Snow still lined the gutters. The double strip of phosphorescence flared and dulled as they approached, turning into ordinary ice melting into slush. He thought that nothing could look more lonesome and ominous than those gutters.

"I don't know how a twelve-year-old girl can shoot a man without hesitation, even in self-defense," said Grey. "It takes a certain frame of mind."

Harris shrugged. "Don't point a gun at anyone unless you intend to use it. She followed the rule."

They turned in at the drive. Snow water thundered in the ditch under the bridge. "When I came to Canada I left her in Galway, in my mother's care," said Grey. His words seemed to move with difficulty, after painful thoughts. "For five years. At the end of that time my brother's wife came unexpectedly from Belfast on a visit and found Elsa in the stable. She had been sleeping there for a week. Sometimes she slept with the lads in their quarters or with the cook, who has a cottage in the village. When Winnie saw her she was wearing a thin dress and a sweater and a pair of the stableboy's boots, and nothing else. In March. Her ears were infected and she had a mild case of pneumonia. She spoke to my brother's wife in Irish."

He shifted down. They had reached the wooded part of the drive. For a few minutes they drove through blackness dotted with yellow and red dashboard lights. The dry beams of the headlamps sucked up yews and pines as they rushed toward further darkness.

"There are things that happen in families," said Grey. "Things that scandalize when they're uncovered. I had no idea. Nor did Gordon and Flavia, who were away at school in England, and stayed with relations there in the holidays. My mother is not a comfortable person to spend holidays with. Another strike against us; that we had no thought of Elsa with my mother, knowing my mother. My father is elderly and deaf, and seldom leaves his rooms upstairs. She was always a watchful child, never very merry even when I was at home. Jasper and Winnie were given to understand that she was a bit retarded. They had no idea either, of course. I, who knew she was of normal intelligence, allowed myself to believe she was attending the local school. I failed to wonder why I never had a letter from her.

"Winnie wired me immediately, then fetched Flavia out of school to look after Elsa. The child's hair was so filthy and matted it had to be cut off. When Fi put her in the bath she screamed as if she was being boiled or throttled. I don't think she'd had a real bath since I left. She wasn't starved: the servants had been feeding her for years, washing her when they could lay hands on her, keeping an eye out for her. They were scandalized, but what could they do?

"The priests had been to the house to plead for her, but even my mother's religiosity couldn't prevail over her aversion to Elsa. She told them Elsa was wrong in the head. They were unable to cajole my address from her to write me for help, and I suppose they hesitated to write my brother. It was calculated, deliberate neglect. The household, the countryside, seemed to cower under a spell that forbade anyone doing anything about Elsa."

They were out of the wood and winding toward the top of the drive. Grey glanced down at his daughter's slumbering head. "The experience made her a strange child. Uneven, somehow."

"Good thing," said Harris, squinting around a drag. "If she wasn't strange she'd be dead."

Grey shot him a glance. "You believe her."

"He knew someone would come down that road sooner or later. Lucky she got him where she did instead of pinking him in the shoulder. He would have turned around and finished her off."

"Lucky?" said Grey. The truck groaned like a bullock rising out of a mudhole. For a moment they hung suspended at the crest of the hill. "There was nothing lucky about it. She's a crack shot. She can put out a rabbit's eye at that distance, from any angle. Unusually fine eye-hand coordination. Gordon wanted to enter her in the marksman trials at Williams Lake this summer, but Iseult wouldn't hear of it. Said it wasn't suitable. If she shot him through the heart, it's precisely where she meant to shoot him."

They drove down into the yard. The house rose on the promontory, its towers black against the star-strewn night.

Gordon allowed the Buick to fall behind the truck until its taillights could scarcely be seen. He was going over the events of the day in his mind. He had said nothing at Wanda Creek about Elsa's trouble, only that Grey was needed at Salthill. His sense of family privacy had forbidden anything beyond that, as he knew his father's had. Not that the St. Oeggers had any privacy left. They had lost their pride, they had lost their sovereignty. A dull anguish had seized him at the Bluffs as he watched Harris walk bare-handed and solitary into the field; it remained with him now. He felt encapsulated in it, this misery of loss, separated from everything as he was separated from the rushing night by steel and chrome. He had lost his place with his father, that mercurial, romantic figure who had seemed to him when he was a child to possess the magic of a god, with his golden hair and mesmerizing smile. It had been given to an upside-down version of his father, as Pan-like, only dark, only scarred, only hard and sly. Even Elsa wanted Harris, with blue shadows under her eyes. All that was left to him was the dryness of his inheritance, that portion given by custom and right that could not be removed.

Chapter Nineteen

FOUR DAYS AFTER THE SHOOTING Sergeant Carradine came to Salthill, bringing with him an officer from the provincial homicide division.

They bypassed the back door, set in an arch in one of the blind towers, and made their way through the fir grove to the front. Yews laden with red fruits grew to an outlandish height among the firs, as if nourished by the stone walls looming like cliffs above the branches. The front faced south into the wood above the highway. Two cedars shadowed a damp green garden. They stepped over a wellspring pooling by a fieldstone wall that separated the garden from the wood, through delicate trails of star moss and fern. The front door was a slab of timber, the vault and piers of its enclosing arch hoary with moss. The knocker was an iron dog's head with a ring in its jaws. Three bears stalked over the keystone, not like those who waddled through meadows by the highways, roly-poly and content, but the ominous mythologic bears of the Viking North.

"God, what a place," said Carradine.

"Not likely to burn down, any road," said the other.

They met with Grey in his study, and the news was not good. Though inquiries had been made by wire and telephone, and photographs taken at autopsy had been distributed to every police district in the provinces, the dead man had not yet been identified.

"She's a minor, she can't be prosecuted," said Grey, pacing the room. "She was defending herself, for god's sake."

The officer, whose name was Heuser, sat with his hat on his knee. He was a type much like the leathery Ned Blaise, with a long, sun-seamed face and light eyes like a wolf's. His blond hair was going thin at the crown.

"Probably that's what your daughter thought she was doing," he said. "This is all going to be straightened out in time. We just wish there was evidence of some kind of threat, some proof she was in harm's way when she raised that British Service."

Grey halted, stared down at Heuser and said coldly, "In light of what you have so far, a stranger fifty miles from nowhere, with no car or other means of transport, carrying a rifle with a scope sight and ammunition but no wallet or papers, sounds a hell of a lot to me like harm's way."

"Probably American," said Carradine morosely. "They've got an awful lot of nuts down there since the war. They come over the border, drift up here and plague our people."

"I don't give a damn if he was an Eskimo. The fact that he can't be identified says as much about him as I need to know," said Grey. "This is the age of identification. Driver's license, hunting license, auto registration, insurance card . . . they're the paraphernalia of modern life. A man can't move five feet without finding it necessary to produce some paper or other, proving he is who he says he is."

"I agree with you, and sympathize with your plight," said Heuser. "But your attorney is going to need a little more to put before the court than the fact that your daughter had a 'feeling' about him."

They left soon after, under a bleak cloud. Grey could be formidable when his ire was roused.

"I don't care who he is," said Heuser as they banged toward the highway. "He's under the law like the rest of us. How old is the girl?"

"Just twelve."

"She's in trouble unless we can obtain some evidence of malicious intent. Damn it, Carradine, we must find out who he was. That's the key to this case."

"I'm doing what I can," said Carradine, gazing sadly out the window.

The aunts came from English Bay for the hearing. Iseult was a tall, stout Irishwoman with watery hazel eyes. Her shock of white hair had once been red, as her skin with its brickish mottling had been freckled. The heavy forearms had a dull gold cast, the freckles blended and faded with age into a dry map that picked up the sun in its longitude. Daisy, a decade younger and much more modern, was slender, an even ivory tinged with olive in the folds of her eyelids and creases of her wrists.

Harris was more amused than irritated by the aunts. Daisy treated him with casual friendliness, Iseult disapproved of him. Not because he was black, but because he wasn't Catholic. She looked at him as if he wasn't finished yet, like a boy all dressed up with dirt under his nails. The first time she got him alone she asked him if he had any religious training. He wasn't annoyed by the question. It made a few things clear. The St. Oeggers were as stuck in their religion as any New Mount Calvary Missionary Baptists back home. He was starting to make distinctions, see things he wouldn't have seen a year ago. It was the clan of her religion, not the tribe of her color, that made the big aunt aloof. It worried her mind that he was going to Hell right in the middle of them. She reminded him of the persnickety churchy women of his childhood, always on the lookout for sin, but knowing a child was in the Lord even when he slid woefully.

The hearing was held in Darmstadt. Elsa wore the blue dress Iseult had given her for Christmas, which was not yet too short. Aside from a flutter of apprehension when they arrived, she remained tranquil and untroubled throughout the proceedings. Everything had been all right since the moment in Piwonka's dining room when she had seen Harris sitting there with that interested, half-amused look on his face.

The courtroom seemed immense, with its walls paneled in polished yellow wood. Elsa was introduced to Mr. Heuser and to the lawyer Mr. Snodgrass, who had been engaged to represent her on Tom Pushkin's recommendation. Her father sat with Elsa in the front row, trim in a suit and smelling of aftershave. Her aunt sat on her other side. Daisy looked thin and citified in a fawn gabardine suit with a kick pleat in the skirt. Her Robin Hood hat, with its shot-green feather riding backward over a smartly turned-up brim, had occupied some of Elsa's attention during the long drive to Darmstadt, and the varied landscape had used up the rest.

A woman took a seat rather gingerly at a post to one side of the stand, and began arranging writing things at a desk. She wore pink lipstick and a jacket and skirt of dark boiled wool. Turning her head like an owl, Elsa marked a scattering of people in the rear of the room. She wondered whether any of them were reporters. Her father disliked the idea of reporters, she knew. It seemed to be one of his chief concerns, and that of her aunts as well.

"All rise," said the deputy.

The judge came out of an inner room, a thin man as dark as her idea of an Italian, with speckled black hair and a long robe on.

"Please be seated." He settled at the bench, then turned his attention to the docket before him. "In the matter of St. Oegger. Who are those people in the back?"

There was a stir in the back. The deputy confabulated with another deputy stationed by the entrance. "The case following, Sir," said the deputy. "And two visitors."

"The principals in this matter will stay," said the Bench. "The rest must leave the courtroom. You may return after this case has been heard."

He sat with an expressionless face, as though thinking of other things, while the room was emptied of all but the small group below the Bench. A flurry of activity ensued. Mr. Snodgrass sorted through and gave some papers to the deputy, who in turn handed them to the Bench. It seemed to Elsa, watching with interest, that everything had to pass through other hands before the Bench could touch it. It was like the pipe that Indians handed around at peace ceremonies, or a king's protectors in the olden days, who had to taste and touch everything before the king could.

He glanced over the papers, then directed his attention to the first row. "This is the girl?"

"Yes, sir," said Mr. Snodgrass. "And her father, Colonel St. Oegger, and her aunt."

Elsa frowned. She hated being talked about as though she weren't there. The magistrate looked at her, saw a young girl in a blue dress, and smiled.

"I will explain to you why you have been summoned here, Miss St. Oegger," he said. "The purpose of this hearing is to determine whether a crime has been committed. If it is so determined, a formal inquest will be held in this location at the assizes when they next occur, which will be in three weeks. At that time you will be called upon to produce evidence to clear yourself of any charges. Have her begin, will you, counsel?"

Elsa was bidden to the stand. Everything was of hard wood; the little cubicle in which she stood, the round-backed chair, the rail which she touched briefly before letting her hands fall to her sides. She listened to the deputy and swore her oath.

"I realize that you have told your story several times, Miss St. Oegger," said Mr. Snodgrass. "For the sake of clarity, the court would like you to repeat it now. Just tell us in your own words what happened. Remain standing when you are through."

She looked down upon her father's head. His hair was parted on one side, showing a thread of pinkish scalp. Daisy sat with hands clasped loosely on her handbag, and the set of her shoulders spoke volumes.

"Just tell precisely what happened to you, my love, and don't fear," she had said the night before, when she came to Elsa's room to press a bedtime kiss onto her forehead. "There's no doubt in my mind that you did exactly what God intended you to. The St. Oeggers are sensible people, not murderers, and you are a St. Oegger in spite of your unfortunate start. One can see that straightaway."

As she began her statement, Elsa reflected that no matter how often she was reminded who she was, she somehow felt unlike a St. Oegger. And being assured "one can see that straightaway" removed the finish from the charm of belonging. If one saw it, why mention it?

When she had finished, Mr. Snodgrass asked questions. "Miss St. Oegger, what first directed your attention to the man you saw that day on the summit?"

"The scope sight," said Elsa. "And the shot he had just fired."

"You were alerted by the sound."

The Bench made a noise in his throat. Mr. Snodgrass beat a smooth retreat. "That is to say, did you notice the shot first? Or the sight?"

"The shot."

"And recognized the sound as that of a gun being fired?"

"Oh, yes," said Elsa.

"You have said that you noticed the scope sight. Are you familiar with these?"

"Yes."

"How is that? Have you used one?"

"My father has one for our rifle. I have used it two or three times."

"For what purpose?"

"To shoot deer," said Elsa.

"Do you know what they do?" he asked. "Please explain the purpose of such a tool."

"They are used to focus in on long-range targets. Some of them are very powerful."

"Do you think this one was powerful, Miss St. Oegger?"

"Not if he was trying to hit anything on the road," said Elsa dryly. "It wasn't very far down."

"Whereas if he were trying to shoot game—deer, for instance—he would have been more likely to be in the field?"

"Yes."

"For which purpose the scope sight would be effective? For instance, in focusing on a buck standing at the far end of a field?"

"Yes."

"Can you think of any reason he would have such a sight on his rifle, if he were not intending to shoot deer?"

"I don't know," said Elsa uncomfortably. This sticky point had been gone over with Mr. Snodgrass and her father, who had made it clear she was not to mention divinations. She cast about for an answer, feeling her oath as a weighty burden. "He would have a better chance of hitting any target with it, I suppose."

They went on in this fashion, Mr. Snodgrass smilingly taking her through the events of that morning. He asked a great many questions about the gunman—what he wore, how he stood, where he aimed, the way he rotated like a guard posted in a prison tower, an image they were all familiar with from the moving pictures.

"Are you skilled at shooting a rifle?" asked Mr. Snodgrass.

"I suppose so," said Elsa, who had an ordinary person's opinion of her talents.

"Who taught you how to shoot and care for guns?"

She was surprised. "My brother, Gordon."

Chapter Twenty

"YOUR HONOR," SAID MR. SNODGRASS, when Elsa had resumed her seat, "it is my hope that with the testimony of my next witness, we will be in a fair way to justice this morning. I now call Mr. Heuser to the stand."

Mr. Heuser was sworn in. He produced copies of some paperwork for the magistrate, who laid them aside and prepared to listen.

"The deceased carried no identification of any sort," said Mr. Heuser. "Identity was secured only two days ago, when Sergeant Carradine notified us from Ontario of his successful examination of some institutional records and photographs." Mr. Heuser coughed absentmindedly into his fist. "The deceased," he continued, "has been identified as Walter R. Snelling, a man forty-three years of age, a Canadian citizen born in Halifax, Nova Scotia. From November 1931 to June 1933, he was in the employ of the Canadian Pacific Railroad."

He glanced at the Bench waiting in expectant silence, then continued.

"Mr. Snelling was dismissed in June 1933 for unsatisfactory work performance and 'mental instability,' as the record refers. He entered St. Dymphna's Sanatorium in Montreal, Quebec, where from August 1933 to December of that year he was treated for a schizophrenic breakdown. He was released in March 1934."

"Had he family?" asked Mr. Snodgrass.

"A sister, Mrs. Jocasta Timms, of Digby Neck, Nova Scotia," said Mr. Heuser.

"Has she been called to identify him? Is she present?"

"Mrs. Timms is on the point of delivering her third child, counselor. One of my detectives met her in Halifax, where she identified her brother from photographs, although she had not seen him for some years. We have her signed affidavit, with attachments."

"Let me see it, please," said the Bench.

The affidavit having been examined, Mr. Heuser continued.

"In August 1936, two years after his discharge from St. Dymphna's, Mr. Snelling enlisted in the Canadian armed services. He was discharged from duty after two years because of increasing mental instability. No further treatment seems to have been undertaken, however, as no record has been found of his confinement in any mental facility in the provinces during that period.

"In 1941, Mr. Snelling found a position working for a warehouse company in Kitchener, Ontario, operating a forklift and loading goods by hand. There he met Mrs. Jean Pleasant, a divorced woman aged thirty-four, who worked as a receivables clerk for the company." Mr. Heuser glanced uneasily toward Elsa.

"Continue," said the Bench firmly.

"Mr. Snelling," said Mr. Heuser, "rented a room in the house in Hamilton, a suburb of Kitchener, where Mrs. Pleasant lived with her two children, in the spring of 1941. On Monday morning, April 9, 1941, Mrs. Pleasant failed to appear at her work. A friend who had taken her children for a weekend excursion came to the house in the evening, bringing the children, and found it dark and the doors locked. Mrs. Pleasant's car was still parked in the garage behind the house."

Mr. Heuser glanced again at Elsa. Mr. Snodgrass and the Bench turned their gazes toward the girl in the second row with her shining blond head, her cornflower-blue dress with its capped sleeve.

"I beg permission of the Court to excuse Miss St. Oegger from this portion of the testimony if she or her father feel it necessary," said Mr. Snodgrass.

"It is permitted," said the Bench. "There is a room to that side where they can wait if they wish until this part of the testimony is finished."

Mr. Snodgrass came over to the family.

"Do you want to leave?" her father asked Elsa in a low voice.

"Of course she doesn't," said Daisy fiercely. "Unless they've no better sense than to drag in a lot of gore."

"I'm sure that won't be the case," said Mr. Snodgrass.

"I'd rather stay," said Elsa.

Mr. Heuser resumed. "Mrs. Pleasant's friend summoned the police, who entered the house on arrival. Mrs. Pleasant was found in her bedroom. She had been shot twice and stabbed with a kitchen knife, and had been dead from her wounds for some twenty-four hours.

"A search was begun for Mr. Snelling, who had spent the day at his work and left as usual at quitting time. A fellow worker stated that he had a knapsack with him. It is postulated that the knapsack contained the gun used to shoot Mrs. Pleasant, a .44 revolver given her by her former husband, which has never been recovered. Mr. Morris Pleasant, who was on a fishing trip with friends at the time of the fatality, described the gun and testified that she kept it in her room with two rounds in it for protection, as they were rather far out in the country.

"As Mr. Snelling owned no car, it was assumed he took the train to Toronto and thereafter transferred to another train, possibly throwing the revolver from an overpass into a lake or river while en route."

Mr. Heuser paused to refer to a page. The room was so quiet the scratching of the clerk's shorthand sounded like Grey's spaniel wheezing in his sleep.

"In October 1941, Mr. Snelling was arrested in Winnipeg when he applied for work at the Canadian Pacific yard. He was tried for the murder of Jean Pleasant, sentenced on sufficient evidence, and removed to the penal mental institute at Ealing, Ontario, to serve the balance of a life term. It was at Ealing that Sergeant Carradine obtained photographic identification of Mr. Snelling. He is to be commended for thinking of checking with them. After this identification we were able to match the prints on file in Toronto with those of the deceased taken June twelve last."

Mr. Heuser paused, looking like a wolf who had just champed on a canary, with feathers floating past his nostrils. The lofty second-story windows commanded a view of the city and surrounding plain. Elsa watched a squirrel whiffling and darting in an alder that coursed before the glass. She was uninterested in Walter R. Snelling, whose measure she had taken ten days ago.

"Go on, please," said the magistrate.

"Mr. Snelling was declared criminally insane at the time of his trial, the diagnosis being given of acute paranoid schizophrenia. With the continuing deterioration of his mental status, he would have spent the balance of his life in the institution at Ealing or another like it. Unfortunately, he escaped from Ealing in March 1945 by garroting an orderly with a piece of wire and leaving the hospital in his uniform, and had not been seen since that time."

Daisy shuddered and put her hand over Elsa's. It felt cold, like a doeskin glove left overnight in the glove box of a car.

"The orderly survived, but the peril to the community was keenly felt, and every effort was expended to find Mr. Snelling," said Mr. Heuser. "Evidently he used the rails as a means of transport, picking up work in small towns or on farms along the way and avoiding being seen. In September

1946 an officer of the Royal Mounted Police, Lieutenant John McAvoy of Lacombe, Alberta, came upon Mr. Snelling, whom he happened to know by sight, entering a boxcar in the CPR yard at Red Deer and attempted to detain him. Mr. Snelling took cover and shot him with a rifle, wounding him in the abdomen. Lieutenant McAvoy was able to identify his assailant, but died on the way to the hospital. Ballistic comparison of the firearm found at Mountain Inn ten days ago on June 12, 1947, has been made with that used in the September 1946 shooting at Red Deer. Both bullets were fired from the same rifle."

The Bench consulted his papers. "Type of firearm?"

"A .99-T Savage, Your Honor. Unregistered, presumably stolen."

"Yes, I see. Here it is. There is no question regarding the 1946 homicide."

"None, sir. Confirmed by victim's statement and prints on the boxcar door."

"Very well." The Bench ran an eye over the St. Oeggers. "Is your witness finished, counselor?"

Mr. Heuser left the stand.

"Your Honor, members of the court," said Mr. Snodgrass. "I suggest that Miss St. Oegger *was* in imminent danger of her life when she happened upon this man, armed and in a remote place, on June twelfth. I further suggest that in defending herself she showed not only courage, but a perspicacity unusual in one of such a young age. Regardless how unrealistic her fears may have seemed *at the time,* Mr. Snelling's documented mental illness, his conviction for a murder done without apparent motive and his connection with another, that of an officer of the law, must give serious weight to the probability that he posted himself on the ridge with the intent of shooting anyone who came along the road. The distance to the road being sixteen and one-half yards measured, it would not be a difficult shot for a man with a good rifle, on a fairly windless day."

"Having identified the deceased, counselor, your reasoning is that Miss St. Oegger was in imminent danger when she fired the shot?" asked the Bench.

"Your Honor," said Mr. Snodgrass, letting out the stops. "I have no doubt she would have been in the gravest danger when her presence came to his attention. And given the intense scrutiny of his surroundings, which I have no doubt of, she would inevitably have been seen."

Her father made a restless sound. Daisy sat straighter. With a mental sigh, Elsa waited while comments were made and directives issued.

She was called upon to stand.

"Elsa Rhys St. Oegger, minor child of Grey Denis St. Oegger of the

Province of British Columbia, and of Alice Sheridan St. Oegger, late of
Carrollton Lodge, Galway, you are hereby released. . . ."

As the words flowed, she glanced restlessly, covertly around the courtroom. The woodwork gleamed between the long windows like honey in
the comb.

"A grand job," said Mr. Snodgrass heartily in the corridor. "A grand job.
His shooting the policeman was helpful. They hate that, you know. Miss St.
Oegger, you may come to work for me anytime when you are grown up;
you would make a fine detective."

"Dreadful, putting the child through this," said Daisy to her father, in the
restaurant across the street. "Questioning her motives, hauling her before the
magistrate for putting riff-raff out of the way."

"He was sick, Annis," said her father mildly.

Daisy sniffed, in a passable imitation of Iseult at her most condemning.
"Is there anything decent to eat here?"

"The omelettes were fair, the last time I tried one," said Grey. "Elsa, are
you well enough? You seem destined for a life of adventure."

"I'm fine," said Elsa.

Chapter Twenty-one

"DO YOU THINK THERE'S SUCH A THING AS EVIL?" asked Elsa.

Grey glanced swiftly at his daughter, then back at the road. They were driving home from town with the month's staples and a drum of molasses in the truck to cut with alfalfa for feed. The dogs rode in back with the drum, their ears turned up in the wind.

"Well," he said finally. "I think good and evil exist side by side."

"I think they do, too. Only evil things aren't always *called* evil, are they? Like someone being sick with a terrible illness. In the old days, people said they were possessed by evil spirits because they didn't know what the illness was. I mean, what germ caused it. Now they just talk about germs and nothing else."

Her father smiled. "So you think science has led us astray?"

"No . . . but everything isn't science. Take mad people, for instance."

He was alert. "Like the man at the Bluffs?"

"Uh-huh."

"Well, he was mad, but that could mean one or two things, couldn't it? He could have been treated very badly once, and it made him insane. Or he might have had something wrong with his mind to begin with. A mind is like a leg or knee or any other body part . . . sometimes it doesn't work correctly—"

"But that's the same as talking about germs. And this isn't germs, is it? He had badness inside him."

"You mean an illness."

"No. Just evil." She sounded exasperated. "Just wickedness."

"Did you sense that when you saw him?" he asked. "Evil? Something malign?"

"Of course." Her smooth young forehead was corrugated with irritation.

"It was all around him like a yellow cloud. Like the ocher paint in my paint box."

"You're fortunate to have such insight," he said after a moment. "Perhaps you're right. I've been in the East, where the movement of evil is observed pretty impartially. It's a simple, stripped-down sort of thing, isn't it? Evil. Like a tar that sticks to your shoe. In the West we are expected to do battle with it so that good may triumph. Unfortunately I don't think we've had much success with it. We seem to have so many foul inventions to our credit. And such foul blots on our history, particularly in this century."

"*I* think it has to do with people," mused Elsa. "Animals aren't evil, not even diseases are really, just humans. And I think you can tell who's good and who isn't, if you're clever. I think going wrong in the world is mainly due to not being able to tell."

He chuckled. "And what are you? Good or evil?"

"Well . . . some of both, I suppose."

"So am I. So are most of us," said Grey. "It's hard to extract the bits of people you want and leave the rest. The good and bad bits are all mixed together."

In Galway as a young child, she had once stumbled over a couple lying in the grass. They were under the ken of some mysterious abiding force, struggling with each other and with the ground in which they seemed to burrow. She stood calmly listening to their labored breathing, the soft grunts like the nosing sounds the cows made when they browsed in the thickets. There was a furtiveness around them, a subtle perfume like the scent of a peach just picked, that she knew had something to do with the upturned sole of the man's shoe, and the woman's knee, bared except for its lisle stocking, bending above the grasses.

The gun cocked in her ear. Elsa woke and sat up in bed. She was in her room at Salthill, with the moon showing through the firs at her window.

She sank back and lay with her eyes open, listening. The dead quiet of country lay in the lanes below and on the moon. Even the cricket songs were too distant to be heard. A breeze stirred the firs and their branches brushed softly along the sill; that was all.

It came again, the cold click of metal falling into a chamber. She got out of bed then, crossed the room noiselessly on bare feet, and opened the door just enough to look out.

The hall floor gave off the luster of a recent polishing. A square of moonlight the size of a kerchief lay in front of Fi's door nearly opposite, which had been left ajar. A figure dim as a ghost's passed before the doorway, momentarily blocking the light. Elsa stood motionless and watched the bare-footed form, in flowing white with a mass of dark hair behind, move down the hall with a slow, swaying tread and reach the stairwell.

She closed the door and got back in bed. It was chilly and she pulled the covers past her nose, feeling her hot breath creep over her face. The bed felt safe, the room safe; even this night with its soundless dreaming pulse that bore her back to slumber was safe, a haven from danger. Here in her father's house nothing could touch her; she would neither drown nor be broken nor beaten. As she closed her eyes and sleep drew near, the memory of the passing image, now moving dimly in and out of consciousness, was followed by a single fragment of thought.

What was Sno-Bird doing on the upper floor in her nightgown?

Late in the fall, Harris came on the Red grazing with the Lapp herd. The reindeer had reached the low meadows in their leisurely migration down the slopes of Mount Endeavour. The valley folds were patchworked in brown and yellow, with streaks of ponderosa rolling out of the notches like green-black fog.

Watching the horse stalk with his long reach over the ground, Harris understood what losing the Red had meant to him. A new and startling concept came to him, of his own nature as a flame that continually consumed itself. That was what Grey had meant, the day he gave back the knife.

He loped the Appaloosa around the herd and moved in on the horse. The Red was thin and rangy-looking. The loss of bulk made his great height more conspicuous. There was a healed wound on his flank and another on his shoulder from a wildcat or horse fight, or from barbed wire. Using a mix of soft words and chirrups, Harris rode alongside the horse and caught him by the halter. A piece of frayed rope dangled from a snap in the halter ring. So the horse had been with someone, somewhere, if only briefly. The Red gave a deep snort and jerked his head back as Harris snapped the lead on.

He was working for Piwonka for a few days. He led the horse back to the camp and gave him a big feed of grain. The other men exclaimed at the size of the horse, the imperial glare that roughing it for months had failed to remove.

Next morning Harris put a stock saddle on the Red. Line-riding was a good way to start a horse working stock. They spent the day roaming through canyons and climbing steep grades. If they found a stray cow, they sent it toward the other strays forming a straggling bunch on the grassland.

The Red caught on quickly, but for Harris the feeling of working with another intelligence, remote and untouched by any influence outside of itself, persisted.

By the time they finished the ride, the Red was "rough-broke" to working cattle. He could outrun any cow with ease and he was surefooted on bad terrain. He could run up the side of a ravine like a mustang, great haunches clenching and stretching, and flush a heifer out in front of him. He learned to stop dead when a calf was roped, then back off while it tussled against the line, keeping it taut so Harris or another man could get down and handle it. Once this was done he sometimes turned on his rider and threw him as well. Harris left the saddle so often the other men made jokes about hog-tying him and branding him with the Mountain Inn brand.

"May's well, you're on the ground so much."

After one of these struggles Harris lost his temper. The rage was more flexible, less deadly than the rage he got into with people. He borrowed a rawhide quirt, got back on and worked the Red over with it, keeping the horse's head up with a tight rein so he couldn't lower it to buck. His face was grim with fury, but he avoided jabbing the horse's mouth. With each blow the Red whirled and squatted, ears flattened to his head, mouth gaping to bare the short, healthy teeth in an equine snarl. Finally he snatched the bit in his teeth and plunged down the long eroded canyon, up the trail and onto the range.

Harris let the horse have his head. They flowed over the ground for what seemed like miles. He knew he had never gone this fast on a horse, that he would never again travel at this speed in a saddle. The old quarry came up, the part that wasn't being used as a dump filled in with earth. New brush grew out of the shallow scar, the only sign left of the excavation that had given up the stone for the two houses in the valley. They ran past it into the mountains. When the woods thickened, the Red made a wide detour, slowing to a gallop along the verge, and turned back onto the flat. They were heading south for the lake. Harris plucked the quirt out of his boot; his arm rose and fell. The Red shot forward, electrified. A long streak of lather struck Harris in the face.

Whenever the horse started to slow, Harris laid on the quirt. His arm ached with the force of the blows. His rage was mounting again and he gave it free play, lashing the wet flanks whenever the horse showed any sign of flagging. The lake came in sight. Points of land jutted into the water, mohawk crests covered with spruce and flaming aspen, rising back into the long clean lines of the mountains. A flock of Canada geese rose above it and flew south against the slow-moving gray glacier of the sky.

The two other men who made up the camp were waiting when the red horse stumbled in, lifting one leg heavily before the other. His hide was soaked black; white lather foamed on the muscular chest and in the hollows of his flanks. Harris sat in the saddle, composed, etched in dust, with the quirt in his lap.

They halted. The Red's head sagged toward the ground. Harris moved the reins forward in the signal to walk. The eyes rolled back at him; the ears flattened, then flicked sideways. After a long pause the horse stepped forward unevenly.

"You're going to have a lot of fun with that bronc," said one of the men with a grin.

They rode back to Salthill after the line-ride. Turned into a box, the Red battered it with his hooves until Harris, afraid of real damage to the horse, let him into a paddock. The Red sailed over the fence and disappeared. Two days later he was back in home pasture, keeping a wary distance from the stallion, who dove at him whenever he came near the mares.

Dai heard the squeals of rage and came running.

"They'll kill each other, the bastard!" he shouted confusedly.

It took them an hour to catch the red horse, who floated around the pasture with the stallion at his heels, pulling away with ease when the stud got too close. At a healthy distance from the mares, he would stop and trot springily back and forth along the fence. When Harris approached him with the lead, he wheeled and trotted back toward the herd. Then the stud came forth again, ears flattened to his head, eyes bulging, head snaking along the ground, and the game began all over.

Harris rode Grey's mare Jonquil into the pasture. She dogged the Red into a corner. When he wheeled and shot out of it along the fence she was right beside him, moving swiftly for her chunky build. The Red's eyes blazed. He flowed over the fence like a river and galloped across the meadow.

Harris rode into the meadow. Like many geldings, the Red had an affinity with mares. As Jonquil approached, he stood with legs rigid, blowing down his nostrils. Harris dismounted and allowed his body to fall into soothing meditative lines. The Red touched noses uneasily with the mare, then snorted and rubbed his muzzle against hers. It was the first sign of affection Harris had seen him make toward anything.

He stroked the horses's neck, which was barely damp after an hour of chasing around, then slipped a rawhide twitch over his muzzle. The loop of the twitch fitted around the soft underjaw and could be tightened by sliding the knot up beneath it, constricting the jaw painfully. He applied some of this leverage. The horse danced and plunged beside him, mouth gaping under the twitch, neck arched and stepping high, subdued for a time.

They put him in the stud barn enclosure. The Red jumped out frequently to course around the country. They would find him grazing on the Bluffs, or in the meadows of the Klaxta reserve. In the stud enclosure, which looked flimsy and small when he occupied it, he paced restlessly up and down in front of the mountains.

"His bloodlines are good and he has great speed," said Grey. "There isn't a fence on this place he can't and hasn't cleared. But to be of use a horse must have a normal mind, and this one doesn't. He's an outlaw."

"He's safe to be around," insisted Harris.

"That was my next question."

They were cooling their horses in tandem. Harris set his jaw. "He killed a man in Toronto. At the track."

"How?"

"A jockey lashed him in the face with a whip."

"What a fiend," said Grey, before he thought.

"The horse dumped him at the start of a race, then caught up with the field and passed it. He was ten lengths in front and going away when he crossed the finish line. The jockey had to walk back to the enclosure. I guess he was boiling mad. He was getting a reputation for doing stuff like that."

"Then what? After he struck the horse?"

Harris focused on a point between his mount's ears. "Stomped."

"Stomped? You mean he . . ."

"Raised a hoof and stuck it through his head."

"My god. And you're telling me he's safe?"

"I don't think he's dangerous."

"Is this a hard conclusion you've drawn or just some sense you have?"

"Both. He's had plenty of chances to hurt me."

"But he fights you."

"That's different."

"When he ran off the day he came, I was relieved," said Grey after a pause. "I was certain he was lying in a gulch being picked over by buzzards. Frankly, I was damned sorry to see him back."

"If it bothers you that much," said Harris tensely.

"No; no. Don't get your wind up, man. He's your horse and this is where he belongs. He's got the entire Skillihawk to roam in if he likes. As long as he doesn't harm anyone, he's welcome to it."

Chapter Twenty-two

IT BEING AGREED ALL AROUND that a change in her situation had become necessary, Elsa was sent in September to a boarding school in Vancouver.

She was late to breakfast one morning, and an envelope with a strange logo and return address was propped against her juice glass when she slid breathlessly into her chair. It was a letter from Flavia. She was engaged to be married. His name was Charles Whitebirch. His family owned the largest dairy in British Columbia, in Penticton in the southern part of the province, and other land besides. His mother was a Haida Indian and his father was a cousin of Iseult's from Connaught. They had been introduced in her aunt's house. Flavia had enclosed a color snapshot of herself standing on the porch at Lisnasheoga, in a chocolate print dress scattered with yellow and purple pansies, next to a tall, brown-haired man who seemed to be smiling foolishly against the sun. The shot had been taken from below and was rather bad, so that Flavia looked dumpy, with a large middle and short, bowling-pin legs.

> I would have written before but we rushed to Penticton to meet
> his family and I am only now able to sit down. O darling, isn't
> it wonderful? I know you'll love Charley as much as I do. I want
> you to be my first bridesmaid.

Elsa studied the logo. *Dade Whitebirch Farms* in green, a severely beautiful silo rising above a fir tree. She stuffed the envelope in her uniform pocket, her face alight with her father's rare smile. She smiled over the rows of heads of shining *fille*-hair, the monitors scurrying between tables with milk pitchers, Miss Gavelline clearing her throat every time she dipped her spoon in her cornflakes. It was at that moment that Elsa felt she was truly growing up. It had to do with being happy for Flavia's love, with being glad Flavia was going to marry Charles Whitebirch, because it was so right for her.

In her room she smoothed the letter open and put it under two interesting stones she had found on a school hike at Lilooet. The stones pinned down a lively drawing of her mare, made using six different pencils, and another of a nude in russet and rose chalks. Her father had sent an irritated response to a note from her art teacher, saying that of course he gave permission for Elsa to draw from the life. So Elsa was driven in Matron's car twice a week to an outside course, where she labored under the direction of a real artist, inhaling solvent fumes and charcoal dust with adults in a cavernous room while rain dripped off the slates outside. There was a little heater to warm the German woman, all knobs and bone, who posed on a dais with a square of carpet nailed to it. On her breaks the woman put on a worn bathrobe and sold hens' eggs, and sometimes a skinned rabbit.

Another note awaited her that evening after classes. It was from Lisnasheoga and was not franked, which meant Mr. Tim Lew the gardener had dropped it at the school office on his way home. She opened it casually, expecting a repetition of Flavia's news. It was from Iseult, the more religious of her aunts.

> My Dear,
>
> Your grandmother, Lady St. Oegger, died last Monday. Daisy and I are going home for a few weeks to make arrangements for your grandfather's comfort. Your Uncle Jasper and Aunt Winni-fred are moving into the wing at Carrollton; Jasper will drive down weekends from the plant. Flavia will stay with the White-birches while we are away. If we are not back in time for the end of term Sr. Ignatius will arrange your train fare to Salthill. I have wired your father and Gordon in Montreal, although of course none of us will be able to attend the funeral.
>
> A novena would be helpful, Elsa. I recommend the prayers of St. Bridget particularly. Certainly she was not much of a grand-parent to you, but she may need them all the more for it.
>
> Love, Iseult.

Without asking permission, Elsa went out the side gate, which had been left unfastened, and down Leinster Road. The cream walls and tiles of Beech's shone soft behind her in the light before dusk. It had once been a seminary, and remained remote and ecclesiastic. Meals were eaten in the old refectory, where the odors of chipped beef and baked halibut seemed to linger in the walls. The classroom fittings were outmoded, the floors worn pine or speckled riverbottom-patterned linoleum that curled at the edges. Beech's was a plain, venerable establishment, not for the glamour-seeking or faint of wallet, offering a solid English public school education, plenty of sports and no folderol. Elsa knew this, having been told so by Iseult on a number of occasions.

The church was at a crossroads behind a walled garden. She went in by the side door and made her novena, then sat in the pew, thinking of Ireland. A few lamps were on. The sanctuary lay in a twilight faintly marbled with color from the stained glass. Except for a narrow light behind each figure, the saints' alcoves were dark. The effect of this seemed dramatic and tender.

Elsa sank to her knees, blessed herself and made a teepee of her fingers. From under her brows she saw a priest enter the sanctuary, genuflect and kneel at the altar. He wore a cassock and his hair was black. She had come to mass here, but he was not a priest she had ever seen.

Staring at the back of his neck, which was narrow and fair like a woman's, she was jolted into memory.

There was a cove by the sea, where the north light turned the water white and clean against the shingle. The headlands ran into the sea there and became narrow bands of rock. A red and white sharpy was moored in the cove. She could see it through the clover and Egyptian grass, lying on her stomach on the cliff. There were two biscuits in the pocket of her dress.

Though the wind was blowing, she heard the footsteps clearly on the path. Someone was coming, and coming with purpose. She slumped beside the rock and clutched the biscuits as if they were good-luck marbles.

She came up the path in a wool suit and a felt hat like a helmet. Her face was narrow and white. She walked with purpose in every line, the stick legs going back and forth in stout shoes. The girl got to her feet with the wind blowing her wild hair about and stood trembling. The face swam at her from under the helmet, blank except for shiny blue button eyes.

"My granddaughter's come for you," she said in a loud voice, as if the girl were deaf, and seized her by the arm.

She tried to pull away but the old thing twisted her arm until she cried out. They rocked together. She bit the hand that gripped her, sank her teeth in as far as she could, not far because it was all chicken skin and gristle, and hung on. The sea, the black headlands and the sharpy tilted. The old thing thrashed about, moaning and hissing like a creature caught in a trap. She shook herself free and hit out at the girl

*with feeble blows. The girl wrapped her arms around the stick legs and made herself
a hanging weight. She could smell the ribbed stockings and the soap she washed with,
the odor of thick wool and scented old lady.*

A cry came from down the beach. "Grandmother!"

*She let go and fell backward on the path, banging her head. A girl was stumbling
over the rocks toward them, a scarf over her hair, a scarlet mouth in a white face.*

"Grandmother, for heaven's sake! Elsa, darling!" And Flavia held out her arms.

*She was being dragged to the grange. There was Flavia pulling off the holey dress
and throwing it on the fire, leaving her standing in her smalls. Flavia outside in the
hall, saying things in a voice that trembled. The bread and butter Flavia fed her, slice
by slice, which she ate thrusting out her neck and opening her mouth, looking first at
the fireplace, then at the door.*

Then Flavia took her away. Flavia took her away.

Elsa began to quiver like the birches by the drive at Salthill when the
winds came. She squeezed her eyes shut and gripped the rim of the pew in
front. A pulse hammered in her throat, making her dizzy.

The priest rose. Instead of going out the side door toward the rectory, he
turned down the center aisle, calmly putting one foot down before the other.
His skirts parted around each shoe. She stared fixedly at the carpet, waiting
for him to pass. When the silence had lingered long enough behind the
footfalls, she looked into the aisle and saw the shoes, black oxfords with thick
soles, planted firmly next to her pew.

Her eyes followed the lines of his robe upward. It was an austere face,
filled with rectitude. The eyes were black and hot with intelligence. She
took his measure as a child does. What one hungers for is not love but
worldliness: acceptance, the facts, truth.

"My child, why are you here at this hour?"

"My child" sounded in her ears like the opening chords of a hymn, and
she heard he was Irish, like the priests on the road in Galway who had greeted
her with voices that fell in a soft rain.

"I am praying for someone I hate, Father," she said.

The Iberian eyes flashed. "Then pray in your own words for her soul," he
said. "For if a child hates, it must be for a reason. You will feel better for it."

Long after he left her, as the evening settled, she prayed. The remaining
light ebbed from the windows until all the scarlet, blue and gold in the glass
was gone.

Dear God, please forgive me. I'm glad the sodding bitch is dead.

Book Two

The Skillihawk Valley
1951

We are all in the gutter,
but some of us are
looking at the stars.

—*Oscar Wilde*

Chapter Twenty-three

THE DEPOT AT FOUR QUEENS rocketed past the windows. Elsa zipped the *National Geographic* into her handbag and watched the platform run backward and slow to a halt. She leaned forward on the seat and crushed out her cigarette. A matronly woman across the aisle frowned at the spectacle: a child smoking. Then the child rose and rose, long and lean, to brush off the lapels of an oatmeal-colored suit and smooth the wrinkles over her hips, and reach for the valise in the rack overhead.

Bending to the window, Elsa saw Harris coming down the corridor of shade cast by the blue station roof. He looked his usual self, alert and a little cross, in a white shirt open at the neck and a pair of jeans gone thin in the legs from wear. She watched him pick her old calf-hide suitcases out of the luggage on the platform, not looking at the identifying labels because he didn't need to, and head for the parking lot with one in each hand.

Elsa withdrew from the window and slumped in her seat in a fiery reverie. Passengers filed past her toward the doors, women in cloth coats with large handbags, the smell of baby powder and stale pressed flowers wafting from the armpits of their dresses, pushing children before them. The odd male sauntered by with faraway look, jingling change.

She ventured to the window again. He was scanning the row of Pullmans with eyes narrowed. He waited motionless, a man who never fidgeted, a man who made no unnecessary movements. Whose watchful bearing had sometimes made her feel like a rabbit. . . . But what was it now that she saw, rising out of the familiar and homely idea that was Salthill? A man, dark, and strong, and exotic.

Her mouth felt loose, her eyes heavy as if with sleep. She crouched forward, nearly shivering, wrapped in a sudden vivid dream: his shoulder, the broad slope, removed from the backdrop of house, barn and field, a tool of work suddenly for *her*; his strong leg against her leg. The press of the secret pouch, the bare foot. The waist and swell of backside under the jeans, seen a thousand times before house, barn and field with no meaning then, which she saw now in a kind of fever.

The sun struck the glass and warmed her like a potpie. Elsa took a breath and rose slowly, gathering her things.

Harris had come to the bottom of the steps. She stood on the top step with her cheeks sucked in. Her mouth drooped at the corners, one foot pointed to the lower step. Everything seemed to stop, the iron groan of the train, the sharp blue sky with its birdsong. They looked at each other. And his eyes understood and agreed and darted over her face in astonishment and fear. And she smiled, wildly in love and frightened, too, and stepped like a cat down the little flight. The valise dropped on the boards at his feet. She reached for the dry hand, felt his fingers tighten and not let go.

He glanced away so she would not see the brightness of his eyes, but they burned her face and neck. His shirt smelled clean and the body under it, clean. She watched him make his face hard.

"Where is Grey?" she said. It sounded like a breathless trill.

"With the MP, up to buy horses." He picked up her bag and they walked side by side toward the parking lot.

They waited at the crossroads to turn onto the highway. Harris watched her lift the braid from her back and let it rest on her shoulder like a tame animal. With cruel instinct she made him more aware of her, a mare lifting her tail at the stallion. He couldn't look away. Her profile was sharp and forbidding, with those brows and high-bridged nose. Where had he seen a woman's face like that before? Because this was a woman.

He tried to think past the confusion he had been thrown into in front of the Pullman. Past the desire that had come instantly at the sight of her red cruel soft mouth, the hawk face and bristling goldenrod and dark silk hair pulled back tight, the eyes that had met his and ignited him like dry tinder.

A book, a European history with woodcuts and plates of old paintings, men in ruffs and queens in gold and white gowns; that was where he had seen that old-looking face. It was a prototype. He knew what a prototype was. He picked up new meanings quickly now, adding them to a vocabulary that had become extensive, a stronghold of happily familiar Latin and Greek roots. It was a face bred to a type, a merging of tribes that had warred for two thousand years over a small green land of mountains and islands. It was a face—what was the word he wanted?—archaic. A medieval face. He was seeing it for the first time, out of the sleeve of childhood.

Harris directed his attention to the road and a dump truck going by with its tail jouncing. He could feel her eyes on him. He could see their ghosts in the windshield, under brows that had reshaped themselves into thick wings.

The car behind them tapped its horn. He pulled out.

They crossed the scarlet bridge in silence. Storm clouds darkened the flight of ranges to the north. The lower edges of the thunderheads blurred into the peaks, except for a jagged black line that was the moving core of the storm front. It was miles away, but it would reach them in a day or two unless it wore itself out. They reached the flat and Harris put on some speed. There was plenty to do at home without spending his time in a truck cab with a teenager. That was what she was. Young. She was Grey's daughter. He would remember that she was Grey's daughter and young.

She didn't look young though. She had that old look on that some very young women got when they were ready for love. For its sweetness and penetration into their strongholds.

She said abruptly into the silence that filled the cab like a fog, "It looks like a country scene from the Impressionists. From the mountain pass into the valley, I mean. The birches and pines lining the drive, the drive like a white ribbon, and the stone house, and those bright green fields."

"Does it," he croaked as if he hadn't spoken for a week. What the hell was an Impressionist? He felt a surge of anger and turned more abruptly into the drive than he should have. The birches cast shade like spilled water on the track.

The guests were on the veranda: Captain Stuyvesant and Lieutenant Brownell of the Mounted Police, Mr. and Mrs. Georgewood and Trinity Georgewood. The shutters were open and the sun lay in their laps and in stripes on their faces. Drinks had made them jolly and a little loud. The men rose when Elsa came in.

"You remember my younger daughter," Grey said with his hands on her shoulders. He was sunburned and smelled of whiskey. "She begins at university this fall."

Lieutenant Brownell looked her over with a kindly expression. "Aren't you rather young for university?"

"I'm sixteen," Elsa said.

"Where are you going to go?" asked Captain Stuyvesant.

"Winnipeg. They have a fine arts school."

"She worked her way through the entire curriculum at Beech's, so we applied for early entry," said Grey. "She had to show her portfolio to be accepted."

Elsa excused herself and went to change for dinner.

Harris had left her bags at the foot of the stairs. She studied them thoughtfully. He had tossed them there to tell her something. What? Harris or Dai had always brought her things upstairs when she came home. Or Gordie. But Gordon was not here much anymore. He had gotten his M.D. last year and was finishing his residency at the Royal Vic in Montreal.

She took the luggage up, two at a time. As she bumped the heaviest one up the steps, she heard a roar of laughter from the veranda, and Bron Georgewood's voice tinkling over it like glass breaking.

Elsa shucked off the suit and went downstairs in her old robe to bathe. In her room, she shook her hair out of the towel and dabbed at it with her fingers. Her hair curled and thickened when it was damp, like a species of sponge. It had gone sable at the roots and layered out, each layer lighter than the one below—dark honey, gold, wheat, a thin silvery top sheen. Her best feature, Daisy said.

She found the sundress with blue ticking stripes in the suitcase. Flavia had sent it, saying they were all the rage. Dearest Fi. She and Charley had been married two years now, and there was a baby on the way. The sundress, held up for review, was a little rumpled but good enough. Elsa zipped it up in back, then rummaged in the case for a pair of sandals. She didn't really want to go downstairs and eat with people. She wanted to meditate alone on the compound of fear and unholy longing that had met her at the station.

She sat on the bed with a sandal dangling, and thought about Harris. Compact, vulnerable, contemptuous Harris, with his air of oppressed gravity. With his air of being permanently transfixed by the memory of some secret crisis. Devoted, her father's Harris. Harris of Salthill. Harris with eyes the color of clean aquarium water. A marine aquarium, not domestic. . . . His arm burned the color of old bark, resting on the door of the pickup.

A Steller's jay shrieked in the garden, above the green fields lying so tenderly beyond the walls. In summer this room always smelled of sweet roses and cardamom. She slipped her hand under her skirt and stroked her thighs, feeling how smooth her skin was, like the thick, soft bell of a lily. She touched herself between the legs. A very little rubbing brought on the tingling, then a luscious warmth at the base of her spine. The warmth spread down her legs to her toes. She lay back with a sigh, dreaming of brown hands, a carnal mouth.

Chapter Twenty-four

THE DINING TABLE WAS LAID with Irish linen and the mismatched Doulton.

"Wonderful," murmured Bron Georgewood. "I can't get my Yorkshire to rise this high. How do you do it, Sno-Bird?"

"Follow directions," said Sno-Bird stonily.

Elsa remembered Trinity Georgewood only as a podgy boy who had danced with her at Flavia's reception at the Elks Lodge after the wedding mass. Most of Four Queens had been there, because Grey believed in sweeping, general invitations. Fi's reception had been as large and erratic as her wedding had been sumptuous and gravely ordered. All the ranchers and their families and a lot of the townspeople had come, and Piwonka and his men. And the aunts, dressed to the nines, and Gordon in a tartan and wool stockings. The Klaxta had played six-pack bezique at one of the tables, and Dee Lachlan's niece Morag had taken a tin whistle from her pocket with the air of a small boy producing a frog and played wild reels for them to dance to.

Harris had been there, in what Grey called his ice-cream suit. He had sat in the pew behind her at Saints Felicitas and Perpetua (because she had refused in the end to be a bridesmaid) with the beribboned snap-brim hat on his knee, and although she had still loved Harris, being still a child, she had not turned once to see whether he rose and sank properly during the ceremony. She did not recall seeing him at the reception; she had been too busy not getting trodden on when she danced, or trying to lead her partner, to look.

Trinity was a grown man now of nearly twenty, as eerily handsome as a storybook prince. His blue-black hair was brushed into a low pompadour, his forehead Greek marble, blue-white and knotted at the lobes. The podge was gone and he looked lean and fit. While the inevitable topics of horses, provincial and national politics, weather and economics went around the table, he engaged Elsa in conversation. She ate heartily—the food on the train had been awful—and answered between mouthfuls.

"You've grown up a lot," he said, smiling. "Do you date?"

"Never," she said.

"Would you like to go to the pictures in Four Queens next week?"

She waited so long to answer that he was affronted. She cocked her head and seemed to be attending to some thought. "All right."

"I'll pick you up Saturday around five-thirty. If it's okay with your dad, that is."

She shrugged. "Why should he mind? He's known you for years."

What a rude girl. Why had he asked her out, anyway? The curvy and kittenish was what a guy looked for. You saw that ideal everywhere, in the picture shows and on magazine covers; girls with cherry lips and bobbed hair. Or women in tight cashmere sweaters, like Lana Turner, who were part of secret dreams. Elsa was thin, flat-chested and dusted with freckles. Her nails were unvarnished. She had a writer's callus on the second finger of her right hand where her pen had labored too ardently. But her eyes, shifting from tawny to green-blue in honor of the sundress, were alive with a contrary intelligence, and she had an interesting, kissable-looking mouth.

"This is a little different," he said authoritatively. "This is a date."

Her mouth twitched. "Okay. Ask him."

After dinner they all went down to look at the horses. Begonias in casks by the stable door lent a dairy creaminess to the backdrop of half-timbered dark green and stone. The prospective purchases were taken from their stalls, gleaming, looking alertly about and snuffing into palms, and were inspected by Brownell and Stuyvesant, with humorous running commentary from the other guests.

They passed the stud enclosure where Elsa's blue roan mare and the Red grazed together, the latter dwarfing the former. The Red was polished to a sheen; his tail fell like a curtain from its high, flaring root.

"Good god," muttered Brownell. "What's that?"

The horse threw up his head and stared, nostrils fluting.

"It's Harris's runaway."

"What a specimen. Is he a jumper?" asked Georgewood.

"He is," said Harris, who had joined the party.

"A jumper indeed!" Grey shouted. "There's nothing he can't get over. How I wish he were at the bottom of the sea! No, Harris's feelings won't be hurt—he's well aware of my opinion. No one but Harris rides him, and he's been thrown countless times. Broke his arm for him last winter, and he had to spend Christmas with me!"

Everyone laughed. Harris grinned. Elsa, trailing behind the others, focused on a spot between his shoulder blades and compelled him by an exercise of will to turn and look at her.

A chestnut mare with a flaxen mane and tail brooded beneath the larches by the drive, her huge belly swelling solidly to her knees.

"What a beautiful girl," exclaimed Mrs. Georgewood, stroking her neck. The mare's large, mild eye turned toward them reproachfully.

"The Duchess of Mag," said Grey. "One of my foundation mares. She bred late; the first heat was false. She's carrying twins and miserable with it, poor girl."

"Does she give you that disgusted look every time you pass her?" asked Stuyvesant.

"No, she usually reserves it for the stud," Grey replied. Everyone laughed.

"Bloodlines?" murmured Stuyvesant.

"Impeccable. By Pantomime out of Faraway, she by King Far. I got her in Ontario as a filly. She's as good-natured, sensible and intelligent as she is beautiful. If any mare can handle twins, she will."

"Is she the dam of any of your offerings?"

"The two chestnuts and the sorrel you just saw. Elsa's mare—the one with the Red—was her first. And if you're wondering how I got a blue roan from a chestnut, I didn't. I bred her to George's roan stud in Wanda Creek."

"I was going to say. That's one of Pepper's all right," said Georgewood. "He bred true as a die, the old boy. Threw out lots of blues."

"She's as good-hearted as her dam," Grey went on. "We thought it would help the Red to have some company, so we put them in together. He seems content to stay with her for the time being."

He went into the pasture where the stallion stood guard between his harem and the visitors. As Grey approached, the stud stepped forward with ears pricked in inquiry and with great delicacy lifted two sugar lumps from his hand.

Harris turned his head as though a sound had alerted him to some danger and stared at Elsa. She felt his look wash over her, and she was astonished by a sudden happiness.

"I've asked Elsa to the films Saturday," said Trinity as they made their way back to the house, trailing behind the others.

"Fine, if she wants to go," said Grey.

"I was afraid you'd mind. I'm a lot older than she is, sir."

"Mind? Why should I mind? I've known you for years. Just drive that road like a man and bring her back in one piece. That's all I ask."

The sun was still warm on the garden walls. Harris sat in a kitchen chair on the grass, drinking Coca-Cola from a bottle. He heard the screen door open and close, and she was there, in that dress. Crumpled in back and smelling of girl. He walked his eyes around the branches of the Jonagold, the leaves transparent against the sky and the deep green leaves of the persimmon behind them. It was evening and the guests had gone.

"Sno-Bird wants to know do you want ice cream," she said. "Dai made it in the crock."

"No, thanks."

"Why not? It's good." She sat on the stoop and wrapped the wide skirt around her legs. "Peach."

"Ice cream reminds me of church socials."

She seemed to accept that, and sat hugging her knees. He listened fiercely to the juncos vocalizing in the lime trees.

With a sigh, Elsa lifted her face to the red, starless glow of evening. "Harris, do you care for me at all?"

"You're his daughter," he said tonelessly. "You occupy a certain place."

"Is that *all*? I just occupy some niche, like Sno-Bird or the horses?"

He let a minute pass. "I know what you're driving at," he said in a low voice, not looking at her. "Don't push it, girl. What you want isn't going to happen."

He had done it, framed the unspoken with words. He couldn't go back on them now. It was like swearing an oath.

She ignored this and smoothed her hands down her legs, reaching for her ankles. He followed the movement, saw the top of the sundress curve out and a pink-tipped breast glow in the gap. A pink nipple like the delicate flesh of a rosebud.

"Do you even like me?" she asked the sky.

"Not much."

"Do you ever think about me?"

"Nope."

"I could make you think about me, Harris. I could make you have to." She smiled at him as if she knew he was lying and it amused her.

The only thing to do was leave, but he couldn't move. He seemed to be rooted in the chair. The gap was smoothed out now. It had been just a second, a blink in time, that creamy little globe, just the size to fit in a hand.

" 'Red sky at morning, sailor take warning, red sky at night, sailor's delight.' My grandmother's cook taught me that," she said. "Her name was Mrs. Terhune, and she would tell me things if she was in a good mood. I never see a sunset without thinking of all those sailors lined on the shore, crying with pleasure as the sun falls into the sea. Then the sea turns blood red, as if a bolus of dye had been dropped in."

"What's a bolus?" Even in the middle of being tormented, he couldn't resist a new word.

"Ball, bowl, dose. A sufficiency. I like the way you sit perfectly still. You make other people look irritable and twitchy. You're not restful though, are you? One always wonders when you're going to leap up."

He was silent.

"Can you think of one, Harris?" she asked. "You know—a verse that pops into your head whether you want it to or not?"

"Yeah. 'He who fights and runs away lives to fight another day.' "

"Oh," she murmured. "That one." She plucked a stray yarrow from the grass and twirled the stem. "Here's the one I like best." She cleared her throat and recited with a galloping intonation:

"There was a young lady from Niger
Who smiled as she rode on a tiger.
They returned from the ride
With the lady inside
And the smile on the face of the tiger.

"It's supposed to be funny, but it isn't, is it? It's chilling. 'And the smile on the face of the tiger.' *Whuff.*"

Rage sprang in him. He bent forward, thrust his face in hers and giggled. "You know what? *I might could* be the tiger," he said. Blindsided, his breath clouded back at him.

She drew her head back sharply. "What do you mean?"

"Leave me alone is what I mean," he said. "I'm not one of your dumb college boys and I don't like being teased."

"I am not teasing," she snapped. "I'm not, Harris," she repeated, in a wondering voice that terrified him.

He set the bottle carefully next to the chair and raked her with his eyes from the crown of her head to her sandaled toes. "Look, I don't want you, okay? Why don't you peddle yourself to that Georgewood boy? You're not much to look at, but I bet he'd be glad to lay down with you."

Her face turned the shade of old brick. "You bleeding son of a bitch."

"And if your daddy heard you say that, he'd whip your ass." He threw himself back, grinning with satisfaction.

She got to her feet and stumbled toward the house. The kitchen door slammed with such force the screen in it fell down.

Chapter Twenty-five

SHE CAME TO BREAKFAST LATE, in jodhpurs and boots and an old sweater familiar from other seasons, with stretched-out sleeves. Her face blazed with freckles. She looked wholesome, good-natured and plain. Her features lacked the symmetry of her father's and had a slight foreign cast, as if Grey had mated with an Arthur Rackham fairy.

Since yesterday he had been telling himself he didn't feel things he did feel, didn't want what he did want. Now, watching her take the chair across from him, his heart jumped in his chest like a Coho leaping in the river.

"Morning," murmured Elsa. "Did the MP buy any horses?"

"Six," said her father. "The best ones, aside from the four going to the shows."

Dai looked interested. Harris shook some jam onto a biscuit. He and Grey had discussed the shows long ago.

"The rest'll be off to the sales?" asked Dai.

"The five-year-olds who haven't sold and a few of the four-year-olds. They'll go in September before the haying." Grey frowned. "I dislike selling at auction. There's no money in it and I like to know a buyer, by repute at least, before I sell him four years' worth of training and care."

They chewed over this oft-uttered statement.

"There's whitewash for the trailers in th' shed," said Dai. "Three gallons. D'ye want me to do them today?"

"Best do it before the rain starts again," said Grey. "The rest of us will work the show stuff. I think you're right about the mare, Harris. She'll go."

"She's got the class," said Dai, twiddling his fingers absently. Harris pushed the biscuits at him.

"And your old pal the Irish steeplechaser," Grey added. "If he shows well, some rich amateur may buy him. He deserves a chance at the sleek life, being driven to local competitions on weekends, eating his head off in a warm stall the rest of the week. Let him try for it."

That was a surprise. "Pete's too old to be a top-flight jumper," Harris protested.

"He's ten. Some jumpers are in their prime at that age. He's been schooled out of his deplorable habits."

"Ah, he'll miss him, is all," said Dai. "He's got a soft spot in him for the old boy."

Elsa plucked a strip of bacon from the tangle on the platter. "Who shall I be working?"

"Sizzle Star today. Near Riot for Harris, since he's soft on daft jumpers. I'll take Lord Edgeware. We'll fit Petronel in between." Grey gave one of his disarming smiles. Things were going well, at least from the horse end.

Harris let his gaze fall on Grey's daughter. She dipped her head a little when she bit into the bacon, and he saw a gleam of small teeth. She chewed slowly, making every movement a movement full of meaning directed at him. She pointed a little finger shiny with grease in the air, displayed a slight frown, the frail vine of her neck. Wordless acquiescence was an art women practiced, when they wanted. It was why going to prostitutes was deadening. Behind the gestures they had turned the lamps off and it was dark and empty in there.

She didn't look much older than she had the night she got drunk at the Klaxta reserve. She wasn't. Under the pushed-back sleeves her arms were the color of the clematis in the garden, pale and dusted with gold. Until yesterday he'd never been drawn to white skin or freckles, or young girls, either. He liked grown women, women older than him, even, like Sandrine. Women brown, yellow, ebony, red; not this ivory, with veins running under it like blue thread. Then he thought of the breasts under her sweater, each with a blushing nipple.

The chestnut was literally too excited to jump. Next to Elsa, Grey squinted critically, watching legs, horse breath, measuring distances. He was used to Harris's riding. He wondered at leisure, when it suited him.

Without whip or spurs, with hands and body alone, Harris moved the skirling horse to the track and kept him there. Occasionally he spoke sotto voce. His hands flowed; his back was gravely beautiful. The downturned profile, sharp with some refining, whittling force, was imperious with concentration. He was a stranger managing a wet-flanked horse into flowing continuity. It was his work and she couldn't enter him while he was in it. She had not found her own work yet and did not know it existed. Without realizing it, she hated this fluttering loose from her personal furnishings.

The chestnut rushed at the fences with ears flattened and eyes popping and cleared them all with feet to spare, throwing gusts of sod against the rails, groaning with excitement on the turns.

"He'll have to be worked between shows," said Harris after a less erratic second round. "He's pretty charged up."

"It's the Holyrood line," said Grey. "All that get is jug-headed as they come. But they can jump all day."

"If they can keep from getting tangled up in their own legs."

They were off. Elsa sat watching Harris's lips move, his beautiful soft lips.

"Take the whole lot twice," Grey said to her finally. "We'll see how she goes."

Elsa rode into the ring. It was another bright day. Even around the horses, the air smelled like clean laundry hanging in the sun. The storm seemed to be diverted, though the weather report from Four Queens, shared as a matter of course by the Georgewoods, was still dire, full of fronts and winds, downdrafts and coolings. There was an unhappy discoloration on the horizon, a plumed line slowly building.

The mare trotted along the track, her ears swiveling back and forth. The gate came up—then two posts—at the next post they'd move out. Elsa touched her heels to the mare's sides and they flowed into a canter as the post shot by. Elsa steadied her for each takeoff. A touched pole on one of the barriers sounded a hollow *tock*, but the first half of the round was otherwise clean. They came around the turn. The water jump lay ahead, improvised from a trough, a hurdle and some pine boughs. A few feet before it, the mare dug in her toes and refused. Elsa brought her around and pointed her firmly at the trough. She refused again. Elsa walked her clear to the water and let her look it over. The mare ran her nostrils along the rim of the trough in a houndlike way and sniffed at the water. Elsa cantered her in a circle and put her at it again. The mare made up her mind, cleared the whole thing with a rush and bounded away, snorting loudly. Elsa patted her neck and praised her extravagantly. They finished the course, went around again without stopping, and cantered back to the gate.

"Good," said Grey. "How does she feel?"

"She's easy to pace." She took off the hunt cap and sponged her brow with the back of her hand. "Never gets too close or puts in a short one."

"Keep on at her with the water jump; she doesn't like it, but she'll come around with care. Good judgment on speed at the takeoffs. Try gathering her more for the oxer, she's sprawling a bit there."

Elsa walked the mare around to keep her cool. She waved at Harris who was cooling his horse at the far end of the ring. He returned the wave with a cold, closed look. The exchange in the garden last night had been a skirmish, ending in a rout. Now forces were drawn to a standstill, gathered and spectacularly resting on opposite sides of a river. She had faced the morning with the same small flames at points in her body, bravado restored. How tough and clever he had been, to parry her love!

Grey took his horse out. He rode with an authority so complete it was a form of elegance. The shirt billowed away from his trim body; his sleeves, gartered at the elbows, revealed forearms wiry with corded muscle. His chestnut finished the two rounds at a spanking pace.

It was Harris next. They stopped, reversed. The lean equine head flashed up and down, fighting the command, then the chestnut compressed himself and took several crisp, interrogative steps backward. Elsa watched them glide across the ring. Riot was a splendid jumper, just raw. Settled in, they rose rhythmically to the barriers. Her father was a top-flight horseman. Elsa knew she was a more-than-competent rider. But Harris on horseback was the artist's holy rood, the exacting, the impossible, made artless.

"Why don't we know more about him?" asked Elsa, trying to sound bored. She had learned yesterday that love does not make the heart light. It makes the heart a plumb-line that drops to your feet and drags your body earthward with its weight.

"Because he doesn't want us to." His horse fidgeted and he brought it firmly up.

"You could find out. He has papers."

He gave her a piercing look. "That would be an unkind, petty thing to do."

"Why does he have to set himself apart from everyone?" she cried out.

"He doesn't. *They* have been set apart. In America they have to use separate rest rooms and drinking fountains. They ride in the backs of public conveyances. They are kept from jobs and education, though given the opportunity they earn college degrees and invent plasma and other useful things, like anybody else. They are hanged without trial. They have no justice. Justice is justice only when it applies to everyone. When it doesn't, it's cant. Or worse."

He said this in a tone so caustic she felt flayed. She felt her father's breadth over her shoulders, the pale flame of his hair. His horse stretched his neck out and snuffed loudly at the rail.

"Oddly, we too are a long-headed race," he mused. "I wonder, was it the purpose of the Almighty that we were to share a history, we whose craniums can be cupped by an adult hand?" He watched Harris's flight past the gate, eyes narrowed. "*That* is one of their warriors. Under that hybrid Englishness are the scars and trappings of the Nubian. I saw through his disguise when he came up our road."

"Was he drawn somehow, do you think? To us?" asked Elsa, awed.

"No. He came because he was starving, and stayed because he could ride," said Grey coolly. "But I owe him his silence, in the name of my race."

Chapter Twenty-six

HARRIS LEFT THE CURTAINS OPEN. The moon was up, the darkness aromatic with resins released like mists into the starry elevation. He read for a while, conscious of the glow of night from the window, the lilac and sage tints in the clouds drifting in fragments in the moon's path, the deep bronze, like caterpillar fur, of the leaves and needles out of range of the lamplight.

He marked the place in his reading with a paper match, left the book on the floor, put out the lamp and went to sleep.

He needed a fix. The car drove by, around the block and past again, crept to the curb. He stood on the corner, sullen and murderous. But he still got in. Still sold himself for two bucks; four, five on a good night. In the hallway stuck the needle in, ripped off the stocking, laid there while the stuff slammed through his body. The city passing by, men and women, screaming children, the numbers runners, shuffling bums, not looking at him slumped there, off in heaven. Or in some room with his mouth open, sometimes in heaven, sometimes in his own puke.

He turned restlessly, the quilt dragging after him in a tail. From time to time a muscle twitched in his flung-out arm. There was a fragrance of something in the air, faint and familiar, like an herb or damp flower.

"*Harris.*"

He rolled away, felt the boot in his belly—the lash—

"*Harris.*"

He woke.

A breeze was playing with the curtains, the panels unfolding with every breath into transparent wings that fluttered, soared and sank. He rolled onto one elbow and with eyes narrowed searched the dark from corner to shadow-webbed corner, sure that he wasn't alone. The pattern of buds and nettles he had idly scanned a thousand times left the wall in a broken wave, changed shape and swam before the moonlit garden.

It was Elsa. She was stark-naked.

Her hair hung in loose disorder over her shoulders. A pubic bush the color of gunmetal fluffed out between the straight, pallid legs.

"Harris," she hissed, nearly running to the bed. "Were you dreaming? You were moaning such things and you looked awful."

Her mouth hung open and she looked lost in thought. He stared at her breasts, a girl's breasts, round and delicate, stiff-nippled with cold.

"Get out of here," he said, scooting across the mattress.

She sat on his pillow, sank back and lolled, knees tucked to one side. "I *told you* I wasn't teasing," she said giggling, waving arms like languid vines.

He got out of bed with the quilt wound hastily around him. "Now look."

"This is what we want, isn't it? O Harris, please don't say no."

"No." *Don't think, don't debate. You'll lose.*

She reared up and kneed her way over the bed. He watched the mattress dimple toward him. "Harris," she breathed mournfully.

He had to do what he'd done in the garden last night—shake her off, get rid of her. But he'd always been a poor-ass liar. *Grey, I want your daughter. I've wanted her since she got off that train. She wants me too, Grey. So with or without your leave, I'll take her. After all she's sixteen, old enough to know her mind.*

"It's because of *him*, isn't it?" The bell of flesh in the center of her upper lip stuck a little to the lower one when she spoke, in a voice like falling leaves. "You're afraid. *He's* what you mind."

"It's enough for me," he said. A remote part of his brain was firing off words, while his body dragged itself toward her mouth.

"Not for me," she whispered. "You don't really care, either. I can tell by the look in your eyes."

"It's too dark to see."

"I see by the moonlight."

"Get out," he said hoarsely. "Or I'll run you upstairs."

"Try."

He clamped his hand on her arm and hustled her off the bed toward the door. His other hand grasped the quilt, feet planted apart to keep from tripping over the trailing ends. She stumbled, cried out in pain and tried to twist away. He held on tight, almost lifting her in the air, glaring in fascination at the downy bloom, like the sheen of a pearl, on the flesh ballooning around his grip.

"You're hurting me," she groaned.

"Then get. Out."

"All *right*. Let me go."

He let go. She rubbed her arm, glaring.

"Do you know what a hound is?" he hissed.

"Certainly," she said crossly. "A dog."

"It isn't. It's a horse with no racing heart."

Her eyes widened. She whirled and stalked away, the loose hair flashing with the swing of her head.

"Don't come back," he said after her.

She went out the window, stepping backward into the shrubbery without bothering to conceal herself. Moonlight defined the planes of her body under the taut ivory skin with its sheen of down. When she cocked her leg over the sill he saw the faint gleam of her sex through the smudge of pubic hair.

She sank into the dogwood with her eyes fixed tragically on his face. She was a girl after all. A grown woman would have looked farther down than his neck. If she had known how close she was to being inside his storm, she would have climbed back in and he would have been gone. But she drew away, and became a ghost blossom among the leaves and real blossoms.

She ignored Harris for the rest of the week, not so obviously that her father would notice, but enough so he would. Harris was as full of relief as if he had survived a fall into a river with a dangerous current.

He sent Sandrine a note saying he would come on Saturday night. He caught four trout in the river, cut some roses from the garden, wrapped the roses and trout separately in damp newspaper. He'd stop for cigarettes, pick up some beer. Sandrine drank beer. She was a grown woman. Maybe they'd go to the movies. The anticipation of Sandrine, soothing, tranquil and real, of lying alongside Sandrine, made him almost light-headed.

As he sat on the bed to lace his boots, he suddenly remembered the pinup in the auto shop in Four Queens where they took the pickup for repairs. He didn't plan to remember it, it was there all of a sudden; a color photograph of a naked woman with the kind of pale skin that looks transparent, lying on a cloth with her legs drawn up, on a windowless wall over the tools and grime. Her arm was curved over her head and her body arched to show her perfectly shaped breasts, full underneath and pointed at the tips. She was smiling an inviting, bright red smile. Her blond hair streamed behind her on the cloth like corn-tassel silk.

But the pinup was a voluptuous woman, and Grey's daughter was a lanky girl.

She had said she could tell by the look in his eyes. He'd seen the look in her eyes too, and it had taken his breath away. It was the female fire that had its source deep in the belly. You had to breathe on it, bring it to the surface with your hands, even with her you would. Women had their private thoughts, their remote ways; they weren't easily warmed. But the fire was there. And when it was going full roar, it was better than anything a man could know.

The pillowcase she had sat on was trimmed with lace, hand-sewn long ago. The cloth and lace were worn and soft. Linen filled the cupboards at Salthill, folded and stacked, with lavender in the folds. Before that they had been in an old country, in a cupboard in another house made of stone. They had journeyed across an ocean and over a continent to this house. He slept under a quilt with his head on old linen, in the winter under a spread-out sleeping bag, a comforting weight when the snow fell. He wouldn't wake to the slow whispering of the sweetgum trees or the rich voices of his people. He would wake in this foreign land and wonder how he had been borne away, why his life had taken him to such strange places.

Chapter Twenty-seven

ON SATURDAY EVENING TRINITY CAME for Elsa in a Chevy pickup with a grille like a mouthful of chrome teeth. When she appeared on the veranda, grave and gawky, he ducked his head with the absent grace of wheat nodding and palmed his Stetson. The back of his hand was silky with black hair. As she climbed in, Elsa caught a whiff of Old Spice. She pulled in her legs so he could close the door.

A children's moon hung midway in a sky spangled with weak stars. When they got to the flat, Trinity rolled the radio knob through a blizzard of static to the only station you could get in the Skillihawk. Elsa stared out the window without speaking, drifting along on throbbing western plaints, steel guitars and dobros. There was an advertisement for Dee's General Store and Gas, another for farm insurance, a weather forecast (more rain), a singing cowboy group. The nasal male voices told their tales of love and loss with a dry forthrightness that was curiously passionate.

The main street was crowded with Canadian and American tourists who, having planned holidays in a country usually sunny and dry in summer, had braved uneven weather to sample the town's delights: fathers in Bermuda shorts with cameras slung around their necks, mothers and girls in matching sleeveless dresses, little boys with heads like thistle burrs. Glum-faced Indians sat on the benches provided by the city fathers while their children played under the struts. Cowboys loped along the boardwalk and cruised the streets in pickups with cigarettes dangling from their lips, hats cocked back on their skulls.

Elsa and Trinity shared a pint of strawberry ice cream with little wooden paddles. She wore slacks and a sweater and cowboy boots her father had given her one Christmas. It was an outfit girls didn't usually wear on dates, but it went somehow with her unpainted face and thick, parti-colored hair. She stalked with the grace of a housecat, swooping to peer into shop windows.

He made small talk because that's what you did on the first date, even though he sensed she didn't need talk. Anything she did say would be frighteningly to the point. It gave him a weird sensation of not being in control.

"Do you remember your mother?"

"Not at all. There was a picture in my grandmother's house in Galway."

"I'll bet you look like her." He studied her face carefully like a photographer.

It had been on a side table. A tinted photo of a woman with an oval face, dark hair like Fi's and Gordie's, scarlet lipstick, a string of pearls. She had stared at it for a long time. "Not really. She died when I was two. Gordie says she hunted with the Galway pack and the Quorn at Meadford. She was English, like my father." She smiled at him for the first time. He blinked, dazzled by lightning. "Actually, the St. Oeggers started in Cornwall. Grey says they were probably a lot of rum-runners."

The opening feature was *Born Yesterday*. Elsa alternately giggled and groaned at loony, bright Judy Holliday. Trinity felt for her hand in the dark and squeezed it gently. She let him.

At intermission Elsa waited in line to wash her hands with corrosive pink soap powder and water that stuttered out of the tap, and dry them with a limp cloth cranked out of the machine over the sink. The restroom was crowded with primping women and children squeaking and rustling like pet mice. Teenagers drawled over their hair. When she crossed to the mirror to look solemnly into her own eyes, a litter of bobby pins crunched under her feet. The girl next to her dropped squares of toilet tissue into the waste pail with a prim peachy mouth stamped on each one.

She felt a sudden rush of panic. It was like dropping in an elevator. She had to get outside when that happened, away from people. She made her way hurriedly and with purpose to the theater entrance, crossed the boardwalk into the meadow and kicked off her boots. With a sigh of release, she stretched her toes in the grass and sucked air cold from the lake into her lungs.

Night had fallen. The tourists had gone back to their campgrounds and motels, little whitewashed courts with totems on patches of anguished front lawn. The cowboys were in the saloon. The street was nearly deserted. A stake-bed truck went past rattling its latches; a few pedestrians wandered along the boardwalk like tired stray cattle.

A couple passed under the marquee light. With a stumble of the heart Elsa saw that the man was Harris. No one in the Skillihawk carried himself the way Harris did. An orange-pink scrap of the woman's dress fluttered between his legs. The light lifted amber highlights from her crown of dark hair, which fell behind them like a swath of brocade.

The pain took her breath away. She headed distractedly into the theater in her stockinged feet and had to go back for her boots. She ran down the aisle, searching for Trinity's dark square head, and fell into her seat.

"Everything okay?" he whispered.

"Everything's bloody fine," she hissed back.

He grinned and patted her on the shoulder.

Elsa sat bolt upright through the next feature. Trinity pried her hand from the armrest and eased it onto his knee. This seemed to calm her a little. Hope sprang in him. He smoothed the captive hand with his fingers. She tossed him a rueful smile.

They walked to the coffee shop. She stalked along with her nose up, fists rammed deep in her pockets. When he tried to take her arm, she jerked it lightly out of his grasp. Her eyes flashed and she tossed her head, making the long hair thrash. Whatever was bothering her, it made her look a lot better than she had at the table at Salthill.

They parked out of range of the bull's-eye lamp left on over the porch.

"You're really an interesting girl," he teased. "Sometimes I think you're kind of sophisticated, the things you do and say. Other times you act just like a kid."

"I *am* a kid," she said. "At times, anyway."

"How about now?" Encircled, she received his kiss. She kept her hands in her lap.

"That was good," he murmured. He dipped into her lips again. "Very good. You're not bad for a kid. Ever petted before?"

"No," she said. "There's this boy, but he won't touch me. He has high moral standards and doesn't want to do anything wrong."

"You're pulling my leg," he said. "What the heck kind of guy wouldn't want to do something wrong? Up to a point, that is."

"Up to and way past the point, usually." She smiled a little. He closed his eyes and let her fingers roam his face, tickling a little, until they found his mouth. He puckered up and kissed her palm equally lightly, tasting girl salt.

"Your lips are chapped," she whispered.

She hitched closer, while he sat hardly daring to breathe. She put her hand on his chest for ballast. When he turned his head and felt for her lips, they were there.

She ran Dai to earth in the bunkhouse.

"Daithi," she asked casually, "does Harris have a girlfriend? I saw him with someone the other night in Four Queens."

"Perhaps an' may be," he said. "Was it an Injun gurl?"

She thought of the fall of dark hair. "Aye."

"That's the one, then. Sandrine."

Her name was Sandrine Gregg. She was a niece of Winston Gregg, the tribal chief. She taught at the government-run native school in Four Queens. Her sister worked at the Indian museum in Clinton.

"What ye call it—collecting the pieces and all, and makin' sure they're kept up proper."

"Curator," she muttered, fiddling with the empty decanter.

Dai took frequent swallows from a glass of whiskey. After each swallow his speech was more slurred. He rolled his eyes to the ceiling, oblivious to her mounting fury, and squeezed a sweet-sour note from the concertina.

"He ought ta marry her, I'm thinkin'. But mayhap she won't have him." Squeeze. "Though she shure has him Saturdee nights, when he drives into town . . . hee! hee!"

The decanter crashed to the floor. The concertina let out a hiccup and swooned into silence. He stared, swaying. Elsa fell to her knees and began gathering the shattered pieces, putting smaller bits inside the chunk of neck with the stopper still attached.

"I'm sorry I dropped it, Dai. Was it worth a lot?"

"Nah. I got it in a grog shop in Kimmage, but it don't mean much ta me. Now sweet Sandy Delight, as I call her, mayn't want to be settin' up house with a black—though 'tis not a good thing annyway, bein' a horseman's wife. Sure, and where would the poor gurl live but in his room i' th' turret—sharin' the house with Sno-Bird—two women in th' kitchen an' then the little pickanannies comin'. . . ."

"I don't want to hear annymore about th' bloody gurl!" she shouted, cheekbones scarlet.

But he was already bending over the concertina.

> "Just pay attention for a while, my good friends one an' all,
> I'll sing to you a verse or two about a famous ball.
> The ball was given by some friends who lived down in Ashe Street
> In a certain part of the liberties where the ragman used ta meet."

Chapter Twenty-eight

SNO-BIRD STOOD UNDER THE JONAGOLD TREE for her portrait. Elsa, who tried to get inside people when she was drawing them, decided that if the eyes were the mirrors of the soul, in the Klaxta the mouth served this function. Sno-Bird's mouth had a brave, hurt look.

She posed in her best beaded doeskin dress, a scarf with fringes, a jacket of rabbit's fur and tooled cowboy boots. Her braids, newly done and not woolly, were finished in timber hitches. The completed portrait was of a tall, full-busted woman, upright as a ship in sail, dressed in the practical, gloriously haphazard style of the range. Pride, irony, sensuality and unscrupulous mettle lay over her features like a series of subtle glazes.

"Elsa, this is amazing," said her father. "You've got her to the life."

"It's perfect," said Sno-Bird in wonder, over his shoulder.

They looked at her with the frank respect accorded those who are able to draw.

"You can have it if you like," she said to Sno-Bird. Her portfolio, a broken-down cardboard one that tied with ribbons, already bulged with drawings and watercolors.

"Not if you take it home," said Grey quickly. "One of your grandchildren will desecrate it. We'll frame and hang it on the veranda."

Sno-Bird shrugged. "Do what you like with it."

"I am doing what I like, my girl," he retorted.

Elsa experienced a flash of déjà vu; not of having heard her father speak to Sno-Bird in that edgy familiar tone, but of having seen or heard something that reminded her of it. The memory, whatever it was, lay scattered like seed pearls over a polished floor.

She made a sketch of the stallion for Grey, who was one of those people who do not enjoy having their likeness taken. She made one of the Duchess of Mag as the mare waited out her gestation under the larches.

"It's the first of July," said Grey irritably. "If she hasn't delivered by next week, Doc Gregory will have to look at her. Those foals need to come out before the shows start and we're too short-handed to care for them properly."

When another week brought no labor, the veterinarian came. The family crowded into the box with him.

"If one of 'em's heading in the wrong direction it'll be a rough labor and maybe one lost," he said to the ceiling, stretching to feel the foals in the Duchess's womb. "If it gets half turned around—aye, you could lose the three."

"I shouldn't think there'd be room to turn in that space," said Grey. "Do you mean one of them may have failed to turn earlier?"

"It happens," said the vet. "Arrgh. There's one now. Hold on."

His face wore the quizzical expression common to men who labor with their hands and minds at the same time. He felt around inside the mare, buried to the elbow in her pursy integument, then carefully withdrew his arm, peeled off the sopping glove and dropped it in the straw. Straightening to full height in his overalls, he towered over them—a man thick as a tree, with red-mottled arms, black hair and a flaming beard.

"They're all right, man. They're in position right enough, just a wee bit cramped. Taking their time w'it, I'd say."

"Would it help to exercise her?" asked Grey, stroking his upper lip with an index finger.

"Canna hurt. Just put someone light on her, bareback. No point adding to the burden."

"I don't think we've got a girth that'd go around her anyway. Elsa can take her, she rides a feather."

So Elsa rode bareback to the river every day, her legs curved like the strings of a longbow around the mare's great belly.

The river ran through a grove of larches, green with the summer rains and fat with cones. Beyond the grove it broadened and grew sluggish, and the meadow became a watery lowland. Silver reed, cress and marsh marigold grew in marginal ponds; lilies big as pie pans floated farther out among the shining green pads. A stand of cedars with pink alligator skins edged the marsh, thriving in the perpetual damp, nurturing winged and toothy ferns.

Elsa rode down the long shadowed avenue around the bog. In a clearing she stopped and slid off the mare, who immediately dropped her head to the pink and yellow wildflowers. Elsa plopped Indian-style on the ground, found a tailor-made in her shirt pocket and lit it with a kitchen match. She puffed industriously, her face enlivened with a fury of passion, and thought about Harris. After a minute of this she slipped her hand inside her shirt and felt her breast. The nipple stood up jauntily under the stroking of her thumb. She exhaled as slowly as she could, sending a thread of smoke into the damp air.

She waited until they were all together, and made her request formal and public.

"I'd like to do your portrait, Harris. Will you let me?"

He looked startled and suspicious.

"Go ahead, do it," said Sno-Bird.

"Yes, do," said Grey with a smile. "Give her a chance to work on her chiaroscuro."

Harris glanced at him. Elsa held her breath, feeling him calculating. Since that night in his room he had avoided her. At the close of day she sat on the bed in her nightgown, looking out at the firs and the moon. He was asleep on the floor below, under a quilt as he had been that night, one arm hanging slack, tender in slumber. How rich and dark he had looked, with velvety pools.

"All right," he said finally.

She knew he didn't want to, but that the rest would wonder if he kept refusing. She knew that underneath that, he yearned to sit before her and be studied.

She drew him in the garden, sitting in the kitchen chair against the white-washed porch, before the little cockade of the kitchen door. He wore what he had worn all day, jeans and a khaki work shirt with the sleeves rolled up. Where the collar stood away from his neck, the chain that was always there lay like a strand of tinsel on the dusky skin. He sat with arms crossed, sardonic and slightly self-conscious. It was evening, after chores. He sat in sunshine with a pillar of shade shooting up the wall behind his ear. Here was chiaroscuro, light and shadow, in one subject.

"Say something," she muttered after she had blocked in head, shoulders, the rudimentary planes of his face.

He cocked his head. The pleasant evening's warmth seemed to draw him out. Or he was like some people, sitting still to be sketched made him talk more easily.

"I was outside looking at the carvings around the doors. White men seem to have a thing for prey animals. It's like some cult worship. All those bears, wolves and lions. Don't you have any cows or goats in your architecture?"

She took her lower lip in her teeth and stared with shining eyes at his graven image. Everything about him was entrancing. He fit in completely, was even more than them in that he noticed these things while they simply lived them. He was a traveling observer. Time and custom had made him ordinary and she no longer saw a Peruvian burial mask when she looked at him, but the brown-skinned man she had lived with since she was twelve. Even his pleasant tenor had come to the surface with years of gentle rubbing. It was a brotherly voice, free of drama, calling her to her doom.

"Why, no. No cows or other herd animals," she said gleefully. "You're right. And definitely no goats."

"Why not?"

"Umm. Goats are symbols of evil."

"If you lived on goats, they'd be a symbol of plenitude."

She mulled this over. "It's because we *started* living on goats that they're thought evil," she offered. "Think what a good drought could do to your goat herd, what power your food supply had over you."

"By *power* don't you mean the winds of fortune that blew your food supply away?"

"Well . . . maybe. But it's the goats dying that causes all the trouble. If you had a primitive superstitious mind, wouldn't you blame it on the goats? You sound like Grey sometimes when you talk. I mean, the words you use. You slip in and out of your other language the way I do mine."

"You mean my 'dumb nigger' talk? I can drop it anytime, just like you can drop that cockeyed brogue of yours. I was raised by a dentist and his wife."

She shivered. "I hate that word." He was holding her off with it, like raising a cross before a vampire or tossing salt on a slug to melt it. "I only meant that sometimes you sound more educated than other times."

"You're ungregarious loners," he continued calmly. "You prowl your territory in solitude, name your children after carnivorous beasts and think more of your dogs than your families."

She reflected, then giggled. "Wolfgang. Ursula. Darragh."

"What's Darragh?"

"Oak. Not an animal but it's something wild."

But she settled again to her task. His exclusion was like a storm wind, carrying the blows he dealt himself and tried to stun her with, like saying that word she knew was wrong out loud.

"Where were the dentist and his wife?" she muttered.

"On an island."

When she worked, it was with a mysterious intensity, an adult authority at odds with the sandy protruding tip of her tongue, the hair straggling from its clamp.

"Come see," she murmured finally.

He took the Bugler can of pencils and crayons off the stool and sat beside her.

"It's good," he said with obvious appreciation.

He smelled clean. She had noticed that clean man smell when her father or Gordon hugged her, which was rare. The only thing you could compare it to was the odor of lemons still on the branch, a tart effervescence shaken out by sunlight. How you wanted to dance under those loosened trees as ancient as earth, with eyes sparkling back in the man-woman gaiety!

"Your face is crooked," she said, studying the drawing, then him. His eyes leaped to absorb her, eyes and brow and cheeks, making her feel luminous. They dropped to her mouth.

A crack like a rifle shot sounded so loud they both jumped.

"Light's going," Sno-Bird said. The screen door slammed shut.

The board lay on the ground. Elsa retrieved it, her heart thumping. "Just a bit more, while I get the scar?"

He went back to his chair, smiling a little. "By all means, girl, get the scar."

She rummaged in the Bugler can for a bit of charcoal. Sno-Bird came outside, bringing with her the ghost of fried bacon, and stood watching with her hands on her hips.

"You know what I'm talking about," he said. "You're one of those waifs that prowls the forest with a wild dog, instead of belonging to a decent tribe of women squatting around a campfire cooking food, with papooses roped to their foreheads."

Elsa laughed. "Are you saying white people are prey beasts?"

"Something like that."

"What are you two going on about," said Sno-Bird. "There are no wild dogs here, just that bunch lapping at your father's heels all day."

"You're moving," she said to Harris. "Turn your head back."

He became a fixed point. Elsa stroked some black under the scar on his cheekbone to pop it up, blended it into the shadow of the hollow underneath with a paper stub. She heard the screen door bang as Sno-Bird went back into the house.

Another touch of black deepened the socket at the base of the throat. If she pressed her lips there, would they meet the pulse's throb? She outlined the lid where the lashes grew, with its delicate natural penciling. With their stretched look the lids were beautiful in themselves, not just as hoods for eyes. Yet he was a plain-looking ordinary man, careful and not showy, who seemed to guard himself.

The porch lay in slanted shade. She willed him to want her; she willed him to fail in his purpose. She was the mongoose stalking the snake, the swift one whose tongue leaves its fricative kiss on the air. If she bent to touch the close-cropped head, the corner of his mouth, what would happen? Would he strike back, or let her slip under his clothing and kiss the shaded hollow? An aching began between her legs. *O throat and eyelids, O veins beneath brown skin, O shadows under the arms, O strong waist.*

His voice came beside her, startling. "I'm going in."

"No." She squeezed her eyes shut. "No." Her ardor was electric, racing like a spark along a conduit.

The sketch pad levitated; there was a tearing sound. The pad descended and swam in front of her with a fresh sheet in front. She watched his wrists turn as he rolled up the drawing.

"You are going to give this to me, aren't you?" he asked.

"If you want it," she said in a low voice, nearly weeping with pain.

"I think I'd better want it," he said, and was gone.

She waited for the screen door to close, then picked up the Bugler can.

Chapter Twenty-nine

BRON GEORGEWOOD HAD STUDIED LAW before marrying George and settling down to run the ranch with him or as some said, *for* him. Even with a daisy-print coverall over her cushiony figure, she looked more like a lady lawyer than a farm wife. She shook hands European-fashion with Elsa, and her clasp was brisk and cool.

"Welcome," she said. "It's good to have a chance to visit."

From the dining room window the view was of cattle, orchards, red barns in rows. The forest spread steeply up the slope behind them, an igneous mass of greens and coppers and the flame of young aspens. As Trinity took her coat, Elsa gazed into the glass at her silhouette with its corona of braided hair, gauzy from the drive to Wanda Creek.

They sat down to chicken with dumplings and new vegetables in their skins. Mr. Georgewood appeared, apologizing for his tardiness, and added the gentle leavening of his humor to the meal.

"I hear Trin plans to take you out behind those two madcaps he trained last year."

"Pop." Trinity frowned, then grinned at Elsa. "They were a 4-H project, the last thing I did before I left for school. You'll see."

"Isn't it going to be hard not having friends your own age at college, Elsa?" asked Mrs. Georgewood.

"Not really," said Elsa. "I didn't have any special friends at Beech's and I'd already passed everything. It seemed silly not to go."

Mrs. Georgewood considered. "You'll have fun. There's a social life for all sorts of people at university. Boarding schools are such a *closed* world."

"Tell 'em what you're taking," prompted Trinity.

"Art courses," said Elsa. "I'm taking my degree in fine art. Drawing and design and painting and art history. And English and math."

"Can't get away from English and math," said Georgewood cheerily.

Mrs. Georgewood watched the two young people walk toward the barns. It was a pity about the girl, when Grey was such a good friend. If it had been Flavia for instance, she would have been delighted. Flavia was a delightful girl. Elsa's lack of looks and that blunt, faintly repelling air must have consigned her to the fringes at Beech's. Her own aversion was instinctive but shameful, really. The poor child had lost her mother at such a young age, it was no wonder she was odd.

"I hope he's not serious about her," she said to Georgewood, who had reached the age of wanting to nap after lunch.

"She doesn't seem romantically inclined," he said from deep in his armchair.

"You mean you think she isn't pretty enough to feel romantic," retorted Mrs. Georgewood. "That's a mistake. All girls do. And he's a wonderful-looking boy. You know what that can lead to."

"Bron, she's from a good family. Don't fuss."

"Family has nothing to do with it." Mrs. Georgewood stared out the window, rising on her toes. "She looks like a precocious boy. She'll probably end up running the place with her father. That art business won't get her far. What a pity Gordon isn't interested in Salthill. Grey says he's going to England on a fellowship. I think it's hurt him a little that Gordon didn't choose something here."

"I don't think there's anything between them," said Georgewood, closing his eyes. The words "fascinating little dame" crossed his mind just then, like a pony trotting over a bridge. Odd thing to think. The girl was only a young girl after all, and perfectly well bred. Her eyes were a striking hazel, but sometimes they were nearly blue. Just as he was watching them at lunch, trying to decide how much anthracite it took to make blue turn back to topaz, she glanced up from a dumpling and smiled at him as though she had read his mind, or seen something further back in his thoughts that amused her. This had not troubled him. He had been married twenty-six years to a woman of formidable inquisitiveness and was used to having his thoughts read. It just made him wonder what lay behind that enigmatic smile.

"He brings other girls home," he said. "Stop worrying it, Bron."

The "madcaps" were a team of perfect bay Morgans. Their manes were shaven Mohawks and their tails were cropped and feathered. Their fat bellies and flanks shone like rubbed rosewood.

"They look like chess pieces!" Elsa exclaimed. "The Red Knight's horses."

Trinity harnessed them to a black-lacquered gig and they fled down a back road with the dust rising behind like smoke from a wood fire. The bays trotted tirelessly, docile and beautifully mannered, their legs flashing and their necks shimmering in their collars.

"Where did you learn to drive?" she called, eyes shining.

"When I was a kid, driving the team at haying time. I used to have to stand up on the seat."

He pulled the gig off the road into a circle of trees. With her hands in her lap she let him kiss her the way she had the first night he took her out.

The Sunday Elsa went to lunch at the Georgewoods' was one of the rare fine days of the summer. It rained that evening and cleared before dawn. By midmorning the next day, the sky was mousy again and the air thick and still. Grey, Harris and Elsa worked the show candidates beneath advancing gilt-edged thunderheads. Just before noon they heard a crack of thunder and looked up to see lightning shiver like a bundle of nerves over the palisades above the lake road. Riders and scholars made posthaste for the cover of the stable, lessons canceled.

By the time dinner was over the worst of the storm had passed. Elsa tramped out to the ring in a mackintosh and boots to exercise two horses. For another half hour she showed a two-year-old how to step quietly in and out of the horse trailer. In the west, the lights of the Klaxta reserve hung in the mist like ships in a fog.

The sky cleared on Wednesday evening, and in the blue heavens stars appeared. After tea Harris saddled the Red. Elsa changed into jeans and a turtleneck and followed him down to the yard to watch them go over the course.

They swept endlessly around, clearing the big ditch-and-rail oxers, the water jump and gates with indifferent ease. Harris rode with a whip in his boot, in a wool sweater Dai had brought back from Bella Coola, his neck lashed a deep plum by the wind.

They cleared the brick wall, which was really wood painted to look like brick, and thundered past Elsa, headed toward the in-and-out. This was a pair of post-and-rails placed parallel to each other a number of feet apart. There were two rails on each set of notched posts, placed one above the other for solidity. The object was to clear the first set, land in the middle between the two sets, take off again and clear the second. It was a jump that required coordination and skill to negotiate when the rails were as high as they were now. During one of the frequent rows between the Red and Harris, Elsa had seen the horse leap over the entire hurdle almost from a standstill.

Leaning idly on the gate with her feet on the lower rail, Elsa was startled to see the Red abruptly leap straight in the air. The great body snaked like a rodeo bucking horse's over the first set of rails and landed widdershins in the middle. They reversed, jolted forward, then crashed backward into the out rails. Harris swayed in the saddle, hands busy. The Red squatted, plunged and kicked, a red swirling streak between the parallels. Elsa heard the racket of hooves striking wood, the cracking and splintering underfoot of the laths supporting the posts. The great haunches swelled ominously over the barricade, which trembled and then collapsed under the driving, backward-rolling weight.

Harris applied the whip with vigor. The Red shot out from the welter of spilling rails into a string of leaps, each a marvel of flight. They slammed against the fence. The boards shuddered and muck splattered high up the posts. The horse's chest bore the brunt of the blow like a door struck with a battering ram; he literally reeled from the impact. As Harris struggled to regain control, the Red went up on his hind legs. Harris flipped the whip like a baton and hit him on the poll with the butt end. The horse rose without flinching to his full height, then staggered and fell backward on top of his rider.

"Dad! Dad!" Elsa screamed.

She squeezed between the rails and flew across the ring. The Red thrashed around on his back and waved his legs, not like an ordinary horse trying to right itself but savagely, whipping his long body from side to side. As Elsa ran up, he rolled over, gathered his legs under him and lunged to his feet. Harris lay sunken and gray under streaks of mud.

"Harris!" She fell on her knees.

Grey sprinted loose-limbed from the stable.

"Goddamned brute," he panted. "Don't shift him, child."

While Dai cornered the Red he lifted Harris's eyelid and peered at the blank pupil. "Get a blanket from the tack room," he said, not looking up. "Let's keep him warm."

Elsa ran.

"Put a hobble on the horse and get him in the stud barn," said Grey.

"He'll kill himself in a hobble," Dai protested.

"I hope he breaks his bloody neck."

Elsa came dashing back with the blanket and covered the prone figure with hands that jerked nervously.

"Can't we carry him in?" she moaned.

"Not till he wakes," said Grey. "He could have a head or internal injury."

Dai trotted up and joined them. They waited, while light dimmed and ebbed from the deepening earth. Harris groaned and shifted his head. The skin around the scar had ruptured near his mouth from some blow or lash, and a thread of blood ran over his jaw.

"Don't hit me," he startled them by saying in a clear, agitated voice. "Oh god, don't hit me." His voice was piteous with terror. "Please don't. Oh god."

They looked away from him and each other, deeply ashamed and moved.

Grey reached for his hand and clasped it, looking grave. After a moment he turned it over and felt for the pulse.

"Goddamn fucking white sumbitches . . . fucking sick white . . . shit . . . jive motherfuckers . . . I'll kill you. I'll fucking kill you." Harris sobbed out loud. Tears seeped from under his lids and washed down his cheeks. They crouched transfixed, their heads bowed in humility, listening as though the voice they heard came from deep within their own centers.

Harris launched into a stream of profanity, uttered with the clarity and incisiveness of a news broadcast.

"Yikes," muttered Daithi, gazing up at the sky.

"Elsa, fetch him some water," her father commanded.

"I will not." She shot him a mutinous look and averted her head.

The profanity deepened to filth, became more inventive as it flowed until it reached a scatologic complexity that seemed to encompass cities and nations and all humanity, to fill the wide, deep, listening sky with violent color. His mouth worked. His head rolled.

"Wake up, Harris," said Grey loudly. "You're at Salthill. You're with us."

The swearing broke off. "Don't hit me," Harris said in a lugubrious voice, like a record player at the wrong speed.

"Wake up, man, for god's sake!" Grey shouted.

Harris's eyes opened, the irises dusty, wrung dry of pigment by tears.

They walked him upstairs. Sno-Bird, who had been about to leave for the reserve, stayed to disinfect his cuts and tape his cheek. He was made to drink a mug of hot coffee with sugar and milk.

Grey examined his pupils with the flashlight. "What day is it?"

"Wednesday July eighth, 1951," said Harris.

"Who am I?"

Harris identified him, smiling slightly. "Look. I'm okay."

"Let's have your full name then," said Grey.

Harris moved his head back and forth.

"You're fine," said Grey dryly. "I doubt you've so much as sprained anything."

Sno-Bird borrowed Flavia's old bathrobe and slept beside his bed in a rocking chair from the veranda. Elsa left the muddied blanket in the wash sink and went down to the barn to collect his saddle and bridle. She did not come of a race that cries willingly, but an unnamable grief kept filling her eyes with stinging moisture. Wiping down the saddle, she burst out weeping. It had been so dreadful: the fall; her father's look as he bent over Harris, a look of naked apprehension; that voice calling to them from the past, loaded with anguish, weeping for mercy without hope. They were all doomed, if behind the veil of consciousness such wickedness dwelt.

She found Grey working in his study.

"It was frightful," she said. "Can't you get rid of the Red before he kills him?"

He looked resigned. "He belongs to Harris."

"Then you should stop him riding it."

"I can't. The Red is his horse. I can't tell him what to do with the animal. You know as well as I do that things like this happen to people who ride."

"But he tried to squash Harris. I saw it."

"I know. But Harris seems to have escaped any serious injury. I'd like to see the brute go, but he doesn't bother anyone else. Harris seems to be his only animus. I can't claim he's dangerous to the rest of us and ask Harris to get rid of him on those grounds."

"What's an animus?"

"In the present sense, a deep-seated hostility."

"Why would he want to own a horse with an animus?" Elsa asked in wonder.

"We all have to master something," he said shortly. "Or court something."

She crept upstairs to her room, feeling lacerated. Her bed was pushed against the open window so she could smell the verbena and roses in the garden, and the rain-soaked grass in the fields. She lay in bed and looked out at the night, fair and opaline, with distempered clouds the color of scorched cotton shining through the trees.

Chapter Thirty

HE WAITED WITH CRAFT AND PATIENCE until in his sleep he heard the creak of the rocker as the Indian woman left to go to the bathroom. Then he turned over, sighed and called out to the empty room.

He stayed in a prostitute's apartment for five weeks while the gash on his face healed. There was one room and a bathroom where he hid when the johns came creaking and chuckling up the stairs. When she was gone he would stand at the window for hours, behind those curtains made of material you could see through, and wait. The housewives tripped past, the ponces strolled in their wide hats. Sometimes he listened with eyes closed to the swish of cars and toot of horns, jazz blaring from radios, the dozens coming up in thin singsongs from kids on the street. Sometimes he opened his eyes, even though he knew what was there. Then he thought that if he had a choice between being blind or deaf, he would pick blind.

He was bored with the view, bored with streets and tenements, even bored with the knife, which he'd cleaned with lock oil and a stray sock. It wasn't real boredom but a kind of frenzy at the sameness of everything, the way he couldn't do anything. His life had stopped. He was frozen in time like Lot's pillar of salt. He could hardly remember the club, dark and whiskey-smelling, the saxophone blurting to a stop. But this view? He would never forget it. From left to right, over and over he read it: a building jutting, then a space, a cloud of tree naked with autumn and the start of another building, all neat and framed in. Shuttered brownstones at dawn, the prowl car loitering, vacant damp stoops with ashcans piled in the alleys. He was bound to leave someday. But the view would be with him for the rest of his life.

He had gone in the club, the prospect of a cheap drunk rippling soothingly over his drug-torn nerves. The woman's face, the man's face white, the only faces not dark. The woman's thin painted mouth like an ugly cut. The piano player hunched, playing on over the shouts. Him whirling to leap through the door, blood flying out of his face. They would say he ran, they would say he flew. But he stooped to get the knife first. No one moved while he worked it out, grunting. It had been the only thing they could do for him. By the time he reached the end of the block the red was throbbing through his pocket.

When Sno-Bird returned, he was lying half off the bed, a leg and arm dangling over the floor. She had closed the window to keep the spirits out. These wraiths had roamed her ancestors' world at night, harmless unless some business important to the spiritual self had been left unfinished. All things must be brought to a close, whether the outcome is violence or peace. She stood by the bed in Flavia's bathrobe and watched Harris for a long time. The scar had shrunk to a polished line; familiarity made it ordinary. In daylight it was still possible to see the holes where the needle used to stitch it had woven in and out. Like all men he looked childlike in sleep, innocent of the mysteries that troubled women, which in the sleep of women made them pensive or hopeful or wise, but never returned them to virginity.

Harris came to breakfast feeling woozy. Everyone was at the table except Sno-Bird, who was standing by the stove. His first thought was of a tableau of the manger scene he had been taken to every Christmas in Barbados until the year he left. Joseph and Mary had to freeze in their poses while spotlights were trained for five minutes on the roof of the church where they were balanced. There was a frozen moment like it when he appeared in the doorway. Sno-Bird in yesterday's coverall, her loose braid framed by a blue willow plate, held the coffeepot in midair. Dai's hand with a piece of bread in it stopped halfway to his mouth.

They all looked at him as if he was going to do or say some strange thing. Then Grey put down his fork.

"How do you feel?"

"Not bad," he lied. "I've got a headache."

Everyone went back to what they'd been doing. Harris took his place at the table, thinking that most of what went on between him and the St. Oeggers happened at meals. It was the only time they were all together with nothing else to do.

Elsa's eyes dropped and she chewed slowly, as if whatever she was eating was hard going. He felt way too shitty to let the girl get to him today. He took advantage of the hiatus, a lucky break almost worth getting killed for, to tell himself that she was a pain in the ass, and ugly too. Georgewood could have her. He was a light sleeper and he knew about the Chevy pickup parked out of range of the bull's-eye lamp on Saturday nights. Being a stranger to the polite ideology of necking, to him the parked truck meant one thing only. Right now, with her roving eyes, fidgety expression and tangle of hair pulled back with a rubber band, she looked like an Alice who'd stayed too long at the Mad Hatter's tea party. Like she was ready to break down and bawl.

He poured coffee, feeling queasy. She wasn't a virgin anyway. Virgins didn't prance naked around a man's bedroom. He let his eyelids droop, seeing through their skins the supple body with its velvet points.

"You'd better take the day off," said Grey.

"I feel fine," he said halfheartedly.

"It's what I'd do in your place."

It was the way Grey always got to him, by putting it on the basis of what he or any other sensible man would do. It was then left up to him, a sensible man, to decide.

He took a couple of aspirins and went back to his room with the coffee. He tried to read. His head felt heavy, and he kept reliving the Red going over with him. He had slackened the reins to help the horse keep his precarious balance and gone for the whip to get him down. He'd belted the horse with the butt end so the tip wouldn't strike him in the eyes. Wasn't that some shit? Who thought of the gloss on a car or damage to the headlamps when it was flipping you into a ditch?

He put the book aside, feeling dizzy. Outside it was raining again, what they called a mizzle, a cross between a drizzle and a mist. At midday the room felt like a confining box, its walls shutting out the routine he craved.

He wandered restlessly from window to chair to bed. Green hospital rooms, Buffalo tenements, custody tanks projected themselves on the faded-rose walls. It had been a while since he'd thought of any of it. He had come to view his life before Salthill with a sense of fatality that was almost as useful as amnesia. He had been like an animal sheltering here, slowly healing its wounds. Why did he feel somehow that the period of healing was over, that things had moved on to some different, more complicated level?

He stared at the homemade shelves that now housed twenty or thirty of his own books. Taking down the Webster's Sixth, he let it fall open on the bed and picked a word at random.

Starets / star-(y)ets: a spiritual adviser who is not necessarily a priest, who is recognized for his piety, and who is turned to by monks or members of the laity for spiritual guidance.

He got a windbreaker off the porch and went down to the yard. Grey was drilling Lord Edgeware in the rain. When he saw Harris he rode over to the fence.

"You had a bad bang on the head," he said. "You shouldn't be out."

"I have to work. I can't handle being shut up in there," said Harris.

Grey looked him over. "Do you remember any of it?"

"All of it until I got knocked out."

Grey pushed the old ranger's hat back on his head. "You could clean tack," he said. "It's the most soothing activity I can think of. Nearly the most soothing, anyway."

Harris had to smile.

"Bad memories fade," said Grey, feeling for a cigarette. "It's one of the benefits of time passing. You won't always remember them as you do now."

"It was no big deal," said Harris.

"Don't con me. You know what I'm talking about."

"Con. That sounds funny coming from you."

"I've read my Mickey Spillane," said Grey with dignity.

He went to the stable to get some tack and the cleaning stuff.

Elsa opened the door to let the steam out of the bathroom while she dried her hair. Male voices wended down the hall from the study, her father's and Trinity's. The house smelled of the corned beef and cabbage they'd had for tea. She put on the Cuban heels she had worn on the train, and shrugged into a houndstooth jacket from which her thin wrists emerged like wands.

Trinity was waiting in the study. She stood in the hall shadows, in a rayon dress printed with orange poppies that didn't go with the jacket.

"Thanks for talking to me, sir," Trinity said, shaking hands with her father.

"Drive carefully," said Grey. He looked tired and restless. He turned to Elsa. "Please don't come in late. Doc Gregory will be here early to look at the Duchess. I don't want to lie awake half the night waiting for the lamp to go off."

"She's still in foal?" asked Trinity.

"She isn't turning a hair. He's going to try something to help her along."

They drove to Four Queens under swag-bellied clouds. *On the Town* was the feature this week. Elsa twisted in her seat, thinking of doom and un-manned tears, while Vera-Ellen pirouetted through the streets of New York with a sailor on each arm.

They parked in the yard at Salthill and listened to the silence of the mountain night. The valley was shrouded in mist, an uneasy, cloudlike vapor distinct from the night in movement, behind which the bald face of the moon lay unsensed.

"Weird-looking place," said Trinity, staring at the house looming through tatters of paler drift. "All that rock."

Elsa rolled down the window. It really wasn't that cold, just damp. "It's haunted with ghosts," she said, face upturned to the mist. "A whole army of wraiths." She sniffed. "Ah, it's good. Dead Norwegians, Nordic gods, dragons and princesses with uncanny powers. There's a knight too, an exotic long-headed knight. He carries a sword and mace, and rides at night with his armor clanking. There's an eye in the visor of his helmet so he can look out, but you can't look in."

"That's right, you're going to be an artist, aren't you?" he said sarcastically.

"Not that. You have to be a little mad to live here." She sighed. "You just don't see it."

"Nuts. Your father lives here and there's nothing crazy about him."

She sagged against the door and examined him. He had withdrawn his suit; his smile was hostile and exasperated. She opened the door and got out. "Good night, Trinity."

"It's been great." He glared from behind the wheel.

"I'm truly sorry."

He relented. "C'mon, Els. It was just kissing."

They exchanged looks. His eyes dropped.

"It was that and more," said Elsa.

"Look, I didn't mean to scare you. You're just a kid after all, aren't you?"

"That must be it," she answered calmly.

"I respect you," he muttered. It was the girl's job to see things didn't go too far. They both knew the code. No hands below the waist, no hands under clothes. No lying down, no unbuttoning, no groaning. Kissing with mouths closed. A stomachache after.

It took some time to get rid of him, but finally he swung the truck around and peeled off, taillights swinging over the coffee-ground earth. Before he reached the turn and the cowboy music had trailed off like exhaust through the trees, she had forgotten him and was waiting.

Chapter Thirty-one

SHE SAW NOTHING BUT DARKNESS at first, heard nothing but the silence of the fogbound, starless night. The air smelled rich with rain. Dew pricked her face and legs and crept down her throat like a potion. Her breasts felt heavy from being touched and the place between her legs warm and full from having her mouth kissed.

She climbed the steps under the disapproving glare of the bull's-eye lamp, carrying these weights like stones found on a beach, and walked though the garden. The grass soaked her shoes and she felt the wet as part of her body, warm and creeping up her legs. Harris's window was dark in its framework of clematis and flowering dogwood. Her own room on the second floor was hidden by an encroaching cedar full of the musk of summer.

Elsa looked into his room through the glass of the long window. The curtains were the gauzy ones that replaced the winter velvet every summer. The dimmest of shapes swam forward, loosened from the night like a celestial body, then his pallet sank behind a scrim like the one the moon could not penetrate.

On the porch, she reached and turned off the lamp. Moving carefully in the tricky heels, she went back down the steps and felt her way across the yard.

The stable door had been rolled to within a foot of the lock. Light coursed down the passageway from the foaling box at the end. Beyond the gap the aisle opened like a yawning mouth with a uvula of light hanging at the back. Elsa slid sideways through the opening.

The lantern was hooked to an overhead beam and the box lay white as a beach under its ray. Harris was offering a pail of mash to the Duchess. The mare was on her feet, her coat still musty with chaff. In the bedding lay two new foals.

The mare swung her head toward the foals with a maternal rumble, then dipped her mouth in the pail. Harris glanced up and saw Elsa framed in the top half of the door. His eyes narrowed. He turned away and with the butt of the pail propped on his knee, looked down at the mare's broad head with the forelock brushed to one side.

"Oh, wonderful!" She unlatched the door and crouched in front of the foals. They lay with their legs folded and their knobby heads erect. They looked sleepy and confounded. Both babies were diminutive but perfectly formed, with damp licked coats and bottle-brush tails.

"Have they eaten?" she asked. A mare often refused to nurse twins, allowing one foal to feed from her bag and ignoring the other. The rejected foal had to be bottle-fed or it would starve.

"They have eaten," he said, in a courteous, distant tone.

She gave an exclamation of happiness, enchanted by the goodness of life, its great propriety.

Harris set the pail aside, picked up a towel and scrubbed his bare arms and shoulders. He wore a grubby singlet with rust-colored streaks across the front. There was an oxblood print on the leg of his jeans where he had absently wiped a hand; his hair was ruffled into little knots and tufts. He looped the towel over his neck and offered the mare water, bringing the pail around carefully before lifting it to her muzzle. His arm rose like a matador's, revealing under the glare of light a bleached armpit with a twist of hair in its marrow. The mare gazed at the water, opened her nostrils and released a long chuff of air. They were dismissed.

"How long did they take?" she asked, watching him drop equipment in the foaling kit.

"About an hour." He unhooked the lantern and left. As he passed, with the swinging glass tossing shadows around the box, she felt the tension radiating like a musk from his body. She stood immobilized at the power that could cause such confusion, pierce his shell so sharply. From deep within the thought came: *This is the power women have always had and I've inherited it.* A surge of emotion made her dizzy. She felt aged and wise and at the same time frightened, as though something immense faced her. Her body was idling like an engine, gently throbbing, hot at points.

"Out," came his voice, clear and hoarse, with the light curving up the wall outside.

She came promptly out of the box. He was back to being his old self. He gave her a sharp look as he fastened the door.

At the spigot he put out the lamp. It flared briefly to bluewhite: she stared into eyes stripped of their leaf color. He set it on the ledge while she stood breathlessly near, splashed his face and mopped it dry. A wan pool meandered into the gap of rolled-back door, the moon shedding a veil.

"You better get on up." He slapped the towel over the pipe. "He'll miss you."

"He's asleep. Let me stay."

"For what, girl? I'm going to bed."

"Harris." She stepped in front of him. "Please."

He snorted. "No way. I've already seen you in nothing. Remember?" He picked up the kit and started up the tack room steps.

She followed on wobbly legs. "*Harris*."

He set the box down and turned, one foot on the top step. She put everything she had—her longing, that gale force, love—into the question. It rang parched and hollow under the loft beams. "Aren't you even going to kiss me good night?"

He was perfectly still. He hissed suddenly, "You sleep with that boy?"

"No." She sighed. "But I let him feel my breasts."

He pulled in his breath, stepped down, lifted her chin and kissed her. His mouth was warm, rich. There was no protocol to the kiss.

He hauled her up the steps. They glared at each other, swaying. He half walked, half dragged her across the room. They stumbled past saddle racks, past humped, covered shapes, bumped into the wall with the bridle hooks, setting the bits alive with a silvery tintinnabulation.

"Damn you," he said hoarsely.

He pulled her into the little sleeping room behind the tack room and kicked the door shut. The room smelled of grease from the old cooker and horse from a stack of blankets left on the floor. She stumbled and nearly fell over the blankets. He pushed her down on the cotlike bed, released her with an exclamation, muttered and thick, went to close the shutter over the window. Her eyes, the only part of her that seemed able to move, followed his rear end in the jeans. The rest of her felt clumsy and hot, bolted to the bed.

He leaned down. A painful sweetness shot through her. His lips were soothing and cushiony, his tongue burned and flickered in her mouth. She lay buried in the kiss, legs loose. He lifted the dress and felt her under it.

A new sensation roused her from her torpor. She was wet between the legs, wet all over as if she had fallen into a warm lake. Her underpants were soaked in the crotch and sticking to her bottom. The wetness felt like a terrible secret pouring out of her, released by this lethargy onto the plain of the bed. In shame and confusion she squirmed away from the reaching, forcing hand and tried to press her knees together. He made a noise as if he were disgusted too, clasped her firmly inside the underpants and stroked the exquisitely sensitive inner flesh that palpitated for his touch.

"Breathe deep," he said in a voice like sliding gravel.

She breathed deeply and went into a trance, unable to stir except in response to what he was doing. Her mind moved across the landscape of sensation like a skittering insect, nodding with fascination, then suddenly rolled up its eyes and vanished. Her legs fell apart and she was boneless, a liquid body with a molten core that throbbed, open and soft, in powerful involuntary spasms.

He pulled off the underpants. Denim puddled on the floor. He climbed on the mattress and entered her, pushing in through the throbbing, inflamed tissue. With each stroke in she was galvanized by pain and sparks flew inside her closed lids, with each withdrawing stroke she shuddered with new spasms. His hand was twisted in her hair and she couldn't move her head. He moaned and she felt him shoot inside her, trembling and moving fast.

He stayed on top of her for what seemed a long time. When he lifted his body, their flesh made a noise like silk tearing. He crowded her legs to one side and sat on the edge of the bed with his shoulders sagging.

They moved slowly about, gathering their things. He cracked the shutter and squatted barefoot to roll her stockings back in the garters. She stood with a hand trailing on his shoulder, admiring the nape of his neck as he labored beneath her. With a gap-toothed comb out of the desk he tidied her hair. His touch was light and deft, what she had imagined it would be. The roots ached from being twisted.

"My darling," she whispered when she was put back in order.

"Get up there before someone comes," he said.

"It's going to be all right," she insisted. And she felt supremely happy; she knew that it would be. She kissed the turned-away cheek. "Good-bye, good-bye."

The fog had lifted, or her eyes had grown accustomed to the vapor and could read its patterns. The line of the house was visible in the trees, the trees visible against the sky, in midnight and sodden tones of gray. She made for the gate, her near horizon, swaying as though drunk.

Chapter Thirty-two

ELSA WOKE AT MIDMORNING. In their adolescence Grey allowed his children to sleep late; they needed it for their growth, he said. Perhaps because of this assurance, they seldom slept in. Even Flavia, the most indolent of the three, had risen in the very early morning to cut roses from the garden or drink coffee with Sno-Bird before the men came in.

The cedar fronds brushed the bedroom sill. Elsa bunched her nightgown around her hips and knee-walked across the bed to the window. A maroon Pontiac was pottering up the drive through the trees.

She gathered her clothes from the floor and went down to the bath. While the oil heater warmed the room, she examined the underpants critically. The crotch was as clean as a little girl's. Elsa went over the dress with equal scrutiny, then tossed both in the hamper. The laddered stockings she kept to put in the stove. She ran the bath, added violet bath cubes and watched them turn to silver-rose foam. Before taking it off, she sniffed down the neck hole of her nightgown. A mesquite tang sweetened the gently stirring air between her legs. Regretfully, she lowered herself into the water.

He had pulled his jeans on before he went to loosen the shutter, as though it mattered after love that she saw him naked. As if she would not want to see him, and the thing men hid until it could no longer be hidden. He did himself up with a small rustle of cloth, and she knew he watched her even in the dark, that being aware of her was his fate. It had been like being possessed again, feeling the gaze of those cold light eyes. Her movements around the bath—brushing out her hair, bending to turn off the little heater—seemed to have a new, pliable grace. Passion stretched inside her like a second self, limber and warm, filled with secret energy. This was what it felt to be a grown woman. A child was one-dimensional. A woman carried this private second self around.

In the kitchen the breakfast things were cleared away and a dishcloth was drying over the drainer. Elsa opened the stove, tossed the ruined stockings on the coals and padded to the pantry for cornflakes and milk. Outside the dogs were barking.

It was definitely going to rain again. The sun was a dull yellow disk midway over the range, the grass lay flat and slate-colored under a shadowy nimbostratus. There was no sign of Harris in the yard. The maroon Pontiac was parked next to the ranch pickup. She could hear Daithi sawing in one of the sheds.

Grey and the visitor, a French-Canadian bloodstock agent who had been to the ranch before, were at the Duchess's box. Elsa examined her father as though he, too, were new. He looked tall and well made in a crisp white shirt under an Aran wool sweater, twill pants and boots. The eyes blazed in his sunburned face. It was a mistake to think blue couldn't burn. The St. Oeggers were of mixed mysterious race; some Scots, some French and something less complaisant, the warriors of primitive Europe. Yet he had a look about the eyes and mouth that was so peculiarly English he couldn't be mistaken for anything else, even before he spoke.

"This is an exciting occasion, mam'selle," said the visitor, whose name was Menard. "A very rare thing."

The foals were making small forays from their mother's side on stiltlike legs. Blond cat whiskers sprouted from their muzzles.

"They have the look of their pappy," mused Menard. "More him than the mare."

"Same bone, same lines," said Grey. "I'm tickled to death at the shape they're in. She was in good hands." He turned to Elsa. "You were there."

Her heart leaped, but she said calmly, "The light was on, so I stopped to look. Harris was clearing up."

"Our foreman," Grey explained to Menard. "He let me sleep until morning, then sprang the news. I can almost forgive him for not waking me."

Elsa was acutely aware of the little room behind the saddles and shelves of equipment—the rumpled cot, the stickiness and roused dust. Had he put everything to rights? Of course he had. He was Harris.

Another car pulled up in the yard; another visitor, summoned by the invisible smoke signals by which country events make rounds. Over the next few days they would climb the pass, cross the red-girded bridge and sweep into the valley, looking for Salthill and Grey and the twins.

"I'll show them in," Elsa offered. "Is Harris here?"

She said it to say his name. She said it to hear it in her own ear. Everything that had ever happened to her, every event momentous or small, tragic or ordinary, belonged to an antique past, the time of her girlhood which was now officially over, the time before last night.

"Gone to Mountain Inn for a few days," said Grey. "I told him to get a decent night's sleep and go tomorrow, but he left after breakfast on that red hellion of his."

The Red was above cheap tricks like holding his breath and swelling up to make the cinch loose. He stood patiently and breathed normally while Harris pulled it as tight as it would go, buckled the straps and slapped down the leathers.

It was early morning. He rode through the Bluffs first, to pass the wash where the sniper had died. Looking down on that face drained of life, he had known he was looking at what they could both do.

The range stretched solidly ahead, darkened at times by passing clouds. It was a colorless morning, warm for that hour. The clouds gathered over the mountains had inky underbellies and the air smelled sourly of damp grass and earth. It would rain before night. The Red snorted and toyed with the bit. Harris shook the reins out and the horse sprang forward, his mane whipping in the wind. They fled across the benchland beneath the shadows of racing clouds to the country of eroded coulees and draws thick with brush that started north of the quarry. It was cattle-grazing country, the feed too sparse for horses to seek out. He could tell the Red had never been here. The horse's ears were forward and he scanned the strange territory alertly as he picked his way up the path.

A lone rider appeared on the skyline, the folds of his slicker cascading over his horse's rump. Harris felt a rush of anxiety. He couldn't spend the next two days with another man, working and talking and eating with him as if nothing had happened. All his life he had fed a need to be alone. That need was hungry now; it was wolfish for solitude.

He had gone up to the house as soon as her light went off, showered and gotten a couple of hours' sleep. He slept instantly, as if he had been knocked out, then woke with a start, his heart tripping and his mouth dry. He had risen and dressed and gone to let Grey know about the Duchess. They walked down together to her box. They went over the delivery, the way the mare had lain there patiently, cramping, until the spasms had expelled the first small body onto the straw. He watched Grey lift one of the foals until its legs dangled, then set it down with a grunt of satisfaction. A healthy, well-boned colt.

"Elsa came in," said Harris. "Right at the end." He wasn't worried about her blowing it, telling her father she hadn't been there when she had. Like him, she would stick to the truth as far as possible. Underneath that she would keep her own counsel and play her hand with resolute slyness. It was crazy, but he knew her.

They walked down the passageway as they had a thousand times.

"I'm going over to Piwonka's," he said. Piwonka had sent a man around the day before, asking for help moving stock to another grazing area.

"You've got time off coming if you want to go into town," said Grey casually. "A man needs to get away from work once in a while."

Harris felt the other man's sympathy for whatever was bothering him. It filled him with the sense of what he had lost. It also filled him with hostility. No way was he going into town or staying here, either. He had to get out in the open, under the sky. He had to get away from everything.

"I'll go to Piwonka's," he said.

The lone rider on the ridge raised one hand in a mild salute. It was Ned Blaise the foreman, who never opened his mouth unless he had to. Blaise on his splay-footed, half-dead-looking brown gelding who made grand champion in roping and beat everything out of the barrel racing most years at the Calgary trials. The grizzled face under the brim of the Stetson was composed and stately. If he had to spend time with any man, let it be Blaise.

They scouted the ridges, flushing out strays. The Red, whose half-hinged brain gloried in sweeping cows out of ravines, was in a cooperative mood. He sucked in the muggy air as they foraged and blew it out in loud wet snorts.

"Crazy as a green-broke bronc, not as good at cowdogging," noted Blaise.

In the late afternoon they found a pitch with water and feed. Blaise tossed him a bedroll and unpacked the camp kit: lighter fluid and matches in a greased waterproof pack, coffee, fry pan, aluminum dishes, a packet of bacon, a tin of beans and a tin of brown bread.

"I'll fix it," said Harris. "You can't cook for shit."

The old cowboy smiled and went to lay out the bedrolls.

It started to rain before they finished eating. They got under the tent, which had stingray panels so they could see the cattle and horses between the stake poles. Blaise smoked and read a paperback with a yellow and red cover. Harris lay down with his boots off and gave himself up to violent remorse. For the first time since coming to Salthill, he was incapable of focusing on the printed word.

He rode in late the third morning, turned the Red out, showered and put on clean riding clothes.

He had beaten himself into submission, sitting under a slicker with the rain pouring off his hat like water out of a drainpipe as he waited for a cow to come out of the brush. Every time he thought of Grey's daughter, desire rushed through him. He wanted her again, wanted to force himself on her. That was what it had felt like, force, even though she started it, said that about her breasts, said she could make him think about her whether he wanted to or not. It was true. That he could have her anytime they could get it, use her and she would never feel used, made the marrow burn like lit sap in his bones. It was him who was had. Even when he sat quiet in the saddle, listening to the beat of the rain, he was hearing her voice. *Aren't you even going to kiss me good night?*

No good at cowdogging, Blaise had said. The Red. Too big, too crazy, too much power. He was no good at this love shit for the same reason. It was too much. He thought longingly and without hope of the small, casual good times.

There were hours to think in. He thought about poor white children in the South, playing by the road outside their houses. That was what she looked like when he crouched in front of her rolling up her stockings, one of those girl-children in a dress a size too small, with scratched-up legs and papery skin. They had stared imperiously when he clopped down the road on one of his charges from the racing stable, past antebellum houses set back in the groves, past their tar-roof shacks up close, the broken fences and cars in pieces and sad, stringy gardens. The leavings of the Civil War, sunk in the poverty Reconstruction never got around to reconstructing, their only pride that however bad things got, by god, at least they weren't black.

He fell into a depression that matched the gaunt landscape. He had made a bad mistake, but it wasn't going to happen again. In the crucible of his mind, resolve flared and cooled to a chill blue fire. The thing was done with. It had happened, yes, but it was over now. Betrayal would become a memory, eventually covered by other things. Like time, as her father had said; the benefits of time passing. Good deeds. Hard work. These things would cover the small pile of rubbish he would bury before it had time to start stinking.

He'd find a way to let her know what he had decided. He wanted to talk to her badly, wanted it in his gut. He had to let her know.

He lit another cigarette and felt that things were going to be okay.

Chapter Thirty-three

HARRIS SADDLED THE CHESTNUT JUMPER. The Duchess was still in her box, sleek and sleepy from eating rich feed so she would produce the best milk. One of the foals was sucking noisily at the teat. His flat little tail wiggled every time he gave a pull.

Grey was at the gate watching Elsa take the mare back and forth over the water jump. She wore jodhpurs and a faded powder-blue polo shirt. Her thick hair was clubbed under a hunt cap. She rode with dash, with a good seat and hands and a look of frowning concentration. She finished the round and started for the gate, pulling off the hunt cap in defiance of her father's rule about wearing it all the time she was mounted. She hated hats. Her body swayed with the loose walk of the mare; her small crooked face looked reserved and peaceful. She would understand why he needed to do this, when he had a chance to tell her.

"Welcome back," said Grey, smiling. And he knew that he really was.

He took the chestnut into the ring and forgot everything for an hour. After that they talked over the morning's work, grouped at the gate. Elsa made comments in the voice that seemed to have gotten huskier over the summer. It was a common scene, the planning sessions on horseback. Once in a while he gave her a level look, just to keep things natural.

"I'm going in," said Grey finally. "This one's had a good workout and we've got the two-year-olds to do. It's going to be a hell of a day."

As soon as he was gone, she turned to him with her falcon's hot look. He knew then how stupid he had been to think it would never happen again.

"When can we be together?"

"Tonight. When everyone's asleep." The words left his mouth automatically. There was no struggle, just obedience to the bidding of the compulsion.

"Where?" she hissed.

He looked at the freckled arms, the hands in pigskin gloves resting on the pommel of the saddle. Her neck looked so young and fragile under its knob of hair.

"My room."

He held her eyes with his until her smile faded and she looked down in submission and confusion. Then he rode back into the ring.

In the evening he walked up the drive to the highway with the dogs. It still felt better to be outside than inside. The moon was quartering in a navy-blue sky, a slice of pearl over mountains hulking like furniture covered with black drapes.

When he got back, Grey called him from the study.

"Let's talk for a few minutes, if it's convenient for you."

He felt a jolt of despair and fear.

Grey was sitting in the big oak chair. Harris pulled up the chair he always sat in. They had a thing they did. Grey kept a bound stud register, thick as one of those old-time family Bibles, on the chair so no one would sit on it. When Harris came in, he took the book off the seat and put it on the floor. It was Harris's chair.

He sat and let his arms lie along the armrests. The mahogany curves turned smoothly under his hands.

Grey poured a shot of whiskey from the bottle on the shelf. "How're you feeling?"

He meant since the fall from the Red, Harris knew.

"I'm not having any headaches," he answered. He did not say he felt fine. He wasn't going to lie any more than he had to.

"Good." Grey leaned back, looking bland. The chair creaked like harness and gave a little beneath his weight. "Have you ever thought of leaving Salthill?"

He went dead calm. Over the creak of the chair and the tick of the clock he heard his own pulse beat in his ears, but his mind and nerves were still. The stillness was a relief, after the turmoil of the last three days.

"No," he said.

"You ought to," said Grey quietly. "You would, if you were interested in your welfare."

He wanted a cigarette. What he really wanted was the whiskey, glowing like a squatty fire in the shot glass. He wanted to toss it down, feel the heat spread in his belly, then drive somewhere, get drunk, stay drunk. But if he'd been asked if what he'd done was worth it, he would have said yes. He would have said yes to both of them, to what they had both wanted from him.

The knife flashed in the air, turned a somersault in joy at its clean steel flight, and landed in the jugular.

". . . inducement to stay. I've been thinking about it for some time. I had a letter from Gordon a month ago. He wants to remain in England after his fellowship."

He sat with his mouth clamped shut. An inducement to stay.

"Perhaps I shouldn't have been surprised," said Grey. "Gordon will inherit my father's estate eventually. My brother is unlikely to have children at his age, and I've no intent of returning to Ireland." He added without irony, "The conventions have always been important to Gordon."

Harris knew Grey's father had some kind of title. A baronet, they called it. Old Dai, that blabbermouth, had told him. He understood the worth of those things to English people, knew too why it was never mentioned at Salthill. It was like Grey to ignore the title and what went with it, turn his back on it the way he had turned his back on Europe. He really belonged in this wilderness. Grey was a maverick, a man who needed frontiers.

Grey smiled that smile that was like a good fire on a cold night. "I don't believe you've any idea of your worth, Harris. You've worked for this place as though you owned it. You've given me the benefit of your perspective when I've asked for it, which has been frequently. For a man of twenty-six you're pretty capable."

"Twenty-five," said Harris. Last week in fact, though his birthday wasn't celebrated at Salthill, at his request. He was sure Grey knew what he wanted to know about him, including his birth date. The small request for correction was meant to draw him out. For a capable man, he had sure fallen into that one.

"You've helped make business decisions," said Grey. "You've lent me your gifts as a horseman for five years, all in exchange for a meal and a ride on a spoiled chaser. I've come to rely on you and I've a very real fear of your deciding to be on your way one day. That's why I'm making you this offer."

"What offer?" he said, feeling stupid.

"Don't misunderstand," said Grey quickly. "Of course it lies in the future, hopefully not too far ahead, if you care to accept it. I had planned to keep this discussion businesslike, acknowledge the importance of our history with a formal interview instead of a casual one. I forget that this concerns you. Are you uncomfortable with the time and place?"

He felt the challenge to his contrary independence. His pride rose. "Of course not."

"Fine. Otherwise we can go in the kitchen and crack nuts, or sweat it out tomorrow over a recalcitrant piece of machinery or horseflesh."

"I won't come unhinged," he said guardedly.

Grey drank off the shot, set the glass down and rose. "It has been good having you here, Harris."

Harris watched him cross to a window and stand with his hands in the pockets of his corduroys, looking at the east garden.

"I've had the feeling lately that something's been troubling you," he said. He sounded cautious, almost apologetic. A man's feelings were private, they both knew that. "Something seems to have happened in the last few weeks to change your life here. It's none of my business and I'm not going to try to find out what it is, but I have wondered whether you're tired of Salthill. There's no entertainment or distraction out here, just a lot of monotonous work. You're a young man. You may want to marry and you've no place of your own to bring a wife to. You may want to be more among your people, be livelier."

"I have no people," said Harris. "This is what I have."

As he said it, he knew it was true. Of course he had no one, in any sense of the word: no people, no family, no race even. All he had was St. Oeggers.

"I'm offering you a share in it, then," said Grey. "In the business of Salthill."

He zoomed in on the man standing at the window with the twilight of the north behind his head. On that look of foursquare integrity that in a white man should have been a mockery of justice and fair play, but in fact was an evocation, at least for Harris, of the very best he could have known. Grey St. Oegger was real. He was perceptive, hard-boiled and trustworthy. Even his flaws were real: his ignorance of his children's needs and motives, his slighting of his son, whatever else he had done; things that might be wrong in the eyes of society but made some secret, perfect sense in his. Even his sexual being was a mystery, not clear as with most men who have married and kept a house, but with a shrouded feel to it. Harris sensed misadventures that didn't fit with the rest of him. Or did they? They were part of what lay hidden in the man, beneath the good stock he was made of. Behind the profile patterned with the lentigo of night shadows, behind the mouth that was a print of hers. It was a face he had always thought he could read easily, or that what he read of it, he had read well.

He rose to his feet. He said, to the best he could have known, "I've admired your strong work."

"What a bracing expression of confidence," said Grey, facing him. "Tell me, Harris: how would you describe yourself? In as few words as possible."

"A tainted man," said Harris uneasily.

"Amazing. I won't pry any further. You've shown me with what poetry the devil's influence can be evoked. The last European to use that phrase probably lived in the nineteenth century."

He would have been amused any other time.

"You could begin by taking one of the Duchess's foals, plus a pick from the yearlings," said Grey. "As compensation in your current capacity. Piwonka bought five hundred acres in Wanda Creek last year from the Dwyer family. There's a house on the land. He wants to move his operation closer to town, stay there during the winter months. He's willing to sell me enough land to extend my northeast boundary through the springs and cedar grove up to the lake road. There are eleven hundred acres available, fit for growing or pasturage or able to be made fit for it, with plenty of room for building."

He said nothing.

"I'd like to buy it with you," said Grey more rapidly. "As an investment. We'd draw up an agreement for repayment at the interest Marvin's thinking of asking. You'd have the land for your use for grazing or building, with an option to buy me out at the end of the term. If you pick a filly and breed her to an outside stud, you'll be starting a new line."

He grasped at the first log in the millrace. "I don't want you to give me any colts."

"I'm giving you nothing but an opportunity. This is prime stock-raising country and Marvin doesn't want strangers in the valley. You've earned his respect and I have reason to believe he'll be amenable to your coming in on the deal. Any help you need to begin with can be arranged on decent terms. Most men here build their own houses; I expect you will too."

"It's too risky," he said desperately. "You always said breeding horses was a heartbreaking business. Things go wrong."

"I'm not denying it. But you've as good a chance of making a go of it as any man. It was you who suggested buying Arabs and breeding them for western stock as well as English riding. I've got a clientele of Arab and half-bred fanciers now. It was you who thought of taking horses to the Seattle sales and getting better prices from American buyers than I could hope for here, even with the regulatory paperwork to contend with."

"What about Gordon? Suppose you die and I haven't met my obligation?" He seemed to have stepped into a world where death had a place in conversation.

Grey made a face. "Don't fret over my children; they're provided for. My Irish properties are tied up in family sentiment, but Salthill is mine to do with as I like. Think about my offer, Harris. You can't work for another man forever. It's not in your nature any more than it is in mine."

He was silent.

"How do you think I've liked using someone of your talent and energy as a hired man? When you could freelance as a trainer to the best establishments in North America, make a fortune and never muck out another stall?"

"I'm black," he said simply.

"Black. Jesus. Go to Europe, then. In France they'll kiss your ass. They may kiss it in England too, if you bear yourself nicely and don't drink from a teacup with your little finger sticking out."

He heard himself laugh helplessly in spite of the pain. "You're ridiculous, man."

Grey laughed too. "I mean it. You're wasted here as you are. Unless you decide to go into business for yourself, with me. But you may not be interested. You may want to walk alone."

"I seem to get in the position of having to," said Harris. He swallowed. "I've liked dealing with you."

"Think it over then," said Grey again. He added ruefully, "I hope I haven't talked you out of what would be most advantageous to myself. This enterprise would give me great pleasure."

"You've shown me the possibilities," he said. "That's all."

He suddenly hated the generosity that had been tossed in his lap. Generosity was just a part of privilege; that's what he told himself when his own poverty showed. There was nothing generous in his nature, just an everlasting fire that had burned a hole in his gut that the wind blew through, and he had to plug it up with whatever was around. But the hatred wouldn't last. He knew now when he was being unreasonable. Grey couldn't help being what he was, either.

Chapter Thirty-four

HE PICKED UP HIS CURRENT BOOK, but he couldn't seem to retain the meaning of anything he read. It was Zora Neale Hurston's *Mules and Men*. He had found it in a used book store in Williams Lake, where he had gone for his yearly holiday. He had been intrigued that a woman would write like that. Sandrine had come with him. They had eaten in restaurants and stayed overnight in a real hotel, making love standing over the furnace vent with automatic heat gusting luxuriously up their forks. He had bought her an abalone-shell necklace with a gilt fish between each shimmering rainbow disk. That had been only last January. It seemed like a long time ago now.

The book had lain around for a while, then he'd started reading it a few days before he picked Elsa up at the station. He'd thought often of what he himself had become, studying peace and knowledge in this valley. He was dangerous no longer. Grey had shown him how much he had to lose. Grey had turned him into a fearful, prudent man.

For a while he thought about the interview with Grey, what they had said to each other, and all the unsaid things. He could not block out the unsaid things. He had to think about them coldly, go over them until guilt invaded and scoured him, and he lay too thickened and roughened under it to fear love. He thought about what was going to happen tonight, what he would strive to make happen. He set the book aside. Where was she now? Her kiss had been innocent, had told him she knew nothing and everything. They were traveling toward each other, down stair flights, flowing through walls. He was flying blind, seeking her mouth like radar. Yet he was lying on this bed, heavy and full of fire, against flight.

At ten-thirty he opened the window on the garden and saw deer crossing the lawn, headed for the Jonagold and the persimmon tree. The gate must have been left open. He counted three weaving shadows. A noise would send them into that jerking, nervous flight that ended in bounding leaps. It was a primordial flight that sometimes entered his dreams. Light fell in patterns across the Turkish carpet between flurries of clouds. He folded his jeans and put them on a chair, then lay down in his underpants and T-shirt. He smoked a cigarette, looking out the window. After a while he smoked another.

He heard scratching at the door. It could have been one of the dogs, but they were shut up in the kitchen. His stomach twisted with excitement.

It was Elsa. She glanced back at the stairway to the upper floor, then stepped inside the room. Her toes peeped out from under a winceyette nightgown sprigged with flowers. Her hair was loose. The changeable eyes roamed his face. He locked the door, feeling pierced through, and tossed the quilt on the floor.

He drew her in front of the window. "Take that off."

Without hesitating she lifted the gown over her head. He ran his eyes over her while she stood and let him look. He kissed her then, not hotly the way he had the other night but slowly, tasting her, letting her taste him.

"Now you," she whispered, arms loose at her sides.

He pulled off the shirt and stepped out of his underpants, and stood naked.

"Copper," she breathed. "The color. I couldn't see, it was so dark."

"Don't talk," he said roughly.

She raised her hands with fingers spread, like a blind girl feeling her way. They were light and cool on his chest. She kissed the hollow place below the medal on the chain. He felt her touch now here, now there as she delicately felt her way down. She put her hand on him and he was big. She butted her head into his chest suddenly. He heard her breath; his own breath.

"It's all right, baby," he said. "It's all right. We'll take it slow and easy."

Elsa failed to come downstairs for breakfast.

"Let her sleep," said Grey when Sno-Bird made mention of it.

Harris was on his second helping of bacon and eggs, eating like a recovering invalid. He put his elbows on the table and spread marmalade on toast while Grey opened mail with the brass dagger a cousin had sent from Samarkand.

Grey pinched the bills open and glanced casually at the damage before setting them aside. There was a letter from the university on milled paper.

The bill from Abercrombie's for grain. The vet's quote for gelding the two-year-olds. Two notes of inquiry, one about stud fees, the other about a young stallion he had kept back from gelding who would make good breeding stock. He was a fine fellow and would have to be got rid of soon; he was becoming troublesome around the mares. A letter from the RCMP confirming transport arrangements for the horses they had purchased. A government communication about watersheds, electricity and the Peace River project, which he put aside to read when he had the time. Power lines were invading the farthest reaches of the province. Part of him welcomed this; a part of him disliked it very much.

There was a letter from Gordon. He was engaged to be married. He and his fiancée were driving to Salthill from Vancouver. A date of two weeks from the writing was given. They could stay the night; they had to be in Toronto the Wednesday after, to leave for London. They were to be married in London in September, in her grandparents' house. Grey read this with eyebrows raised. He put the letter to one side with the government communication.

"Engaged? Why didn't he tell me when he wrote last month?" he said to Elsa later. "He must have met her before then, unless he's gone love-mad, which I doubt. There's never been anything impulsive about Gordon. Now he wants me to come to the wedding, as if I could leave this place at the height of summer with no notice. Jasper and Winnie will have to stand for me."

With her first child due in August, Flavia couldn't go either. Gordon had chosen to be married at the most inconvenient time of the year.

"Why don't they stay in town?" suggested Elsa. "It would save them driving another hundred miles. It's not as though she'll never see Salthill. Her parents live in Victoria."

"It's not very welcoming," he protested.

"They're only staying the night," she said dryly.

"Well. It is sensible of you to think of it." He looked pleased. "You're getting to manage this sort of thing as well as your sister."

"The Pioneer Days festival is that weekend. We could go first and look at things, then have dinner at the Plaza Hotel."

Harris felt refreshed and strengthened, as though last night had given him a secret source of power. He saddled a horse and rode out on the grassland. The stud was covering a mare on the fringe of the herd. He dropped down as Harris passed, the long, ruddy penis dangling outside his body. It would disappear soon between the powerful quarters, like a cobra backing into its nest.

He rode toward the north coulees, turned and came back through the Bluffs, getting his horse used to the rough terrain. It was a young horse, afraid of everything or wanting to be afraid, neck arched and skittering with life. He let the colt sniff around and spook at nothing, showed him a few obstacles and let him pop over a fallen tree branch.

The rampart of tamaracks was miles away, then a hundred yards away. It was a clear cold day, full of oily resin from the firs. He was to remember that summer as one of storms, of long slate skies that ruminated over the land, opening almost daily to drench it, and of the few good days as full of this cool light. The sun struck the stone of the house and transformed the window on the second story of the turret into a medallion that turned and flashed as if it hung from a chain.

In the yard Grey was saddling one of the jumpers.

"Give me to the end of summer to think about your offer," said Harris. "That's how much time I need."

"Certainly," said Grey cheerfully. "Just don't leave."

"I'm not planning on it." He stared down at the autumn-leaf head.

The hinged square in the ceiling in his room had a recessed place in the center with a knot in it, a belly button of some kind of rope. He'd always thought that one day when there was time he'd see what was up there. The ceiling was high. He had to stand on the bed and poke at the knot with a coat hanger to pull it out of the hole. It was the end of a cord about two feet long, made of hemp or sisal, knotted at the other end to keep it from slipping through the hole. He pulled at it. The square snapped open and turned into the hinged door of an opening. He tested the mattress with feet spread apart and jumped lightly. On the second try the coat hanger twitched out a handful of knotted cord. A rope ladder tumbled past his knees.

He studied the trap door, then hooked one bare foot on the first rung. His body swayed, but it held his weight. It took strength to hold the rope taut for each foothold, but the rope was stiff, with a texture like straw, which helped. The opening swallowed his body to the knees. He pulled himself up the rest of the way by his hands, and was on the upper floor of the turret room.

The vault of the roof was waffled with crossbeams. He padded around. A few cartons pushed against the wall, marked in grease pencil in a foreign alphabet, showed how long it had been since anyone had come up here.

The floor was laid in close-fitting planks smooth as sand under his feet. There was about six square feet of dusty floor in the center.

He padded to the window. It was a long drop to the ground. The upper branches of the trees moved below the glass, shifting the light around. There was no rustle of leaves, no flutter of birds. He was on an island between earth and the sky, afloat on his own private atoll.

Chapter Thirty-five

GREY AND ELSA WERE WAITING in the Buick. Their faces swiveled toward Harris, alert and uncooperative, with pink and tan skins and thick eyebrows like two Scotty terriers. He experienced the sensation, not new, that they were more of a mystery to each other than he was to them. That he was the divining rod they used to locate themselves. Grey's fedora was on his knee. He still wore a hat when he thought the occasion called for it. Elsa had her oatmeal suit on and a scarf over her hair with the ends knotted in back. He got in behind the driver's seat and she let in the clutch.

On the other side of the bridge a lone man walked, in new jeans and a blouse with beading. They slowed down. Grey leaned out the window.

"Need a ride, Elmer?"

"If you don't mind, Grey," said the Klaxta, removing his hat politely. "Hello, Miss Elsa."

He climbed in beside Harris. Once Harris would have been glad to sit in tacit communion with Elmer, tasting the wind on his lips. Now the cares of passion kept him paralyzed, obliged to sense only her. He didn't need to see her face to know how he weighed on her. Since the other might he had been sure of it. He had the power to move her too, and he was going to use it.

Between the trees the lake was a sheet of hammered tin. They drove past the crossroads to the CPR station, past hillocks of cow vetch and ditches bordered with trefoil and red clover. The main street was strung with colored lights; a Pioneer Days banner snapped in the breeze; there were pots of flowers on the window ledges. Even the balcony of the defunct whorehouse sported a row of geraniums in clay dishes. The sidewalks were lined with trucks and cars and crowded with festivalgoers. There was no place to park. They let Harris and Elmer out across from the movie house.

"We'll be at the Plaza at six if you change your mind," Grey said.

"He doesn't need me there," said Harris.

"I'm sorry you feel that way," said Grey, eyeing him. Grey knew Harris didn't like Gordon. Grey knew a lot of things he had no intention of discussing. Elsa was staring out at the banners. The wild hair was bundled on her neck like a sack of sweet wheat. Those two, father and son, stood between him and what he wanted. Yes, the father loved Harris and he loved the father. What a mistake it was for men to love each other when borders of stone lay between them. Inside those borders, daughters and earth and gold were guarded from other men. Chaos came from careless love. He was an intruder looking past guards into a stronghold. They were not of him. He had known since the night he took her into that room, known since he opened her dress and touched the pink buds that he was never going to be of them.

Harris watched the sedan roll away without regret, even though it meant not seeing her for many hours. He wasn't about to go to that dinner. Gordon was a bigot. He was the worst kind of bigot, an imperialist. Gordon made him yearn to smack his fist into that lofty, pale mug and watch it buckle.

Tourists wandered around idling cars on the main street. As always, when he passed the slow-moving surge of plaids and florals and dragging sandals and cameras slung on chests, more than one looked away, politely avoiding eye contact, as though at the sight of a man grieving or a man with pustules or a smell, or set apart by some freakishness. He heard the thoughts: *Why isn't he on a back street, in his little house, wherever they live? Are there more like him?* These thoughts being interruptions of their larger consciousness, forgotten as he was forgotten, soon after he was out of sight. A brief disturbance on the landscape, because after all he was a solitary Negro, only one of him. These ones were the Americans. The Canadians, the Germans, English, Scots, Finns, took him in as stolidly and cautiously as they took in each other, the historical buildings, the daguerreotypes and Gold Rush pans and pickaxes in the local museum, the bunting, the food booth offerings. They accepted. They migrated into the folds of the hills, big red-blond men with freckled wives, thinking of real estate and settling down. There were a few dark, ruffled-looking Quebecois honking French down their noses. A family of Jews, the women in city dresses, the heavy men in dark suits and round-brimmed hats, with faces buried in spongy black beard, rumbled past like a collection of boxcars.

He turned down a street of bungalows with yards fenced with chain-link and yellowing privet hedge. There were as many vacant fields as there were bungalows. He followed the dirt path between the trees, skirting dried–up horse clods.

Her house was shuttered. The Virginia creeper over the porch was dry in patches. There were two newspapers with the rubber bands still on lying in the purple deerhorn at the edge of the drive. He turned them over with his shoe. They were the last two editions of the *Trump,* which came out once a week. He tossed them on the porch, feeling his tension mounting, the roiling of his guts that had become familiar in the last weeks. What in hell was going on?

He walked around the back. A bicycle with a plaid seat was chained to the stoop, its rear tire sunk in weeds. He'd bought it for her. She had tried to make him ride it. He had refused, not wanting to tell her he'd never been on a bicycle. She had guessed anyway.

"Don't tell me you can't ride a bike after riding horses," she scoffed. "You have wonderful balance. Look, try it. It'll take you ten minutes to learn. You'll like it, it's like flying."

She had been strong, a strong woman. He had needed that, not because he was weak. In the world he came from, being a man didn't have enough to do with what happened to you. He understood that now, though the knowledge had come slowly and hard, and left scars like troughs, because of his insistence on his superiority. He had been born superior. It wasn't some idea put in his head by inheriting light eyes and skin from the plantation-owning mulatto his uncle had taken care to let him know of, a man who went out at night to fuck the African women he virtually owned, women who could not refuse him no matter how exhausted they were or who they loved. His superiority had been his intelligence, his sense of its rightness in seeing this and doing that, and he had been scornful that everybody did not possess it. The idea of subjugation had taken bitter root at last, as it had to, but subjugation had not. He could see men conquered in Africa, making themselves little, scurrying under cover of rule like insects under leaves; he could not see it in America. To be in America was to be in exodus from every ancient form of slavery of the mind; it was to be separated from the antlike masses of Europe and Africa to stand alone. He was already America, it was in his blood. There was no more relation between him and some African on his mound than there was between him and the Englishman in his field. He prowled a borderless world with a looser-fitting skin and a brow full of pale thought and dark thought. So subjugation was not a reality, but still he could not plot his own destiny. In a world where a black man could not look a white man in the eyes, where the white man looked politely away to spare the black man the necessity of looking away, where a man never knew where he would be next week, or next year, there was no room for any woman but a strong one. You had to know she was there, even when you were going to leave.

He stopped at the grocery store to buy cigarettes. It was there that he remembered where she had gone. She'd told him in July, told him the last time he'd seen her that she was going to her sister's in Clinton for three weeks. He'd forgotten completely about it. Everything had been wiped out of his head by what was going on at Salthill.

The shop was crowded. He stood in front of the cash register and the Coca-Cola sign, feeling change being pressed into his hand. He pocketed it and wandered outside in a daze. People passed him, not tourists this time but people he knew, ranchers, shopkeepers, farmers, the dentist and black-smith with their families. They appeared on the street suddenly like a colorful bunch of released balloons. They had come late after finishing chores, some driving a hundred miles to spend the evening in town. Under the bobbing lights their faces were plain and work-worn but reflected contentment with what they had. Many smiled at him or nodded in recognition, or said his name. Young children who had never seen him goggled and got behind their parents when he passed. It didn't bother him. He stood out. The sun had darkened him and the scar was a tight seam running down his face. He knew it made him look ominous, but the truth was that he was simply unhappy.

Music wavered thinly from somewhere near the lake. An Indian wearing a choker of salmon pearls and bear teeth rode a good black horse down the street, the crowd parting around him like the Red Sea around Moses.

Harris sat on a park bench, still woozy from the shock of going to Sandrine's to break up with her and finding her gone. He had made some dumb mistakes in his life, but sleeping with two women at the same time wasn't going to be one of them. He had too much respect for the shaman power of women. He had even thought of the reason he would give, knowing she wouldn't believe him but would have to accept it in the end. He couldn't tell her the truth, that this other thing had swept him up like a firestorm and he couldn't get back. Women had their pride too.

He remembered someone telling him once about a jazz musician whose wife walked into the club one night when he was playing a solo, took a gun out of her purse and shot him dead. Seemed like she couldn't take him fucking around on her no more. Sometimes it was better not to love too

much. You had to remember your position and not let your heart mess with
your head.

He stopped in the saloon. It was warm and dark inside, good for drinking
when you were looking up the wrong end of the blues. Cigarette smoke
drifted under the dim ruby lights and a game of darts was in progress. One
or two men nodded at him in greeting. He sat at the bar.

" 'Lo, Harris," said the bartender, an Englishman, wiping down the
counter. "The usual, or are you going to drink whiskey like a decent fellow?"

"The usual," he said. When the ginger ale came he lit another cigarette.

If only he could get her out of that house, take her away somewhere.
They would do nothing but make love, eat and sleep. He would hold that
supple body in his arms, he would kiss the pink and fawn highlights. He
would feed her with his hands, spoon food gently into her mouth as if she
was a bird or baby animal. He would stroke her hair, cup in his hand the
delicate skull that held such mysteries and feel her mysterious essence burning, licking toward his fingers. He would touch her and it would be the
same as touching himself. With her in the turret room, on the quilt with the
night air cooling their bodies, he had experienced a voluptuousness that was
like the few times when being drunk or loaded had worked, when his whole
being responded lazily and freely to a force outside him. That was the way
he responded to their nakedness, the way it felt when he was in her. He
strangled the yearning and turned it into touch.

He rubbed his throbbing temples. The ginger ale tasted gassy and he
remembered that he hadn't eaten since breakfast. He thumbed a dollar out
of his wallet and paid for a sandwich. There was a Seattle newspaper on the
counter, left by some tourist. He opened it and read while he ate. Some
people had filed an anti-segregation suit, *Brown v. Board of Education,* down
there.

When he left it was drizzling, a mist so fine it was like standing in the
middle of a cloud. The tourists were gone, but the local people still wandered
in the twilight with their coats buttoned up, smiling under folded newspapers. An umbrella bobbed, but nobody was going home. Everyone ignored
rain in the Skillihawk.

Chapter Thirty-six

PERHAPS SHE WAS SO HAPPY because between the two men, Harris and her father, she felt completely safe. They loved each other so much that some of it fell on her like a soft rain. She felt marvelously flexible, which she wasn't most of the time, and greedy. Greed was a new thing—perhaps part of this new grown-up womanhood? She felt full of energy and rushing, pumping life.

"I don't think things have ever been better," said Grey. "For us or for Salthill. Don't you agree?"

"I do." Elsa kissed his cheek.

"You haven't done that since you were small," he said. As though following a train of thought, he added, "I've invited young Trinity. He's going to represent the Georgewoods."

The lake appeared, winding around the points. The jibbooms and gaffs of a sloop nosing the dock piles lifted in slender clusters toward the clouds. A tall curved light, yellow as a daffodil, appeared in the belfry of the Anglican church.

Dai and Sno-Bird were waiting in the lacquered gloom of the Cattleman's Room on the ground floor of the Plaza Hotel. Trinity Georgewood met them in blue jeans and a powder-blue shirt with pearl snaps on the cuffs and pockets. Blue was Trinity's color and he knew it. Even the blossom-pink and white skin was faintly blued at the jawline. Elsa stared bemused at cream lizardskin boots, thinly shingled like mail armor, then was guided to the table with his hand in the middle of her back.

The table was laid with darned linen and railroad dining car flatware. The waitress wore a dress instead of her uniform.

"You're my last of the evening, Colonel," she said with an air of determination. "I hang up my apron at eight sharp."

"And so you ought, June, so you ought." Grey received the menu. "But treat us well while we're here, will you? This is a very special occasion."

Gordon arrived with a diminutive girl in a skirt-and-sweater set. Grey embraced her without ado. She sparkled with relief in his arms, shy and bridelike; Grey had that effect. Her bob, the shade of dull fallen leaves, framed a face with buttonish brown eyes and rather marsupial cheeks. Elsa, rising from the table to be introduced, towered a head over her.

"She's mousy," she said to Flavia, years later. "She's dull as ditch water."

"Nonsense. She's a nice English-Canadian girl of a certain type," returned Flavia. "You just don't belong in the Junior League and she does."

She thought Gordon looked doctorish, with that inscrutable expression doctors put on to shield themselves from their patients. His gaze had a film over it as though he were looking at the world through thick lenses, although in fact his vision was perfect. People often thought he wore glasses when he didn't.

They had medallions of beef and a bottle of Drambuie. Grey offered the toast.

"To the happy young couple, Gordon and Nell. My fatherly blessings upon you both, and may the wind be always at your backs."

"*Sláinte*," muttered Dai.

"*Sláinte.*" They brooded, and drank.

The orange-gold liquid slipped around the bottom of the bell, leaving an oily residue. Elsa swallowed. Its descent seemed to outline various parts of her anatomy. She made a face and put the glass on the cloth. The brandy lingered in her mouth, fiery and pungent, with an overlay of oranges. Trinity winked at her. *The dirty rascal,* she thought, *not even the grace to look ashamed, with his hand down my dress.*

"Like it?" he asked, possibly wondering how she kissed when drunk.

"It burns awfully. It's rather attractive, though."

"Sure is."

She finished it.

Gordon seemed lonely, not because of his expression but because of the way he sat in a little cloud without saying much. His eyes met Elsa's and he smiled genuinely, then became vague and clouded again. He wore the chloroformed look of the male who is biding time until he can decently leave. Few words passed between him and his beloved, yet they seemed already a unit, tethered with some invisible last as tough and flexible as the new plastics. He was alone, but he had Nell. Gordon, remote and upright, facing his private disappointment with Nell at his side, leaving for the Old World and his own life.

I'm the only one here he can stand except for her, thought Elsa. It was why there would be only the one evening with him. The realization was so spontaneous she nearly sputtered into her brandy.

Her father's voice projected over the general conversation. It was a beautiful voice; she had never realized how beautiful. It was a little too dry to be plummy which made it lovelier and more real. . . . "One of us will be up tomorrow with George's mare. Let him know, will you?"

"Good sir," said Trinity. "I will."

The bottle was going around.

"Valkyrie," said Dai with a sly grin. "What a name."

"She's an awful pig to ride," said Trinity.

"A veritable iron maiden," said Grey. "Wouldn't stand still for the stud. I'd half a mind to turn her out with the herd and let him roll over her like a locomotive, but he gave her a clout and that finished her."

They laughed.

"Aye, he's a bright one and no mistaking," said Dai. "Knows his job."

Nell blushed, which made her look livelier and more accessible. Sno-Bird sat impassive, eyes moving over their faces as though memorizing them. She never looked at Grey but seeing his coffee cup was empty made a majestic sign to June to bring the pot to the table.

Elsa drank off her second brandy.

". . . shooting anymore. I'll miss that." It was Gordon, making his confidential farewell. He smelled of aftershave. This close, his gaze was clear. "D'you still hunt, Els?"

"Not much this year," she said. Her lips felt rubbery. "Grey goes when we need game. Ever since that thing happened he's only let me go where the shot can be heard."

"Take care of him, will you?" he said. "Sometimes I think he needs it."

"Grey?" She smiled at the thought. "Harris takes care of him."

"That nigger." His eyes went blank, the lapis lazuli frosted over. "They're getting into the schools down there. The blacks. They're trying to pass a court injunction to integrate."

She drew in a wobbly breath. "Gordon, how in hell can you use that word?"

He looked annoyed. No, more than that. His face was pinched and bleak.

"I know what I'm talking about," he said sharply. "Your language, Elsa—"

"You don't know anything, you effing prig. Sewer inhabitant. *Your* language." She was trying to get up, she was weeping. From a distance she heard the clang of a chair going over. The dishes were rocking on the tablecloth, flatware cascading into glasses, the smell everywhere of fire and sour fruit.

"*Whoa, whoa,* hold on." Trinity, startled and laughing.

"Look, Elsa—"

She tumbled forward as the table raced at her.

Chapter Thirty-seven

"YOU SEEM TO HAVE NO IDEA what constitutes enough drink," said Grey. "I wonder where that comes from."

She plucked at the sheet. Her father shifted his weight on the bed.

"What on earth happened? One moment we were all happy and together, the next you'd fainted. Where was young Trinity?"

"I don't know. Nothing happened, really. I just got dizzy." She spoke ponderously as though he were being dense. Her eyes looked heavy but he didn't think she had been crying.

He sighed, thinking of the horses. They were so much easier to deal with than his children. "How much did you have to drink?"

"A couple of glasses. The bottom, you know. Not all the way up."

"Of course not. You'd be sick as a cat if you drank that much."

"It was awfully strong."

"Brandy is. I should have been watching you. Every time you drink something happens. I hope you don't drink when you're out on those dates. Do you?"

"Never."

"Well, that's good," he said. "Somehow I can't see you fainting. You've always had a good head."

"Maybe on top of the ice cream and steak. I feel fine now. Really."

"I'll be in the yard if you need anything," he said, and left.

Elsa went downstairs in jeans and a shirt and made a sandwich in the kitchen. She really did feel fine. Outside the windows, the trees were making a shivery green papyrus sound. The drive looked dampish so it must have rained again, though the midmorning sun was bright and warm. She couldn't remember much of last night after she had been revived and given some coffee. Her father had driven them home, and she had fallen asleep on the way.

A kind of irritable rage returned when she thought of Gordon. She remembered the exchange perfectly. How dare he talk about Harris that way, or any black person. Black people lived under the umbrella of her protection because of Harris. They could be in the schools, they could do anything they bloody wanted.

She wondered whether she and Gordon would ever meet again without hostility. He was lost to them all, gone to England with Nelly or whatever her name was to become a conservative creature who worried about his practice and money, the fundamental decency that had seemed part of him lost forever on the long, flattening train trips over the plains from city to city. He had gone, leaving a gaping tear to be filled, and she didn't know what to fill it with.

Sod him, she thought.

She stood at the veranda door in her bare feet and wolfed the sandwich. In the yard the Georgewoods' horse trailer was hitched to the back of the truck with the gate down. Harris, wild-eyed and with his hair ruffled into spongy points, sat in the cab with his legs in the door, staring out at the east wood.

She put on her moccasins and went down to the stable.

"He's taking George's mare back," said Grey. "She's bred."

"Can I go?"

"Ask him. Though I don't think he's in the mood for company." He used a comb on his hair, then sounded amused. "He was out all night."

Elsa felt a drag of fear, the first since she had known she would have Harris. Out all night where?

She got in the passenger seat. Harris looked startled.

"I'm coming with," she said airily.

There was just enough gold in his eyes to give them some warmth. He used a comb on his hair, then got out and slammed the door. She waited while the mare was inspected and loaded into the trailer, hearing the men's voices thin out on the Sunday mountain air.

"Please thank Bronwyn for the eggs," said Grey through the window. "I forget what we had with them."

"An omelette, I think. Mushroom," she said.

"Don't drink anything but tea or Coke," he said, smiling.

Her color changed, but she said nothing.

They rolled down the highway. Elsa fished a cigarette from the pack on the seat and lit it, blowing smoke nervously.

"Sometimes he talks to me as though I were ten," she complained.

"You're not, are you," he said woodenly.

"No." Her hand crept along the seat.

"Don't."

His voice was harsh, but a bronze note trembled in the bottom of it. Desire was a pool of sensation at the base of her spine, a sharp warmth spreading from there to her breasts, her moistened armpits. The countryside was already blurring, as though her eye were a camera lens that focused on a single object and edited everything else out. She closed her eyes, slumped against the window, and let the wind take her hair.

They took the road around Lake Endeavour, driving first through the straggling settlements north of Four Queens, then beside the forest and meadows of the provincial park, marked with blue metal signs. He drove faster than usual, pushing the vehicle with a leaden foot, keeping an eye on the rearview mirror and the contents of the trailer. His mouth was too full to form a tense line, but there was a grim look about its usual soft shape.

"Suppose they ask us to lunch?" Elsa asked apprehensively.

He snorted. "They won't. Know what I like about you St. Oeggers? You're so goddamned unworldly."

"Really?"

He slowed for a curve. "How many times have you been with a man?"

"Once," she said, sounding surprised, as if he should have known. "A boy rather. A college boy in my art class."

"When?"

"In April. We went to his room. It smelled like mildewed boots and milk left out to sour and there was a hot plate on the bookcase. We had to clear books and laundry off the bed so we could lie down."

"Not Georgewood?"

"No, not him. He wore a safe—the boy, I mean. He looked so funny trying to get it on. I think he knew what to do, but that was about all. I didn't really feel much, just drippy." She gave a deep chuckle. "He thought I was another college student. He was horrified when he found out I wasn't even sixteen. Rushed me to the door almost gibbering, he was so anxious to get rid of me. What a fool. I'd have had my tongue cut out rather than tell. Even Fi doesn't know."

"It was bad loving," he said happily.

"It isn't that way with you," she said in a doleful voice. "You fill me up.

Between my legs, and all up inside, so warm, and my mouth, and everything. Even my breasts feel filled up when you love me, like cups instead of mounds. My mind is filled, my stomach is filled." She shivered. "O I feel sorry for you that you're not a woman; I grieve for't. What a loss it must be, not knowing the loveliness."

"The good part is causing it." He cleared his throat to get rid of the gravel. His voice got hoarse when he was aroused. It had embarrassed him more than once.

"Please," she said, as though she wanted candy, but that piece of candy was a matter of life and death.

"Stop keening," he said, "or I won't be able to get out of this truck."

She stopped, and they drove in silence. They turned onto a side road and drove beneath the woodburned sign that read: WANDA CREEK RANCH, G. GEORGEWOOD, PROP.

"I'm sorry you missed Trinity," said Mrs. Georgewood while the mare was being led to her stall. "He and George went to Lockerby to look at a tractor."

Bron Georgewood was dangerous. Bron Georgewood could penetrate to their desire where a father or brother would not. Standing hugging herself, shoulders hunched a little though the sun was hot, Elsa shifted her moccasined feet and scratched her elbow, and was glad she hadn't brushed her hair before getting out of the truck.

Harris came out of the barn looking his surliest, backed the truck into the parking area and detached the trailer from the hitch.

"I would ask you and Mr. Harris in for a cup of coffee," said Mrs. Georgewood, "but I have to go out myself."

"I don't think he planned on staying," Elsa returned.

They drove sedately down the drive and under the sign.

"She says she's leaving," said Elsa. "She'll be right after us."

"The hell she will," he said.

They turned onto the main road and the truck roared into life. The landscape revved up and shot past like a speeded-up film reel. At the junction Harris turned right instead of left and drove toward the park with the speedometer needle climbing. Somewhere between the junction and the park she put her hand on his thigh, feeling it flex when he changed pedals. He made a nearly inaudible sound and moved it between his legs.

He found a service road and drove down it for a half mile, then turned onto a dirt trail. The trail seemed to end in a grove of trees, spreading wide and shade-making on old river sand. They made for it, leaning forward eagerly with lips parted and faces frozen in anticipation. The truck bounced and clawed at the rutted pumice; deadwood crackled; sprays of fallen foliage snapped under the tires. They pulled beneath the drooping green fringes of the trees, whose roots flowed through a ground fall of drift like crocodiles in a pond, and stopped. He cut the engine, set the hand brake and took her in his arms.

There was no room to lie down, but for the moment they were unable to move. They kissed as though they were inhaling a lifesaving draught, eyes closed and their features distorted with heavenly pain.

The ground was dry in patches. They got out of the truck and looked for a smooth place among the roots. Harris got a blanket from behind the seat and they lay down on it. They crushed the leaves like rolling pins with their backs and behinds and knees; the stiff curled edges left points on the naked flesh that strayed from the blanket.

"Is this what you want?" he ground out, the silver chain trickling on her breast like a rivulet of water. "Is this it?"

"No. Yes. Oh, Harris."

"Fucking little bitch." He kissed her and went into her. Her legs were long and white alongside his before she drew them up; the fine-boned feet stayed turned out, the toes spread in pleasure.

They lay and listened to the birds. She sat up, eeled out of the wrinkled shirt and said calmly, "Next time I'll wear a sweater."

He wanted sleep. Repose was the great gift sex gave men. He dozed with his hand on her ass, thumb cradled in the silky crease where it started to flare out. The sun came down through the trees and warmed their backs.

Elsa blinked, sat up yawning and rose to walk under the trees, close to the trunks where the oldest branches spread like fans above the ground. She prowled in a circle, frowning at the prickles under her bare soles, then squatted and urinated. He lay watching her, aroused by seeing a woman urinate, her dreamy look of relief, the leaves shining. He wanted to put his hand there and feel the last drops beading in fur the shade of a thrush's wing.

She came back scuffing up leaves and stood over him.

"Don't call me a bitch again," she said, stringing every word out.

"Get down here."

She got down. "I mean it."

"I won't, baby," he whispered. "I promise."

They dressed reluctantly among the quiet trees and bird rustlings, in air luminous with afternoon sunshine. He tucked in his shirttail, sat in the door of the cab and drew her toward him. She stood between his legs like a child being called to account.

"I wish we could stay here forever," he said.

"We can," she said calmly. "You'll never have to give me up. We'll talk to my father and get married."

He shivered. "I don't think this is in his plans."

"It won't matter. He thinks you're a Nubian warrior."

"A what? You don't know anything," he said harshly. "I'm not asking Grey."

She shrugged. "Do as you like." She turned to wiggle her feet into her moccasins.

They drove back down the trail and out of the park.

"You think the sea's going to part for you because you found out about fucking," he said. "It makes things more complicated, not less."

"Do you love me." She was winding the loose hair on top of her head, a supply of hairpins from the glove compartment tumbled in the fold of her legs. The hair was coming down as fast as it went up.

He pulled off the road. The last houses were behind them. He held her face in his hands. The bones were fragile, the eyes had a wild look. The hair grew prettily around her temples.

"I can't live without you."

"That day at the station," she whispered. "I watched you waiting for me to come out—for me!—and it was as if I'd never seen you before. You were always just Harris until that day. Then suddenly you were a man, with a soul, and a body. Does it always happen to women, I wonder? When they want the man do they see his soul at the same time?" She raised his hands to her lips and solemnly kissed both palms.

"I don't know," he answered, dazed. He had never had his hands held and kissed in his life.

He started the engine and pulled back on the highway. Remorse would come later. All he wanted now was to avoid detection. He was the post-release warrior, watchful and quick and muscular again, because safety was foremost in the jungle.

"I'd no idea lovemaking was so wonderful." Elsa sighed and stretched like a lioness beside him. "I couldn't see what the fuss was about the first time. You wanted me, didn't you? The night I came to your room."

"I wanted you," he said.

"It seemed almost incestuous, you know?" she reflected. "When I realized I loved you. Then I saw how right it was."

"How was that?"

"Because we started our lives here together," she said impatiently. "Sitting alone and frightened in that kitchen, hardly able to speak. Our mending process began here under the same roof. That's why."

"I was not frightened."

"You were hungry and frightened." She sighed again contentedly. "Then you weren't hungry anymore. How I stared at your woolly hair and that terrible scar. Fi kept pinching me under the table to stop me goggling. My father made friends with you and you started to feel safe. You found that man at the Bluffs. You acknowledged me when I was surrounded by my judges."

And he had done it with no more than a smile, admitting her to his dark fraternity; a young girl.

"If he'd been alive you would have finished him off. You would have crushed his throat with your foot."

Her words seemed to move in the air around them like music from some strange, simple instrument. He pulled into a turnout and kissed her again, holding her in the curve of his arm, dying to hold her forever.

"Maybe I would have," he said. "For Grey, not you."

"What difference does it make?" Her voice dropped to a whisper. "*It makes no difference.* Ah, your lips are so soft and full, my love. They're speaking when we kiss, telling me everything about you. How you'd like to break me in pieces and grind up my bones because you don't like feeling the way you do about me. Aye, that's the part of you that's dangerous. You might do some dreadful wild thing out of't, like leaving us. If you left I don't think I could bear it. But your kiss is so sweet I know you'll stay. I mind how I found you wandering out on the moor one night—or were we both wandering?—and came on each other's fairy lights in the dark."

"Fairy lights?" He snorted. "You sure like to talk, girl."

He got out of the pickup and walked to the edge of the turnout. Beyond the pass the woods billowed like the green rim of a volcano around the lake. The lake was glassy and contained; the Enid behind them spread untamed in oxbow bends and irregular wooded sloughs over the floodplain.

The road was empty except for a red station wagon making for the pass. He could already pick out the wood slats on the sides.

He looked back at the truck. She was sitting framed in the window with that smile on her lips. He wanted to love her again, kick his jeans off and sit her on his lap while she breathed that warm girl's breath on his cheek.

He pictured Piwonka roaring by, the look on his face when he saw her with her wild hair curtaining him, riding him like a pony in a point-to-point.

"Let's move," he said, getting in and starting the engine. "Piwonka's on his way past here."

She pouted. "Such a shame."

"Fix yourself up. You look like you just got out of bed."

"I'll wave at him," she said, and giggled. "You can wear your usual sour face."

Chapter Thirty-eight

HE BEGAN A SERIES OF DREAMS, which lay in wait for him two or three nights a week and projected themselves on the walls of his sleep. They featured different segments of his life so far. His mind made commentary on them from the distance of years.

One night he was back in jail.

lying on the bunk reading a book. He didn't know what had made him want to see the printed word. The book was Alice in Wonderland, *which for some reason was in a box of stuff donated by some group.* Alice in Wonderland *in the joint. He had taken it because of the pictures. By the time he finished it he knew that reading was the way to stop his mind from running. It was a silly book, but he was concentrating on what went on in it, not the sweaty desperation in his head. It wasn't what happened to you that fucked up your life, it was the way you handled it inside. He had not known that before. Books were his first clue, his Underground Railroad to freedom.*

Before that he was in the hole for stabbing a pimp with a piece of glass for putting the make on him. They thought they could mess with him because he was young, fuck him over. Well fuck them in the ass. Blood all over the fucking place. Scalp wounds bled bad. Then they'd stuck him in this cell with a rusty-headed honky with blue eyes they called the Dago. He was sure they'd been put in there together so they could kill each other. The prison was unofficially segregated, blacks and whites automatically paired up to keep things peaceful. He was no more like the other blacks than the Dago was like other whites. Most of the blacks were okay. There were a few sharpies, razor-scarred and crazy as shit, a few killers. Most hadn't done anything but get hooked on heroin or been in the wrong place at the wrong time, something he knew all about now. Some of the junkies were musicians in there for using. When they tried to get him to hang out with them he would drop into polite well-bred West

Indian. It put them off. They laughed, but they knew when they weren't wanted.
They had learned to read those signs early. They left him alone.

The Dago told him in a croak as rusty as his hair that they were in a separate
cell because they were under twenty-one. Way under. Too bad for one of the juvie
places, too young to be in the pen with the others. He shouldn't have been in that
cage with the pimp, said the Dago, but he'd done good. That was the way the Dago
talked. The Dago bragged on his first kill, wanted to hire himself out to the mobsters.
Harris used to lay in bed at night afraid that this was what he could look forward to
being.

When the visitor was announced he laid the book aside and slouched off the bunk,
hard and composed, a man who had lost inexperience for all time. The visitor wore
a uniform with a crust of decorations on the front. Only someone important could
have gotten away with wearing a fucking general's uniform or whatever it was into
the joint. Glen Miller wire eyeglasses, short hair that curled the way white men's hair
curled, like they had a finger in an electric socket, blind eyes like a lawyer's, scruti-
nizing without letting you in. That was what he saw.

A guard waited outside the cell. The visitor introduced himself. He ignored Harris's
hostility, just gave him a piece of newspaper.

"I thought this might be you."

He took it. The clipping was brittle and tan with age. Newsprint has a short life.
It was a photo of a man jumping a horse over a hurdle, the shot taken from below
so the horse's body arched dramatically across the lens. Horse and rider were etched
against the sky. The caption gave his name and the horse, Strider, at a competition
in New York. Owner, Juliette Treat.

In the dream (lying uneasily asleep in the turret room), he held the scrap of print
and thought how she had been nothing to him. She was a woman he worked for, a
middle-aged woman. His life was a hallway in a haunted house, too narrow for
company; she was one of the ghosts who came and ultimately went as he passed one
door after another in his slow tramp toward an exit. She was a drifting white face
along the way. Now (in the dream) he knew her. A Jewish woman, haggard and old
before her time. She spoke good English with an accent. Her father had taught dressage
at a cavalry school in Austria. Skin the shade of palm driftwood, chain-smoked, voice
like a Cat Cay dockworker, she could ride. She had taught him equestrianship, using
words like principles, *and* elements, *shouting them across the ring over the clip of*
hooves and slap of leather. She was literally the first human being he knew who didn't
care what he was or where he came from. He was used to being identified so that he
could be ignored or feared, all measurements being taken within the context of race.
But she ignored America. She viewed life through a different glass, a mirror tarnished
by history. She was from someplace else, a Europe he would never see. He never saw

her eat an American hamburger or drink a Coke; she brewed Darjeeling, ate dry toast or herrings or noodles out of packets. She did not come from what he knew, and this had made him free.

She told her story in casual bits and pieces over nearly a year, until he realized he was hearing fabric being woven, the screech of thread, the give of the last. It was a story of borders, jewels sewn into skirt hems and trouser cuffs, a death in a boarding-house, lying under shrubs while boots marched past, going without food for days except for pig swill. A gun thrown down on a dirt road. A helmeted boy dangling upside down in a tree with blood draining out of his throat. He listened to the dead of Europe speak for the first time in history, saw the masses of Europe pouring over the plains in movietone black and white like the cattle in Red River, the tribes that were not of Ham, their misery and toil given voice while he was still tongueless.

Take this, she said, and gave him the medal and chain. It spilled into his palm. The medal was copper chased with silver, engraved with a man carrying a child on his back. He didn't know who the man was. This belonged to someone I knew once, it will give you luck. But you must not take it off, she said. Harris never had, until he came here. It was locked up in the warden's office.

He handed the paper back.

"That's me."

"I watched you ride in that competition. I had no idea you were so young." The lenses flashed like twin mirrors, checking the thing on his face with its look of bad healing. "Would you like to come out for an afternoon? It can be arranged."

What did this ofay want? Two hours in a hotel room? He still thought like the junkie whore he had been, what seemed like a lifetime ago. Well, not this time. He was done taking it in the ass.

He never knew how it happened, just that the man was a trustee and on the parole board. A West Point graduate and silver spoon who had Harris picked up and driven to lunch in a shirt and slacks lent by the warden, where he stood surrounded by roses, indifferent. He knew all about rose gardens, two-acre lawns, fine big houses, stables full of Thoroughbreds, elegant women like the one he was introduced to, who gave him a frozen smile and repeated his name through lips that hardly moved. Not a nice polite nigger who answered when spoken to but a black boy half crazy with hate who didn't bother to hide it. Bet the General had a hell of a time explaining hisself in the bedroom that night.

The dead head lolled in the backseat under the hickories in the grove, the stocking buried deep in the neck. Even though he had never seen it, he went over and over it in his mind. It was a spell that had been put on him, obeah, witchcraft; even he believed at times that he had done it. The voodoo men (smelly and white, with faces like roots) by their belief in his murderous lust had turned him, an ordinary boy with a boy's foolishness and pride, into the mythic oily savage.

And yet there was that in him that was chivalrous in a way they would never be, one immemorially known by the voodoo men who had wandered far and now could not return, panicked at the sight of him who had never left.

Why would a rich man want to subject him to lunch in his house, not knowing if he knew a salad fork from a dinner fork, or if dining with the white man could be a form of torture? He'd taken out his manners and used them. His Barbados aunt used to rap his knuckles with her knife, Sunday dinners. Napkin spread on his lap, peanut-headed boy with eyes sliding. His lips moving, saying his prayer in front of the shining silver.

Now, in the dream, he saw that manners had meant nothing that day. The General's invitation reflected the indifference to color and class that marks a certain type of man, the man who prizes ability over his own superiority. He could have come in a loincloth and sucked the butter off his fingers and it would have been fine, because Clarence Westbrook had been in the stands the day of the New York competition.

"You have an accent," said Westbrook. "How long have you been in this country?"

"Since I was twelve," he said. "How about you?"

Westbrook took him to the stables to look at the horses. He had a beautiful, aloof black gelding brought out. The horse eyed them distantly. Harris stroked his neck, as bright as satin funeral ribbon; he spoke sweet words. The dogs nosed under the borrowed trousers and sniffed his ankles until a groom pulled them away. The horse glared like a grand dame through an eyeglass, then dropped his muzzle into his cupped hand, nosed around his chest for a treat.

"I'm amazed," said Westbrook. "That horse doesn't make friends with anyone."

He had given the gelding two lumps of sugar and more words, then saddled him. They rode down a long avenue through a plantation of beautiful hardwoods. He was transfixed by the smell of fresh air and the clipping of hooves, riding through a covered bridge toward a circle of sunshine. The best part of the afternoon hadn't been the horses; horses were always with him in a way. It had been being free of the colorlessness of the joint, the smell of canned vegetables and urinals, the continual coughing and yelling and snoring and farting of dozens of men living crammed together.

"If you stay away from drugs there's a job waiting for you here when you get out," said Westbrook. "A horseman of your caliber will work as long as there are horses to ride."

A thin warmth trickled through his icebound soul at the offer of a job. But in spite of the horses, he didn't want to work for this man. He couldn't work for a white man again. Not yet. Because who else could he work for; who but the white man?

His cellmate greeted him with a sneer, jealous of the favor he'd been shown. The kid didn't mind bunking with Harris, even seemed to kind of like him. They called the kid the Dago because he used knives. He told Harris he was Boston Irish, and he could use a knife better than any wop.

"Call me one thing," said Harris, "and I'll poke the eyes right out of your head."

"Yeah, fucking sir," said the Dago with his lewd, loony grin.

"I am no friend of yours, white motherfucker."

They seemed to get along okay.

He woke. It was raining again. He lay listening to the patter broken by occasional gusts, and wondered why these people not only crossed his life but seemed to wallow in it. Why he always seemed to be looking into their lives instead of his own, learning them instead of himself. Juliette Treat, he thought. Clarence Westbrook. Grey. Now a girl who tried to make him forget the color of the skin she kissed, whose color, hair and nails and belly, was not his own earth shade.

Harris packed his gear for the shows: breeches, riding jacket, shirts and stocks, extra boots. In the back of the chest of drawers, when he lifted out his socks and underwear, was the drawing she had made of him. He pinned it up next to the mirror scattered with silver shot. He wanted to see it before he went. She had made this thing of him. Oils from her fingers had seeped into the paper, her breath had charmed the soft tooth. He still felt incredulous when he looked at it. It wasn't just the resemblance, which was perfect. He admired that as he would any work well done. It was the revelation, penciled and stroked in, that fascinated him: of the surly, hopeful, sinning, intelligent, suspicious, yearning self, the man he was. Lonely. A man of slowly growing thoughts. The eyes weighty as stones, saying how tired you could get of the eternal struggle to be a good man, what a relief it would be to let go and sink into the bad. That was why he had put the drawing away, afraid to let anyone see it. She had transcended his silence and guile and dug into him like a gardener with a trowel, uprooted him and planted him on paper.

She served at tea. If she felt guilty over their wrongdoing she made no sign of it. It was hard to believe she had lain with him under those trees. "Ah, god," she had said, and cried out beneath him. He knew that desire was a river inside her, a sweet deep delta. But the look on her face when they were alone was not the long face she had on now as she slid the soup bowls into place.

Her braided hair was pinned in a coronet around her small skull. It was hot in the kitchen; she was flushed, her forehead baby-damp. Outside the sun hung in a smoke of storm-drained clouds edged with tinsel. When she reached over his shoulder with the platter his nostrils took in the essence of her underarm. He wanted to press his mouth to the damp cloth, breathe it in drunkenly.

Then they were in the yard.

"Don't you ever think about *him*?" he muttered.

She was going over the chestnut with the scissors, removing excess whiskers and hairs, while he rubbed blacking on the hooves.

"Grey? No, why should I?" she said, snipping.

He struggled for words. "It's disloyal."

"Why? He's my *father*. What we do in bed has nothing to do with him." She moved around to the same side and stood with her legs touching his back. He heard her giggle over his bowed head.

She was right as far as she went. When he wasn't so dead set on getting her alone that nothing else mattered, he knew this. Children owed parents no loyalty in bed. Maybe it was the way in families; every loyalty was owed but that. He was the one who had sworn fealty to Grey, a man not of his blood. It was his allegiance, not hers, that Grey demanded.

They loaded the horses last. Harris was driving Piwonka's station wagon, filled with cases and tack, the trailer hitched behind it with Riot and Sizzle aboard. Dai had the second trailer carrying Petronel and Lord Edgeware. His face was a wizened apple through the Buick windshield.

Grey leaned in the window. "I hope Daithi watches his drink, at least at the wheel."

He didn't need to say more. Harris would take care of Dai.

They left the yard, the snugged gate bolts tittering and the tires squeaking on the gravel. At the bend into the trees he looked in the rearview mirror and saw Grey still standing in the drive. He was smiling like some lord, and his bare head gleamed like polished straw.

Chapter Thirty-nine

WHILE HARRIS AND DAI WERE GONE, Sno-Bird's son Javier rode to Salthill on his bay cob every morning to help feed and muck out stalls. He brought weather reports gleaned from his one passion, ham radio, and dispensed them morosely with dinner.

"Storm coming down from the Yukon. They're having a hot wet summer up there. Plenty mosquitoes."

Grey and Elsa schooled the horses who were trained to the saddle. They lunged the younger ones, standing in the center of the ring with a long pointer while the colt walked or trotted in a circle at the end of a lead. If the colt started to drift toward the center, the tip of the pointer was used to touch him gently back onto the periphery. They helped Javier with chores when they had time, groomed the saddle horses and checked their hooves. There was a slow stream of buyers, generally arriving unannounced and remaining for dinner as was the custom. Grey sold two green colts to an American broker and two young broodmares to Menard, the bloodstock agent. Gordon's mare Zuleika delivered a late stillborn foal with the cord around its neck, putting Grey out of humor. He hated losing a foal. A flurry of mares came to the stud from farms in Williams Lake, Gold Bridge and Lac la Hache. The mares stayed in boxes in the stable, waiting to be declared bred before their owners fetched them home. A couple from Victoria, looking for a jumper for their daughter, bought one of the geldings destined for auction.

In the mornings Grey emerged from the house in riding clothes, his old hat on at an angle, ready to work. He ignored heat, flies and the rain squalls that came after hours of torpid humidity and hurled through the valley with the force of important storms. The fields sprang green and furred after them. Home pasture and the riding ring gave birth to ponds that had to be ne-

gotiated on horseback or slopped through in Wellingtons. The truck tires
gouged long runnels in the wet silk of the drive.

Elsa sat at tea in the afternoons with a listless, abstracted air.

"Your hair's in a tangle," said her father. "You're letting yourself go again."

She squiggled her shoulders.

He would have to speak to Daisy about Elsa. He had the horses to deal
with, after all, and they were trouble enough.

On clear evenings Elsa sat on the veranda with her legs hanging over the
basket chair and read. The windows were thrown open to the sky, and she
often abandoned her book to moon over the valley and its sharp blue ridges.
She vibrated for Harris. His phantom roamed the house, slipping from one
room to another, always just ahead of her. She dreamed of his room, which
she had never seen before this summer but which drew her now like a secret
cove filled with treasure—his furniture, odor, boots, clothes; the quilt on the
floor, another sea but a warm one, ruffled by full and slivered moons. Shaving
things on the washstand. Books, she had not realized how many, piled on
the chairs. The foxed mirror in which her own reflection, watery and stained
with liverish macula, saw itself briefly. White, with used mouth, triumphant.

Her father returned from a trip to town looking businesslike.

"I'm sending you to Flavia for a few days," he said. "You look as though
you need a rest."

"I don't," she said crossly. "I feel perfectly well. I'd rather stay here."

"Daisy will be there. I've just spoken to her. Come now, you'll have a
good time."

"There's too much to do."

"Your well-being comes before work. You'll be leaving for the university
in three weeks and I can't send you off in this state. You'll be a comfort to
Flavia; Charley's busy and you can amuse her while she's waiting for the
baby."

"Flavia never needs to be amused," said Elsa.

She packed without interest. She was familiar with her father's methods
and knew she would be subjected to a kindly but firm working-over in
Penticton. She would return no longer chewing her hair, in her bag a pancake of pressed powder in a tortoiseshell case, gift of Daisy, a rosary of ha-
zelwood beads, gift of Iseult.

Even the prospect of seeing Flavia failed to cheer. She was doomed to
spend her days with the wraith of Harris, distanced from everything that
wasn't Harris. Going to Flavia's meant not seeing him cross the yard or ride
against the trees even in her mind. She wanted him with a glow that left

her ashy and whitened outside, like the cindery leavings of a fire. Her sketch-pads and charcoals lay about unused because she lacked the experience to translate her woe onto paper.

She put out the lamp and composed herself for sleep. First she memorized the three times Harris had made love to her. Then she lay supine like a figure on a sarcophagus, legs straightened and hands overlapped on her breast, and stared up at the molded ceiling left by the Norwegian. In this pose, stream-lined for transportation, she awaited the return of Harris and the delightful equipment of love.

Grey went into the stud enclosure with a flake of alfalfa on the end of a fork: The door of the box had been left open so the Red could go in and out.

It was just after dawn. A fog rolled through the valley, edged with a skirt of wheat-yellow banded with green that was the seemingly roving plain beneath. From the far end of the enclosure the Red appeared out of broken patches of vapor. His head was high and his ears pricked sharply forward, not in inquiry but as if he strained to hear some message of vast, urgent importance to his brute self.

"Come on, you silly sod," said Grey, advancing with the alfalfa, which he intended to drop in the hay net in his box. It was easier to enter the box through the paddock than walk around to the entrance, which for some reason had been built inconveniently facing the east meadow.

The Red moved forward, body swaying, even the upraised tail flicking so the ends lashed his flanks. As he broke through the foam, the dew pearlized on his coat and flattened into damp striations. A few yards away the horse stopped and laid back his ears. He nodded his head as though in violent agreement, then swung it from side to side. This strange exercise could have been to enable him to see Grey clearly with both eyes, since horses had poor forward vision. While he paused, bemused at this thought, the horse bolted straight at him.

If it had been any other horse, Grey would have stood firm or stepped out of the way. Confrontations like this were nearly always a bluff. But this was the Red. Grey sprang aside and made for the fence. Hoofbeats poured in a closing thunder behind him. His imagination leaped ahead to the great chest slamming into his back, the hooves driving him facedown and sprawl-ing. Anticipation made the hair stand up on his neck. He simultaneously dived at the fence and was knocked violently forward, cracking his jaw on the post as he fell through the rails.

The horse swerved and galloped off, eleven hundred agile pounds of muscle and bone, tossing his head in frustration.

Grey got to his feet on the other side of the fence. The Red slowed at the end of the paddock, turned and headed back toward him. His head was outthrust, the lips were peeled away from his teeth in a simian grimace. The eye didn't roll like a grazing animal's, but stared instead with the fixity of a prey beast's. It was an intelligent and baneful stare, with a yellow luster to the iris.

Anger coursed through Grey like a lightning stroke, but he had worked too long with horses to indulge the adrenaline-induced rage that came after a close call. Fear was there too, but he ignored it. He reached between the rails and dragged the fork to him by the handle. The Red swerved and minced across his line of sight, tense as a rocket. The fixed eye seemed to expand and fill itself with his image, until he was looking into a mirror at his own dark figure.

Grey pushed the hay off the fork with his foot and stepped back through the rails.

There was no one about. The rolling fog brushed along the ground, vanishing when it encountered anything solid. Cold condensation dashed at his face. He walked forward with the tines jutting. The words came without reflection or intent. "Come here, you son of a bitch, and I'll ram this down your throat." As he said them a frisson of hatred went through him.

The Red whirled and bolted. Grey waited until the horse was nearly on top of him, when all he could see was the grimace and torn ends of mane skirling wildly against the backdrop of sky and fence. Then he stepped aside like a matador and jabbed with all his strength at the mad eye. As it swerved he smelled the strong horse fragrance radiating like heat from the steaming hide. Even the hooves of a horse had an organic odor, of clean saltless rock and desert plants. He managed to stay on his feet and hang on to the fork. A loud moan tore the fog. The Red swerved across the paddock with a laceration gleaming on his neck. In the only gesture of its kind Grey had ever seen a horse make, he came to a halt, craned his neck violently to one side, raised his foreleg and pawed at the wound like a cat trying to reach its face to clean it. The cry could have been air forced through his windpipe and out his mouth, creating that exhausted bray.

Grey licked his lips and stepped forward. *I've lost my head,* he thought distantly. He could feel the oncoming rage, majestic and uncivilized like the tantrums of his childhood. *"Come on."*

The Red lunged at him. The narrow snaking head was an elongation of the neck. The wound gleamed under his mane and wet its strands with darkening scarlet. Grey drove at the flying legs with the fork. The horse bounded to one side as though on springs, skidding in the strewn flake. Hay shot up like scraps of green sunlight. On the far side of the barn Sno-Bird's hens, flurried by the racket, squawked discordantly in their pen.

The Red swept around the paddock, then bolted out the open gate with his tail up and ran along the outside rails. Shaken, Grey stood gripping the fork and followed the horse's flight until it was swallowed in the smoke.

He saddled Jonquil after dinner and rode through the parkland along the river. He took the loaded Winchester along. Sanity had returned, and the kind of sensible compassion men have so often for animals, so seldom for their fellow men, but there was such a thing as prudence.

The fog had burned off and although the day was dull he could see across the range through the trees. The avenue was sodden, the lowland turgid and thick with white lilies and masses of purple-red stachys. Mosquitoes hovered in clouds over the standing water. He rode through a garlicky stink of vegetation, past rush-collared ponds, and crossed beneath the Bluffs to the lake. From there he searched the eastern fringes of the reserve. Piwonka's red barns grew larger as he made his way south, dropped down onto the flat, and rode past the remuda and a stock pen of heifers, buildings ringed with corrals and holding pens.

Piwonka's office was a pitchpine add-on to the barn. Like most big ranchers, he spent as much time in the office tending to paperwork as he did outdoors. Grey wouldn't have traded places with him. Marv was growing a paunch, the soft middle bulging over his belt.

"Come on in," said Piwonka. "How 'bout this weather?"

"Better than a drought," said Grey, brushing the dew off his hat.

"Depends. 'Thirty-five was like this, rain and floods most all year. I lost a hundred head of cattle alone in flooded rivers and that damned quarry. No feed crop, either; had to truck it in all winter. Took a real beating in the market."

"Think it'll be dry enough for a decent crop this year?"

"Better be. If it holds off a few weeks around harvest time, from August, first of September, say. Get some good sun and dry out the ground."

Piwonka gave him a mug of briny-looking coffee. Grey poured in tinned milk until it was the color of iron rust, added three spoonfuls of sugar and stirred well. He had drunk Marv's coffee before.

"The Red's run off again." He sipped cautiously. It was boiling hot.

"Why does Harris keep that brute?" snorted Piwonka.

He shrugged. "Because of the brute's ability, I suppose."

"The hell you say. Suppose he puts a hoof through someone?"

"I'll shoot him," said Grey without smiling.

"He's gone, ain't he? Harris."

"To the shows, with Dai helping. Though Dai hasn't earned his keep lately."

"Boozer." Piwonka wagged his leonine head.

They talked watersheds and drainage systems, the overflowing Enid, politics, stock and hay prices. Piwonka brought up the land offer.

"I'm pretty well fixed on you as a buyer, if you can stand the pain. I'm not sentimental about business or I wouldn't be where I am, but I like having you down the road. We can start negotiating next spring after the shipments go out, winter if things look good for the market. You'd have to drain that bottomland by the cedars though. It's pretty much gone to bog."

"It's sumpy." He didn't want to show too much interest. Marv was a businessman, as he had pointed out himself. It was good rich flat land, ideal for expansion. *I'll keep the cedar grove,* he thought. A vision came, briefly: a house in leafy shade, for Harris; the stream dammed, troughed and bound, flowing past his door. Grey was filled with a sweeping sense of order and comfort. "I'm working on a few ideas, Marv. I can't talk about them yet. By the end of summer I should know what I need to know. Anytime after that will be fine to go over options."

"Sure thing. Just don't let them put any phone lines up."

"Lines have to come through eventually."

"They can run 'em south of here on the government land. I want sky over my head, not poles and wires."

Grey rose and stretched his neck. "Thanks for the coffee."

"Javier says you're alone over there."

"Elsa's gone to Flavia's in Penticton for a few days. All I've got is the hope of an odd letter about the shows. He said he'd write."

Piwonka gave him a shrewd, comradely smile. "You think a deal of that boy, don't you?"

"He's turned out well," Grey said evasively.

"Nuts. You're as close to him as if he was your own son."

Grey chuckled. "He is. Had a dust-up with a lady in the Bahamas a few years ago."

"Get stuffed. I admit he turned out to be not so bad, once he got past his little problem with trying to kill people he don't like. If I did that, the Skillihawk'd be strewn with bodies."

"Marv, that red horse. Tell your men to give him a wide berth if they see him. I think he's gone loco. He could be dangerous."

"Okay," said Piwonka. "Maybe his bad spirit got into the horse, aye? Harris's? Left him and got into the horse."

Grey halted in the doorway. "For god's sake, Marv, you sound like an old Indian. You'd better get out of the mountains and move into town."

Chapter Forty

HARRIS HUNG OUT HIS RIDING HABIT and pressed his shirt and stock under a handkerchief. The motel manager brought a fan and plugged it in. It made a noise like a nest of stirred wasps, but the rotating warm air was better than the stagnant warm air.

"It's fair hot today." She wiped her forehead with an arm from which a swag of loose flesh dangled. "Riding in the horse show, aye?"

He was standing in singlet and trousers, sweeping the iron over the cloth, nosing the tip around the collar. She watched him put the iron on the soleplate and shake the cloth out, pick up the iron and finick delicately around the buttons.

"Where on earth did you learn to do that?" she asked, amused.

"In prison."

"Ooh!" She laughed heartily. "Goodness! You gave me a turn. Well, it's nice to know they teach people *something* useful in those places, isn't it?"

They were in the lower end of the province, out of the path of the rainstorms. He walked to the show grounds after dinner, over a country road and through a stretch of wild mustard to where the first buildings lay. The ring was nearly Olympic-sized, but the course was laid out tightly, the turf a dark ocean around an island of hurdles, broad jumps and walls decorated with green shrubbery. Harris paced off the course, gauging the number of strides his horse would take between each barrier and how handily they could manage a round. In a knock-down-and-out class the object was to jump clean without touching or knocking down a barrier, falling or having the horse refuse more than twice. Three refusals and the horse was disqualified. Some jumping classes were point-graded on form, some on speed. He planned strategies, speed versus horse versus ground between to be covered versus height versus type of barrier. He and Grey were both good at eyeballing a course, never needing to walk it over more than once, or watch the riders going before them to check how many strides they took between jumps.

He waited in the collecting ring with the other entries. He could feel glances through his black broadcloth jacket, like fingers touching his back. With the jacket he wore regulation-dress canary breeches and black boots, a black velvet-covered hard cap with fitted protective skullcap and chin strap. His shirt was patterned with small jumping horses and finished with a white stock. The scar on his face was shadowed by the beak of the cap.

He knew he was a strange sight, a black man in a formal English riding habit, mounted on a Thoroughbred jumper. At a racetrack stable he would have been taken for granted. In a show ring he was a curiosity.

One of the exhibitors, recognizing him from another event, saluted him with a gloved hand. Harris saluted back. His own hands were ungloved. A white pasteboard number had been fastened to his coat by the judge's assistant. The chestnut was polished like an apple. Harris had shampooed and thinned out his mane and tail, which shimmered loose and long, like a collection of silk scarves. He felt the horse's electric inquiry through the reins. *Where are we? Is this going to be all right?* He laid his hand reassuringly on the lean neck.

Grey had said once to a guest, "Jumpers are the most difficult of all horses to ride. They're independent, fastidious and full of all manner of quirks. Riding a racehorse is straightforward compared to getting a jumper over a hurdle it doesn't like. You school a racehorse to the barrier and make basic decisions—whether it needs the whip or sulks under it, whether it likes mud or hard track and so forth. Taking a jumper over a course is like performing gymnastic feats with six legs, on an animal capable of changing its mind at any moment. There's no such thing as a flawless ride under those circumstances."

A leathery Englishman drew alongside him. "Hullo, Harris, ready to trounce the competition again this summer?"

"I've got some good jumpers." Harris smiled at him. "Your gray doesn't look too bad."

"I'm devastated anyway. You'd win on a bloody mule running in the wrong direction."

"Stop shucking me," said Harris, amused.

The man laughed, showing long yellow teeth. "What does that mean in plain English?"

"It means you're being egregious."

Harris heard his number over the loudspeaker. He collected the chestnut, touched the visor of his cap and shot through the gate. In the ring the announcer's voice, thin as if on water, gave the horse's name, his name and Grey's, Salthill Farm, Four Queens, British Columbia. The stands fluttered with color and noise. He noted absently the mosaic of parked vans and trailers, blue-tiled stable roofs, blocks of yellow hay, clusters of wandering and seated brightly dressed spectators. There was the occasional gleaming dot of a horse being led or ridden through the colors. Three men in cowboy hats and pastel rodeo shirts were leaning on the fence near the gate, in an area shaded by some willows. As he came into the ring, he thought he heard a hoot of laughter. The ring was a lunar plain.

The chestnut screwed his head back and plunged with excitement. Harris cantered him in a circle to buy him time to calm down. They sped toward the first jump, a post and rails banked with brush. He let the chestnut look at it. Somewhere a band was tooting a Sousa march. He shut that out and focused on the ten feet before the jump. The chestnut's ears pricked forward, his attention complete. They rose over the rails in a smooth arc.

They were off, sweeping around the ring at a controlled gallop. With this horse, the chief goal was to maintain focus. Harris steadied him for each jump and the chestnut leaped cleanly off his hocks. Being still green in spite of having been schooled over similar hurdles at home, he tended to overestimate and leap higher than he had to. Harris knew there was a lot of clean air under his stirrups. But overjumping was better than hitting a pole, and by the time they were down to the last three jumps he knew that barring some scrape, the round would be clean. They cleared a snake fence and galloped past the stands, past people crowded along the rails. He stood in the irons as they came around the turn, floating above the buoyant, fleeing body.

Suddenly the chestnut shied violently beneath him. It was only by luck that Harris kept his seat. A wave of moans surged from the stands, sprinkled with laughter. It must have looked comic, that wild leap to one side.

They bolted around the turn. Harris brought the excited horse under control in a few strides. He spoke to him in a matter-of-fact tone and turned him to the next jump, a triple bar, as though nothing had happened. He was swept with a sudden passion for the huge frightened creature, who sought his assurance like a child blindly seeking the pressure of its parent's hand. Power flowed from his hands through the reins, steadying and comforting. The chestnut lengthened his stride with renewed confidence and skimmed over the triple bar. They cleared the last hurdle, a gate, and rode back into the collecting ring.

"Good on you," said the rider who had gone before him, with a nod of approval. It was a compliment either on the clean round or staying seated during that strange leap.

The three men he had noticed when he came in the ring were leaving the willow-shaded area. Harris turned the chestnut out of the gate and trotted into the grove, moving away from the grandstand, ducking his head as he passed under the weeping lances. When they came out into the sun he was in front of them. The chestnut blew down his nostrils and spun in a circle the size of a hat while Harris looked them over. All three faces were studiously blank.

In the cooling area he dismounted, loosened the girth and went over the horse's damp body, his mouth tight. There was a wheal on the loin behind the saddle area, the skin around it broken and crusted with a little drying blood.

Chapter Forty-one

THEY ATE DINNER IN FRONT OF THE STALLS, stale baloney sandwiches and Cokes, sitting on overturned buckets. Evening sun spilled like runny egg yolk over a different set of ridges.

"Someone clipped Riot with a piece of buckshot in the first round of the knock-down-and-out," said Harris.

"Jhasus. What kind of muck'd do that?"

Harris looked into the wizened face, amused. "Trashy white people," he said succinctly.

"Ah, them." Dai grinned. "What'll you do if you catch 'im?"

He mulled over the time-honored ways of getting even. "Maybe I won't."

"If ye get lucky, give them a salute for me. If ye get my drift."

A scattering of applause had accompanied him out of the ring. It had been a tough competition. Forty minutes later all but the chestnut and one other entry had been eliminated. Then the black horse with the white coronets had knocked a rail off a post and Harris had come back in for the ribbon, with the chestnut dancing and making a spectacle of himself, as Grey would have put it.

That night he dreamed he was being attacked by men with knives. Their acid spit pelted his face. A serpent writhed on the ground at his feet and he strove to lift it with both hands like a sword and strike back. It whipped out of his grasp and slid toward him with its jaws unhinged, baring ivory fangs. He woke with his heart banging in his chest.

It was a muggy night. Harris tossed back the tangled sheets, sat on the edge of the bed and lit a cigarette. Out the window, beyond parked cars and horse trailers, the countryside lay in darkness.

An hour, he thought, dragging the ache into his lungs with the nicotine. *Just an hour with you, girl.*

Maybe he hadn't lost Grey yet. He could marry her, do what she wanted and ask Grey for her. It could get him back to Grey. He and Grey would be partners, they would all live together in the castle. Or Elsa and him, in a house he would build above the meadows not far away. She was young, though, real young. She didn't realize what the race thing meant, even in this wilderness where hard work was the prevailing value and distinctions in caste or color were seen as faintly frivolous. But he was the only black man in the Skillihawk. The part where he told Grey about being in love with his daughter was a blank screen, with no picture or image to fill it. He had mistaken value for equality once before. His naïveté had nearly cost him his life.

What his mind couldn't make was the leap, like the black horse that afternoon, over the last set of rails, raised higher and higher over his conception of his life and their lives until he was too tired to clear it. It was the foreignness he couldn't get over, the Anglo-Saxon, stoic, sovereign people he had come to live with, with their teas and their food, their language that tinkled across the meadows like sheep bells at twilight, the dark furrowed mythical North they labored under. There had always been them on one side of a river and him on the other, standing there looking across, and seeing no reflection of himself on their faces or in the water that separated them. He smiled grimly into the dark. Marriage, merging with that baby-butt paleness, a life spent like an exotic in the Tower of London, caged and fed and far from the savanna; it was crazy to even think about it.

He put out the cigarette, rolled on his back and felt his cock. It stood up in his fist. He jerked off watching himself, hearing the rasp of his breath, the dry sound of the cock being worked. At the other end of the room the fan swished back and forth, still plugged in. A car horn sounded outside, like one always did at three in the morning, all over the world. The ecstasy was miserable, sweet buckshot rattling behind his eyes. The chestnut screamed in terror.

He slept uneasily.

stopped, and they were black. An old couple in a junked-up truck. They communicated with each other and him in the telepathic language of fugitives. First they rolled him in the back of the truck. Their faces were petrified wood, the woman's eyes stony with old grief. They began to pray out loud while they made him as easy as they could, calling on sweet Jesus to save him. The man hid him under empty feed bags, the woman added her cloth coat. He shivered so violently his teeth snapped and his body jerked. They drove through the night while he lay under the bags and coat, fainting over and over. They left him at a black hospital in another state. To go that long a way they must have had gas in the back of the truck. He didn't remember them stopping to fill the tank, only coming to at times and seeing the same starry night.

He woke in a green ward filled with black faces that stared tiredly away from him, people who pricked him with needles and made the bed under him. He was naked under the sheet, the bloody pants and shreds of shirt gone. His body was lacerated, bruised and swollen, violent purple, orange and rotten-fruit-yellow, his nose and ribs busted, a wrist broken. His belly and groin were crisscrossed with long red welts and thin gashes where the whip had cut through. They wet him down with rags soaked in cold tea. He sobbed with pain.

After they glued him together and set the broken wrist, they put a tube up him so he didn't have to pee. They held his head and dragged his mouth to a paper cup of medicine that tasted like puke.

One of the orderlies cleaned him up, swearing under his breath. Then he saw the man was weeping. He stared away from the filled-up eyes, stared up at a mustard stain in the ceiling where water had leaked, one rain. If he thought at all, the grinning white faces loomed like Halloween pumpkins. There was morphine for the pain, but not enough to blank them out. That came later, on the street. Plunge in the needle, yank off the stocking, weave and nod. Forget those faces, those blows.

The doctor came and stood over his bed, tall and thin and weary, with skin the color of dried orange peel.

Where do you live, son?

He didn't answer, just stared at the place on the ceiling.

I understand how you feel. The folks who brought you here didn't say either. Of course you can't go back. But you need some money, some kind of identity, to be able to move on. How old are you, son? Seventeen, eighteen? You can tell us. You're safe here.

Fifteen, he thought. I'm fifteen.

Chapter Forty-two

HE SOLD THE CHESTNUT TO AN AMATEUR rider eager to own a difficult horse.

"He'll be dragged all over the shop," said Daithi cheerfully. "There's nothing in that creature's brain but baked noodles."

"It's the Holyrood strain." He was going through the paperwork. "But they can jump all day and they're good at it."

Dai got drunk in Penticton and stayed in a fog of low-grade inebriation. Harris found two pint bottles of whiskey under the seat of the Buick and drained them into a ditch. He bought a six-pack of Molson's to help him taper off. The inside of the Buick stank of spilled beer and elderly, regretful male. He composed sandwiches on the tailgate.

"Jhasus," muttered the little man. "I can't stomach this pap. Gimme a whiskey."

"Eat," said Harris, standing over him.

"Jhasus." Dai chewed slowly, his face comic with revulsion.

At a show in Ashcroft they watched an RCMP exhibition: uniformed men in red and black in drill formation, the inside horses stepping in place while the outside horses fanned around them at a canter. The Maple Leaf fluttered and snapped over the lead horse. The air smelled like flowers, horse dung and roasted peanuts. A brass band played in a field nearby.

He went looking for a toilet and found two portable outhouses in a buckwheat field. It was deserted at the moment, and so quiet he could hear insects hopping. The door of one opened and a man stepped out, tucking the tails of a pink rodeo shirt into his jeans. When he saw Harris, he looked startled.

"You dumb motherfucker," said Harris, and punched him in the throat.

He made sure the man was down, then rolled him over and went swiftly through his pants. The buckwheat kissed his arms and sizzled like hundreds of tiny snare drums. There must have been a hawk over the field; as he flipped through the wallet he heard a shriek of torment, so distorted with pain and fear it was hard to tell whether a rat, bird or rabbit was being murdered. Driver's license, hunting license, entry ticket to a barrel-racing class that afternoon. Harris took the tickets out, tossed the wallet on the grass, and dragged him by the collar into the hazel shrubs behind the outhouse.

"I see your sorry white ass near a show ring again this season, I'm going to run a horse over it," said Harris. "Do you hear me?"

The man rolled his eyes, still gagging.

Harris yanked at the collar. The pearl snaps rippled open. He flicked out the knife and laid the dull edge of the blade at the man's throat. "You hear me."

"I . . . hear . . . you."

"Now get the fuck out of my sight."

He was back before the finale, slightly breathless.

"Did ye fall in?" asked Dai. "Yer durty-lookin'."

"You can stop watching for buckshot."

A smile flooded the old man's face. "Ah, ye've been at it again. Where's the famous shiv o' yours, now?"

Harris pulled it out of a back pocket and showed it on his flattened palm.

"That's the one you whittle with," said Dai.

"That's what it's good for," said Harris, putting it back.

They sat in a companionable silence and watched a riderless "freedom" horse jump over a tea table set for four, complete with thin sandwiches, teapot and china cups.

"Wonder how many o' those he scattered before he learned," mused Dai. "Annyhow, t'anks."

"For what?"

"Taking care o' me when I've had a drop too much. Yer not a bad one, fur a black."

He was still as a totem, eyes digging holes. "You sons of bitches just can't let anything get by, can you?"

"Don't take yerself so damn serious," said Dai. "I used to think you was a prig, bein' so tidy in yer ways and niver takin' a drink, and all. But you're more than that, arun't ye? Yer what th' English call a right boy. That's a wide boy, gone right. Ah shit, I'm tired with the week that was in't. All this rollin' on the road's makin' me sick as a damn cow."

They drove beside the Fraser, a gorge with the water rolling far below, clay streaked with tan froth. There were farms on the spacious banks, woodlands and violet mountains behind the fields. The air grew sharp. He smelled the sea.

They never talked about the sea, the St. Oeggers, even though they were an island people. They never talked about the sea, but their eyes brightened when it was mentioned. The old Irishman made a journey every year to the coast, to walk along the estuary and watch the tides suck in and out, and buy popeyed bass from the Salish fishermen to cook for his boardinghouse tea. He brought sightings to the table at Salthill and spread them on the cloth: moon phases and currents, salmon seiners, gale venues. Navigation by stars, without roads, across the heaving plain to Alaska and the Beaufort Sea. They listened with grave interest to the reports, broken with swallows and sips and chews. The words stung like poetry, a salt that abraded the mind.

Harris didn't give a damn about *his* ocean. His people had never worked it as theirs had. The sea had never been a thing to conquer, to come home from in triumph, in long boats broken by storms. If they had, it was lost in time. *Their* violence was still new, the blood was still fresh on their mouths. Who was the invader? He knew them. Their history had seeped into his bones, while his stayed secret, sealed in blockhouses on a different shore.

Vancouver clustered around the bay, a bunch of white, pink and buff boxes and sandstone towers. "Sure, with her harbor and buildings along the green shore, and her grand span o' bridge," said Dai when they stopped to sniff the air and relieve themselves. They wandered like buffalo through the waist-high grass by the road. Harris stood thinking deep things, looking seaward with a cigarette dangling from his lip while the mare whinnied down her nose in frustration at being locked in the trailer.

He left the horses at the fairgrounds with Dai and drove alone into the city. He walked streets crowded with sailors headed from the wharves, men in business suits and soft hats, gangs of tourists. Cars went past, their tires shushing like sprinklers hurrying over lawns. He passed Chinese women in flat shoes and midcalf tweed skirts. No ugly style of dress could rub out the allure of those downcast eyes, the neat graceful limbs. An air of tranquillity hung over the sidewalks.

He headed toward a tangle of ships' masts, looking down alleys with money in his wallet. There was no feel of a rough district even near the wharves. This wasn't America, with its relentless spawn of pirates and criminals, jackbooted and defending against all comers. It was a land of quiet people, industrious clean-living agrarians. The north wind ruffled everything into order here. Heat made you want to lie alongside a woman in a tropical funk or get in a fight. Across the quiet surface of the harbor, Russian freighters carrying wheat to Siberia jostled fishboats and luxury yachts for space like traffic in a rush-hour jam. A neon-lighted gas barge threw its cool salmon and blue light on the water. He walked restlessly along the harbor road, watching the sun turn the sea to tarnished plate. Asian markets appeared among the commercial buildings, warehouses and shipping houses. Down alleyways cobbled with bronze stone, bazaars offered bamboo furniture, rhinoceros horn for sexual luck, teak and jade.

He should have gone into one of the restaurants with red and gold marquees that cluttered the skyline along with poles, lines and rigs, where mahogany-glazed ducks hung in the windows. He should have eaten pork and jasmine rice out of blue-flowered bowls upstairs while the kitchens crashed, banged and shouted downstairs. Instead, he turned back to one of the English eating houses near the hotels. In a room with linoleum floors, chrome fittings and tea smells, he had a bowl of watery canned soup and a triangle of white bread that stuck to the roof of his mouth. It was a bad meal, British-bad. Sno-Bird cooked what Grey had once said was the rarest food in the world, properly prepared British food. Food, he said, out of reach of tourists and corner houses; light, beautifully cooked stuff not served outside private homes. For five years he'd eaten mulligatawny and lamb, curries and roast beef, rarebits, Yorkshire pudding, soda bread, bacon and cabbage, poached salmon, Irish cheddar. He'd eaten the moose stew and cedar-smoked steelhead of the Klaxta. He'd eaten berries from the meadows, plucked and sweetened and deep in cream.

Outside, the sidewalks were damp. He stopped in the doorway of a saloon: a long bar, sconces on the walls throwing dim quarter moons of wattage, men in coats sitting hunched. Beer glasses, a sailor's beret nodding like a dinghy on choppy water. A woman's face bright as a candle, the soft red of her dress blotting up the darkness. Her gaze seemed to reach out from an untouchable, swimming center. Her eyes passed over him again, slower, as if they were trying not to drift, poignant in the face that flickered and wavered like softly burning wax.

Women liked him. He knew it without conceit. He liked them too, their softness, their smell, their talk, and all the good things they had that were different from what he had. He'd been pretty busy with that once. But eventually you grew up. If you were lucky, if you had something to grow up for. Got picky, though once in a while you forgot picky, said to hell with it and got funky instead. Rolled in it like it was the last time you were going to get any.

There was a card in a barbershop window, the kind of place that looked like they didn't sweep the hair off the floor. He read it by the light of the street lamp. MASSEUSE, CALL GLORY, and a number. He pictured Glory, a blonde with big smeary features, in a dress with a keyhole neck. What if he picked up something? He'd bring it back to Salthill, steal in with it like some germ-haunted ground fog. A gift from him and Old Glory, an English or Russian professional, from Vancouver by way of Odessa or Liverpool.

He turned away, undecided.

He dreamed

He was naked and riding the Red. They were galloping down a road. At the end of it was Grey, with maple-leaf hair. He knew Grey was in danger, that only he could save Grey. He spurred the Red on, crouched low on his neck with fists buried in the cedar mane. As they raced toward Grey he saw Grey's eyes open wide in terror. Then he knew it was his nakedness Grey feared, his nakedness that was the danger. He tried to swerve away from the eyes that saw him unclothed. But the Red was bearing down on them like a missile. He heard the horse give a scream of rage. They were going to smash—

He woke. Tears of anguish ran down his face. He fumbled blinking in the duffel by the bed and found one of the handkerchiefs, blue-white from washings, that Sno-Bird had put in with their stuff. He wiped his eyes and blew his nose, then balled it up and threw it on the floor with a curse.

The dream hung over him, was his twin. He lit a cigarette and prowled the room, full of dread. In the other bed Dai was a lump coughing stale tapering-off beer. He turned on the lamp and went through the duffel for writing paper and a pen.

Grey,
    We've finished Penticton where we got first place in the jump-
ing competition and the knock-down-and-out with Near Riot,
and first in the hunter class with Sizzle Star. Riot is sold.

He pondered. Grey liked details about buyers.

His name is Frederick Corwin as you will note, and he lives outside Vancouver. He is a lawyer who competes on weekends. He has one other horse, a black mare who looks "made," which he stables near Cherrywil. He rode her in the hunter class and she jumped by herself. Hope he will keep in mind that Riot is not that seasoned. Am forwarding his check made out to you which I had the bank guarantee in exchange for the papers. It is in the upper range of what we discussed, very good for him. . . .

Reached Vancouver yesterday. It is cool and dry. There are a lot of competitors and the exhibits are full. The Knock-Down looks good for Edgeware. I entered Petronel in the open jumper class before it closed, so he will be showing both days. Sizzle is in Handy Hunters again. I am sure she will arouse some interest, as she is in form. Elsa has done a good job getting her over water.

I met some of the exhibitors from Penticton. They are going on to Victoria after Vancouver. Gil Janus sends his regards and says he'll be up there sometime late August, so keep a lookout for a good green colt. Wilfred Humphries asked about stud fees. He has two half-Arab mares from the Salud line and wants to get a couple of three-quarter-mix foals. He said he would be in touch. The heavy hunters aren't much this year. . . .

He sealed the letter that turned into an envelope. He got back in bed and slept, and dreamed of the persimmon tree outside the turret window, its ebony heartwood and fruits red as fire.

Chapter Forty-three

"THE RED'S OFF AGAIN," said Grey. "He's been gone two weeks. George saw him in the mountains when he went to move his traps."

Harris swore.

"He bolted out the gate one morning. Like a fool I had left it open. Not that he couldn't have jumped the fence."

It was their first meal back home. They were having it on the veranda, shepherd's pie snowcapped with whipped potatoes. Sno-Bird sat in the basket chair with her legs folded to one side, smoking a cigarette. He put his fork down and felt around with his tongue for a papery corn kernel.

They went over the shows and the sales. Dai remembered everything he knew about. Like many alcoholics he was shrewdly observant, noting details drunk that a lot of people sober would have missed. Harris made a mental note of the shrewdness.

In the middle of the meal the door opened and Elsa walked in. She carried a brace of rabbits and the Winchester tucked under one arm. She was in jeans and a leather jacket and her hair was tied in a knot at her neck. Her face was dirty.

"You're back," she said, on the threshold.

He sat frozen and helpless under her aloof smile.

"Put those in the pantry for now," said Sno-Bird. "I'll skin them later."

Her gaze flicked over them impartially. She disappeared in the kitchen with the rabbits, marching slowly on those long legs.

That night he waited for her to come. He lay on his bed ready to throw the quilt on the floor and love her in the moonlight. They would lie together and watch the stars, hear a wildcat scream in the rooks above the range. He fell asleep and woke at dawn to cold air lifting the curtains into the room. It was time to get up and feed the stock.

The vet had been around to geld the colts. They looked over the new geldings, languishing in stalls while their wounds healed.

"I don't like waiting until they're developed," said Grey. "They look showier when they're gelded at four or five but it's hard on them, and risky at that age." He dropped his hand from a colt's neck and moved on to the next, speaking without a change in tone. "Harris, while you were away the Red made a serious attempt to put me out of business."

He felt bludgeoned. First she hadn't come, now this. "When?"

"The day he got out. He tried to trample me first. I fended him off with a pitchfork."

Harris had a vision, painfully lucent, of the man beside him waiting on the road in his dream.

"I'll put him down," he said.

He was sluggish with shock. The Red had finally gone crazy. He was crazy too, waiting like a fool for her in the dark. There were men who spent their lives doing this shit, jive artists who got so tangled up in deceit they didn't know what the truth was after a while. He wasn't one of them. That was what was wrong with him. He could only tell a finite number of lies in a given time period.

"I'm glad he didn't get you," he heard himself say.

"I cut him with the fork," said Grey. "He'll have a wheal on his neck." His voice was distant, as though the Red wasn't a subject he cared to pursue.

He knew now that he'd do anything to have her. He would let no chance get by. When she schooled a horse he waited; when she drifted past him in the yard with that little smile on, he waited. He waited while she and Sno-Bird snapped beans over a paper bag, the strings and nubs rattling on the paper, the way those beans had when the women of his aunt's house sat with bags torn open on spread laps, the strings dropping into them and the beans plunking in the bowl while their talk ran on.

He saw how important work had been to him. It defined and shaped him and filled him with a surly vitality. He was one of millions who labored, part of them because he shared the common need to prosper. Work had always given him a sense of power. Sometimes he looked across the range and saw a golden sea of humans toiling on the rich, round ball of earth; the men striking and bearing, lifting and carrying, the women the same, lying in labor, then rising up with children in their arms. The men coming home weary with their tools, groups of women preparing food. For centuries this had gone on. When he came to the door with his hat in hand they let him in, as they nodded to him on the street, because he worked; he rode, cleaned, planned, chopped, strove, wore out his body.

Other times he saw only the stooped backs of dark people over the cane fields. To be a slave was to work without reason.

Now he went through the motions of work, losing himself only briefly in effort. He spent his days waiting, his nights in fitful sleep. He never felt tired and he was never rested.

She ignored him. From time to time her wild gaze burned him like the flame of a match, then moved on as if he was nothing. It was like he had never touched her. This made him crazy. Had Georgewood gotten to her while he was gone? Georgewood looked like a fucking movie star. He shook the thought off. It had been too good between them. She was no fool. He calmed himself by remembering her devotion from the start, how she'd sat between his knees as a girl and wiped the bits while he cleaned bridles, running her little mouth about Ireland and the cove by her house. The rock-strewn points called *skerries*. He was better in the sack than Georgewood anyway. He knew how to make a woman happy.

He wanted to follow her when she rode out and lower her to the grass, not waiting to take off her clothes (a convenient flimsy dress), see that solemn face under his, the eyes that followed his movements and seemed to follow his thoughts. Sometimes the fear made him cruel; he wanted to see fear creep over her like a blush when he lay her down.

The fourth night after he got back, he was at the sink barefoot in his shorts, brushing his teeth. He rinsed his mouth and dried his face and neck. He had given up waiting for her that evening; as before, she had made no sign she would come. He had read a book earlier for an hour, an anthology of poetry, and way too many of the poems had been about love. He skimmed them restlessly. For a while he stood looking out at the garden, wondering whether he'd be able to shoot the Red when the time came. For the first time since he got back to Salthill, he wasn't thinking about Elsa.

When he came out of the bathroom, she was sitting on his bed, hugging herself with both arms as if she was cold. She wore a nightie with a ruffled hem and he had never seen the point of this garment before. She turned to him at the sound of his step, and the look on her face wasn't like any look she wore during the day.

He sat on the bed beside her and took her by the shoulders. They looked fiercely into each other's eyes. She didn't speak and her speechlessness moved him more than any love talk. She spoke with her eyes and body. He held her face in his hands and kissed her, savoring her mouth like a starving man. He lifted the nightie and touched the long warm body.

He forgot to ask if she'd locked the door. The notion sped through his mind and was gone. There was nothing but this.

He tossed the quilt on the floor and they lay down in front of the cold-spangled window. What he remembered afterward was the mute, fearless way they watched each other. She took his hand once and placed it where she wanted to be stroked. He groaned inwardly with happiness at knowing what meant the most to her, what he could give her. He made himself wait until she was completely his for that sweet moment when he completely surrendered himself to her.

The air grew spit-colored and heavy. He had to get up to shut the window on the mist and the garden. Lying together like this in silent communion was one of the things he'd longed for most. He nosed the musk of girlish scalp and let her kiss his temples, feeling both a perfect peace and his body gathering itself again, like thunder rolling from a distant mountain.

Grey sat up in bed and put aside the covers. He had been wakened by a noise from outside, somewhere in the yard or the fields around it. While his eyes adjusted to the gloom he listened closely.

His room was large and the walls were papered in a floral design, the pattern broken by pieces of the mahogany suite his wife had brought to their marriage. An Albert lamp and flashlight were on the bedside table, along with the book he was currently reading. While he listened, he observed these things with more acuity than he did in broad daylight.

Finally he identified another sound, that of hooves muffled in wet grass. He rose quickly then and began to dress. No animal galloped before dawn unless something was after it.

On the porch he struggled into a sheepskin-lined jacket and Wellingtons. The young coonhound he had added to the household sniffed the backs of his legs and politely asked leave to join him. He let the dog out and walked down to the yard, planting his feet carefully on the slick steps. The air had a dank, fertile smell. In the gradually lifting darkness the yard was visible, but not the line of trees behind the meadow. The mountains had been sponged out of the canvas entirely. He could have been looking out on a bleak desert, a horizonless Sahara, instead of a valley ringed with peaks. A fine rain rich with oxygen stung his face.

The Red was galloping around the riding ring like a watchworks horse.

As Grey approached, the horse came to a stiff-legged halt, wheeled and started off in the other direction, running swiftly and mechanically along the rail. The powerful muscles gathered and slid automatically under his rough coat; a creamy excrescent lather worked between his legs and in the hollows of his flanks.

As the horse swept past him, he looked into the staring eye. It was dark and sheened, like a burnished fur that absorbs color. There was no rim of white as the eyes of crazy horses were said to have. Loco, they called them here. Rogues, they were called in Ireland and England. Rogue horses. The eye bulged knowingly, its iris and lighter concentric ring aflame with an intelligent madness. He wondered what paranoia the brute harbored, if he was capable of thought. In spite of his antipathy, Grey couldn't help pitying the animal. How keen his suffering must be. Perhaps this compulsive flight was an attempt to stem the torture of his unreason. The horse scrambled around the far end of the ring, gathering himself and leaping forward as though lashed from behind, landing sprawled then wobbling on, his gait disintegrating. Coming around the turn he skidded in the mud, went down on his knees and lunged to his feet with a violent effort. His breath poured in ragged gasps across the space between them.

At Grey's feet the young hound uttered a single yawp. Grey spoke to him, then turned and retraced his steps to the house.

The kitchen was still dark, but its furnishings were beginning to stand apart from their shadows. The tin flue of the range loomed like a cliff, drawing light from the embryonic dawn. It was possible Harris was awake; he often was at this hour. Grey stopped in the passageway and rapped with the back of his hand on the door of the turret room.

"Harris," he called, keeping his voice low.

There was no response at first, then he heard footsteps. He waited, staring down at the piece of worn Persian runner before the door.

The door opened. Harris stood naked to the waist, fastening the fly of his jeans. He exuded a fug of sleepy masculinity.

"The Red's back," said Grey. "Pelting hell for leather around the ring."

"I'm coming."

He disappeared, leaving the door ajar. Grey heard a drawer open and close. Harris came out in a sweater and boots.

They stopped for the Winchester, which Elsa had cleaned and left on the veranda. "I'm not going down. This is your affair," said Grey, watching him load it with cartridges. "You're not operating under my orders."

"I know that," said Harris. "Come on."

Grey responded to the urgency in his voice. "All right, then."

The sky swept them downhill, a flume of water filled with topsoil. Wet earth sucked at their boots.

Grey cursed. "Damn this bloody muck. I'm sick of wallowing in it."

Harris carried the Winchester with the stock under his arm. His face was blanched and flayed-looking. A scrim of some emotion shut them off from each other. This was rare; they lived in such constant easy communion. With a mental shrug, Grey left the lad to himself. Putting the Red down was not going to be easy.

The horse was standing at the gate. His head hung nearly to his knees and he swayed like a tree in a storm, weaving on splayed legs. The sunken eyes glared without focus. Harris stepped through the gate with the rifle and cupped his hand over the horse's nose. Suddenly the Red raised his head and pushed his skull into Harris's chest. Harris held the head to him and stroked the twist of mane behind the horse's ears. Under his supple and tender hand, the chilling glare stayed fixed on the near distance.

This is the time, thought Grey. A single shot to the brain, and the great body would sag and drop to the ground. They were conveniently near the gate. Clem Lemuels would have only to open it and drive in, raise the carcass with the winch and drag it from the ring. It was a dirty morning to get Clem out in, but worth it.

"Give him one more day," said Harris in a tight voice. "I'll ride him into the mountains and destroy him there."

With an effort Grey concealed his exasperation and chagrin.

"He'll be food for a mountain cat or wolves," he said when he could speak. "Perhaps it would be more fitting. Forgive me. I could have put that better."

"You put it fine," said Harris.

Chapter Forty-four

THE BROOD HERD DISSOLVED into the dove-gray clouds on the slopes. Harris put the Red in the stud box with the bottom half of the door fastened. The horse stood staring out at the damp fields, his feed untouched.

"Wait until the weather looks like holding," said Grey abruptly at tea. Rain spattered the kitchen windows at intervals like water from a hose.

"Wait for what?" asked Elsa, examining them in turn. Her father, wearing his opaque, rather dreamy look, didn't answer.

"Get rid of the Red," said Harris bluntly.

She put down her coffee. "The Red? Whatever for?"

"He's gone loco." Harris pushed his dessert away and leaned back in his chair like the bad boys who hung around Olney Gibbs's car shop, loafing and cadging beers; what Gordon with curling nostrils called louts. Olney Gibbs's son was in the reformatory and both his daughters had had to drop out of high school and get married. Harris's T-shirt stretched like a tight second skin over his chest and stomach. He looked dangerous and cheap and full of himself.

"Loco," she repeated. "You mean *mad*?"

"He went after Grey while you were gone," he said.

"I'm sorry, Elsa," said her father. "He's a beautiful animal, but there's something wrong with him."

"Oh, *no*." What a blow this was, to make him so careless and hard-looking at the thought of it. She let her eyes rest on Harris, taking mental snapshots: the body under the shirt, his neck and the graceful way his head was set on it, the thighs under the washed-out jeans. A dull ache started between her legs. Her distress for the Red was honest, but passion swept her past tragedy to a more urgent place. A loss for Harris meant the role of comforter for herself. She longed to be his ballast.

"Aren't you gonna eat that pie I slaved over?" Sno-Bird asked him crossly.
"I'm full." He reached for his cigarettes, to show her.

She whisked the untouched slice from in front of him. "I'll put it in the pantry. You can have it before you go to bed. Skipping dinner and wasting good food."

Harris grinned. "Yes, ma'am."

The weather remained fitful. Gilbert Janus came from Vancouver the next day, bought two colts and ended staying the better part of a week. Humphries's man trailered up the two half-Arab mares. They waited in their boxes to come into heat, diminutive girls with dished faces and cow eyes. Sizzle Star's new owner arrived to fetch her. Grey gave a dinner party for Piwonka, Janus, Sizzle's new owner and the Georgewoods, who brought their own houseguests. There were two fresh-killed lambs from Wanda Creek. The headless trunks turned on spits over a trench in the east garden, giving off the primitive odor of roasting meat.

Midway through the roast the sky filled with storm clouds with bile-green fringes. Harris, turning the spit, glanced up and caught a fat drop of rain in the eye. He and Grey threw up canvases over the cooking area, but it was hopeless; the rain swooped on them like a seaborne squall. In minutes the canvas was on the ground, the trench swimming in water, the water full of bobbing, spitting coals. Garden, roofs and hillside disappeared from view.

In high good humor from either the unaccustomed adventure or the effects of scotch whiskey, the guests rushed out to rescue the barbecue. Rain dashed at their faces; gusts of wind rocked them like clumsy bottom-weighted toys.

"Oh!" shrieked Bron Georgewood, holding the skirt of her golf dress pinned between her legs, while the back ballooned up.

Sno-Bird added extra wood to the range. The women pulled the lamb off the spits, hacked it up, laughing and shouting, and loaded it in the oven. A pile of damp towels blocked the pantry door.

" 'S pissing-down rain's gone on too long," Dai said, groaning, letting himself in.

"What a place!" said Sizzle Star's owner, amused. "No phones, when lines are up all over the province. Wood-burning stoves—"

"No gas, Crosbie!" shouted Grey.

"Peace River's positively citified compared to us," declared Piwonka proudly.

"There's talk o' building a Val-U Mart in Four Queens," said Dai.

"Shush, man. That'd spoil the look of the place! Who needs smelters and power lines and department stores? We've got cattle and tourists!"

"Real runoff problems is what we're going to have if this rain doesn't stop," said Georgewood. "The river's boiling like a millrace."

"Tell me! I'll lose my grazing land if the plain below the pass floods," said Piwonka. "I've spent the last week getting my stock up to high ground. If this keeps up every spread in the Skillihawk'll have to be reclaimed from the McKenna, system or no system."

Elsa played hostess for her father in the new peach linen sheath Flavia had made her buy and her hair in a coil, helped with last-minute touches and saw to the comfort of the guests. They ate on the veranda, perched on chairs, crowded around the fireplace with plates on their knees, robust with drink and food: Grey and Elsa, Piwonka, Sno-Bird and Javier, George Torenose, Harris, Janus and Crosbie, the Georgewoods and their guests.

The following day was clear again. In the morning Grey and Janus made an excursion to Mountain Inn. Piwonka rode back with them, and the rest of the party left at noon to lunch at Wanda Creek Ranch.

Elsa exercised her mare, then rode into the stud barn to look at the Red.

The barn had two oversized boxes, one on either side of a short passageway with a lofty overhang. The Dutch doors were bolted shut on both the paddock and passage sides, but the top halves had been left open. The Red snorted at the sight of her and Elsa looked into the staring eye. His body slid past her close enough to touch, like a train going past a window. His coat looked dry and coarse, with hollows in the flanks.

She dug in the pocket of her anorak for a carrot and offered it on her outstretched hand. The red horse sniffed her, then lipped the carrot from her palm. Even with that gesture, so light and negligent, she felt the power coming from him like a blast from a torch.

Harris appeared in the passage entry, looking ferocious.

"You didn't go with the others," he said.

"I don't like Bron Georgewood. Are you really going to destroy him?"

He shrugged. "He's not eating."

"He just ate a carrot," said Elsa. "Why don't we get the bag and see if he'll have more?"

Harris filled a pan with carrots from the feed cupboard and gave them one by one to the Red while she watched. The air around them was bright with tension.

"Would a mash work?" she asked. "A hot sour mash?"

"He's not an invalid," said Harris in a surly tone. "He's gone crazy. He tried to run your father down."

"The devil's in him," she said thoughtfully. "It's himself in there, with the yellow fangs and claws and all. When can we be alone?"

He felt the long shiver down his spine. "How did you get away the other night?"

"I just went upstairs after you both left. Harris, I'll be gone in a week."

"Gone?" He honestly didn't know what she meant.

"Off to school, you mutt," she said with intense humor. "Where have you been all summer? D'ye think I don't lie awake nights thinking how to get out of't? Ah, if I'd known ye were waitin' the day I'd have not said I'd go."

"You have to go," he said automatically, flushing darkly. "It's your school." He had a sudden vision of the three of them in the house all winter if she didn't, sharing the ground floor in a claustrophobic fug with the snow like thick bars outside. He wouldn't be able to get near her for weeks, with her father sleeping on the veranda. Anyway, she had to go. It was her fate as a St. Oegger. Schooling, that rite of initiation he had abandoned long ago, was for them a tedious but secure passage, taken for granted and half disliked.

She sighed. "Oh, if this bloody rain would lift and all these people would go away we could meet at the lake."

"It was good." He clasped the knee under the snug twill. She sat with lips parted, basking in the heat of his touch while the mare nosed in the pan. He thought, *If he walks in now, even if we aren't wrapped around each other he'll see. He'd have to be blind not to see.*

"The lake," she whispered. "If it clears."

"No. We can't both be missing at the same time, outside."

She looked approving. "It's clever of you to see that."

Desire made him clever. This urgent, naked need made him clever. It was one of her ugly-kid days. She was freckled and bony and her nose was too big. Her eyes looked too close together even though they weren't; it was just a trick of those brows. She'd gotten rid of the boots and socks and her feet hung naked out of the stirrups like flowering white tubers. She bent from the saddle with drooping lids, the anorak wheezing, for his long kiss.

"Harris, my darling life," she drawled. "Is making love always this wonderful?"

"For us it is," he said, a little dizzy. "You're the best I ever had."

She sat up. "You know," she said stiffly, "that's a silly remark."

"It's true."

"You're afraid of me."

"I'm scared shitless."

She laughed down at him. "I love your blackness," she whispered. "I love the little shaved-off wool on your temples, and your brown skin, and the way your behind grows. I like the way your hand looks resting on me. We've always been meant to do with each other, Harris! Let's hurry to your room."

Arrangements were painful. It meant taking out his obsession and discussing it.

"Forty minutes," he said. "Meet me there."

He watched the mare walk out, swishing her cream-colored tail.

He went upstairs as soon as he could. She was sitting on his chair with her hands in her lap, having cleared the books off and left them lying all over the floor. She looked shy, as if the minutes spent with his possessions, inside their textures and odors, had turned her back into a virgin maid. Harris lifted the curtain aside. One of the Connemaras had found its way into the garden and was eating out of the circle of lawn. It was crazy, making love with these people coming back any minute. It was crazy, but he didn't give a damn.

He closed the window and let the curtain fall, and bent her back like a sapling.

"You're all in your dirt." She giggled.

"You like dirt," he breathed, working his way around her mouth, lifting the hair from her neck.

"Don't stop," she ordered. "Please don't stop."

He pulled the chair up and stood on the seat. She put her foot beside his, to compare it with his foot. To note every detail of him, to look for irregularities, the uneven expressions of nature's art, was delightful. For instance, her toes were stubby and the little toe of each foot had a claw, thick and curved as an owl's talon, instead of a nail. His were long like his fingers, with thin nails trimmed straight across. She lingered over the pearl-pink moons.

It was as bright and airless as a hothouse in the attic. The sun lay in dusty oblongs on the floor, in ridges on the blanket he had left there for this moment. He drew up the ladder and closed the trap, sealing them off from the world.

Rounding the corner with a handful of mint for the lamb, plucked from around the waterspout in front, Sno-Bird saw Elsa coming up the path from the garden with her hair tousled and her face emptied and serene. She walked like a cat, seeming to lift a paw and shake it delicately before setting it down. Her hips rolled. After her came the pony, stopping every few feet to snatch at the leafery. Sno-Bird stepped quickly into a niche in the wall that sheltered the garden from the wild slope below and stood, breathing quietly, until the smell of crushed mint brought her to herself.

Chapter Forty-five

HARRIS TURNED THE RED OUT with the two half-Arab mares. The horse kept his distance. He poured oats on spread-out pieces of canvas. The mares came forward, swinging their lowered heads gently in anticipation. The Red watched them for some minutes, then crossed the paddock, dipped his muzzle and tasted the oats. He ate rapidly and methodically then, moving his head along the ground like the bucket of a steam shovel, chasing grains over the cloth with the wind from his nostrils.

The guests were gone. Elsa was in Four Queens with Sno-Bird buying groceries and shoes for school, Dai was napping in the bunkhouse. The two men ate dinner alone. Grey sliced his fruit with a kitchen knife, Harris with his switchblade, wiping the blade carefully before retracting it.

"If they'd seen that they'd have jumped in their cars and driven off," said Grey good-humoredly.

They walked to the barn and saddled up. Massed rain clouds drifted toward the horizon, leaving a broad wake of sky.

In the late afternoon they rode to the Lavender, where the brood herd was grazing. The lake was swollen out of shape. Water looped in brown coils around piles of sludge and filled the hollows above the beach. The salt grass that had once been the bed crop of an ocean was drowned to its silver tips. Two colts were playing in one of the pools, rearing and pawing at the air. They wrapped their forelegs around each other's necks in a rough embrace, bit and kissed each other, then dropped back on all fours.

The stud nuzzled Grey's breast pocket for the treat that was always there. Grey spoke to him reproachfully, then produced two lumps of sugar.

Harris rode away from them along the shore toward the point. The smaller pebbled beach was gone. From the rearranged shoreline broken by black flints and rubble, the lake spread out under the milky sky.

He turned back. Grey was following the shore in the other direction, the stallion ambling at his side. He stared at the distant figures.

"Harris."

He woke. She was sitting on his bed in the winceyette nightgown. The window was open, the air sharp with the smell of pine. Outside the sky shone steel-colored, with a few stars caught in the clouds. The moon turned her hair into a silver-and-gold cap. He reached out and saw his own hand washed by moonlight, with a violet tracing of veins on the back. She grasped his hand. He sank back, feeling her hip press against his side. In mutual peace they watched night walk through the garden, stately in her furred, starred robe.

He raised the blanket. She dropped the nightgown on the floor and crept in, sighing against him. They kissed.

"I'm leaving tomorrow," she whispered, letting him feel. "Make it be good."

But when he closed his eyes the Southern night road, the rattling of the old truck, the sickness, the green walls pressed on the insides of his lids.

"Harris . . ."

"What."

"*Harris, I love you so much.* Do you love me too?"

Her smile seemed to waver in the steely light. The moon moving before clouds made her radiant, swam over his body, which swam through dark and light to her. It crossed his hand, clamped on her stomach like a sucker on a coral reef. Maybe they had both drowned in this weird, rainstormed summer.

"I'm not sure I know what love is," he said. "Can you live with that?"

Her mouth drooped; she seemed to get smaller inside the nightgown.

"Maybe we don't either of us know," he added.

She twisted away and buried her face in the pillow.

He sat up and turned her over. She studied him, composed, lips dark against the pallid skin. Her kissed her roughly. "Still want me?"

"No. Get away, damn you." She shot him a look of hatred.

He slid down and kissed the insides of her thighs. She gave a little gasp and pushed at his head. He caught her by the wrist. Whimpering, she tried to snatch her hand back. He tightened his grip. Her pulse fluttered under his fingers.

"It's all right," he said. "It's all right."

He pressed her legs apart with his other hand. After a minute she stopped struggling, and the long creamy legs untangled themselves slowly from the sheets.

He kissed her dazed mouth and whispered, "Taste yourself." The pulse was pounding in his neck. It was like when he shot drugs, that feeling that everything hung just right, that you really had taken leave of your senses and rode above them. The high was power. He could do what he wanted, make anything happen.

He heard the door handle turn.

She heard it too, a minute click. She turned her head toward the sound. Her ear was a haphazard leaf, pale and pointed under the strewn hair.

The door was locked; no one could get in. He got up quietly and stood with head bent in concentration, trying to absorb the presence in the hall outside. He crossed to the window, closed it and drew the curtains.

She was kneeling on the carpet, gripping her hair. Her hunched nakedness made something give inside him. He squatted and held her shoulders.

"Don't leave me," she whispered.

"I'm not leaving, you're leaving," he said. "Tomorrow."

He put on shorts and went into the hall. The dining room door was open and a rod of light from one of the gunwales lay across the floor. Nails scrabbled on the kitchen lino. One of the dogs padded toward him, head down, ears flat, and sniffed his legs. He smoothed its head and it went back to its place, comforted and reassured.

He roamed the lower floor noiselessly, past the dining room, the parlor, the staircase, the front room. He checked the kitchen and veranda. Her suitcases and trunk were by the door, waiting for morning.

When he got back Elsa was standing in the doorway.

"Jesus, girl," he hissed, steering her inside and locking the door. "Are you out your *mind*?"

She was laughing silently like a fox. The gown flurried against her legs, soft lean poles wrapped in cotton.

"Do women do that to men?" she demanded.

"What." He ran his hands down her sides.

"What you just did to me."

He smiled. "Yeah. They sure do."

"Show me."

He shook his head. "Maybe next time."

"I'm *leaving*. I can't wait until next time." Her lips brushed his lips, then his throat. "Tell me what happened first," she whispered. "All these marks. How did they get there?"

Damn it, she was a witch, she was clairvoyant. He felt sick suddenly, trapped on the night road, unable to leave, afraid to stay.

"Some things are private," he said. That sounded stupid.

She tugged the shorts down over his hips.

"Look, I'm not a horse," he said. "It won't work."

Her hand on him. "There's one right where your hair grows," she said dreamily.

"Get up here," he breathed.

"Don't be a fool, I'm going to do this." She grasped his prick, scowling a little. "How does it work? This way?"

"Use your hand," he said, giving up. "And your tongue and lips." He guided her, felt the scrape of a tooth, a second of humor, a blink of hope, standing away from himself untouched. Then his eyelids dropped as if they were weighted. He let his hand fall on the crown of her head and rest there. With a sigh, he gave himself up to her mouth. She was clumsy; it was so good. As she gained in cunning a voluptuous sweetness swept through his body like a honeyed flood racing down a canyon. All the potency was being drawn out of him. It filled him with sensual delight, this transfer of power from his body to hers. He stood with legs apart, submissive, locked in its hypnotic charm. He felt the sexual convulsion coming and controlled it, unwilling to end the pleasure of giving in to her. Then he flinched away and moaned. She stared wonderingly at the fluid pulsing over her hand like water from a fountain.

She kissed his stomach.

"Tell me," she whispered. "Ah, tell me."

"How will I live without you?" murmured Elsa.

"You'll live." He hefted the suitcase down the steps. She clattered alongside him in a pair of cream-colored shoes with Cuban heels. She wore the same suit she had worn that day at the station, with a checked blouse he had never seen. Her hair was in a loose knot at her neck. A beret shadowed part of her face. Most girls of her class dressed like their mothers, but she'd managed to avoid that. She had managed to look like no one but herself.

"Where did you learn all those wonderful things?" she asked. "Like the one last night. What you did."

"Women, I guess."

"Bad women?"

He scowled. "Women who know what they like. Some folks like to think it's bad." He slid the suitcase in the bed of the truck, next to the trunk and the boxes of art stuff. "There isn't much point to fucking if you don't do what you want," he added.

He sniffed the wind and examined the sky. The summer had been one of watching weather. They had all been watching and waiting, for storm or shine, for weeks.

"You've got that wolf look on," she whispered. "Oh, if I could kiss your arm, right there where the sleeve is rolled up. The inside of your arm where the skin is so smoky and tender around those marks."

"Cut it out," he said tensely.

"If I gave you a friendly good-bye kiss, which I'm surely entitled to since you're one of ours . . . but I'd fall on you, they'd have to pry me loose. It would look *very* bad."

Her laugh and that faint gloating tone were making him angry. So this was how she was going to take leaving him, smiling and swishing out on a current of irony like some movie heroine. Then he saw that she was in pain and disordered, that her eyes were shining with tears.

Grey was on his way down from the veranda with her old calfskin suitcase with the finish worn off in patches. She glared at Harris, got in the passenger side and began to rummage with bent head through the duffel she used as a handbag.

"I'll be back by noon Wednesday," said Grey, buttoning his jacket.

"The Red'll be gone," he said. "I'm taking him up there today."

Grey hesitated. "He seems better."

"You know I can't take the chance."

"I'm sorry. I wish it were something that would pass."

Elsa had left the door open. When the engine turned over, Harris went to close it for her. She had learned everything she needed to know about manners in the aunts' house. Men closed doors. That was traditional between men and women. When they got to the college, that place that was going to absorb her for four years, except for summers, which she would spend at Salthill tormenting him, her father would come around to the passenger side and help her out. That was tradition, too. He thought of the bare feet taking her down the hall in dance steps after she'd drained him dry. Everything about her was neatly made. Her irregular features had a certain elegance, like the chipped Doulton in the sideboard that was still Doulton, not Woolworth's. The beret was tilted at the right angle, yet he knew she'd just clapped it on and skewered it with a hatpin. She'd have style one day, the kind he'd seen in New York women and the good-looking colored women of New Orleans, casual dash with breeding running under it like fine veins. She was going to be something else someday, and he had been in on the beginning of it.

He watched the truck go up the drive and disappear around the bend of the green close.

Grey shifted into high gear on the highway. The billiard-green turf that only rain could make grow rolled past the windows.

"Is he really going to destroy the Red?" asked Elsa. "You won't have to worry about Harris being hurt then, will you?"

"I'm afraid there's not much choice."

"It's sad," she said mournfully to the windshield.

"Animals aren't as complicated as humans," said her father, in his companionable, sorting-things-out voice. "Their responses are provided by their genetic makeup, and there aren't many variables. Horses are clever and playful. Nature gave them a clearly defined intelligence that raises them above other grazing animals. I've been bitten, kicked and subjected to mock attacks and various tricks over the years. So have you. But a horse doesn't attack a human being with the intent to kill unless something has gone wrong with its mind. It's still a horse, not an inherently savage beast of prey."

"You never liked him, did you? The Red."

"The animal gave me the whim-whams, frankly. You didn't say good-bye to Harris."

"I did," said Elsa. "Before you came down. He knows I'll miss him terribly."

Chapter Forty-six

HIS PLAN WAS TO RIDE the Red bareback into the mountains, then hike out with the bridle and the Winchester. If he cut through the reserve he could probably get a ride home from Sno-Bird's husband Ashtash or one of the other old men who spent their days tending the vegetable plots or minding grandchildren. He had ridden down from the reserve more than once with a truckload of small kids.

As they came out of the box, he heard the stallion's trumpet on the grassland. The Red ignored the call and strained his head toward the riding ring and the set-up hurdles. The horse was rigid with tension from his out-thrust head to the root of his tail. He snorted through barreled nostrils and plunged forward in leaps that lifted Harris nearly off his feet.

That morning he had opened the door to the small room behind the tack room and seen the old cooker tucked against the wall, the bed striped with uneasy daylight. Had they really lain there? He thought of her breath catching in the dark, her eyes shining. The rough way he had her. She had made him do what he wouldn't do. He had invaded her, the girl at the kitchen table; he had invaded them all, the sovereign, sufficient people.

The room was cold and stuffy. It was there, standing in the doorway, that he felt the first stirring of a desire to ride the Red again. There wasn't any connection between the red horse and Elsa, they occupied separate areas of his mind, but when he thought of either of them he felt wrapped in shame. His encounters with them had shut him out of ordinary life. He had failed to tame the horse and make him the champion he deserved to be. The living thing that had signaled his first steps into a decent life would be no more after today. And he had failed her. Because what did he have to offer but trouble? *Harris, I love you so much. Do you love me too?* She wanted love, and it could destroy her. . . . He had wanted nothing this cold summer but a union that filled him with self-disgust, then with guilt for seeing it as anything but the union of man and woman, old and frank as stone; she deserved that respect no matter who she was. . . . There was no promise of another sweet night with her, just him moving in this shame. There was no promise of the power the Red had created in him whenever he got into the saddle, just a trek into the mountains and a hike back alone.

A fiery exhaustion crested inside him. The day was humid and windless. Even the tamaracks were still with the weight of a coming storm. He saw himself returning from destroying the Red, slogging down slopes in the rain, confused in his senses. Now, under the horse's red coat with the gloss restored by feeding and grooming, the long flat muscles twitched under his hand.

He got the Pariani with the knee roll out of the tack room and saddled the Red, changed into riding boots and rode into the ring with the whip in his boot. He was ambidextrous but preferred it on the right. He had never had to carry a whip with any other horse.

The recently furrowed track smelled of turned earth and acridly of horse dung. As they cantered down it, the Red leaned into the bit, giving occasional loud snorts that seemed forced out by his bounding stride. The jumps were spread out in a rough oval. In the center was a set of cavalletti, a row of poles set close to the ground on crosspieces, for schooling beginning jumpers. A scrap of flag hung limply on a standard by one of the big uprights. When he collected the red horse and turned him toward the first barrier, he felt the unfurling of power as though he was bringing a great ship about on an ocean.

They swept around the course. Harris felt a sudden rise in his spirits from the good going, the energy beneath him lifting, soaring and falling. Every obstacle seemed taken with contempt, and his loss and confusion, and the craziness of the horse, were transformed into flying exhilaration. There was no real sympathy or trust between them, there never could have been. But here and now, on this track, they were united.

He raised the rails on the oxer and pulled two jumps together to make them broader, then mounted and went around again. The hurdles coursed at him at speed, turning and reappearing—a gate, a brush box full of junipers, the water jump with the standards dragged apart and the trough boggy with rain water. The saddle tapped him gently on the ass as they shortened stride for the turns. He stood in the irons, feeling the humid air begin to stir, a breeze kiss his forehead.

They took the in-and-out where he had come to grief in July. Then the oxer, a staircase of graduated bars with potted trees in between, the highest

bar now over seven feet off the ground. Only one other Salthill horse, Petronel the steeplechaser, was expected to get over it. The Red lengthened
his stride, rose, and the wall flowed under them.

They were airborne. Harris felt a knot in his throat. They had left earth,
they were soaring into the sky; that was how perfect the locomotive power
was beneath him. He was riding the swiftest and canniest horse he would
ever ride. In an hour it would be dead.

They touched ground. The Red took off in a long, snaking leap. Harris
kept his seat, not by chance but by foreknowledge. The horse squatted and
spun on his haunches, trying to snatch the bit, ears crimped and his neck
curved toward the saddle like the polished bole of a tree. Harris took the bit
away with a short jerk, swearing. As he was whirled around, he reached for
the whip in his boot. His mind darted ahead of his hand, seeing the whip
cut and draw blood, blood flying while he struck over and over, out of his
mind with rage. Suddenly the Red flung his head back and struck him
heavily in the face. He knew the blow, the pain and outrage of having his
nose smashed, but nothing clearly after that. He felt himself leave the saddle,
slumping out of it as consciousness went in an explosion of light and dark.

His fall was broken by something hard. He lay in a daze with his head on
the track, the jump painted to look like a brick wall supporting his upflung
legs, and blinked at a sky streaked with green light. Spots yellow as sego lilies
floated in front of his eyes, popping and re-forming.

At the sound of hoofbeats, he rolled over and away. There was a solid
chunk of flesh meeting wood as the Red hit the wall, then the tattoo of the
wall bounding over the turf. He scrambled to his hands and knees, climbed
dizzily to his feet. The Red swung toward the outside fence, ducked away
from the rails and galloped back toward him, eyes bulging, teeth bared.

Harris ran for the nearest shelter, a post and double rails with white bars
raised against the sky. The cavalletti were suddenly in front of him; he skirted
them while the breath of his assailant poured in ragged gasps behind him.
He smacked into the hurdle before he could collect himself and it went over
under the force of the collision, taking him with it. He rolled violently over
the spilling poles and landed spread-eagled while they rumbled around him.
The steel-shod hooves made cracking noises behind him, kicking the cavalletti to splinters.

He got to his feet and fought through the rails, keeping them between
him and the horse, stumbling in the long riding boots. The water jump was
close by. He ran behind the fir boughs. The Red rocketed along the front
of the trough on the other side, the empty saddle perched on his back like

a leather bird. Harris grabbed one of the standards that backed the greenery. They were light; it was the rails that weighted them down and the three-point spars on the bases that gave them ballast. The Red came around the stile and bore down on him. The wild eyes were ringed with white. If they had bulged any farther out of their sockets, he would have seen the nerves and fibers that attached them to the skull.

Harris ducked in front of the trough. Seeing him on the other side, the Red wheeled in midflight and rose on his hind legs to clear the rails. Harris lifted the upright with muscles that seemed to tear with the effort and chucked it at him, aiming high for the brisket. The post hit the horse squarely in the knees. The giant body streamed over the hurdle and fell to the ground in a tangle of legs.

He ran.

The stable was an oasis of cool dark. The loaded Winchester was on the desk where he had left it. Harris jogged back with it. His legs felt stiff and heavy. The ring was empty, the gate latched, the poles and flimsy battens scattered over the ground. The sky was a steel color through which the green light shone like a patina, moving against a black grid of storm clouds over the railing.

He threw a stock saddle on Frederic Remington. Petronel was faster, but the Appaloosa was surefooted and tough. The rifle went in the sling under his leg. As he jerked the cinch up, he noticed blood oozing from a shallow cut on his forearm. He mopped at it absently with his sleeve before getting into the saddle.

Hoofprints cut deep into the sodden ground cover that grew nearly to the rails. The saturated grass hadn't yet sprung back from under their weight, and Harris could see clearly where the horse had gone. He tracked them across the meadow, past the windbreak and onto the range. He was sick to his stomach and his head ached where he had been banged in the face. He thought of the Red running loose through the Skillihawk, bridled and saddled, deadly to himself and anyone who tried to catch him, and nudged the Appaloosa to a gallop.

All over the valley streams were rushing with the abundant summer rains. He stopped at one to drink and bathe his face. The range was a livid green broken with lines of fencing; the tan mounds of the Bluffs rose in the east against a screen of black sky. Moist, whippy air flowed swiftly past him, smelling of rotting vegetation, while the earth moved beneath him in another direction. As if he was the only living thing that stood still.

He wiped his mouth and got back on his horse.

They traveled west. Lights glowed dully in the trees, the storm-warning lamps of the Klaxta households. To the south were the lights of the ranch house at Mountain Inn, on high ground like the house at Salthill. Mount Endeavour loomed ahead, its long, naked spills mustard-gold in the eerie storm light.

George Torenose had taught him some about tracking, told him that though the Klaxta had not been familiar with horses or hunting on horseback before the Europeans came, they had learned much since then.

"We Klaxta are better cowboys than whites. We're not afraid of any wild thing," George said. He added darkly, "Besides, it is wise to be adaptable."

His face was damp with tears. He dabbed them away with the back of his hand, surprised at tears that seemed to come from nowhere and fall for no reason.

The hoofprints vanished on a hillside edged with Russel fencing. He angled across the field, trying to pick up marks in the spongy turf. A marmot scuttled out of his path. A moose and her calf, knee-deep in floating yellowstars, moved deliberately away from him toward the trees.

Frederic Remington made the rumbling noise deep in his chest, shooting abruptly to a shrill whinny that is a salute to another horse. Harris reined in. Twenty yards down the field, the Red left the trees and slipped along the edge of the wood.

Harris reached for the Winchester and laid it across his lap.

He swung the Appy away from the verge and galloped along the crest of the field, avoiding the hole-pocked marmot settlement. Below and ahead of him the red horse floated, empty stirrups banging against the saddle and the reins looped over his head. His ears were flattened and his mouth gaped in a sneer, the gums fiery above the pulled-back lips.

The swell of the field was crossed at its lowest point by another, flatiron-shaped field. The eastern side of the reserve was rich with meadows like these, small, steep and grassy. In the fold of the two slopes, buried in shrub and blackberry bramble, was a narrow gully. The Russel fencing wound through it, marking the reserve boundary. On the other side the field feathered into a low ridge of spruce and aspen, its backward tide lost in a smoke of low-hanging cloud.

Harris reined in his horse and sat listening to the silence. To the north, the upper field narrowed to a point where it met the flank of the mountain and the wood. The field was empty.

He dismounted and walked, carrying the rifle. The slope was so steep he had to angle sideways to keep his footing. Pain throbbed between his eyes and across the bridge of his nose. The wind had died and he could feel the air gathering, warm and rank with the smell of fetid undergrowth, so heavily moist the sweat trickled down his ribs and the groove in his back as he plodded. He heard crackling, then a roll of thunder. The sky rustled with blue-green light.

The Red broke out of the trees above him, running like a deer. Harris raised the rifle. The horse galloped past, tail a red streak, made a wide sweep at the end of the field and started back, headed toward him. Harris snugged the stock to his shoulder and tried to line the lathered head in his sights. He concentrated on the forehead, but it was the rimless eye that seemed to speed toward him, like the headlamp of a locomotive. He squeezed the trigger.

The shot snapped in the overheated air. Lightning slanted across the field. The gun kicked slightly to the left. He dropped it and flung himself in the other direction as the Red burst over the spot where he had been standing. Harris hit the grass and felt the heat of the horse's body, the dull thunder of his hooves in the soft earth as he rushed past and on up the slope.

He climbed to his feet. The Red swept up the crest of the field, then flowed back down the slope, headed past him at an angle. His mouth gaped open; the bit flopped on the jerking tongue. Feeling sick, Harris retrieved the rifle and started down the field. Momentum carried him down the steep incline faster than his legs could follow. He went down on his hip, slid in the gumbo and got up with long wheals of mud down his legs, his heart slamming in his chest. Near the bottom of the field he raised the rifle again and tried to keep the swift-moving horse in his sights. It was hopeless. He had never been a marksman. If *she* had been there she would have taken the rifle from him, raised it to her shoulder, followed the target with a cold eye, a sensual flowing thing tracking a sensual flowing thing, then with one shot released the horse from his life.

Below him the Red was crossing the field on a diagonal, headed full-speed for the Russel fence. Harris lowered the rifle and heard his own voice bark flatly back at him. There was no pause to gather for the leap, no break in stride. The Red was in the air in one smooth thrust. For a second the head was framed forever in his memory, red and snakelike against the sky. Then the horse's unfolded front legs struck the fence with violent force. The huge body, propelled by its own momentum, shot over the fence and gully, over the shrubs and vines that filled it, and struck the earth head down. He heard the great weight ram the head into itself and snap the neck like the trunk of a tree in a storm. The fence shuddered and swayed.

He ran, staggering in the deep grass.

There was a place in the gully cleared enough to climb the fence, swearing and with brambles ripping at his hands and clothes. Harris threw himself on his knees beside the Red. The horse's head was twisted at a right angle to his neck. The legs twitched and hammered, receiving faint signals from the dying brain. The eyes rolled, but they did not see him, they saw nothing, they were filled already with the bloodstain of death. He stared into the wild glare and saw the irises darkening and the light going out.

He got to his feet. Tears welled again, but he ignored them. It wasn't grief that dying animals needed.

In a blur of tears he found the rifle where he had thrown it down to climb the fence. He stumbled back to the red bulk that twitched and gagged, waiting for him to bring easeful death. He couldn't stop sobbing; nothing could stop this wild grief to which he had learned no resistance. He couldn't release the contortions that stiffened his features, or stop his mouth from filling with the saliva of agony. His eyes started brightly at the pressure behind them, of the bitter grief falling on the green meadow.

He wiped his nose on his sleeve, lifted the rifle and took aim.

Chapter Forty-seven

"COME IN HERE FOR A MINUTE."

He followed Sno-Bird into the kitchen. She had taken the old Albert lamp off the mantel and set it on the table, as she did when she stayed past her going-home time. Yellow light pooled on the oilcloth. He sat down and put his head in his hands.

Her footsteps came, the gasp of the percolator. "Drink this," she said.

While he drank, she laid a loaf of bread on the board and got the knife out of the drawer. Her arms were strong and rounded; her movements had a heavy, leisurely grace. She wore a flowered coverall over jeans. He watched two slices of bread curve and fall away from the knife.

She went to the pantry and came back with a dish of butter and slices of tongue wrapped in waxed paper. She must have been near that age when women suddenly become old, yet she looked no older than she had the first day he saw her. The thought drifted away, rootless and fragmented like all his thoughts.

She tossed the paper into the stove's mouth. "I'm sorry about your horse."

Harris shrugged, staring at leafy ash.

He had gone back for the saddle and bridle, riding Petronel bareback under a long slicker because the Appaloosa was tired out. He had eased the bridle over the ears, lifted the bit out, removed the saddle from the gross corpse sluiced with rain that seemed to be already sinking into the earth. He saddled the chestnut, hooked the bridle over the horn and rode off without looking back.

The dead horse was on reserve land, close enough to the Klaxta homes for scavengers to be a nuisance. He had stopped at the chief's house and arranged for George's team to drag the carcass away. He saw it being tipped into some gulch, bouncing and rolling down with the head lashing on the broken neck.

When he got back to Salthill, the brood herd was huddled under the overhang of the stable roof.

"I can't get near 'im," Dai bleated, rolling his black currant eyes. "Every time I go in he runs at me like he's gone daft."

He looked around at the shambles, the hurdles tossed like matchsticks in the ring, the bleak, rain-darkened buildings. "He thinks we're trying to separate him from the mares," he said.

He swung the gate open. The stallion came around the bunched-up herd with steam rising from his coat, saw Harris and bugled a note of recognition. They watched the herd stream through the gate toward the stable. In the dry passageway the mares crowded around the hay Dai had forked out, nosing each other out of the way and occasionally lashing out in irritation with hooves and teeth. Unnerved by the stallion's presence, the saddle horses circled their boxes and rattled the door latches. The foals nursed noisily from their dams. The vaulted space was steaming and noisy and alive with animal warmth.

He sent Dai upstairs to get his tea, then went in the house by the front door. He showered, doctored his cuts with hydrogen peroxide and his aching head with aspirin. He put on dry clothes and returned to the yard to finish the chores. The old man tottered back down the steps, stopped and raised his cloth cap, which had been drying on the hearth while he ate, in the gesture that meant both hail and farewell, and made for the bunkhouse down the muddy trail.

It had been a long, wet, bad evening. When everything was done that had to be done, Harris sat on the tack room steps smoking one cigarette after another. It seemed like neutral ground, the stable. In the ornery way of weather, the downpour stopped at sunset and the clouds parted like curtains to reveal a limitless, star-filled night. The air was chilly and fragrant, the sky vast, with a watery moon. He had walked up the hill then, to the porch inside the walled garden.

Sno-Bird put the sandwich in front of him and started wiping the counter. Harris ignored it and lit another cigarette. The thought of eating buttered tongue made his stomach churn.

"I know about you and Elsa," she said with her back to him.

He froze in the act of tossing the match into the saucer. She laid the knife in the drawer and closed it. He noted with the absentmindedness of shock how thick the braids were that fell between her shoulder blades, how brown her fingers looked in their silver rings.

"How?" He heard his voice crack.

"She looks a certain way. And other things."

"Nuts. You're crazy." But he had given himself away. The denial was too late, and it had no force.

She said in a melancholy tone, "Grey doesn't know. It takes a woman."

"I'm getting tired of what it takes women to know," he said.

She sat down across from him. He eyed her warily.

"Thing is," said Sno-Bird, "I don't want *him* to find out. Not for her sake. She can take care of herself. For *him.*"

You love him, he thought. The revelation felt distant.

They sat in silence. An owl gave a watery hoot from one of the cedars in front. It seemed like a sound from another life.

She sighed and stirred. "I don't guess you can stop."

"Mother," he said, his voice still husky, "I know I should. It's got a hold on me and I can't shake it off."

She nodded sagely. "Sometimes it takes you that way."

"When I'm with her I feel like I'm in a whirlpool. Like I'm drowning." He stared at the tablecloth, hearing himself with wonder, hearing it come out at last.

"You love her? Some people set a heap of store by love."

He turned cagey. "I got feelings for her."

"Maybe what you got's a feeling for what kind of woman she's gonna be."

"There's nothing wrong with her," he said swiftly.

"I never said there was."

"Don't you."

"I never did. Just men are going to be important to her, is all. She won't like it." She studied his face. "Grey finds out you're lying with his daughter, it'll kill him."

"Why the fuck would it?" he snapped.

She shrugged. "It's just the way it is. My cousin's girl, now, she got a baby from one of those albinos you hear about. German boy from Kleena Kleene. Looks like he fell in a bucket of whitewash. Her father hit her so hard he broke her nose. Had his shop mate's oldest boy picked out for her, with a good job working down at the bindery. Anyhow now she's got this yellow kid with orange hair. Every time my cousin's husband thinks about her he wants to get drunk, and he doesn't drink. He's never even hit a woman except that once. What if you get her in the family way?"

"I been careful." Except for the first time which had taken him by surprise. His head was whirling. *Sometimes it takes you that way.* Was this what happened to love? He watched her shake a cigarette out of the pack on the table.

"Know what's wrong with you, Harris?" she said. "Aside from the fact you're like a lot of white people, always worried about being noble and doing right, then going and doing bad anyway."

He got irritated. "I'm not white folks, mother. Use your eyes."

"You are since they finished with you. Where's your tribe now? Where are your stories?"

He was silent.

"There's a tradition among the native peoples in this country," said Sno-Bird. "At a certain age a young boy is sent into the woods to seek his spirit-self, which is supposed to direct him in his life and work." She exhaled. Smoke lingered in soft, spreading donuts. "Now in old times with the Klaxta, a boy was sent out into the forest with food and water, his trap and knife and fishing tools. He had to stay in the wilderness alone for twelve moons and fend for himself. He had to hunt and fish so he could eat, and protect himself from wild animals. It didn't hurt if he got a big prize either, like the skin of a silver wolf or a wand made from the horn of a giant wapiti. At the end of twelve moons he returned to his village, a fully self-sufficient and independent being. That was how he found his spirit-self. When he left he was a boy, when he came back he was a man. You're having your year in the woods, Harris. Nothing's going to get you out until you learn what you have to know to live."

"Shut up, old woman," he said quickly.

"It would be better if you went," she said. "She'll be back, and some things don't change."

He pushed the chair back and went out on the porch. The verbena in the garden smelled lemony and earthy. Over the wall and the branches of the fruit trees, the moon had shed its veils and come to rest on the black band of the horizon. He breathed deeply, staring up into the night at the piece of broken chalk.

He went back in the kitchen, ghostly with exhalations floating loose on the light, and stood over her. "What would I tell him?"

"You'll think of something," said Sno-Bird.

He studied the smoke-stained molding traced with leaves and flowers, the tin flue, the deep-set windows. "This crazy place. You ever hear of King Arthur?"

"Nope."

"He was an English king, a long time ago. Centuries ago. They don't even know if he really existed."

She waved an airy hand. "That's not important."

"His favorite knight fell in love with his queen. If it had been any other knight the king would have had him killed, but this knight was first in his heart."

"Did the knight love her from far off?"

"No. Close up, every chance he got. But he served his king, too."

"Then you serve, in your own way. Leave. It's the only loyalty you have left to offer. Grey isn't any more noble than you are. I have seen him as a man. A man you can feel in your bones, that's a man worth hurting, right?"

He sat down and picked up the sandwich. "You love him."

"I have known him," she said with dignity.

He bit into the tender salted meat, wondering when and how often she had.

"It was your cooking," he said with weak humor.

"It was much more and much better than my cooking." Her smile was small and complacent.

For the first time in days he could eat. He felt a sudden rush of euphoria. He savored it; it was going to be brief. It would burn away fast when he was alone in the turret room. What he had, had not been enough. He had needed too much. Loss lay ahead of him: lost love, lost pride, lost home, lost friend. Behind him was loss too, not long in the past. Only in the small space between, in the time of work and golden fields, had he really lived.

He would never forget the day he arrived here, plodding up the road with his kit in his hand, light-headed with hunger. As he climbed, the landscape had seemed familiar, as if he'd followed this track before, on another evening golden and thick as if with pollen. In the same way, he had seemed to recognize the house on the hill. He had never seen anything as weird and funky as that castle with its towers striking into the sky. Yet its image had appeared on his lids, known and strangely soothing, when he closed his eyes that night in the bed they found him.

There would be no rest for him tonight. The mad horse would enter his dreams to haunt him with the message he couldn't understand. Behind the mouth with the iron bit and the sweet obsession with its iron grip lay the road out of the valley, winding away over the plain. Sometimes you just wanted suffering to change to a simpler form, something you could deal with because it wasn't a mystery; something that could have an end.

He said, "After he gets back from the auctions. I have to give notice."

"You gave no notice you were coming."

"That was five years ago. It isn't the same anyway, going as coming."

"No more'n a week's notice, otherwise he'll have time to tell her. He's as innocent as a baby picking death caps in the wood."

It was what he had wanted. Innocence. He had wanted to meet it with his own stillborn innocence. He put down the sandwich, feeling cold inside. "I can't do it."

"I'll make you a rhubarb pie," she said, leading him gently forward. "You won't have to stop for anything for a long time. Think of him. *I* know how you feel about him. How long would it be before he found out?"

He thought of the attic above the turret room, voices like swallows dipping down the hall. A rap on the door. He stood looking over the drop, dizzy with the height and depth, knowing one more step would send him spinning out into the void, and feeling her breath on his neck as he lifted his foot.

Book Three

Vancouver
1957

That realm is never long in
quiet where the
ruler is a soldier.

—*The Duchess of Malfi*

Chapter Forty-eight

THERE WAS A SETTLEMENT called Lodenstock, built by a German for the men who worked on his logging operation and oil rigs after the first big oil field was found at Leduc, Alberta, in 1947. The discovery had led to a swell of derricks north of Vancouver. This place was on the Pewit River, which emptied into the sound at Howe. Besides the rigs on the broad sand-bars, the inlet was full of booms anchored and under tow, mile-wide neck-laces of joined timber circling batches of logs cabled in by donkey engine.

Since the war the settlement had been left to the rough workmen and the drifters who were naturally drawn to those places. The Mounties sometimes detoured from the highway to check that it hadn't burned down, driving past the tavern with its tin roof and windows boarded with plywood. There were stabbings and shootings. It was a dangerous place and a ninety-mile-drive from Berrysville, but it was the only place where he could go to do what he wanted.

The air in the bar was suffocating, a pong of booze, sweat and smoke that seemed to have soaked into the linoleum and rough lumber of the walls. A man Harris knew was a priest was drinking at the rutted bar, looking furtive and miserable. The long patrician lines of the man's face and neck, starred with the scarlet of age and excitement, were made for a collar and black dress. Harris slid onto a barstool as far away from the priest as he could get and ordered a whiskey.

There was no bouncer. If violence broke out, the other men settled it. There had been no live band since the night a customer stabbed another customer over what tune they were going to play next. A jukebox controlled from the bar blared country western over the roar of men's voices. The bartender had not only seen it all, he had done it all himself. He had crossed the border of humanity into the land of the walking dead; a little beach of grotesque silence stretched around him wherever he moved. He never touched the women or spoke to the men. It was like he would never need to prove himself again by dealing in human traffic, even on the most rudimentary level.

The whiskey came. Harris drank it off. *Whiskey, ah*. Glenlivet. Not Old Tennis Shoes. From Steinbeck, that would be. *Poor ol' Doc, died drunk in his lab. Poor ol' Doc*. Nope, this was okay stuff. Even this place had to serve decent booze. There were serious drinkers in this toilet.

It rippled down his throat like a snake on fire, backed up prickling into his nasal tubes. He lit a Player's, hunched over the empty shot glass, until the pleasant necessary warmth had risen and spread to his brain. He ordered another. The dirty-aproned figure removing the glass, the gleam of the bottle being tilted were a little out of true, as if he was seeing them through a subtly distorted lens.

He was radiantly aware of the whiskey in his hand, shining like a gemstone touched with swimming, darting gold. It was mute, but it seemed, slurring in the glass, to have a shouting life. He squinted lazily. It could be any liquid to look at it, tobacco juice or horse pee or spit. He breathed in the fumes, its potent drag.

An alarm went off in the back of his head. *What's wrong with you, man?* he said to it. *You better get out of that mode. You're here and it's the way it is.*

He drank the shot in two swallows and sat feeling it make its way into the various channels and recesses of his body. The cozy heat expanded, tingled in his feet and fingertips and head. He was liberated. An inarticulate gasp of pleasure sounded in his ears, the cry of a bird winging too high to be heard.

He ordered another.

A woman in the working outfit of a doxy sat two stools down: skin-tight skirt, tight fuzzy sweater, red boots with high heels. For a second he thought it was Minnie because she was black, but she was too big-boned. She wasn't Minnie anyway. Minnie was dead. Her skin was smoky in the backlight, solid and with a greasy cast. She had a squashed nose, heavy bitten lips painted red.

"Give her one too," said Harris. "Out of the same bottle."

The shot came down. She swung her head toward Harris like an enraged cow. He raised his glass briefly and said, saluting the corrupt eye:

> *"I walked on the ice of the sea*
> *And wondering I heard the song of the sea*
> *And the great sighing of the new-formed ice."*

"Eskimo," he added. "Poetry."

"You pay for poontang, bub, you don't sing to it," said the man next to him.

"Mind your fucking business," said Harris.

"Suit yerself."

He sipped at the whiskey. "I don't like that word."

The man swiveled with an evil grin. "What word, bub?" He wore a bandanna head rag. A cigar lay in the saucer in front of him like a dog turd with tooth marks.

"Poontang."

"She says it herself. She'll give you a blow job you won't ferget, bub."

"Fuck off."

"Suit yerself. Don't have the brass fer't, aye?"

He didn't want a fight. He was here to drink.

"Look, why don't you talk to somebody else?" he said more pleasantly.

They went back to watching the rows of bottles.

The whore sashayed off. The heels of her boots were worn so far down she jerked forward a little when she walked, like a train inching up a hill. In the back she was joined by another whore. They leaned on either side of the door, eyeing each other like gladiators. *Which one gonna win the fucking prize*, thought Harris, watching in the mirror. He lit another Player's. The roar of voices escalated; he heard shouts. Then he was hit a glancing blow on the shoulder that spun him backward off the stool. He swayed, then toppled, trying to untangle his legs from around the rungs. Breaking glass tinkled above the roar.

He wandered past a room. Two women were performing on a rickety love seat. A few men were watching. He weaved, spellbound and out of focus. The bodies seemed to crouch at each other, blurred at the edges. Something hot flared inside him expertly, the rest of him stayed stupid. The women looked stoned and dazed, searching each other with tongues like pointed instruments, with kisses sloppy and vague, and rough dirty groping fingers.

"Don't touch the black-haired one," said a man in front of him. "She bites."

The other laughed, then saw Harris in the doorway and stopped laughing.

One of the women was naked, the other wore an evening gown of slippery dark green. One breast was out of its cup. He wanted to touch the hot breast, but he couldn't move. Suddenly the love seat collapsed on one side, emptying the women onto the floor. And suddenly they were laughing, the men swearing and shouting coarse remarks, the women swearing and shaking with laughter. He moved, concentrating on where he put his feet.

He bought two fifths and walked down the dim hallway with the bottles in one hand, listening at doors. In one of the rooms where the whores received the men, a crude room not much more than a closet with a bed, not even decorated with posters and record liner notes with pictures of doo-wop and Delta blues singers the way they did in Louisiana, was a lone woman. She reared on her knees on the mattress, a pale dazed column, some older, sandy tits, a discolored tooth in front. The gown was on the floor. It looked black in the shadows, like a cast-off fur, but the light from the wall lamp picked up a gleam of green.

"Got any dope, honey?" she said.

"Don't got no dope," he said. "Got money."

"Got money?" she repeated hazily.

He closed the door gently behind him.

He holed up in the room with the woman and drank. The black woman came in later, lured by the smell of activity, and he gave her money too. There was no heat in the room and it was cold this far north in mid-June.

Sometime in the early morning he was wakened by the screaming protests and scuffling of the women being dragged out of the room by a big West Indian.

Harris leaped to his feet. A ragged stroke of pain flashed through his head. He fell back, stumbling over a bottle, which skidded glossily between and around all the feet. The West Indian gripped a woman in each hand.

"Dey got men waiting for dem," he said.

"Fuck off," said Harris, picked up the stool that had been tossed nearby and hit him in the face with it. The West Indian crashed to the floor.

"Shee-it, now you gone done it," said the black whore, rubbing her arm.

"Shut the fuck up." He started to dress. His hands were steady, but he knew he was going to vomit. Any eye movement caused arrows of pain to shoot behind them into the delicate jelly of his brain. Every pang made his stomach swarm restlessly.

"I never seen anything so fast in all my born days," said the white whore, slumped knees apart on the bed.

"You good as called that spade in here, bitch," said the black whore.

"I never," said the white whore. "You're s'posed to be working the room, not me."

"Huh. This whey the work *wus*," said the black whore. "You should of got your sorry ass out front before he come looking."

"Hush up," said Harris.

"The man what own this place, he gone kill you," she told him. "Thas his main boy."

He was almost dressed. His stomach started the heaving pattern, rippling toward his diaphragm, that meant he wasn't going to make it. He hunched over beside the mattress and vomited whiskey and bile.

The West Indian was still down, jammed like a log between the bed and the door and keeping Harris from leaving. Harris stepped on the outflung hand to immobilize it and bent over him. The nose was puffing up. The eyelids fluttered. Harris picked up the stool again—one leg was hanging half off—and clipped him on the side of the head. The man's skull hit the floorboards with a hollow *clop* and rolled loosely to one side.

"Keep quiet if you know what's good for you," he said to the women, who were watching him warily.

He stood on the bed. There was a window above the mattress, the sash welded to the frame with coats of old paint. He tried to rock it loose, but it stayed stuck. He stepped off the bed and dragged the West Indian away from the door. Then he sat down and put on his boots.

It was still midnight in the hall lit with a weak bulb that picked up tags of smoke but swallowed its own wattage. Harris closed the door without a noise and felt along the wall for the outside door to the parking lot. It was locked, to keep customers from sliding out without paying.

He shrugged and passed through the door into the bar, trying to look casual. His steps fell with the airborne lopsided feel of drunkenness, as if he was walking on floors of different heights. The men, the bar glittering in the darkness that was like a smoke, thick and heavy, the fogged mirror over the counter, the rifle in a rack over the sink, were vague woozy impressions. But a corner of his mind was sharp, enlivened by the sense of danger, and his coordination felt only slightly off.

As soon as the door swung behind him, he had to have another drink. Every step screamed, *Drink, drink, drink,* to the lined-up dusty bottles. He halted at the bar.

"A scotch," he said.

"Where's the other one?" said the bartender with his dead cod look, sliding the glass over.

"In there fucking his brains out," said Harris. He tossed the shot down, pungent, bad-fruit tasting and -smelling.

"Can't," someone sang out. "That nigger lost his balls in a crap game."

He threw the glass at the voice and heard a scream. Other voices came at him, shouting, growling, swooping. Someone punched him in the ear. He recoiled and slammed against a wall, into a fist; another fist caught him in the belly. He grunted, winded and fought back, slap quick kick quick. His ear burned wet and crushed. He took the path of least resistance, swarmed half carried between the heavy thumping bodies and hands clawing, fists punching and missing, grimly toward the door.

The parking lot was a dirt clearing between the bar and the encroaching trees. Overhead a nebula of light appeared atop a rig thrusting its black proboscis into the sky. He ran, with icy air pushing at his face. No footfalls came behind him, only the racket of the jukebox, clamoring when the door was thrown open, muffled when it closed. The truck was unlocked and the keys were in it. Harris gunned the motor and backed swiftly out from between two other cars, jouncing high in the air as the back wheels shot over ruts and roots. By the darkness, which looked black but was really a deep gray, separated from night by the minute creep of dawn, he saw a figure running toward him from the building, around parked cars and into the clearing. Harris heard a pop and sharp whine, but there was no flash. The truck seemed to leap by itself. He floored it and bore down on the figure running with raised arms between him and the road. The windshield ground filled; he wrenched at the wheel, swearing. The figure spun, then disappeared under the hood.

Chapter Forty-nine

HE WOKE IN THE LIVING ROOM, sprawled on top of the sleeping bag. The floor felt grouted in around his backbone. The phone was ringing.

He rolled to his feet, his head shrilling chaotically. The phone on the kitchen counter seemed to jump with every ring, like a cartoon phone. Harris snatched it to the crust on his ear. "Yeah?"

"Harris, it's Joe. Where the hell have you been? I've been trying to get hold of you for two days."

"Out drinking," he said before he thought. His head thumped loudly and aggressively in his ears.

"You're kidding. I never saw you take a drink. Look, I'm calling about the mares. The gray should be in heat soon. Should I go ahead and breed her?"

"If she comes in. I can't get there before next week anyway." He groped for the percolator. Yesterday's grounds were still in the basket, sticky and cold.

"Make it two weeks. It'll be safer for her to travel and I'll know she's bred. How does it look? The place."

"The way he left it."

"You sound kinda low. Everything all right?"

"Everything's fine," said Harris. "I just got up."

"Must've been a real toot. Hey, you're entitled once in a while. Let me know how it goes, will you? Call if anything comes up."

"I will. Thanks for everything, Joe." He cradled the phone.

Harris put some coffee on, then opened the kitchen door. It was a nice day. He stood naked in the doorway, feeling sick. The clearing with its guardian half circle of trees looked like the one behind the bar. He could call up every shadow, dim-lit stone and stick of that parking lot. He never had blackouts.

He was always aware on some level of what he was doing. Afterward he would relive through a painful fog of apprehension events he seemed to have gone through at a remove, like an effigy of himself.

The sky was as blue and cool as a sugar mint and a few clouds were playing tag over the fields. Impressions raced through his mind like those running clouds, but they were brooding and black. He stood in the contrast between the noon brightness and the twenty-four hours just gone, and his fear leaped alive. His body smelled like something scraped off the bottom of a foot, the sour and salt lifted out by the pleasant beat of the sun. He shuddered with revulsion. And last night? When he thought of the escape—from being shot or clubbed to death maybe and left in the river—the whiskey seemed to come out of his pores in a fog of dread.

What in hell had gone wrong with him?

He hadn't run over whoever it was had tried to shoot him. Before he turned out of the drive he had looked in the rearview mirror and seen the figure separating itself from the ground, climbing slowly to its feet. But the rest was bad. The women, those poor crappy broads. That nutless asshole whose nose he busted. The hours lost drinking.

It had been six years since Harris left Salthill. In the early period of loss he had learned misery as a refining disease, an affliction that could be borne; that could, if he did the right things, pass on to something else. His obsession with Elsa had lifted slowly over time. From this he had learned that the nature of obsession is ephemeral, and that what he had experienced was not love but something not as frightening. It had been a spell, grounded in the physical, the chemical. He knew it now. Sometimes, idly, he compared Elsa with alcohol.

Nothing had tempted him to drink. He had gone without a drink for so long he had forgotten how to want one. Abstinence had become a habit; sitting in the saloon in Four Queens with a ginger ale, sipping punch at Flavia's wedding when everybody else had been joyfully high on champagne. First he had created an identity for himself that did not include alcohol, then he had become that thing, a man who did not care what alcohol was. And beyond that, did not know what heroin was. Heroin sat behind alcohol on a throne, a pernicious deity inspiring disgust and fear of a high order. Heroin made him whimper; he came close to revolution at the thought of its terrible sweet sleep. He had grounded himself with other things. He had never told another living being of his conflict. Only one other living being had guessed at it.

. . .

Everything had changed four weeks ago, the day he had taken possession of this cabin. The date was marked on a calendar from a feed store in Oregon that now hung by the icebox. May twelve, 1957. He looked at it sometimes when he was in the kitchen. It still said May twelfth.

That was the morning he had packed his bags and checked out of the hotel in Vancouver with a rush of intense relief. He was clearing out of this city; he was going to take hold of his birthright as a man and walk free on land he owned. From now on he would be too busy to think. He would get past this unease at being in their precinct, 250 miles from the past. That was about how far he was from Salthill.

His new place was between two larger properties. Harris turned off the highway onto a dirt drive lined with conifers and an occasional cedar and jolted down that for a half mile. A stream crossed the drive under a wooden bridge. He drove over it, feeling the boards spring under the tires, and wondered if it was solid enough to keep holding the weight of traffic. You thought about stuff like that when it was your property—value, worth, repairs. He'd busted a gearbox once outside Calgary on a road like this.

The place looked even worse than when he had first seen it in February, muddy and colorless under a winter sky. Now it was submerged in an ocean of grass, wild hay and lamb's quarter, the buildings sunk to the roofs like ancient ruins. The farms on either side had trim barns bordered with wheat. The boundaries had been weeded and his neighbor's near field laid out in some vegetable. The contrast between the military furrows, moist from irrigation, and the dried-out jungle on his side was complete.

The cabin was made of finished timber and buried in overgrown hemlocks. Behind it a grove of tamaracks, sprinkled with young cedars that would later overshade the larger trees, grew in a yeasty compost percolating groundwater. Cauliflowers of filigreed coral and moss sponged up the decay. At the bottom of a neighboring field, a cherry orchard was in bright pink bloom.

He climbed the steps to the porch. Part of the chimney had caved in; he had to step over brick and crumbled grout scattered in the windfall. Jasmine grew in a tangle over the rails, following the sun through chinks in the shade, its dusty fragrance stirring as he climbed. An opportunistic Japanese wisteria had choked its latticework to splinters and was creeping along the roof. The fronds drooped over the windows like a bridal veil.

At the front door, Harris tried one of the keys from the set the bank had given him. Everything had been painted off-white. The rooms smelled like the cheap paint he remembered from rented places. There was a main room with a rough-beamed ceiling and a kitchen, the wall in between cut down to counter height. There was a fireplace with built-in shelves and cabinets on both sides. A passage off the main room led to a bedroom and bath. The bedroom had been left unpainted. It felt like a garage, with dark untreated planks and a single north-facing window set too high for light.

The only furnishings were an icebox and a stove crusted with petrified grease in the kitchen. Harris went outside and turned the water on at the main, then tried the toilet and faucet in the bathroom. The toilet flushed. The faucet gave a hollow roar, then coughed up rust-colored water.

He descended into the cellar. The walls were lined with cinderblock shelves of preserves in Mason jars, waiting in the silty darkness to be opened. Maybe Humphries had been into canning. He imagined Humphries, massive in an apron, moving slowly among steaming pots and boiling fruit.

The bottle of whiskey was on a lower shelf. Harris raised it impartially to the light. He felt nothing except curiosity; it could have been a jar of tomatoes or ginger peaches. The glass was thick, the color of clean river water in its dusty sleeve. The whiskey, curving sinuously against the glass as it turned, was maple syrup gold. The foil label glinted under the ceiling bulb. One of his nails made a bright sound on the glass. It was not a brand he remembered, but it didn't look cheap. He carried it upstairs by the neck and left it on the counter. Maybe he could find somebody to give it to.

He had known what effort lay ahead of him but that day, facing ten acres of abandoned land, he experienced a sharp loneliness. He followed the boundary fence to the end and back to the riding ring, stopping to grasp a rail, rock a post.

The first thing was to get a phone in. He would need it to do business. They had to be on the phone in the Skillihawk by now, he thought. Salthill and Mountain Inn. There were lines up in more remote stretches of the province. He had wanted to hear Grey's voice once, wanted it in the worst way, but he had never called. Maybe that was the deal he had made with himself, a lifetime of no contact in exchange for what he'd done. Maybe he was a man who had to keep his life compartmentalized, all the different periods lined up like boxes on shelves in a closet.

He unloaded the truck and brought everything in, plowing back and forth through the windfall. In the kitchen he unpacked fry pan, coffeepot, utensils, a box of strike-ons, a carton of cigarettes, bowl, mug and plate, jelly glass, two bars of Ivory soap, four rolls of toilet paper. Everything a man needed.

There were no back steps, just the back door hanging out over the foundation. A piece of the rail was attached to the house like a stuck-out finger, draped with a rag dried to the texture of bark. The rest of the steps lay in a loose pile on the ground. He jumped down and sat on a log, smoking a cigarette and thinking about the small but polished and highly efficient horse ranch this mess was going to be someday. He savored the view of the mountains behind the fields, the yellow and purple of the afternoon light, the patterns of lengthening shade in the grove. Fifteen miles away, on the other side of fields and woodlands, was Vancouver, city on the brink of a sea. How insignificant men were in this country. Their settlements were no more than stars that exploded and fell to earth, distant sparks dying on the flanks of a giant.

He remembered the evening clearly. He had gone into Berrysville for a restaurant meal, since he had nothing to cook, and tarried at a movie. It was late when he got back. He fought his way up the steps through the debris and turned on the inside light. The bulb in the ceiling sucked the light out of the walls. The broken chimney and the damper hanging loose, which he would have to figure out how to repair, meant he couldn't make a fire, and it was cold. Harris roamed the cabin with his spirits sinking. It felt cramped and dingy and full of ominous corners. It was crowded with the past; it seemed to insinuate all the possibilities for ill fate and bad endings. The beauty of the afternoon had created a kindly assurance, but now the sense of death and loss he felt was overpowering. Afterward he couldn't bring to memory exactly what that death, that loss had been.

He tried to reason with himself. The place had been empty for three years, what had he expected it to look like? He was lucky it was in this good shape.

He found a broom to clean up the windfall he had tracked in so he could lay out his bedroll. As he was sweeping the grit out he noticed, under the flattening glare that etched each mark more deeply, the kind of light women examined their pores in a mirror by, a faint stain on the floor. The floor was oak, worn but scuffless except for a few marks where the furniture had gone out. Humphries had shot himself after mailing a letter to the police so his body would be found soon. The letter reflected a determination to stick to the fundamental decencies in the teeth of a silent desperation that could be lived with no longer. Standing with the broom, Harris realized that the stain was blood that hadn't been scrubbed away. It had gone as if through a hundred washings to this shade, a soft umber streak that had become part of the grain of the wood. A man had lain in death there. More men had come to scrub away his shape, his failure to master life.

He stepped coldly over it. As he did, it came to him that he was also a man who had tried to kill himself.

He left the broom on the porch. Back in the house, he opened the bottle on the counter.

He was never able to think clearly about the feelings that preceded what happened. If he had a sense of anything it was helplessness, a gleeful rush of fatality. His hands seemed to work of their own will, disconnected from his mind. Every movement was executed in a supernatural silence where nothing chirped or brushed or stirred. Even his footfalls were erased in the breathless hush that seemed to fill the kitchen. He had to rap the bottle sharply on the tile to loosen the cap and break the seal. The sounds crackled back through time. He got out the jelly glass, poured it half full of whiskey and drank it down with his eyes closed. He wiped his mouth and set the glass thoughtfully on the counter, in a silence so thick it sounded like the roar of an ocean.

Since that night he had done nothing but drink. He bought another bottle the next day, a cheaper brand. He drank to blot out the realization of having done something horrible to himself, of having pierced a vital organ so the blood would seep from his body as from a pressed sponge. In the evenings he had a couple of belts, enough to get dressed and drive to Vancouver or Lodenstock. There was no place to drink in Berrysville. His excitement rose when he saw the bar roof in the middle of the huddle of bad dwellings, or the lights of the city where it was safer to drink and the booze was cheaper. There were no real slums in Vancouver, but it was still a city; there were still places a man could go to lose himself. He found those places as if he had never left them, quickly; as if he had been waiting those thirteen years for his chance to get back. The monastic life was carried away on a tide of whiskey. He always came to at Humphries's in the late morning, remembering remotely what had gone down, filled with that sense of doom. Once he met himself in the bathroom mirror with a swollen eye underscored by a bruise the shade of a mango. He must have been really out of it not to feel that happen. He had inflicted punishment in return; he never hesitated to and knew that even drunk, he was good at it.

In the daytime he laid in his sleeping bag smoking and dozing, ignoring the work to be done, by not looking past the shadows of the evergreens, the foliage blocking the windows and rustling dryly against the sills.

Chapter Fifty

AFTER SHOWERING OFF THE SCUM of Lodenstock, Harris drank water and urinated until the urine came out straw-colored, then downed a bottle of beer to settle the queasiness. There was a small beefsteak in the icebox. He fried it and ate it methodically, thinking about Joe in his kitchen in Oregon, with account papers and books spread on the table, and a view of the stable and tracks from his window. And the mares, who were supposed to be picked up in two weeks. Could he get the place ready in two weeks? Sitting on the fireplace mount with his legs stretched out, Harris felt that he could if he started tomorrow.

His neighbor came over to ask if he needed anything. She must have seen his truck parked in the drive and planned her move. She looked surprised when he came to the door, but she had the aplomb of the successful farm wife, able to take anything in stride, even this hard-looking, cat-faced black man. She had brought along a pie and her husband. Harris accepted the pie and stepped outside, closing the door and effectively cutting her off from entering the house. They sat at the bottom of the steps. The sun sifted through the tower of jasmine and made a pleasant heat; their dog eeled through the long grass after a quail. Two milk cows stood under a tree at the boundary fence, too dumb to switch the flies off each other with their tails the way horses did.

"On your own and no furniture, aye? I've got a deal table you can have," she said. "Don't we have some things in the shed, Ray?"

"There's a box spring an' mattress," said Ray. "Mattress is dusty, but it'd do."

He had that Anglo-Saxon economy of emotion, sitting heavy and pale in the sunlight with his freckled hands on his knees. They made good detectives, because you never knew what they were thinking. What they were thinking, of course, was that you didn't know what they were thinking, which was just fine. When two or more of them were together this made for a very quiet gathering.

"Thanks," said Harris. "I appreciate it."

"Poor old Humphries," said the wife cheerfully. "Place all gone to seed. Who would've thought this would happen to him?"

"Wilf and I put in the fencing and bridge," Ray said to him. "Good locust wood. Wilf had a fancy for it. Said it never rotted."

"It doesn't," he said. Locusts grew in the East, in limestone soils in lush green woods.

She sighed. "Now you're probably wondering why we didn't buy it ourselves and level the buildings. It's good growing land. Truth is, we never fancied it. Ray felt uncomfortable about Wilfred. Being there and not there, if you know what I mean. The Jesingers on the other side, they felt the same way."

Ray grunted sleepily.

You never put him to rest, Harris thought.

She leaned toward him. "You're going to raise horses, aye?"

Suddenly he was frightened. They had been Humphries's neighbors. Humphries had known the St. Oeggers, had bred his mares to the Salthill stud. These people were all tight with each other. If the girls or the aunts came to visit they wouldn't have mentioned him. But Grey might have, if he had ever met Ray.

"What makes you think that?" he asked.

"I suppose because the place is laid out for it. But, well, truth is you don't look much like a farmer." She laughed.

"Huh-huh," said Ray.

"What we were thinking is, our daughter's living in Toronto now and her good riding horse is out in the field eating grass," she said. "Bluebell's getting kind of wild, you know how horses are when nobody's been on them awhile. Why don't you keep her over here and exercise her? We'll provide the feed. Ray can cut your grass for you in exchange."

"That would be fine," he said, startled and relieved, then pleased. That would make three horses, with the mares.

The pie was lemon meringue, his favorite. He made a piece of it be his dinner.

In the afternoon Harris picked up the mattress and box spring and a frame, then took a load of wash to the laundromat in Berrysville. It was going to be fine to sleep in a bed again. That evening he dressed and drove into town. He had to get away from Humphries's. If he got back at a decent hour he could start work early tomorrow, get stuff done. Ideally it would be better to stay in, at least one night, but as dusk fell he knew it wasn't going to happen.

When he went outside to get in his truck, the sun was sinking behind the hills and a spectacular sunset was in full force. He seemed to stride inside a jewel flowing liquidly past the black flaws of the conifers, bathing the stars in fire. Even the dust under his feet, floury from lack of irrigation, and the hay-filled fields were a dark rose red, a deep coarse gold. The roof of the clapboard stable appeared, faintly golden in the darkening field, in his rearview as he drove over the bridge.

In Quebec he had gotten back in the habit of going to clubs. They were in basements there; you went down a flight of stairs and into a funk of cigarette smoke, booze and fried chicken grease. The Black Bottom. The Ellie's Tune. Le Club Jazz. Le Sourir. American blacks ran the grills and played in the jazz bands. It had been a joyful, jumping noise that he had needed when he could get into town, even when it had meant sitting in a corner with a Coca-Cola.

> *Down in Black Bottom, put your money in your shoe*
> *Down in Black Bottom, put your money in your shoe*
> *'Cause those women in Black Bottom, they got the take your money*
> *blues.*

The *boites* were different from the red-light house in Louisiana he had been taken to as a boy, where there was always a piano playing and the soldiers went in and out. In Montreal he had gone out of curiosity and stayed all night, emerging into the winter dawn in a daze, feeling like he had spent a year in another country. The fresh snow on the sidewalks, the men in topcoats, their dark faces authoritative and satisfied, the laughter on the air— laughter of complicity, laughter of children who had fooled the devil and stayed up all night—was part of that country.

The Starlite Grill had the lounge feel of clubs in English Canada. The walls were peach with cream trim, the doorways fluted casbah-style, with candles in glass sleeves on the tables. The barstool seats were cracked Moroccan leather. The floor was covered with Persian carpet except around the bar and blue-lit dance floor, where nobody ever danced.

He ordered a scotch and water and started on the long road to making it last. He was going to get home early tonight.

The crowd was a mix of black and white, with a sprinkling of Asians who looked like tourists. The atmosphere was altogether classier than the roadhouse. There were some fine-looking black women in cocktail dresses, their shoulders polished under the lights. A couple of them eyed him speculatively because he was a man alone, their glances darting to the stand like nice girls turning their attention back to the preacher. One of them passed behind his chair and her hip fiddled with his jacket. He glanced around. She smiled triumphantly at him over her shoulder, a woman in a pink Chinese cheongsam dress. He smiled back, amused, and watched her going away. Her rear end wagged slowly back and forth like a clock pendulum under the tight brocade. His eyes narrowed and there was still a smile in them.

Half a scotch made him introspective. *You made a mistake,* he thought. *You came back.* But he hadn't felt that way seeing the Lion's Gate for the first time in years. What he felt then had been unnamable, confusion vigorously thrust away unsorted. He sure as hell hadn't decided to settle here because of St. Oeggers. No way. It was because of the harsh winters in the rest of Canada that he had come back. He was a southern man. The climate here suited him. He told himself these things.

He listened to bebop for a set, observing without irony the subtle transcendence of the dark man over the white man in this small, cordoned-off area of society. The band played the break tune: *Deededly-op! bom, bom, bom, bom, a-deededly op! bom bom, bom, bom.* The musicians put down their instruments and straightening their jackets, tugging at cuffs and running their hands over their heads, left the stand in a kind of trance.

Harris saw the saxophone player walking between the tables, accepting greetings and comments with a little smile. At Harris's table he stopped suddenly.

"Scarface? *Man.* Is it really you?"

Memory flew him across the years, to the pen in upstate New York. The joint. An older man who used to sit with him at the noontime chain-linked tables, unasked. Bring his food over and sit down. He was taller than Harris, thickened with the years, neck puddling over his shirt collar. Harris had a sudden picture of himself sitting in front of an untouched plate of food, eyes burning in a raw face, a boy alone. The old man (he had seemed old then) had talked to him in a kindly way, tried to draw him out. He remembered the man telling him how he had worked on the Red Ball Express during the war, a truck route in Europe that brought supplies to the front.

"Time we got there, we'd grab guns if we had to, help with the fighting, you know? When I got home I couldn't get a job in a factory, man."

He had been speechless at that. He couldn't believe any black man would fight alongside his mortal enemy to save a country that refused to accept him as a citizen. That was the way he'd seen it then. He'd been on the outside looking in like he always was, not seeing it was the only country the man had, that he maybe loved his green mountains and rivers no matter who people thought they belonged to, because they were his home.

"Noble," he said, bringing the name up out of nowhere.

"How're you making it, my man?"

"Have a drink," said Harris.

The musician sat down heavily. "A Coke'd be fine. I'm boozed enough for one night. Now what the hell are you doing here?"

"I bought a place outside town."

"Yeah?" Noble leaned back with a soft grunt. He wore the jazzman's air of conferring a gentle presence on his surroundings, of not being surprised by much. His smile had a detached, mildly gloomy sweetness. "You look like you come a long way from the States. Hadn't been for that souvenir on your face and them eyes, I never would've known you. Never did know your name."

Harris told him.

"You stayed clean all this time? Been keepin' out of jail?"

"Ever since then."

"Glad to hear it, glad to hear it. Me too." Noble swallowed a yawn and massaged his eyes gently. With eyes closed he said: "Now that drummer, some nights he's higher'n a motherfucker, foaming at the mouth and about to fall off his stool. He just chippies around though. He knows I don't like working with real bad junkies, so he plays it cool." He chuckled.

The barmaid reappeared, slapped wet glasses and a ticket on the table.

"How long you going to be here?" Harris asked, eyeing his second and last scotch.

"Another three weeks. Stop by some night, bring your lady."

"Don't have one."

"Now what's wrong with you? Fine young cat like you with no lady. They's plenty stuff here if you look around. See that gal sitting over there with some others? That's the piano player's wife. Follows him all over the country, making sure he don't get too taken with anyone. Now that girl next to her? That's her sister. Nice-looking girl."

"Sure is."

"Not that you wouldn't have to mind your p's and q's with her. There's the one by the bandstand with her legs crossed and her skirt hiked up. French girl. Went home with the bass player the other night. Some of these women are right up front."

"Must be distracting," he murmured.

"Hell, yes. They do it on purpose, try to drive a man crazy. There you are up there blowing away and you got to keep your eyes closed because if you open 'em you be looking at them fine legs and dropping notes all over the place."

The piano player's wife's sister was checking him out. Strong features, tilted eyes, straightened hair pulled back in a roll so tight and polished it looked like a hunk of lacquered wood. Good shoulders in a dress cut to show the shoulders. She gave him a brilliant glance, haughty and confused and sweet. He looked away, feeling marked.

He threaded his way through the tables behind Noble, glass in hand, and was introduced. The piano player's wife looked him over swiftly, eyes stopping at the slash mark on his face.

"He's cool, Mimi," said Noble. "He just looks bad, he's really a pussycat."

"He's lying, I'm bad," said Harris.

The women laughed. He took a chair, feeling suddenly cheerful.

He paid attention to the girl, whose name was Freddy. When her group left, he cut her out of the pack and walked her home, the two of them trailing behind the others.

"What do you do if you aren't a musician?" she asked, as if a musician was the only thing worth being.

"Train horses." It seemed like the easiest way to put it.

She looked surprised. "Hadn't you ought to be in your bed?"

He smiled. "Now how do you know about getting up early?"

"I grew up on a farm in Ohio. Daddy always had a couple of trotting horses behind the house."

They were in front of her hotel, named after some commodore or a flower. He wanted to move in on her, but he knew the time wasn't right.

"Maybe I'll get to see you again," he said.

She whispered, "We're at the club most nights, but if we aren't, this where we staying."

"I can see that, girl," he teased.

She giggled, eyes cast at her feet. He liked her delicious neck, weighed down with that club of hair. A classy lady. She looked like she'd been reared with a strict hand. A lot of musicians married into families like that, good stable people. They must find a security there they needed to make it on the road.

He walked to the club through the lamplit streets and sat at the bar getting drunk. After he solved his problem, would that be the time to move in on her, or anyone else? She was beautiful in her dark skin, with that sandalwood essence around her wherever she stepped. What was his problem? This became a problem itself, something to do with bottles and the fire in his belly and limbs that wouldn't move. He was using the problem to erase the problem. Only when he was fully drunk could he acknowledge this. Only then could he face it with a little smile, and light another Player's.

Chapter Fifty-one

HE COULD TELL IT WAS AFTERNOON by the way the sun slanted in through the windows and lay its light dust on the institutional green of the walls. Harris sat on the bunk, listless and hungover, and listened to a phone ringing and being picked up, a voice whining in another cell. A typewriter clacked and clattered somewhere.

The cell was furnished with sink and lidless toilet, in working order and decently clean. God bless fucking Vancouver.

He had washed his face and dried it on the square of terry provided by the city. His braces were gone. The shoelaces were missing out of the oxfords under the bunk. This grimly amused him. No way was any man going to hang himself in their precinct. No, he would be suspended instead in lingering torture, held dangling over life until the last juice had drained from his body and the last breath been legitimately seized by natural causes.

It seemed symbolic that this visit felt less traumatic than the night he had spent in jail in Four Queens. Still, he wanted out. He wanted coffee. Behind these concerns, insistent as the burring of the phone, was the historic shade of Minnie, a specter that traveled without heat, that coolly bonded with the atmosphere, the mote-laden light and his own ectoplasm. It must have been the whore at Lodenstock that made him think of her, this morning of all mornings. They were in the same business. But compared to the whore at Lodenstock, Minnie, though tough, had been the girl next door. Minnie was embedded in his contrite heart.

"I got the dope," she said, coming in the door. She threw down her jacket and stepped out of her parrot shoes all colors of the rainbow. "I brung a customer back, though. He's down there payin' the cab. Get him over with first."

He slid off the windowsill and went in the bathroom, feeling the knife through his jeans. He heard the door to the hall open and close, the slide of a man's shoe. Marijuana punk seeped into the room, light as cat dander. She laughed that hoarse laugh like a cough.

She let the john out and came in the bathroom in her shift. Cheap fabric loved Minnie, clinging to her pine-cone breasts and long shanks like silk. She pulled the shift over her head and ran water and bubble bath in the tub while he hunkered against the wall.

"The bar is name Stokey's, and he is dead," *she said, splashing. "You be crazy, or just out your mind? Stabbin' some white hoodlum. Don't you flash them eyes at me. You are out your* mind."

He said a few words carefully, his first out loud. The stitches plucked at his mouth like guitar strings.

"So he pulled a shiv," said Minnie. "We all know that. Why didn't you run like hell? No, you had to stick him back. Some ofay. *Seem like sum you mens ain't got no sense when it come to staying away from them people. You in deep shit now, Red Johnny boy." Picked up a piece of soap, soaped up. "Damn. Now you* know *I ain't no angel of mercy. You know I don't have time or money to be hiding you in my home. Why I opened that door and let you fall in here is more than I know. The police, they going to be coming 'round now, give me all kind of trouble over what you gone and done."*

She sounded flinty, but he knew she approved of him for the whole neighborhood. For all the heads that got hit and the nights spent in jail for doing nothing, being expected to help win a war then coming home to no jobs and the back of the bus.

"I hope you enjoyed yohsef," she finished moodily.

"I'd do it again," he said.

"You ain't going to be around long with that attitude. Chile, they is folks what know how to get on and folks what don't—"

He let her run her mouth, not really listening. Her titties bobbed in the bubble bath, nice and wet and slick. Uh-uhm.

She gave up and grinned at him.

"You like white pussy like some black men?" she asked idly, twiddling her toes in the water.

"Not 'specially. I like it all fine." He got honest. "Only been with one them women anyway."

"Bet she use you like they all do," said Minnie. "Some of them loves that dark meat when they gets it. Just don't be thinking they going to help you when they get they white asses in trouble. All you is to them is a nigger in the straw."

"Girlfriend of one of my bosses," he muttered.

She ran her eyes over him. All he had on was his jeans. "That what all them scars be from?"

"Yeah."

"Look like it was a close one."

"I got away." Hatred feathered up his spine, making him dizzy.

"You been a lively motherfucker for your age. How you been making it on the streets? Been running for the numbers men?"

"Been whorin'."

"With them queers?"

"Yeah."

"You queer, too?"

"No."

"You like it anyway?"

"I need the money for junk."

"Oh, that. Stick with dope, chile. A key of good shit don't cost that much if you know the right people."

She stretched a leg out of the water with the toes nicely pointed. They watched the soap bubbles glide back down it.

"Ain't no one going to know nothing nohow, no matter how many question they get asked," she said. "The man you done kill, he showed up in that bar every month with this fancy ugly white woman. Picked up his take from the man what own the place and sit drinking his whiskey all night."

The wound worked moistly under the bandage. He gave up talking and wrote on the notepad that he kept by him with a stub of pencil. He held the note up for her to read. She could just make things out if it was written down plain.

She sniffed like one of those old white aunties down South.

" 'Do-they-know-what-I-look-like?' Huh. Don't you know we all look the same to the man? Just keep out of sight. They see that thing on your face, they going to bring you in for sure."

It was a lie to say he'd given up fear. All he had to do was think about being in jail, even up here in the north, even for a night, let alone all the days and nights he'd be in there if they found him. Then fear came back and hung itself around his neck.

Harris heard the cell door being opened.

"You can come out," said the warden, in a blue shirt and midnight-blue trousers. In America there would have been another guard behind him, hand on a gun.

At the desk a pleasant-faced English policeman handed over a bag with his stuff in it. Everything was there: braces, wallet, shoelaces, his jacket.

"You will of course go straight home," said the policeman, meeting his eyes directly, unlike the warden. They were blue, with early lines around them. "You have no prior convictions, but if we find you driving inebriated again we'll be obliged to do more than take you to the station to sleep it off."

"That makes sense," said Harris, and meant it.

He had to shell out fifteen dollars to get his truck out of the impound lot, so there was some punishment after all.

At the cabin he showered, put on clean clothes and made coffee, moving more slowly than usual. He felt curiously grounded and mentally absent, as though under an incantation. It was, after all, life; it was only when you looked too closely that the nausea came. What did it matter if he drank himself to death? If he descended more deeply into his fate as he had into the cellar that day, until the peculiar dark overcame him for good? And he couldn't ride or work or, finally, stand to live? It would come when that cherry orchard lost its color, but right now he could see the blossoms throwing their flames into the sky from the bottom of the field, a cheap pink like the cotton candy you bought for a penny at carnival time. The wiry sugar had stuck in calluses to his lips. That flame would be gone that jiggled with happiness in the lost, long-gone streets. He knew it. Right now he had it, and if he could have as much of it as time would allow, and keep his sense of fatalism, maybe part of him would remain intact and free until the end.

He thought this over coldly. It was a thing that demanded pragmatism. Otherwise you would go crazy with fear and make a blubbering ass out of yourself, erasing your hard-earned manhood, shaming humanity before the animals who even in their fright died with dignity and a sense of death's awfulness.

He went to his neighbors' to pick up the mare. Bluebell, what a name, like a cow. She waited in the field, head up and alert, a breeze riffling her mane, a chestnut with a white chevron on her face, a smaller blaze between the nostrils, leggy hind stockings.

> *Two white feet and a white nose*
> *Cut off his feet and throw him to the crows.*

He felt the drama of her presence, the bulk and big bone of horse, quivering and sensitive to his humanity. For thousands of years he had approached horse, on plain and steppe; for thousands of years horse had inclined his head, regally curious, to sniff.

Harris stroked her nose and snapped the lead to her halter. She rolled a large blackstrap eye and fell in step beside him, snorting liquidly. Toward the fence they broke together into a trot. His head, punished enough for one week, was jarred from the base of his skull to the bottom of his spine. Still, the hangover seemed to lift; he had lost weight, not eating much lately; now, aware of her legs flashing beside him, her hooves thudding on the soft earth of the path, he felt a surge of almost euphoric pleasure; he felt lifted into the air himself. He nearly laughed, thinking of the saddle waiting. Bluebell, what a name.

While he was getting out the Pariani with the sheepskin knee roll he had had rebuilt at a saddler's in Oregon, a vision came of the precinct officer who had handed him his belongings at the station. A man with that fresh complexion you saw in Englishmen that made the blue eyes start out. They were not as fine or as purely blue. The irises had been clouded with a willow brown, the lashes straw instead of sable. But the directness, the bearing, the diligent health of eye and mind, the decency that overrode every dark impulse to contradict it—he had handled Harris just right, without condescension, brutality or fear. A man who was not afraid of him or anyone, a man who was his own man.

He tossed the saddle up, smelling seasoned leather and oily wool, and thought:

Grey.

He sat on the log out back and meditated under the purpling mountains. What was it Joe had said? That Joe had never seen him take a drink? What was the difference between Oregon and now, between every place he had lived since Salthill and now? The difference was that he was in British Columbia. He was back at Salthill's gate.

Harris went inside and got a beer so he could think. He sat on the log, rubbing his unshaven jaw absently between swigs. Could he have come back for a purpose other than the ones he had laid out like ducks in a row when he went into this? Could he have secretly intended to see Grey again? Could that intention have guided him, from the first gleam of interest when he opened the classifieds of a bloodstock magazine and read the notice of a farm for sale in the north, to this hour when he hovered edgily in front of the truth's possibilities?

For six years he had refused to think about Grey, had put Salthill behind him as part of the past. He had done the best he could in a bad situation, had acted with what honor he could salvage. But time had not brought the relief of perspective. He had betrayed and dishonored friendship, and betrayal was immutable to time.

There could be no real amends. Hell lay in that direction. But to travel to Salthill and present himself, speak past the reproach, unspoken but necessarily present, that lay between them and break it down, surely break it down: could this be what he was supposed to do? It was a stupid, bad idea, because what could he say that would not bring pain?

In a murk of indecision he fixed dinner and forced it down, a little beef stew, a tomato from the wild vine outside the dog run, the last sliver of the neighbor's pie. Then he drank two shots of whiskey and got into bed.

In the middle of the night he woke. He had never been a sound sleeper, but now it happened frequently that images like dreams but with stronger shapes came to him when the world was most deeply asleep. This image transcended its distortion: the face of the policeman at the station house, turned toward him with an expression of such secret meaning and urgency that Harris sat up with a strangled cry.

He lay back, groaning. To wake in the night meant drinking. He could feel the fire of need crisping his gut, uncounted trillions of unfed cells yowling for alcohol. He got up, sighing, and went to the kitchen for the whiskey.

He drained the bottle, then sat naked on the edge of the mattress and waited for release. That was when he thought of Minnie again, her hand going cold in his on the last morning. It was when he thought of Grey. In the minutes before release overcame him he saw why he had turned again to alcohol. He saw it with a sharpness that clicked inside his head as he slid into sleep. Grey was embedded with Minnie in his contrite heart: the hand grown boneless and soft as an empty glove, the policeman's face heavy with insistence. He had tried to drink away the calls for penance, but their weight had been more than he could handle. He had fallen groaning under them, and was lying trapped.

Chapter Fifty-two

HARRIS TURNED INTO THE DRIVE at Salthill. The old gravel and dirt had been tarmacked. He rumbled over the culvert and into the silver birches that still towered gracefully overhead. The yews were overgrown and the burdened lower branches lifted, sighed and knocked at the roof of the truck. On the other side, the pasture, which had always come in full view at that point, stayed partly hidden by a new plantation of unidentifiable trees, with rubbery dark leaves and yellow bark. The small changes—tarmac, overgrowth, foreign trees—loomed alien. He shifted restlessly at the wheel, filled with dismay at the premonition of change.

The curve of the hill seemed less pronounced than he remembered, more like a swelling plain than a mountain road. Harris waited for the towers to creep above the crown. Maybe the house would look dusty and insignificant, the way he had read things did when you came back to them as an adult. The battlements and gunwales and bad-teeth parapets could be gone, replaced by a wraparound glass-and-wood hacienda like ones he had seen in the suburbs around Vancouver. Then he saw the roofs rising above the trees and the house on its projection, the blind-faced towers black against the soft June sky. His heart turned over at the sight of it, at the bronze yews east of the house, the poplars and limes—a new forest of undersized limes with chalky trunks—below the brickworked wall.

Harris shifted into low and nosed the truck down the drive to the bottom of the dale. He had had nothing to drink since noon the day before and he was sweaty and a little giddy. Other than that, he felt hopeful.

He had never been a praying man. Religion had been not been part of his life since he was a young boy, when he had gotten plenty of it. Maybe that heavy indoctrination was why he had made the connection the other night between the whiskey and this guilt that had taken on a renewed life after six years, like a bad cold coming back as pneumonia.

If they could just talk a little . . . Harris could go away relieved; they would talk again soon. He went over the last words they had spoken. Funny how he remembered them: the words in the study, the less formal words later, scraping their toes in the dirt as if to signify in dusty scrawls the confusion and apprehension inside. His thanks had been leaden; he had been in such pain, in such need to escape that he could hardly say anything. And Grey had known he was in pain. There was only one other person who had ever been able to divine his thoughts like Grey. And she was the reason he had left.

A little discipline and some rusty prayer could have kept him from doing the wrong thing. Maybe now he could do what was right, or at least find out what he had to do. He still had a chance at a sober life.

A new fence and gate separated the house from the yard, covered with a vine bearing stellate white flowers. There was no sign of life. It could have been the first day he came, the same stillness prevailed. A different pickup was parked by the gate, the same color and model as the old one.

He had promised himself he would stay calm until the house was in sight. It had been the only way he could get through the valley without pulling to the side of the road. Without turning back. Now, as if his emotions were on tap, fear and anxiety gushed through him. Harris turned the ignition off and set the hand brake.

He tried the house first. Beneath the keystone with its vined molding the door was unlocked. It had never been locked. The veranda was empty as usual in midday, the windows open on the garden, the sky soaking the floors with a Mississippi of dusty sun. The flank of the other turret, the one that had always been used just for storage, swelled against a sill on the other side. The room was airy with the spring smells of freshness and revival. There was a familiar underlay of past cooking, the combination of foods used here— flour, onion, nutmeg, sage—superimposed on the odor of granite and fireplace ash that was the house's own essence.

Harris walked through the coarse ground cover to where the other turret fluted out of the hill. A man in a white shirt and jeans and a high-crowned white hat was crossing the east meadow. Harris knew he was Indian because of his braid, and that he was young by the way he walked. About ten mares with foals were grazing in the other pasture. A flock of sheep, burly and dripping with fleece, were sprinkled in the grass near the river.

With his heart beating fast, he went back down the steps and into the barn. He walked rapidly down the dark passage, lit only by the sun falling through the windows on the bodies of the few stabled horses. He reached the end of the passage without seeing anyone. Could he have gone riding? Harris checked Jonquil's stall. The buckskin was inside. She gave a snort of recognition and rustled bright-eyed through the straw in his direction. He retraced his steps toward the entry, feeling desperate.

At the door to the tack room Grey was waiting, propped between a pair of metal crutches.

They stared at each other. Harris's eyes fell without volition down the thin legs, the metallic rods gleaming in the dusk cast by the shut-up room behind, like chain mail or jail bars.

Grey wore trousers and a brown corduroy shirt. He had lost his vital muscularity and was dried up, like a vine starved of soil and mineral food. The face that had glowed with vitality, with sheathed heat and elasticity and sun, was a sickly white stroke in the gloom. More color seemed to leach out of it as he inclined toward Harris. Only the eyes, flaring like newly struck matches, had color.

"So you've come to offer your regrets."

"I have no regrets," he said. "I wanted to see you."

"You've seen me. Now leave." He looked as if he was going to start trembling. The trousers fell loosely, outlining bulk no longer there, like sleeves mysteriously emptied.

"I can help," said Harris.

"I have help." Grey balanced himself clumsily against the doorframe, eased one foot and seemed to regard him more calmly. "What are you doing now?"

"I bought a ranch near Vancouver," he said, swallowing.

"A ranch. You, with a ranch? Where did you get the funds for such an enterprise?"

The attack made him angry. "I worked for it," he said sharply.

"The terms must have been favorable for your patch of dirt," said Grey. "You had your time here, got what you needed and moved on. I like to think it wasn't spent in vain. Now, as I said, please leave. If you really have no regrets and I am satisfied with the few minutes I've given you, there can be no reason for staying longer."

The flare of blue was gone. Harris looked into eyes like dry stones.

"Good-bye," he said.

At the entrance to the drive, Sno-Bird emerged from the trees, riding a brown cob.

Harris stopped the truck. She shaded her eyes and looked at him over her bosom. He had the sensation of being viewed from a far distance.

"I don't want to talk to you," he said in a friendly voice, over the idling engine. A cigarette hung loosely between his lips. The sun felt hot on his arm.

"Go," she said, "to the old ham. There you will find what you need."

Her hair was undone, falling sooty and thick like dried hemp past her waist. She looked no older than the day he had first seen her.

"Thank you," he said simply, and put his foot on the gas.

He didn't stop until the vast rough reaches of the north were behind him, until the neat and consolidated farms began to appear along the rivers of the south.

At first he did nothing. He went to bed, thinking, *I'm having a nervous breakdown*. He had read about breakdowns, but had thought they only happened to women. Men died by gunfire or booze, women went mad, like that crazy Sno-Bird pronouncing on him from the bushes. Men did not get in bed and stay there, the way he wanted to, forever.

He drank until he passed out. When he woke it was dawn. Harris lay in bed, wishing he still slept in the front room, which had more light and a fireplace to look at. Only when he put his feet on the floor did he remember Grey and the ill-fated trip to Salthill. Then shock, grief and pity swept through him at Grey's fate, at Grey's rejection, at his own fate, sealed as surely by the sick man as if he had murdered Harris.

He drank whiskey for breakfast, pouring it in his coffee. The sky was getting light, he had better feed Bluebell. Why did animals have to be fed at dawn? Because dawn woke them, and their bellies too. He climbed into the clothes he had dropped on the floor and went outside.

The earth was bathed in the diamond light of morning; the long sedge, glistening with dew from the night, wetted his legs. He lifted his face to the silence, monastic and birdless, of the plain. He wandered around, stepping over trash scattered as if it had dropped from the sky: old buckets, newspaper, half a roll of asbestos tiling, dog feces ripe yellow to crusted ash in color and composition, part of a stepladder, a dead rabbit with the eyes pecked out and ants pouring into the sockets, a dead rat, more rats. Rusted nails spilled from an overturned coffee can. A scrap of harness. A used condom in a nest of squashed yellowing grass. A coil of baling wire, a rusted-out oil drum, the oxidized crust so eaten through in places he could see grass through the holes.

He walked down to the stream. It hummed along the drive and into the hay, rough-bedded with stones, the only thing that had stayed beautiful and clean. He lingered with his hands in his pockets, staring at but not really seeing the water, or the yellow columbine and horsefern growing on the banks.

The paddock gate swung on its hinges like a hanging victim. The riding ring was filled with grass and chickweed. There were only a few sags in the fence, but the paint was worn down to the wood. The stable was peeling and weathered a yellowing gray, the sluffed-off paint in piles on the ground like autumn leaves. But it was in good heart inside, the vaulted roof sturdy and the boxes clean-timbered, with no sign of rot.

Bluebell was pacing in her stall. When she saw Harris she trumpeted with hunger, darted to the door and flung her head up and down, haranguing him. Harris let her into the paddock where he had laid down a feed of oats. She dashed past him with piercing cries, nearly tramping on his feet. He left her nosing and crunching and wandered away from the stable. His head was starting to work. *I've come here for nothing/I can't stay here/he hates me/o god he's sick, he's dying, ah shit he's dying, Grey . . .*

In a shed that had probably housed a horse van were a few tools; rake, shovel, a scythe, a cobra-headed hoe, a claw hatchet between two nails. A wheelbarrow was propped against the wall. Harris turned it over onto the wheels, feeling cobwebs settle like lace around his arms. As he rolled it out, bumping over earth as hard and dry as stone into the soft crust of the yard, he felt tears gather in his eyes. He stopped to dash them away irritably and hurried, nearly running, toward the stable, stopping every few feet to toss junk into the barrow. Bottles, cans, barbed wire . . . soon it was full. Where had it all come from, this mysterious spoor?

Was she taking care of him? Sno-Bird? What had she meant by that cryptic statement about ham, and how he would find what he needed by going to it? Why did she think he needed anything? It was Grey who needed . . . Grey hated him. Had he somehow learned about Elsa? Was that the reason for his hostility? The thought made him feel sick. No, that wasn't it—that couldn't be it. Grey was angry, disappointed because Harris had left him and his plans for them both, had run away from his love . . . How could two men talk about love, how could they do more than silently hate each other for having loved each other?

Harris drove the junk in truckloads to the dump in a kind of frenzy. He stopped at Berrysville for a bottle of whiskey, uncapped it and drank freely at the wheel, shooting darting glances around for cops. It was a weekday, there was hardly any traffic. Back and forth, up and down the highway, the dump miles away near an industrial site, one picture haunted him, replacing asphalt, scenery and slag heaps, becoming distorted and wavy as the afternoon wore on: Grey walking up the aisle at Flavia's wedding, tall and whittled down in dark, formal clothes that turned his skin to ivory and his hair to spun gold, with the bride on his arm. He had danced the first dance with her, virile and elegant, light as a god on his feet, smiling down at the crown of her head, then at the lights as they shot and swirled around the floor.

On the way back—it was nearly sundown, it had taken him all day— Harris decided to go to a bar, where he could get stinking drunk away from Humphries's. But he couldn't see the road; it undulated back and forth under the tires and the painted stripe down the middle kept vanishing. It took all he had to turn into the drive and wobble up it at a slow pace, sometimes running the truck onto the grassy shoulder and having to stop and back it off. He lurched to a stop in front of the cabin, got out and vomited into the dust-addled weeds. Fumbling for his shirttail and wiping his mouth, he climbed the steps, clutching the rail, feeling vines scratch and tear, and fell in the door. The cabin received him, a remorseless tomb, barren except for his own drab stuff, which he stumbled over blindly, cursing.

He was sicker the next morning than he had been since he'd started drinking again. Harris poured a shot of whiskey to steady his nerves, watching his hands surreptitiously. They weren't shaking yet. He thought of the winos in the streets with their palsies and red sores, the dead who haunted his sleep, and roamed the kitchen in desperation, skirting grocery bags full of empty bottles. Brown liquid seeped onto the linoleum from under one of the bags.

Later he remembered what he had sometimes noticed, a tendency to act on a thought running so deep underground he was unconscious of it. All he knew then was that in the middle of his pacing, he suddenly stopped and opened a small cupboard under the counter. On one of the shelves was a telephone directory covered with dust. He must have taken unconscious note of it when he was unpacking.

Harris plopped it open on the counter. It was musty and outdated. It had probably been in the cupboard since Humphries lived here; it had been thumbed through and consulted by Humphries. With an internal shudder, Harris flipped through the pages toward the letter *H*.

He was really going to have to get a chair. He eased onto the window seat and, with the sun making dusty patterns on his shoulders through the wisteria, ran through the list of every business and name that began with an *H*. Ham. Ham. *There you will find what you need.* There didn't seem to be any message here. Humphries was listed, which wasn't surprising as he had been alive then, but that was immaterial. There was nothing he needed in this place except to get his shit together. *Grey.* He blinked, and fanned forward.

St. Oegger would be listed under *S,* not *O.* Harris lifted a half inch of directory upon *S.* There were a number of Saint Somethings, but only one St. Oegger, *IM.* That had to be the aunt, Iseult.

The classifieds were listed by category. It looked as if he would have to read every page. He flipped to the O entries first—Office Supplies, Oil, Opticians—then back to the beginning. He saw it right away because it was under Art—a display ad with an ink drawing of a building shaped like a barn, and under it in dignified type: *Oldham Gallery, Fine Art.* That was what she had been saying. Oldham. The address was on DeHaviland Street. Wasn't DeHaviland somewhere downtown? He could have sworn it was near the hotel he had stayed in before he moved into the cabin.

Art gallery?

Elsa.

He parked the truck near the hotel and went cunningly on foot.

The boulevard was packed with cars and buses, inching across the intersection in both directions like lines of tramping beetles. Harris crossed between idling engines and entered the park. It was laid out around a maze of graveled paths, shaded with red-boled cedars and ginkgoes. In the center was a lake with a scarlet bridge which he veered to cross, his dull interest quirking, because it was there. He leaned over the bridge and watched three swans glide from under the arch, uncoiling their necks as they came out into the sunlight. The water was so clear he could see lava rock and speckled stones on the bottom, and some kind of weed streaming toward the surface like a tattered dress.

DeHaviland was a street of old frame houses, some of them converted into professional offices with shingles over the doors. There were a few close-faced shops. Three blocks from the park a scattering began of possible art galleries, with paintings on easels in the windows, like dummies in a dress shop. But the Oldham, standing alone on a corner with a shingle over the door, had no windows. It looked important and fastidiously tended in its creamery-butter shingles and an ogee roof of gray scales. Harris felt diffident. A pair of doors stood open above a flight of steps lined with holly in pots. He had the impression of a plain of blond light reflected from varnish or new paint, but a wall or partition cut off his view.

He stood in front of the entrance like a man waking from hypnosis and wondering where his senses have been.

There was a bus stop at the curb. He withdrew and lit a cigarette. The building looked tranquil, like a library or old men's home. He waited, a man waiting out a siege. The open doors leaped at him, repulsed, became a distant shore. The post-hangover headache vanished, as if its only purpose had been to make him desperate enough to get him here. In its place came a dry, intense pain. Memory, rising toward consciousness, swam back and forth under his thoughts. He felt nausea at the invasive prodding, moved deliberately, breathed shallowly, put the butt out with a scuff of his shoe and nudged it into the gutter, swearing under his breath.

Memory, suddenly sharp, turned up the bellying of a curtain in a night breeze.

He hadn't kept the drawing. He had taken it with him and burned it in a motel room in Medicine Hat. The paper had curled toward his fingers, turning into a brown cigar that broke in fragments when he tossed it away. As fear had kept him from enjoying the amazing reproduction of himself, fear had kept him from grieving as he watched it disappear.

Goddamn all St. Oeggers. Goddamn them and that cracked woman for dragging me here! So she paints? So what? Got nothing to do with me.

He turned and walked back toward the park.

Chapter Fifty-three

AS SOON AS HE WAS IN THE TRUCK, he had to have a drink. A panicky dew broke out on his forehead. He had drunk up everything in the cabin. He cursed Grey and himself and whiskey. It was broad afternoon. He could make the store before it closed.

He was driving home by a different route. Harris passed a restaurant on a spit of land between the highway and one of the ubiquitous rivers that flowed around the city. The pink and blue neon sign was a fish blowing a circle of bubbles around itself. He made a U-turn, parked the truck in a lot fenced with privet hedge and went inside, nearly running.

The telephone was in a niche by the restrooms, the directory chained to the base. He opened and riffled it hurriedly; this one was current. There was another St. Oegger above the first one: St. Oegger *ER,* with an address on Aubrey Road. Elsa, another name for Elizabeth. *ER,* Elsa Rhys. He would call her. His amends to Grey had failed. Now it was her turn.

The cubicle was suddenly washed with the swimming golden red of Glenlivet. His mouth filled with saliva and his head spun.

She would slam the phone down in his ear. He made a note of the address and dialed the number. While he listened to the line ring, he stared blindly at rows of red booths and chrome fittings.

A deep female voice answered. "Hullo?"

A wrong number. He held the phone dumbly, feeling hope plunge. "Hullo? Hullo?"

Then he heard the accent.

"Elsa," he said.

He heard a sharp intake of breath. "Who is it?"

"It's Harris."

He stood with the receiver tucked between his jaw and shoulder and listened to the hollow sound that meant they were still connected. Red and yellow lobsters marched over the plastic covers of a stack of menus on a nearby table.

"Elsa," he said.

"Where are you?"

He could hear her young girl's tone resonating under the adult one, like a ping at the bottom of a bell. Domestic noises lapped around it—tap water running, the clink of crockery, a dog barking.

"I'm here. In Vancouver," said Harris. "Elsa, I want to talk to you."

He could hear her breathing, light and anxious.

"What about?" she said finally.

"Nothing that will upset you. I promise."

"I can't think of anything about you that doesn't upset me," she said, and hung up.

He stood there holding the receiver.

Elsa clutched a tea towel in one hand and listened to the children shouting outside. There was a softball game beyond the shrubbery that hid the road from the house. The road was lined with trees, birch, cedar and jacaranda. The latter had just come into bloom. Although they had no fragrance, the profusion of pale purple blooms, hanging in clouds from the branches and drifting in masses along the lawns, filled the air with a cloying presence not unlike cheap scent. It was still far from dusk, yet as she stared out the window a teardrop of light appeared over the hedge, then another farther down; the street lamps coming on one by one.

She had been rinsing a saucer when the phone rang. It clicked loudly against the sink. Elsa stared at it with a blank expression. Chipped. She made a whimpering sound and hurled it out the window with all her strength. It shot across the garden and into the shrubbery, taking its place with the pot scrubbers, the odd toy, a mummified orange. She was an outstanding pitcher but not much of a housekeeper.

She shuddered and looked at her hands. They were trembling.

Sophronia came in. "I told them to put their bikes away. Leaving them laying in the drive. What's wrong?"

"Nothing. An obscene phone call. I hung up."

"Ugh, them." Sophronia leaned against the sink. "Dinner ready?"

"It is," said Elsa. "If you start dishing up I'll fetch them."

"Smells good. I thought you couldn't cook."

"Not can't, won't." She fumbled with the lid of the fry pan, releasing a wad of scented steam. "Goulash, the cheap version. Jay likes it. Hamburger, onions, canned tomatoes and noodles, with one precious scoop of sour cream. Not very exotic, I'm afraid."

"Sounds fine," said Sophronia with an air of resignation.

Elsa went outside and called the boys. They came running through the garden, past the flowering planters and wild shrubbery, the scattered tools and cat dishes. She stood in the doorway and they ran panting under her raised arm.

A milling about took place. Jay wandered in with a magazine and found a seat while the boys struggled over soap in the washroom. Elsa shifted a stack of books off the table, poured milk out of a carton, pushed a drawer shut with her hip. At the table the boys made noises with their chairs and fumbled for the bread.

"Hands off," said Sophronia, eyelids heavy but voice like a smack. "Grace first."

Jay sniffed, but put down the magazine and sat with his hands on his knees.

"They're all wound up," he said from under his brows. The boys snickered.

"Sit still," said Elsa absently. "Scottie?"

They bowed their heads.

The siege lifted at times, and Harris became relatively sober. Then he slept, exhausted, and in waking hours laid plans like a frenzied soldier constructing a bulwark against invasion. He had gotten his books out of storage, and now he opened the boxes and put them on the shelves. The rows of gold and blue spines, spines the brown of saddle leather or with crackling dust covers in primary colors, were a statement to the cabin and its ghost, to St. Oeggers and everything else lost, that he intended to stay. He balanced his bank statements, noting coldly that there would be no money left in one account after buying the mares. The money he had set aside for loan payments was still in the other account, but he had drunk up his prudent reserve. He was going to have to make some deal soon, get some horses to board or train, or he was going to be in trouble.

He saddled Bluebell and followed the brook into hills that seemed to fold softly on either side, leaving the farms behind. The brook widened into a river with a deep sandy bottom, running fast between high thicketed banks, the path beside it shaded with hazels and oaks. Clumps of brilliant green and silver sedge dazzled in the gaps between trunks. The trees extended their branches over the brown river the color of good beer, deeply clear and with a small foam around the rocks, casting it in shade except for the center, where a stripe of sun bobbed and shifted. Ray's dog went along, sometimes running ahead to sniff out a rabbit or jump onto half-drowned stones to snap at darting fish.

He never knew why he decided to go back to the gallery. No voice spoke to him, and he had no warning dream or premonition. Neither had he thought again about Sno-Bird's weird pronouncement. Elsa had paintings in there; she had become a real artist. That was what she had meant.

It seemed easier to drink himself blind every night than plan the next move. If he phoned Elsa she would hang up on him again, and he didn't want to confront her in person. Everything he knew about Elsa forbade that. He had to somehow convince her to meet with him. A spiritual wisdom came to him between the second and third shots, when he was in that golden glow of release and his mind became almost playful in its dexterity. The right words would form when the time came, because he had once loved these people and from that love had come his own good. The healing syllables of peace would flow from his lips. He felt, after the third or fourth shot, that the St. Oeggers were suffering from a malaise brought on by his deception, that their lives were haunted by his prolonged and extravagant silence.

In the daylight of reality he knew that he had been forgotten and that they would have been surprised to know he thought of them more now than he had in years. That they had assumed a terrible immediacy as if they occupied the cabin with him and dead Humphries. They moved with him from room to room and watched him wash himself and cook.

Still, there was no reason for him to dress in town clothes that Friday morning, six weeks after he picked up the keys to Humphries's. There was nothing to propel him toward the city, no vague sense of business left undone. To the last day of his life, he would think of that afternoon as something slated to happen, the way your car started down the road to meet the truck in the collision that ended your brief excursion on earth.

On his way out, Harris heard a tractor engine start up in the next field. It was Ray on his Harvester, wheeling onto Harris's land through the gate in the boundary fence. The long grass swayed in front of the tires, then swooned and splintered as Ray pulled the mower sideways through the opening and jerked the lever back to spread the cutters. His hand went up in a casual salute. He wore a billed cap that shaded his face. Harris lifted his hand in return. A cloud of starlings rose from the grass in front of the mower.

The day felt slow and peaceful in spite of the racket the Harvester made grinding along the fence. It was as if Harris was hypnotized by the sun-filled sky and fields into walking ahead to the truck, instead of staying to watch his place rise out of shorn land. Yet he was unconscious of any enchantment, either then or on his way into town. It was crazy. He tried never to go back to anything once he left it. He didn't like the different periods of his life, stored in those mental boxes, to overlap even briefly. It made him feel as if all the ghosts would get together and compare notes on him, and a motion would be made to declare him inferior and drum him out of his own existence.

This time he drove past the park and straight up DeHaviland. There was no sign of life around the gallery. How did they sell anything if no one ever went in the place? Maybe they didn't sell pictures, just put them up for people to look at. He was a stranger to this whole art thing. He found a parking spot under the trees. His truck looked rough beside the sedans and two-doors lining the street. Harris climbed the steps and walked slowly in through the double doors.

The partition that had cut off his view was part of a narrow alcove. Beyond it was a small room with a beamed ceiling. The walls were pale cream, the floor hardwood with a pecan finish, full of knots and whorls. He could see through a doorless entry another room of cream and pecan, vast and immaculately bare. A desk scattered with papers and books blocked the entry. There was a lamp on it with a green glass shade, a lidless enamel box of business cards. Harris glanced at the desk, then walked around it into the other room.

The room was deserted and full of an alien silence. Pictures were hanging on partitions in parallel rows on the polished floor, along with a few statues scattered around waiting to be bumped into. He could see a painting on the back wall, something red streaked with yellow, like a Rome apple. Light fell to the floor from windows set high under the gables.

It was his first time in an art gallery. Most of the paintings seemed to be landscapes in heavy gold frames. He stopped in front of an ocean with waves crashing on the shore. The froth sucked away from a ledge of beach the smooth gunmetal of a carpenter's plane, baring rocks crusted with silver barnacles. There was a violet tint to the storm clouds gathered over the waves. It was too ornate, too decorative, too dumb. Her things had spoken in some way. Not that he told himself this in so many words. His reaction was simple and ignorant. He looked, and knew it wasn't hers. He read the typewritten label mounted on a strip of Lucite next to the canvas. The label gave the title of the painting, the artist's name, what kind of material had been used in its construction and the price. The artist was somebody else.

He worked his way swiftly back to the front on the other side, rejecting snow-covered mountains, the pine-fringed shores of Queen Charlotte Island, a Chinese market, even a refinery at Kitmat. Everything belonged to the other artist.

The first painting in the next row was hers. He knew this not because of a difference in style, or because it spoke to him. He knew it because the first painting, an unframed canvas wider than his arms could reach, was a view of the Skillihawk Valley. The paint lay in curling glossy shapes, like a windfall of leaves, and it was only when he stepped back that they melted together and took on form. Then the golden benchlands appeared, and the mountains speckled with glaciers, disappearing range on range into the northern twilight. The texture was loose and the details sparse, but what he was seeing was clear. It was the Skillihawk in its dry, prewinter mood. She had captured it perfectly.

He read the label. *Autumn. Acrylic by Elsa St. Oegger, 1955.* Her name in print filled him with unease. The price was a month's earnings for an average man.

He was seized with a violent reluctance to go on. He continued down the row, pressed steadily on by some force. There were only a few paintings. She was twenty-two; how many pictures could she have painted? As he approached each one, his body seemed to take on an extra load of weight. He looked and moved on, finding in the next frame worse memories, the first dread beginning to flutter in his belly.

After the Skillihawk painting were two watercolors of a lake the color of a fresh lime, seen through a stand of birches, that looked like the country around Four Queens. Standing with hands behind his back, he examined the white skins of the birches, laced with pink and gray knots, and the sheen on the water.

Then came portraits. Harris stopped dead at the sight of human faces. He did not want this. He did not want to come on Grey St. Oegger frozen in paint, or Sno-Bird Williams in paisley and leather, smiling dryly from the porch at Salthill.

On the other side of the room a door stood open. He retreated and stood blinking in the sun at an empty parking lot. The shadow of a cloud loaded with rain gathered from some storm at sea lay over garage roofs and back gardens of snapdragons and sweet peas. He listened to the urban grizzle of traffic, frightened in a way he never had been at Humphries's, frightened by phantoms rising at his back.

He turned back into the room.

There was a pencil and charcoal portrait of two Indians, sitting on the grass in their ceremonial blankets. The blankets, in browns and rust and dingo yellow, were so finely detailed they looked eerily real, like old photographs gone mustardy from being stored in drawers. But the fabulous blankets were cheapened by the dignity of the square-hewn faces above them. They had forgotten themselves in the act of displaying their wealth, and their souls emerged from the hardness of their faces. Their eyes were the eyes of captive wolves, bright with staring resignation. In a moment so sharp he was lanced with sorrow, Harris saw the defeated warriors who had sat in the grass with him at haying time.

There was a sketch in red chalk of a girl in jodhpurs and boots, standing the way girls that age did, with her stomach out. Her gaze was aloof and enigmatic, already glazed with the mystery of femininity.

After that came a portrait of a woman in a blue dress sitting in an armchair. Harris stopped in front of it. The figure was strangely elongated, and looked struck by some sleeping or fainting disease. The hands resting in her lap were long and weak, the face long, white and empty. The blue dress dominated the painting and gave a listless air to the head on its stemlike neck. He read it easily. A woman who disliked sex, a greedy woman who expected nice things, gems and clothes and status, who hated the moisture between her legs, disliked the penis. Inbred, dried up. She would wash and wash to be clean, and give nothing. If he was that woman he wouldn't have the picture in his house. It was as honest as a blow, full of coarse power. He was impressed.

He had reached the end of the row. There was a partition behind it, angled against the wall, on it a single painting framed in stained dark wood. Harris started, hesitated, then moved forward in disbelief.

It was a portrait of himself as a child.

That was his first reaction. It was a portrait of a young boy, and it was him. The light green eyes were outlined with dark lashes. The nose was his before it had been broken. It was the one studio photograph ever taken of him, on the mantel in his first aunt's house next to photos of her own children. Someone had taken it out of its red leather frame and out of Barbados and it was hanging here. He was staring at the childish version of the face that had looked back at him in the mirror all his life.

He stepped closer. The colors, faintly odorous with turpentine, gleamed in the silent room.

The boy was seated in a bishop's chair, with the curved back rising behind his head. He looked kindergarten age or less. He wore a white shirt open at the collar to reveal his tender brown neck, and blue shorts with a belt. His arms lay on the armrests of the chair, too short to reach the ornate knobs at the ends. It was a dignified pose. The chair stood by a window, maybe a parlor window. The parlor window where a chair like that had stood, the last time he had seen it. Sunlight poured in on the chair and the boy, falling on part of his face and body, leaving the rest in shade. The white shirt, touched with pools of blue and yellow, was more brilliant than the small face. But it was the face that dazzled. The eyes, the green of pond water, touched with amber like reflected sun or the movement of aqueous life, gazed at a point beyond him with an expression of sweet honesty and self-possession that was a world to itself.

Everything was fading in and out like a radio with bad reception. It was only after a time that Harris could turn to the label. It was a long time before he could read the words typed on it.

Seated Child. Oil by Elsa St. Oegger, 1956.

Chapter Fifty-four

HE ENDED UP GETTING A ROOM in the hotel where he had stayed before. He couldn't face Humphries's tonight.

While he was checking in, Harris saw the apprehensive look on the face of the woman clerk. He glanced in the mirror behind the desk and didn't blame her for being nervous. He looked ferocious. This struck him as blackly funny, which in turn bred an elaborate courtesy, as if having lost his mind, he was reaching out for the last remnant of sane behavior available to him. He towered over her while she fluttered with papers, a devil with a scarred face, a man no lady stomached, a chain-gang fugitive with flared nostrils and smile that menaced, ready to suck up the innocent. Then the manager came out from in back and remembered him, even remembered his name. They spoke to each other. He pulled himself together for the trip upstairs.

It was early evening, near suppertime. Harris opened the door on a bed with a puke-green chenille spread, chairs covered in tired chintz, maple with peanut-brittle varnish, a tinted photo of hop fields in the Okanogan Valley. He threw down his keys, shrugged out of his jacket with a cigarette hanging at the corner of his mouth, winking at the smoke, and picked up the phone. Waiting for the call to go through, he paced back and forth as far as the cord went.

"I have your party. Go ahead, please."

"Joe," he said.

"Harris. On your way yet?"

"Soon. Did you breed the gray mare?"

"Not yet. I held off a few days to make sure. She looks ready now. Let's see, I can take her to the stud Friday, he's booked before that."

"Don't do it. I've changed my mind. If I need to I can find a good stud up here." He lit another cigarette. "Joe, I may not be able to get there as soon as I thought."

"Anytime is fine if you're not putting her to the stud. How's the place going? Getting stuff done?"

Harris dowsed the cigarette in the Coke bottle on the nightstand. There was quite a collection growing in there, a glass temple of butts soaked in gray ash.

"I'm getting more done all the time," he said.

The streets were quiet for a Friday night. Harris walked to the boardwalk and watched the sea turn primrose under the setting sun and the first stars appear. When the harbor lights came on, he tramped back past rows of docked fish boats and stopped at the first bar.

He drank whiskey facing the door. His throbbing head felt disconnected from his body, a hot weight pressed into his hand. Everything seemed distant; the whiskey burning, his thoughts wavering, like his vision, around the room, the barmaid's legs lumpy in black nylon, the bar loading up until the mirror reflected an ocean of humanity and choking smoke, the toilet where he stood, weaving, to piss a gallon of relief, everything but the one fact that shouted over and over.

He bought a tin of aspirins and washed two down with another whiskey.

"You all right, mister?" asked the barmaid, idling for a second. "Need a cab?"

"Shut the fuck up," whispered Harris, turning away. Even those few words caused intolerable anguish, as if his mouth was a wound that tore itself wider with every word that escaped.

He ran out of funds and his last drink was a Black Horse. He set the empty bottle on the table and listened to it overturn. Only slight corrections were necessary to reach the frosted porthole that identified the door, because he had a good sense of direction. The street was dark, very dark; he stood with legs braced to steady himself, feeling the salt air sting his face. He stepped forward. The moon must have gone behind a cloud or one of the ships tethered like buildings to the skyline, massive in the inky, oily blackness of the harbor sea. He stepped on air and plummeted into darkness that shot triumphantly to meet him as he shot down. Like a dolphin he thrust occasionally with shod feet, plunging below bobbing garbage and tar-slick, then spiraling upward. Something loomed, a hull or pile, and slammed into him. He trawled blindly away from it and broke gagging and spitting to the surface.

. . .

He climbed the stairs to his room, shoes squeaking. His teeth had stopped
chattering; between somewhere and now he had sobered up. He stripped off
his clothes and stood under a hot shower, gasping and letting the water
bounce out of his mouth. His cigarettes were still in his jacket pocket; he
squeezed the pack out and chucked it in the wastebasket. He washed his
underwear and socks with complimentary shampoo, draped them over the
radiator, hung jacket, shirt and slacks on hangers to dry. His shoes went under
the radiator. They were ruined, but he had to have something to walk in.
Then he climbed naked into bed and got ready for a sleepless night. He
thought about Joe. He hated to put Joe off, but he didn't know what to do
about the mares, with this other thing that had happened. The other thing
made him sick. When he tried to meet it squarely all the fuses blew and
stopped his mind dead in its tracks, cracked like a piece of glass. He couldn't
handle the pain.

He fell asleep. Bad dreams made him twitch and moan. When he woke
it was late morning and he was hanging out over the floor, the pillows
upended like marshmallows on the carpet. His eyes felt gritty. The relation-
ships had sorted and rearranged themselves in his sleep, and he rose with a
leaden acceptance of their reality.

Ray had finished mowing his land and it looked better, the long clean lines
of field and buildings mellow in the afternoon haze. Harris felt a momentary
sharp exhilaration that seemed borne on the air along with the odors of
cultivation, fertilizer and cut grass. The hay and junk were gone, magically
leveled, and he was sure of one thing. He was meant to be here. Grey's
reception of him two weeks ago made sense now. Harris had not only thrown
love back in his face, he had stomped on it and mangled it first.

Before leaving town, he had stopped at the public library. It was the
biggest he had ever been in, marble and mahogany in the lobby, grids of
stacks in leather shades inside. The national and local newspapers had been
put up on poles in the reading room. Harris unhooked the current edition
of the *Sun* and found back editions stacked on shelves. He took a random
sampling of Toronto, Montreal and Vancouver papers, threw in one from
Winnipeg and another from Seattle, and sat down at a table in his wrinkled
clothes to read through the art sections.

It took forty minutes to find a reference to Elsa St. Oegger, in an article
listing different happenings in the art world: *Miss St. Oegger, a native of British*

Columbia who trained at the Slade, London, has won this year's prestigious Winnipeg Foundation Prize for Canadian Art. Miss St. Oegger resides in Vancouver and teaches art at Simon Fraser University.

Not a native of British Columbia. They had that wrong. They had been hypnotized into thinking this was one of the genus *Canadiana,* freckled and hearty and plumb full of common sense. Painter, she was a painter . . . an artist. Yes, he saw that. She had shown him what he needed to know through pictures, like a mute girl. A mute girl telling a blind man.

He went through a stack of Canadian and American art magazines and found a paragraph about her in an article dated October the year before. There was no photo. The paragraph plunged into a discussion of her work.

> *. . . a promising young artist whose primary interest is the discovery of hidden motifs in ordinary subject matter. Unconventional use of colour and form draws the viewer's attention to often contradictory inner life, and to the minutiae of human emotion. Themes are developed with a sensibility that make her canvases among the most idiocentric of colour composition imprimaturs. . . . . An artist of unusual maturity.*

A twinge of humor stirred in him, so he wasn't dead yet. He flipped the magazine over and eyed the cover. Minutiae of emotion, huh. He wondered whether she believed all the stuff she read. Not unless she had changed beyond recognition.

At this knowledge of her as she was, he felt the first needles of fear. He started to perspire in his shirt, at his dread of her judgment.

Harris drove by the house on Aubrey Road the next day.

It was an old clapboard, two-story bungalow shaped like a chimney stack. There were lemon trees on the lot and more in the vacant lot next door, so the property had probably been part of an orchard once. The lower story was hidden behind an unkempt hawthorn hedge.

He drove by slowly, feeling conspicuous. There were West Indians in Vancouver but no black faces around here. He circled the block. The gate to the drive was closed. A bird of paradise grew by the fence, one of its orange and purple heads wound through the chain links. A brown Cadillac was parked in the drive. It was in good shape except for a tinfoil crumple in the bumper. Harris felt another flicker of amusement like the one that had greeted him in the library.

Through the garden gate he could see a bicycle parked by the door, a

marmalade cat sitting on the stoop like a piece of pottery. He imagined the
radio going in the kitchen—there was a squirt bottle of dish soap on the
window ledge left of the door—sweaters and mackintoshes piled in the entry,
cat hair on the sofa. Home elegance had always been low in the St. Oegger
priorities.

He drove on down the road, passing a school. Was it *his* school? It looked
shut up for the summer. Or was it Sunday? He had lost all sense of the days.
He had been flung into space; he was whirling suspended in time.

A sign at the turnoff said the neighborhood was called Mount Delphin-
ium, even though there weren't any mountains, just houses like hers, with
old orchards behind the garages. Ancient walnuts and live oaks grew on the
lawns. The sidewalks dissolved into dirt shoulders at the end of the block.
The roots of the oaks grew over the spits, burst through the asphalt and lay
in the road like knotted legs and arms. Jacarandas closed over it to make a
tunnel of graceful dark trunks and foliage shaggy with light and shade.

A middle-aged couple walking on the shoulder stared at Harris suspi-
ciously. It jolted him into anger. It was as if he needed an excuse to lose his
temper. He floored it and left the neighborhood, finding an open road and
driving fast and hard through fields of wild mustard.

Her house would look like Salthill inside. Ranch life was organized around
work. Everything—character, history, private thoughts and longings—had
been peripheral to the central core of labor. There had been nothing to talk
about. There had been no curiosity about him. Sloth or inquisitiveness would
have surprised them, but he had been a stranger to both. He had understood
the way they wanted to live, had blended into the fabric of their lives,
become part of its weave.

He hadn't been set loose after all. He had never left.

He returned to Aubrey Road that evening, driven by a craving, like the
craving for liquor, that seemed to intensify at the end of the day. Then he
wanted— But what was it he wanted? His curiosity fed? The longings he
had throttled and buried satisfied, even though he now knew he had never
known what they were? That had never been what he thought they were,
body hungers, or superior urgings for happiness and accomplishment? The
vision in the gallery had left a trace across time, like a star shooting past the
impervious planets; he was destined to live his life forward from that vision.
There had been moments like it in the past. They had marked discovery; he
struggled to remember a passage from the New Testament about seeing
through a glass darkly and removing veils. They were long strands of life that

carried his being toward its end. Even though he cursed and fought against the journey, it was the mystery of his being that he longed to master, the longing its own unending search.

He drove under the trees with their bowers of purple, stopped the motor and sat with the window rolled down, listening to crickets scraping in the citrus-laden twilight.

Suppose he got out and rang the bell? He imagined an angular woman in the doorway, the adult version of Elsa, wheaty hair bobbed or in a horsetail, as he was the adult version of the child in the painting. There was no color or fire in his speculations. He would step past her toward the dark inimical being waiting inside. He would touch the small hands that had rested on the chair arms; he would speak the unspeakable.

In the midnight hour he brooded over the secret he had kept. It hadn't been a secret to anyone for a long time. Not Grey. Not Sno-Bird or Piwonka or old Dai, Piwonka's cowboys or the waitresses at the Plaza. The fiddlers and tin whistlers, the cattlemen. The Georgewoods, the Lachlans. The library lady and the red people in their shotgun houses. Being what he was, no one in the Skillihawk. He hadn't even been able to spare them that. What if he'd given in to one of those impulses to phone Salthill the last six years? He wasn't good-humored enough to see anything amusing in standing bug-eyed while illusion was stripped away by a cold voice at the end of a line. If a man was a rogue, so be it. No man enjoyed being a buffoon.

The front door opened. A woman stepped out and paused under the fanlight.

He watched from the shadows. In the light her dress looked like orange paper, polished and crisp. A turban nodded among the leaves, like one of the heads on the bird of paradise. He let the breath slowly out of his nostrils. She turned from the light and went down the steps, moving with the imperial, practical grace of an African woman. Harris watched her close the gate and get into a Pontiac parked in front of the drive. He slouched on his tailbone and stared at the house across the street, a Victorian with a tricycle left out on the porch, until he heard the Pontiac start up and move past him. Her headlights flashed across his mirror on the passenger side, drowning shadows, and slid away.

Chapter Fifty-five

EXPLOSIONS OF SUDDEN COMPREHENSION and resolution sometimes burst around him like artillery fire, lighting his feet instead of his head, falling in showers into the dark. His hunger for the sight of this child he now knew he had grew until it filled his waking thoughts. Harris had never had anything to do with children, and had observed them seldom. He felt a pity for their fragility and lack of worldliness. One night in an alcoholic stupor he dreamed that Grey had rejected the child savagely, that Elsa had put the child away with his connivance, that Grey and Elsa came to him on a beach, where the warm gray ocean met the cool gray sky, and waited with the wordless gloomy avid patience of the dead for him to tell them what to do with the child. It was not the young Elsa that he saw in his dream but the teller at the bank, a middle-aged woman who always wore sweaters and looked like she felt the cold.

He wrote a letter.

In Berrysville to buy feed, he picked up a packet of airmail paper. He sat down at the deal table with a cup of coffee and a notepad.

> Dear Elsa,
>
> I realize you don't want to see me. You made that clear when I called. Please give me a few minutes of your time. I won't ask to talk with you more than once. Maybe we can come to a friendly conclusion, and when you think of me it will be without the anger you obviously feel.

Harris bit his lip, pondering, then changed "obviously feel" to "seem to feel." The ballpoint squeaked under the pressure of his fingers.

Otherwise I hope you won't mind if I call Grey. However, I would prefer to talk to you. If you agree, please meet me at King Seafood on the River Road this coming Wednesday at 7:30 PM. If you aren't there, I will take that as your final answer. If you need to say anything before then, you can call me at PL32239.

Harris

It was almost as long as the letters he had sent to Grey, driving from show to show that last summer. Longer than the letter he had written to Clarence Westbrook to take him up on the offer of a job made eleven years earlier. It was through Clarence that he had gotten back in the training business and started working with Joe Clark.

The part about calling Grey was good. Grey was the touch that would flush her out of that house on Aubrey Road.

He was surprised at the rawness of his desire to see this boy he had fathered.

It was Saturday. If he mailed the letter today it would be there by Tuesday at the most. Harris copied the letter out on clean blue paper and dropped it in the post box at Berrysville. Back at the cabin, he poured a whiskey and listened to big band music on the radio while he put groceries away. The telephone squatted on the kitchen counter, a Bakelite monster with the power to stop his heart.

The restaurant backed up to the river. A dinghy nosed willows at a small dock by the back door. Harris parked the truck next to the brown Cadillac and got out. The Caddy windows were open. He looked in, pleased to be intruding. That was his current mood. He had been sober since late last night. As soon as this deal was over he was going to go somewhere and get pissed.

The inside of the car smelled like sun-baked leather and some kind of solvent, and a little like perfume. Books were scattered on the back seat. One, face up, was poetry by Christina Rosetti, which he had read. It had been in the library at Salthill.

Love, strong as Death, is dead
Come, let us make his bed
Among the dying flowers.
A green turf at his head,
And a stone at his feet,

Whereon we may sit
In the quiet evening hours.

Another was *Inside Europe* by John Gunther, with a cracked spine. Another—
he had to stick his head clear in to see it lying on the floor behind the
driver's seat—was a picture book with a grape and tomato-red cover, the
title partly hidden by a stained rag: *Art of Egon Schiele.*

He withdrew and straightened his clothes. He wore the jacket and slacks,
dry-cleaned to get the wharf out of them. They were the only town clothes
he had. He ran his hand over his hair and walked toward the restaurant.

Venetian blinds had been drawn over the windows to protect the inside
from the fiery glance of the sun. At the end of a row of red leatherette
banquettes and chrome jukeboxes, a waitress was filling shakers with salt. A
few diners sat over coffee or dessert. It was past the dinner hour, but the
odor of seafood lingered, blown around by an unevenly skimming overhead
fan. The cook's hat moved silently along the rear wall behind a screen separating the kitchen from the dining room.

The only woman alone that Harris could see was sitting in a booth by
one of the windows, a glass in front of her on the table. Her hair, all different
shades of blond, was tied back with a ribbon. She had raised the blind and
was gazing out the window, her profile dissolved in a glare of light that turned
her lashes white and lay in coins and a spreading map on her cheek. Her
hand fell. Her gaze left the window and moved toward him, and any idea
of his ever having seen her before vanished. It wasn't Elsa but a woman with
a superficial resemblance to Elsa, a female of the same racial type. You saw
them all over Canada—English, Scots, Irish, Scandinavian, blond women
with sharp features and fair, speckled skin.

This one was a beauty. Breasts snug in the bodice of a snuff-colored sleeveless dress, long graceful neck, sensual mouth drooping at the corners. A pair
of shapely legs were crossed under the table. She was a woman men would
notice. There was nothing artificial about the strong beauty he was admiring,
disappointed that it wasn't her. It was the wrong one, another woman, a
sisterly lookalike. . . .

She was staring at him with an irritated, apologetic smile on her face, the
kind you greet someone with when you realize recognition isn't mutual. He
moved toward her then between the booths, hardly knowing where he put
his feet. She rose from her seat. The eyes with the dark winged brows, the
hair and her mouth were all that was left of her. The rest was gone, shed
like a moth's pupa, leaving this womanly imago in its place.

"Hullo, Harris," she said, in the deep female voice. One day, when she was growing old, it would sound parched.

"Hello," he said.

She glanced over him casually. "You look haggard."

"Thanks," he said.

She sank back into her seat.

Harris sat down, keeping his face blank. She had no makeup on. She didn't need any. The generous drooping mouth was unpainted, the delicate flesh of the lips slightly chapped. She smelled like scented soap and cigarettes. She reached into a pocket of her skirt and shook one out of a pack of Dunhills, throwing him a slanted look. He offered his lighter. She sucked her cheeks in over the flame and etched a smoke figure above his head.

He anchored himself to her mouth. She watched him with a little smile, following the movement of his eyes, and he watched her mouth. The deep, light voice filled his ears. He watched her mouth.

"Well, here we are," she said. "What was it you have to say, Harris? Your 'few minutes' are ticking away."

She had made a fool out of him again. *He* hadn't changed beyond recognition; she had seen the man she expected to see. But then, he always had been at a disadvantage with her. He had never had the power to anticipate what she could do or be.

"Don't rush me," he said curtly.

The waiter came, a crewcut boy with an Adam's apple that looked like he really had swallowed a small apple. Harris ordered coffee. "Do you want another one of those?" he asked, indicating her glass.

"No. What are you doing in Vancouver?"

"I bought the Humphries place."

Her eyes widened. They were gold because of the dress, a pansy gold touched with violet. "Humphries?" she repeated. "He went all to pieces and shot himself. About three years ago."

"They couldn't find a buyer," he said. "I guess people were afraid of the house."

"You weren't," she said.

"No," he said. Not then.

"He came from Northumbria thirty years ago. He never married." She seemed ready to stay on Humphries. "I always felt rather sorry for him. That means you're near here."

"Southeast, near Berrysville," said Harris. "About fifteen miles on the river route."

He watched her take that in.

"Why in hell," she said conversationally, "did you have to buy a place here? Why not on the other side of the country?"

"I like a long growing season," he said.

Her lip curled. "Don't make jokes."

"All right," he said. "None of your business."

The boy set his coffee down. Jukebox music drifted over their heads, spread by the fan. *Now it's crying time tonight, you're going to leave me.*

"Was there any stock left?" she asked.

"Everything was gone. Don't you want to know where I've been?" He had no intention of telling her where he had been. He just wanted to get this stalled conversation lurching forward.

"I'd rather know why you left." She stubbed out the cigarette and leaned on her crossed arms. The movement strengthened the shape of her breasts under the dress. "Not that I care passionately, just feeding a mild curiosity. Grey wrote a month after you left, saying you were gone. He didn't know where you were. You never called or wrote."

"It seemed like the best thing to do."

"Best thing to do," she repeated coldly. "Then why not stay lost?"

He studied her. "I've seen him. Grey."

"How did he look?" she asked, wary.

"More haggard than me."

"What did you talk about?"

"Didn't he tell you I was there?" He was watching her.

"No."

"He wanted to know how I got the money to buy a ranch. Then he told me to leave."

She seemed to relax. "How did you? Get the money."

"I worked for it. Any man can make money if he wants to enough. I—Grey—"

She drew in her breath. "Grey. He was why you left. He was always between us, like a policeman. Like a rival."

"He treated me like his son. Of course he was between us."

"The great betrayal," she sneered. "You didn't tell me you were going. You said *nothing*."

"Elsa, you would've blown it if I had."

"Me? Ha. You're joking."

The discussion was veering around like a car with one wheel off. He was talking to a woman he had never met, this lush, pallid woman with the orange brandy voice.

"You'd better leave if you feel that bitter about it," he said.

Color seeped into her cheekbones. "I want to know who you are first."

"So do I," he said lightly.

"Stop it, Harris. You didn't manipulate people with words at Salthill. You didn't drag them with letters and phone calls to places they didn't want to go."

"No," he said. "Manipulating was *your* thing."

She looked surprised. "Don't try to put the wind up me with that nonsense. I'm *not* manipulative. On the contrary I'm very direct."

He sank back, almost panting. Was he yellow instead of black, was he really haggard and wasted? Could he get her? He searched for words with care, not for any truth they might hold, but for the answer he wanted. Because he wasn't going for amends anymore. His life was laid out for him like the map of a country he had thought he would never see again, and his way had never been this clear.

"Elsa," he said. "I'm sorry. It was the only way out. For all three of us."

"Pfaugh! You were bloody frightened, in fact."

"I was young! I wasn't much older than you are now." Feeling squeezed internally and driven by foul spirits, he said, "Elsa, I truly regret the pain I caused you. Please forgive me."

Her face was white except for the blotches. It was an arcane face, made for passion and destruction, all angles and a big mouth that worked helplessly. He didn't give a damn about her pain. He wanted her, he had never wanted anything more, and he couldn't afford sympathy now.

"I should, I suppose," she said stiffly. "Even though you take everything too seriously, like a goddamned old maid, and drag everyone down with you while you're at it." The mouth quivered suddenly. "You have no idea how much pain you caused me. I hate seeing you right now. It gives me nothing but pain to look at you."

They went outside in the open air like fighters going out into the street. They moved away from the traffic noise lapping over the hedges, toward the darkness around the river. The tobacco-colored dress seemed to sink into it, camouflaging her in the last details of light.

"Did you love me?" she asked angrily. "That's all I want to know. Was there ever anything there?"

Suddenly he was angry too. He let anger ooze out of him like a pulp. "Love had nothing to do with it," he said. "All you wanted was my dick. The rest was romantic bullshit. We saw, we wanted, we got. Whatever the price was we were willing to pay it. So shut up, because we both paid."

She swallowed. There was no color left in her face, it was a ghost of the moon at her shoulder.

"Didn't we?" His hands itched to slap her, touch her.

She worked her jaw silently.

"Where in hell did you get this thing?" he muttered to the Cadillac.

She shot him a single queenly look, full of malevolence and sly triumph. "From someone I knew." And he knew the someone was a man. She laid a hand tenderly on the leather of the seat, her thoughts turned inward and an enigmatic smile on her face.

He had cut her off with the remark about the car, she had met it with her own blow. He panted to be a leather cushion under her hand. He wanted to lie down like a dog at her feet, and be stroked and petted.

She pulled the ribbon out of her hair and tossed it on the seat, then cast him another look, chin lifted and eyelids slanted as if she was about to laugh at a secret joke. "You'd like me now, wouldn't you?" she drawled. "Too bad, Harris. Your day came and went. I've gone on to other memories."

"Not if I had a Jaguar," he said without thinking.

She slapped him. "You bleeding son of a bitch."

"I don't want to hear about your men," he snarled, holding his face.

She flounced into the Cadillac and slammed the door. He looked down at silver-gold hair falling loose in the dark. She turned the key in the ignition, fed gas, let out the brake.

"Let's not do this again," she said. "All right?"

"Go to hell," he said.

The car stalled. She started it again, making it shriek like a buzz-saw blade. Her profile jerked forward, hatchetlike with rage. He watched the Caddy rocket out of the lot in a gust of exhaust and turn onto the road.

Chapter Fifty-six

FIELDS SPED PAST, GREEN AS PARKS. He overtook cars and trucks. Once he passed a tractor rolling from field to field along the shoulder. It was eerie, driving in a mindless void. Approaching cars stood still; cars ahead of him floated aimlessly as soap bubbles before he shot past them and made them pop.

Harris parked in the gallery lot, ran in through the back door and nearly tumbled over a food-laden table. It was afternoon of the next day. People were standing around on the pecan floor with plates and glasses in their hands, or wandering gesturing between the partitions on a tide of sound. Harris edged past a couple of men helping themselves to slices of coconut layer cake at a table and an aproned woman arranging platters of little hot dogs speared with toothpicks. If the men noticed him they gave no sign of it. They looked prosperous and absorbed, not like bankers but as if they made their living off their minds. The woman smiled at him a little stiffly. Even though he was decently dressed, not caring to come to town and visit the bank in work clothes, he was obviously not one of this party.

Harris made his way across the floor toward the picture. A white-draped table appeared with rows of glasses of wine on it. He picked one up and drank it down. Champagne, maybe. The glass was plastic. He gave it a look of disgust and tossed it in a wastebasket full of napkins and bent glasses.

The picture was still there. Harris stayed long enough to see it actually in its frame, struck again with amazement at its perfection, the way the pools of color, like the leaves and crusts of paint on the Skillihawk Valley canvas, magically formed the unphotographic image. It was so untrivial. She was untrivial. She made other women look banal and rabbity. She was still young; she would frighten men later unless they were strong. There was no one like her in this room and there was no one like him either.

Then he left. If whoever ran the place saw him next to that painting, they would know who he was. He shouldn't even be in the room with it. She hadn't seen fit to tell him he had a son. All right, he wasn't going to let on that he knew.

At the bank, he purchased a cashier's draft for the amount of the picture. Except for the loan payments and a small amount of cash, it was all the money he had. That was what the picture cost him. Two mares.

Elsa was avoiding the Oldham. At noon she left the advertising agency, where she worked when she wasn't teaching the class at the Fraser, for her lunch break.

"Go on *down* there. Listen to what they're saying," said Jay in his trim, faintly singsong Torontonian English. He was cutting masks, working on his feet in a litter of X-Acto blades and film scraps, a man with the build of the teenage boy he was mistaken for until you saw the fortyish face and astute small eyes bracketed with lines.

She lingered at the table. "I thought we were done with those. When are they coming to look?"

"They'll be out of town another week, so not to worry. I'm moving to your Skillihawk by the way. It's wonderful country. Whyever didn't you have me drive them up before?"

"Don't move there; you'd be bored in a week. It's very quiet and inartistic."

"Go to the gallery."

"I was there last Saturday for the one you said counted. You know I hate receptions. All that nonsense about form, and my feet on fire in those shoes."

"You sound remarkably world-weary. It's only your second show and you're lucky to have had two at your age. Some critic may drop in on his lunch hour to encourage you."

She walked aimlessly on the streets instead, sometimes almost running, stumbling over her feet and at curbs. The sandwich she had eaten at lunch, sitting on the back steps looking out on what had been a back garden, lay like a brick in her stomach. Creativity was a shy faun, capable of going into hiding for long periods. It had withdrawn to some distant corner of her consciousness, lay curled on itself like a petrified leaf or insect, because Harris had come back.

Elsa turned into the courtyard of the theater next to the Toronto-Dominion, sat on a bench and shivered among the potted plants.

Harris had driven away her muse, and for what? A miserable half hour, an explanation too late, an apology for the wrong wrong. Why had she responded to that letter? He couldn't know what a threat he was, couldn't know what a call to Grey would mean to all of them. And that visit to Salthill! But apparently nothing had come of it. If she'd ignored the letter he might have given up trying to make contact. Elsa smiled bitterly at a *Monstera deliciosa*. What a stupid thought. Harris never dropped or gave up anything unless he wanted to.

I answered the letter, she said silently and harshly to herself, *because I wanted to.*

Now she knew why people swooned from emotion. It wasn't silliness; it was a vertigo of the heart. The worst ten minutes she had spent in a long time had been at King Seafood, a name she would never forget, waiting for the door to open and the flesh to reappear after six years of being spirit.

He looked the way he had always looked, except that his color was bad and he *was* drawn, and rather thinner. His essence had been entirely familiar, like a remembered odor; he could easily have been pulling up a chair in the kitchen at Salthill, to sit and bore into her with that pale, atavistic stare.

Going over it later (lying in bed last night, with the Sevres clock Daisy had given her when she finished at the Slade telling its pale green hours), she had perceived, through the cloud of panic and love in which she seemed suspended, that Harris had no male pride in the normal way men did. He wasn't outfitted with a dire masculinity that had to be protected. Something had flayed or knocked it out of him before he ever came to them, and he had flattened beneath it and simply grew sideways, like one of those succulents that need little water, and root in soils that starve other plants. The only other men she had known with this adaptability were her father and Piwonka, and an artist at the Slade who had been her mentor. Their chief personal characteristics were success in work that absorbed them and a dislike of fanfare. They were men who if they married went back to their work immediately, relieved at no longer having to hunt; who kept tidy out of an almost military sense of order; who never made the error of thinking themselves handsome, important or stupid.

But worse had followed. As Harris approached, looking ordinary—not family as he had once been but an ex-passion, a different member of the same gallery—she had suddenly grasped his innate nature. His remote, uncharted interior had unfolded before her, not its current whims or motives but the contours of his mind, like a clearing seen ahead in a forest. It was in acknowledgment of this vision that she had risen, trembling inwardly, to her feet. And the cloud had risen with her, so that she became faint-headed in its mist.

After that, there had been nothing to do but fight.

He was here in Vancouver and he wasn't going to leave, not if she knew Harris. Once settled, he had a low opinion of change and moved cautiously around its periphery, as though it were a live volcano that would consume him in its maw. Elsa did not know what to do.

She got up with a mental cry of pain and dusted a few stray crumbs of ornamental bark off her bottom. He had been thin, brown and intense last night, a man somehow miserably at odds with himself. And how did she know that he was?

On her way back to the agency she passed a beauty salon. The windows were curtained for discretion and photos of women in different hairstyles had been arranged on stands between glass and cloth. The brunette models looked like Rosalind Russell, while the blond ones—unapproachable, coifed in spun gold—looked like Greer Garson. She went inside.

A woman in a smock and knot of Grecian curls swam toward her. "Yes, miss?"

Elsa, who had never been in a beauty salon in her life, dragged her fascinated attention from a row of resigned-looking women with shod feet starting delicately from beneath forensic gowns; from an imaginary canvas of a Roman arena filled with female gladiators in peach togas, advancing in formation with metal rods springing from their heads.

"Do I have to have an appointment to get this hair cut off?" she asked. "The entire lot. Very short."

"I can fit you in." She added with a delicate frown, "Are you sure you want to cut it? It's lovely hair."

"Please," said Elsa.

Harris got to the bank before the doors closed the next day, where he signed for a parcel wrapped in oiled paper and bound with twine. It was heavier than he expected. He horsed it into the truck. Wedged between the passenger seat and the dashboard, it assumed a reality that seemed to invade his bones and turn them into juice.

He unwrapped and propped the picture against the bed. The colors glowed rich and dark as an oil slick, drinking the *aqua fortis* of the watery light. He switched on the lamp and examined it grimly from every angle. It was his sole property now. Buying this meant he wouldn't be able to go on at Humphries's. Without stock, he couldn't raise more stock. Without a foundation of two mares, bred and turning out foals to be trained and sold or kept for outbreeding, he couldn't earn the money to pay off the loan. What dreams he had dared to begin dreaming after learning the Humphries place was in probate! All he had now was his truck, his clothes, and this thing staring quietly at him from under the lamp.

Harris covered it with the paper and went out to the kitchen. The dirty dishes were still in the sink from his last meal. The can opener was on the drainboard and there was an empty Campbell's tin in the paper bag that was the trash pail, so it must have been soup.

He got the old .44 out of the bedside stand and stuck a few rounds in it from the box of cartridges in the drawer, noting how steady his hand was. The current bottle of whiskey was on the kitchen counter with the cap off. Harris opened the back door wide and tossed it out. The bottle flashed above the grove and pile of back steps, pinwheeling booze. He shot at it with the Colt, missed, fired, missed, fired. Glass spewed over the whine of the slug.

He dropped the gun on the counter and put his face in his hands. *This is the end of it, God. I got a purpose now.*

Chapter Fifty-seven

THE JAGGED LIGHT-STRUCK SKYLINE of bottles repeated itself in mirrors. Harris picked his way between the tables, here because he was afraid to be alone. Alone, voices would start asking painful questions. Alone, he would slide the oiled paper away from the picture, stare at the small face, and shiver by himself in the sad cabin as he had for the last two nights.

The clubgoers' faces had a dry zombie cast in the candlelight. Noble Brownford was playing saxophone in front of the band, his face plumped and sooty with perspiration. The piano player's wife Mimi and her sister Freddy were at a table by the bandstand. The girl smiled at Harris as he took a seat nearby. She hadn't seen him since the night they met, the one he had finished in jail. Harris smiled back with just the right amount of friendly courtesy, making the right eye contact for a man who is appreciative but otherwise engaged. Elsa was right. There was something old-maidish about him, a fastidious core that stayed remote from the low life he had been living. Personally, he thought life had a way of whipping your sorry ass into prudence.

He ordered a ginger ale. He had spent the day mending fence and taking Bluebell out for a long ride. His head was clear. He had even gone swimming in the river, wearing a pair of cut-off jeans, working his toes in the brown sandy bottom while the neighbors' dog laughed at him from the bank.

Some people stood up to leave, milling briefly in front of him. As they sorted themselves and drifted off, Harris saw the woman who had come out of the house on Aubrey Road, sitting at another table near the stand. The woman's hair was turbaned the way it had been the other night. She wore a green-gold dashiki that outlined her in an elegant smoke. Before Harris had time to react to this strange juxtaposition of the Starlite with Aubrey Road, a voice came at his shoulder.

"You son of a bitch."

She stood before him with her hair chopped off, a white stalk, her face luminous and wild in the fish-tank glow of the stand. The dress tapered into darkness, low in front, leaving the lily face and lily breasts. She was a woman men noticed.

"You knew, when you met me at that place. You knew!"

"Sit down," he said. The drum solo had just started.

"*I will not.* We're going to talk about this now!"

He marched her between tables to the crash of cymbals and roll of drums toward the doorway with the pink neon exit sign. They staggered against each other, passing a blur of heads; his own face felt full of pounding blood. Her scraggly low-rent hair flamed in the blue light. They were disgorged into the lobby. An energy whispered behind the door to the street; it was raining outside. Umbrellas stuck like quills out of a few cheap stands.

"Cool off," he said to her.

"It's mine!" Without the anchoring weight of her hair the face that glared back at him was a bright young hound's. "It's mine and it's not for sale. Give me a cigarette."

He lit one and handed it to her. She exhaled roughly. "I went to the gallery this morning. I had to, on business. That was clever of you, signing the check 'Brown.' "

"How did you know it was me?"

"Sudden intuition." She looked savage. "Then I called the bank."

He shrugged. "The draft was cashiered by the bank manager, the signature's legitimate. His name really is Brown."

"I feel sick," she said suddenly, and plunged into the women's room.

She was gone awhile. Harris waited in the lobby, tingling with sudden zest. Did the feeling that things were playing into your hands ever happen more than once in a lifetime? The synchronicity of it (a word he liked) was so pleasing that even if nothing came out of it, he would always be warmed by the small chance happiness of this placement in time.

Elsa came out looking gaunt.

"We met in that place for a half hour and you *never said anything*," she said.

"I was waiting for you to say it," said Harris.

"Why should I? I've no obligation to you. Did you know this could happen, Harris? I've always wondered. When I came back that winter and faced my father, it would have been a comfort to know I hadn't fallen for some old trick."

"Of course I didn't," he said, the slow surprise in his voice. "It wasn't a trick."

"That's what you have to say about it?" she cried bitterly. "That's *all*?"

"It's enough. You know, you St. Oeggers are something else. You think life's a fucking soccer game, with everybody following the same code of fair play and honor. You know nothing about the dark side of life, about murder and hate and the lies that tear people apart. Even your cold-blooded brother won't admit evil exists."

"That's so people like you will have a sanctuary to go to," she retorted. He was silent.

"We do know it exists. I do. But we're not part of what you're talking about."

"You mean you won't own to it."

"You're driving me mad. We've nothing to own to. I—we—prostrated ourselves to be real to you. My god, how we struggled to bring you to life." She glanced at the door; a few people were straggling out. "I'll come for the painting, of course. Or you can return it straight to the gallery. That would be better for both of us."

"It stays with me," he said simply. "I own it."

"It's not for sale," Elsa returned with exaggerated patience. "Of course I'm not going to sell a portrait of my own son! The gallery borrowed it to fill that white space at the end of the exhibit. Someone priced it and put the label on in error. I hadn't been there since the opening, so I didn't realize what they'd done."

"I don't give a shit. I paid for it and I'm keeping it."

She goggled. He crossed his arms on his chest and smiled. "There's not much you can do about it, is there?" he said.

"I'll give you a check for the amount."

"No."

"You won't get anything else out of us. I'll see to that."

"Fine."

Harris watched her walk back inside the club. He waited some minutes in the lobby, gathering his wits, then went after her.

The drum solo had ended and everyone was coming together down the home stretch. Harris walked through sound and blue light to her table. She opened her lips once, as if to receive a pearl or morsel, then swung her head away. He laid a compelling stare on the nape of her neck, standing back on his heels with his hands in his pockets. If he was going to get slapped down he wanted to earn it.

"Elsa," he said deliberately.

"Go away," she snapped.

The other woman was looking him over. Her skin was electrum, a dusty alloy of gold and silver. The nose was aquiline with flattened nostrils; beneath the Egyptian brows her eyes were elongated and light in color, possibly the shade of sugared almonds. He saw that she knew everything, and was irritated by it.

He introduced himself.

"Sophronia Trudeau," she said, offering a hand. "Sit down." Harris pulled up the third chair. There was just enough room at the table for all their knees to meet. He felt Elsa swing hers away.

"Buy you ladies a drink?" He smiled.

"Brandy Alexander for me," said Sophronia cheerfully.

"Scotch," muttered Elsa. "With a water back."

The drinks were brought. From lack of space they were forced to sit squashed together. Elsa felt her arm being pressed, then scoured by the fabric of his jacket, a contact she experienced as a series of intensely irritating, shocklike jolts. It was like being half of a Siamese twin, conjoined and miserably inseparable. Why didn't she stand up and leave? Sophronia was used to her ways and wouldn't mind. Why did she stay rooted in this chair?

She studied his profile. The fine-grained skin was slightly coarse at the jawline. She had a sudden strong mental picture of the bristles curving back into the beard, having to be picked out of the flesh with a needle as he looked patiently into a mirror with his braces hanging. And how did she know he had to do this? Because he had always gone out on the porch where the light was good to do it, using an old makeup mirror that hung by the icebox. It had been the only visible item of his toilet. She used to watch when she was young, although he would stop at times and glare at her between spread fingers, annoyed by her dumb, awful attentiveness. At this remembrance, she thought she was going to scream.

She turned away from her scrutiny, filled with self-disgust. A moment later she was back to it.

His lips had a threadlike outline of lighter color that made the pursed insides look darker than his skin. The sideburn grew over the scar where it started at the temple; the small wool was trimmed close around it. The scar coursed down the cheekbone, tactile and shining like a worm in a book of organic *natura,* something that slid through leaves and soil, alive though it had no face. A blade had slashed and caused to open the inner flesh, layering tissue fruitily veined down to the incisors gleaming out of welling red. Her gorge rose.

"Pardon," she said, rising abruptly.

Noble and the drummer joined them on the break. Harris was not pleased with this. They seemed to know the two women.

"Now what'd I say?" said Noble to him, fetching a chair from an empty table. "I tell you to stop by, bring a lady, and now you here with my cousin!"

"Cousin?"

"Sophronia. She's a cousin of mine. Comes here all the time to hear me play."

So that was how Elsa had known where to find him! Noble might have said something to Sophronia. But more likely Sophronia had approached Noble. Not knowing he knew Harris from the past but just: *You ever see a man looks so-and-so in the neighborhood, maybe comes in to catch a set?* He would be easy to identify. The sister had that smile on that a cat wore creeping through tall grass. Elsa had tracked him here to tell him off and get the picture back, and having finished the first part of her mission she didn't know what to do with him.

Now they were all together at the table overflowing with glasses and loaded ashtrays. The musicians leaned back with ties loosened, releasing a powerful effluence of content.

"Like another drink?" asked the drummer, nodding at Elsa's empty glass.

She shook her head. She had come back from the ladies' room, or wherever she had gone, looking tense and angry, but that made no never-mind to the drummer. He was about Harris's age, a slim man with the face of a young panther and alert black eyes. Harris watched him light her cigarette, smiling an easy smile. The hand that held the lighter had a ruby signet ring on the pinky finger and the stone reflected the light as it turned. There was a faint, magnetic hesitation before he snapped the flame off, as if he was reluctant to leave the sheltering aura of her lips.

Fucking pimp, thought Harris.

Elsa sat back, exhaled and gave the drummer a little smile.

"You two friends?" he asked her.

"Harris used to work for my father," she said, croaking like a frog in the thick air. "I've known him since I was a child."

"Lucky man." *What a damn boring subject,* his flattened tone implied. *Let's talk about you.* His gaze dropped lightly to her breasts and slid up her shoulders as if her body was in the way of something he wanted to see. He smiled his good-natured predatory smile, and his eyes over the rim of the glass were entirely free of guile or insinuation.

Harris pressed heavily against her, weighted and sagging. Her skin, a little sweaty, gave off a delicate female odor that penetrated even through smoke and booze, a compound of her own milky salty scent and some flower.

Noble glanced at his watch and got up.

"Staying for the last set?" the drummer asked Elsa.

Harris heard her draw a shaggy breath. He saw a strange room, coats flung over chairs, whiskey in water glasses and sexual oblivion. He made his arm a rock cliff face.

"I think we're going to."

The drummer smiled his panther smile. "Buy you a drink later?"

"I'd love it." She smiled back.

At one forty-five the break tune was called for the last time and the band started packing up. The crowd pushed out in a restless tide, leaving chairs and tables scattered, cases gaping open on the stand, bartenders mopping. At one end of the bar stood a short lineup of desperadoes gulping final shots. At the other end were members of the select group who gathered after hours to drink the owner's cognac and sample each other's dope.

By that time Harris had decided to throw the night away. She was going to do what she was going to do, probably because he was there, and the hell with synchronicity. He retrieved the women's coats from the cloakroom, having no difficulty telling them apart. Sophronia's was a sleek black raincoat with a tapered skirt. Hers was a tweed that looked like something off a peg on the back porch of a fish cabin. The lining was faded around the neck from its original burgundy to a rusty yellow. He bet the dress was old too; he bet she didn't have any money. In the middle of his rage and despair he was touched. He sniffed the cloth before walking back into the surging crowd.

Sophronia was by the bandstand with a man he hadn't seen before, talking to Noble and the piano player. Elsa was sitting at the table watching the drummer pack his set.

"Here's your coat," said Harris.

She stood reluctantly and allowed him to slip it over her shoulders.

He was introduced to Sophronia's escort, a West Indian from Trinidad about forty years of age who looked moneyed. They shook hands. Harris felt Sophronia's eyes run over his face as they had a few times during the evening, as though its planes and bones and eye sockets were still a revelation.

There was a party going on after hours. Harris didn't want to leave the club until Elsa did, but that problem was solved when she left with the drummer. One minute they were talking over the packed-up set, the next they were gone and so was the set, leaving a square of dustless floor where the cases had been. He checked outside the back door where the drummer logically would have left his car. There was no sign of them and no car either.

The pain this inspired would have called for a fifth at least, in a life that seemed curiously distant. But Harris felt disengaged. It was like he couldn't take anymore, least of all the idea of losing Elsa, and everything went stone calm on him. He decided to join the party leaving for the party. No way was he was going back to Humphries's tonight to lie awake until dawn.

He and Noble and the guitar player walked down a street of stone and brick buildings, apartments first, then commercial buildings and warehouses. It had stopped raining, but the air still crackled and stung with damp. The harbor gleamed at the ends of the alleys, the riding lights and a few stars floating above it through mossy strings of cloud. They went up a flight of outside stairs. A door opened, and a brother stood to one side and let them into a loft.

As he waited to go in Harris saw the women approaching on the street below, Sophronia and a couple of others, escorted by the moneyed Trinidadian, then Elsa with her collar turned up and the moonlight on her ruffled hair. He stood on the top step absorbing her wildness. She seemed older than twenty-two, already cast in one piece, refined and steely. Women that age were usually still girls. Wild, scary, confusing, vulnerable, all nose and eyebrows and glare, he had seen her with the drummer, which had told him what he needed to know, and at the same time he knew he knew nothing. She trailed behind the others with feminine mystery shining out of her like the moonlight on her hair, like the moon on still waters, more woman than he had seen coming toward him in a long time.

Chapter Fifty-eight

THE LOFT WAS THE TOP FLOOR of a shipping warehouse. Spars crossed the blackened arc of the ceiling, the hobbed ends hanging like stalactites between metal-sashed schoolhouse windows. Light softened by the frosted panes sifted into shadows, gray, striated and black, broken by the shapes of human heads. Except for a lamp with a red scarf flung over it and a bulb by a door in the far wall, there was no light. The guitar player, a gaunt bespectacled man who reminded Harris irresistibly of a stork, was stepping across the room toward the bulb.

Harris picked out Sophronia by the sheen of her dress, Elsa by the confused lily oval of her face and hands like stars at the ends of her coat sleeves. The two women came together briefly, then inched along the wall over rippling waves of legs. She was the only white woman in the room, the only white human being other than the guitar player. It was a black party. She was there on sufferance, out of tolerance. The faces that looked or did not look out of the gloom were dark, with spread noses and full lips and remote expressions. The silence was like no silence he ever heard in a room of white people. It had an appreciative, peaceful busyness to it. Marijuana punk wavered through the cigarette smoke on its own thin scow of burning weed.

A man came out of the door under the weak bulb. Harris leaned against the wall and watched him sit on a stool near the red light and lay a guitar across his lap. He was a shamblingly built man, with a roman nose and ebony skin that shone in patches on his cheekbones and the bulge of his forehead. There was no extra meat on the rangy arms that cradled the guitar or the fingers that tried a few notes out on the strings.

(chord)
"One of these days

I'm gone show you just how nice a man can be
I'ma buy you a brand-new Cadillac
If you'll only speak some good words bout me."
(chord chord)
"Hear my phone ringing, sound like aaaa long-distance call
Hear my phone keep ringin', sound like a longggg-distance call
When I pick up my receiver
Party say theys another mule kickin' in yoh stall."

The voice was rough, full of feeling and a menacing masculinity. Harris shut his eyes, lost in the lean shape of the songs, entirely at home.

"On the seventh hour
On the seventh day
On the seventh month
The seven doctor say
You was born for good luck
And that you will see
I got seven hundred dollars
Dont you mess with me.
I'm a hoochie-coochie man
Evvrybody knows I am."

The bluesman rested the guitar on his lap and rolled a cigarette.

After about an hour Harris saw Elsa's appealing silhouette and fluorescent tuft of hair undulate from the floor up into the light. She let herself into the head, carrying the fish-cabin coat. A string of Christmas lights revealed a glass of violets on the toilet tank before the door closed. Harris watched her come out and leave the loft by the entrance, sliding past two men whose eyes wandered like soothing oil over her body. He waited long enough, then followed.

A few people were gathered on the sidewalk. He stood on the stairwell above the *tick-ata-bong-a tock-biddy-bong* of a steel band coming from a portable radio. Elsa was down at the curb, shrugging into the coat. Sophronia passed him coming down. She stopped at the landing, her skirt lifted elegantly above the steps.

"What part of the Caribbean were you born in, Mr. Harris?"

"Bridgetown," he said.

"Really." She looked lively with her eyes, the way West Indian women did. "I am from Castries myself."

She continued on down.

Harris joined Elsa at the curb. The headlights of a car guttered at their feet.

"You going home?" he asked.

"I am."

He gentled his voice. "With your friend?"

The steel band was rolling down the sidewalk. A man and woman—Sophronia—were dancing in a space that cleared as they swept forward. Her head and torso snapped gently back and forth, side to side, on and in back of the beat, and all around it. She gathered her skirt and wagged her bustled rear end. Every part of her body seemed to be following a different joyous, slapdash rhythm. The man crowed with laughter, patted his hands softly and shuffled in a circle around her, moving inside his own goosey rhythm.

"She's busy," said Elsa. "I said not to bother."

"I'll give you a lift," he said, and held his breath.

"All right. It'll be easier than finding a cab at this hour," she said. "You owe it to me, really."

Harris pulled the truck up to the curb. He started to get out, but she shook her head violently and stumbled in the passenger side without his help.

"You bought this used," she said with an air of satisfaction, settling herself.

"What makes you say that?"

"It's a red truck. You would never buy a new red truck. You bought it because it was in good shape and the price was right, and in spite of its being red."

He had to smile.

"What was his name?" she muttered. "The guitar player."

"Muddy Waters."

She closed her eyes. "It's a different world, isn't it. Like an essence, very concentrated. And like theater. Theater of the air because that's where the music goes. I'll come back someday and paint him."

"He'll be gone," he said.

He drove as slowly as he could, while she gazed out at the night like a rider on a train, sealed in silence.

"I'd better tell you how to get there," she said once.

"I know how to get there."

"You know every damned thing, don't you?" she said. "You've been spying on me, 'buying' my pictures so-called, bedeviling my father, a sick man."

He looked at his hands on the steering wheel, the wrists shooting out of the cuffs and the long fingers, the skin on the knuckles darker than on the joints. "Tell me his name, Elsa. When was he born?"

"May thirteen, 1952. It's Sheridan Keith St. Oegger."

Pain swept over him. "That's some fine name."

"Sheridan after Grey's wife, Alice Sheridan," she said in a grainy, exhausted voice. "I did it on purpose. It was spiteful, but that's what I was then, a spiteful adolescent. I meant him to be called by his middle name, but we've always called him Sherry."

"Is he home?"

"No, at Salthill. He went with Sophronia's son, who is a year older."

The fanlight was on at Aubrey Road, throwing a yellow pattern on the walk and casting the hawthorn hedge into darkness. This time she waited for Harris to open the door.

She said, "I can hear the night stirring around you, cooler than your shade, and that jacket that seems to give off its own woolly heat."

"Like those sheep your father has now," he said, standing in front of her, blocking the light.

She shuddered. "You can't imagine the almost nauseating resistance I feel to you, Harris. Your clothes, your smell, that pitted and pored shaven jawline. Everything about you is alien and mismatched and repugnant. Revulsion washes over me and leaves me limp. I feel a terrible lethargy."

He kissed her on the mouth. She accepted it, standing with her hands hanging and her head back, while he gripped her arms through the coat sleeves.

"You think this is everything, don't you." She made a face.

"No," he said. "I think it's part of everything."

"What do you want?" Her expression, expectant and irritated, the way she stood with her arms tight to her body, her feet trimly together on the walkway, her head back a little so the planes of her face came sallow out of the dark, meant she wasn't going to give him much more time.

"I want you to marry me," he said.

She did not look surprised. "Harris, you are an ass," she said. "Of course I won't."

"You don't know how it would be," he said.

"I don't bloody care." She looked him up and down. "Odd, isn't it? I've lost my desire to be with you permanently and exclusively. I think that's the way you felt about me at Salthill. Now you want it, don't you? Permanence. It's why you stole my painting."

His body was on fire from the taste of her mouth and that weary contralto. He was ashamed and enraged at his weakness. He fought diligently for control, standing in ice-cold showers, tramping uphill in deep snow.

"That's right," he said coldly.

"There are too many other things for me to do now, Harris. So many more than there were then. I have pictures to paint, worlds to see, my life to be lived. I'm standing on the threshold of my own eternity, looking out on a limitless golden vista! Even the dark places ahead intrigue me. I want to surrender to all the cruelty and pain waiting for me personally. I can't have this business with you. Otherwise I would be leaving myself before I'd even begun to be."

"Be wicked. Go to the dark," he said. "Let it be on my time. It would still be your life."

"You don't mean that." She dragged her hands down her face, sighing. "If only you could. There's one image I keep seeing, even in my best hours: your image stamped on the Skillihawk, like a double exposure. Remember the way the sky meets the horizon, the way the land becomes one long streak of color under the sky? On that image. But it's a country we've left behind, Harris. You're trying to drag me back there against my will. I'm not going back. I will *not* be cast into disarray by you or Salthill."

She unlatched the gate and went into the house without looking back.

He got in the truck and slammed the door, nearly weeping with frustration and lust and loss. His body felt hard, but weakness surged through him in waves. *I'll be damned if this is the end,* he thought. *I am hers. And my son, Sheridan. Sheridan Keith. It's a fine name. She'll have to let me spend time with him.*

But he understood what she felt. Not because it had happened to him; oh no, he had never had the experience of standing in youth with life in front of him to be savored in all its wonder and stupidity. He had been hurled into life before he knew what it was, he had torn into it and damaged himself, and youth had scattered on the wind. Yet he knew that the dry necessity he felt now to take risks, to strive to succeed, to vanquish his demons, was no different from her desire to do and know everything possible before her own death. With him it was trying to recover loss, make the rest of his time better and call it dreams; with her it was golden possibilities. She had had a baby without being married, a bad thing, true, but women had babies. Babies came out of their bodies and she was strong, and it was a good thing, he thought. When he thought of having children it was with pleasure, because now he could think of it. He had to savor that more. You wanted to be able to look back on life and know you had rolled in it enough so that good or bad, you hadn't gone to waste. And so he would willingly have been her fool.

After an hour he fell asleep, cold and cramped on the front seat, and dreamed.

"You aren't going out?"

"Course I'm goin' out," she said with her back to him. "We got to eat, don't we? I got to pay the man his rent."

She had that worn-out look on and a purple welt under her eye. For the first time he wondered how old she was. He lay on the bed and watched her roll her stockings and zip her dress up in two stages, reaching behind with a long thin arm. The dress was black bamboo shoots on an orange background. It was so tight he could see the muscles in her back gather and slide. The satiny orange picked up the highlights in her skin.

"You got a twenty off that asshole," he said. "You could rest up awhile."

"Thas for safekeepin'." She got into ho shoes with clear plastic insteps. "I'm layin' it by."

"Don't go," he said. "It isn't safe. Suppose he comes looking for you?"

She turned on him. "Look, what am I suppose to do, get a job in a office? They ain't no jobs. This all I knows how to do."

"We could go back to the country, you and me."

"I ain't goin' nowhere. It's you going back by yourself, soon as the coast is clear. Stop peddling your ass to trash in the park. Get away from the drugs and lowlife and head out of town. You won't never make it here."

"This thing," he said, feeling his face. "They'll see it."

"Jee-sus. You ain't the first black man wid a cut-up face. They ain't going to make no connection between you and some other nigger."

"They will. It got in the papers."

"Then first snow what come, walk out of here with a scarf up to your eyes. Man, do I have to do your thinking for you?" She finished painting her mouth and capped the lipstick tube with a snap. Pooched her lips at the mirror one more time. "You got to get on with life, Red Johnny. You think the shit done passed you by, but if you don't let life scare you off there be plenty more. Just don't be saying, What was that? What happened here? Don't look down, or it will be over for your black ass. Now

give me a kiss, sugar." She leaned over and left cinnamon red paste on his mouth.
He smiled and watched her switch out the door. What a woman.

He could still see that big motherfucking dope dealer standing down on the curb
last night waiting for a cab with his gun, wallet and clothes gone, just an overcoat
over his naked frame. Motherfucker shouldn't have hit Minnie like he did. That was
why Harris went to the window and looked for Minnie through the glass. The thing
worried his mind some. He wanted to make sure she was cool.

She had left the sidewalk and was crossing the street, a little orange flame on the
blacktop. He looked down at the part in the crown of her head and felt a stab of
jealousy at the easy way she came and went. She was down there, free, and he was
up here, trapped forever.

So it was that watching and full of envy he saw the car appear suddenly that had
been nowhere a second ago. He saw it crawl across the road like a fly on glass, wiggling
and changing direction until it found Minnie. He saw Minnie's body fly up in the
air, loop-de-loop, and hit the street. He was two stories up, but he still heard the flat
pancake sound of her slapping down on the pavement, the motor gunning, and the
car roaring off.

Screams rose, scattered and floating. Then silence settled on the street below.

He ran down the green tunnel lined with pipes that made ocean noises. No doors
opened as he sped past. He was alone on the upper floor and the lower one as he
took the stairs, legs pumping. He sprinted down a hall between a double row of doors,
then across the lobby past a row of mailboxes. The lobby smelled like cooking, had
smelled like his own blood the night he ran in, a smell like sweet iron.

The glass doors were propped open, rubbish already scudding in the track between
the carpet and the sidewalk. He halted, panting, and stared out.

Minnie Love lay flung down in the middle of the street, all soft and loose-looking,
with her face turned to one side.

The wail of a siren came not too far off. There were always cops around in a
ghetto. But there was no sound in the street, no shouting or wailing or moaning. No
mouths or eyes moving. Just one "Oh, Lord!" from a doorway, a sanctified cry of
grief.

He moved forward in the silence of a dream, through the doors propped open and
waiting. No crowd formed around her to erase her orange shade, Minnie Love with
her head on backward, lying asleep. There was no sound, just the empty, vibrating
air. When he stepped out, the sun felt so warm on his naked back and shoulders,
warm and blissful on his face and the flame of the scar. He squatted beside her in the
road. Her chest seemed to flutter for a minute, under the bamboo shoots.

He bent and straightened the skirt down around her legs. Then he picked up her
hand.

"I'm here," he said.

The circle never formed, even though he could hear them breathing in the doorways, waiting and listening. He was still sitting there, holding her hand, when the police car pulled up and the doors opened.

"Minnie Love," said Harris in terrible sorrow, and woke.

He was still in front of the gate on Aubrey Road. The peaceful, secret night had passed and dawn was coming in broken streams through the trees. On the other side of the hawthorn hedge, at the end of the walk with damp patches slowly vanishing on the concrete, the house came out of the dark like a knowing figure. He struggled upright against sorrow, blinking at hot pavement, a dangly earring splashed against a cheek, in the crease between waking and sleep.

Then he started up the engine and drove away.

The door to the room at the end of the hall was open. She stared at herself in the mirror in the black dress. The fumed lilac of a crape myrtle pawed gently at the window. The floor was a glossless dark pool out of which her feet and ankles rose white as moonflowers. Behind her the bed, old and wide-lapped, sagged on iron legs, its spread seeming to lift toward her out of the gloom.

She tore at the jagged hair with both hands and sank to the floor. Her sharp cries flew to the walls, into the dawn and the garden. *"Oh god no, no, no. Oh god, help me."* The couple next door smacked their lips in their sleep and turned away from each other, dreaming of cats mating.

Luckily he had turned the mare into the field the night before so she could crop grass and fill her belly if he got in late. Harris fed her and added fresh water to her bucket before he did anything else. Then he went inside to brew a pot of coffee before getting to work.

He worked outside all day, stopping only to make a trip to the lumberyard for nails and wood. At night he opened a can of beans and ate with the radio on. Then he took a shower and went to bed. He lay sleepless, his still detoxing body twitching spasmodically, or sweating and drying out, as if with ancient humors. He thought about paint and nails and salt licks. Those dog runs that were partially torn down would have to be cleared away. He could use the machete in the toolshed to take down the rest of the grass.

The next day he borrowed Ray's power saw and cut down the hemlocks in front of the cabin to let in some light and air. The trees lay where they had toppled, in dusty sheaves; he would cut and cord them for firewood when he had more time. The wisteria he kept, because he liked its hot, wild shade. He left the saw on Ray's front porch with a gallon of gas for a thank-you.

He mended fence until it was too dark to see, tightening it up, rehinging the gate, replacing broken rails with fresh lumber, reinforcing a post. That night he fell into an exhausted sleep.

The next day he bought a gallon of phenol compound and creosoted the fencing. The air was wavy with the stink of coal tar. He coated the stable roof with mastic to keep it watertight and swept out the eaves and gutters. Then he worked out how to fix the damper. The chimney drew in spite of the crumbled brick in the stack. He organized the small tack room. There were built-in racks for saddles, sturdily riveted, and a cabinet that he stocked with neat's-foot oil, Lexol, liniments and tincture of violet.

A lone duck waddled after him, pecking up grains left by the mare, greeting him with a flat, squishy honk whenever he stepped outside. Harris finally carried it to the stream under his arm like a lapdog and launched it on the water among the horsehair ferns and stones.

"You're as stupid as I am," he said bitterly to the white tail. "Working like a mule on a place I can't keep."

He didn't know why he was doing all this. His plans were gone, and the new mission laid on him awaited further instructions. He had a sense of things coming unwound, purposefully and inexorably. There was nothing he could do about them but stay busy.

Chapter Fifty-nine

HARRIS DROVE TO AUBREY ROAD three days later and parked in front of the hawthorn hedge. The gate was unlatched. He walked like a thief through the sun-heated garden, past the Caddy in the drive. His footfalls made no sound.

The wood of the front door needed refinishing; an arrow of varnish plummeted to the mat as he turned the knob. Inside the house was disorderly, littered with casual stuff and slightly funky-smelling. Beyond the kitchen was a long hall with windows on one side overlooking the garden, a canyon with featherlike terraces of unweeded columbine and purple stalk crowding a worn pathway. There was a room with the door closed, before which he hesitated a moment, then a flight of stairs, narrow and carpeted with stained drugget. He climbed them to the top floor.

The room was whitewashed, filled with sun and racing cloud from a window in the ceiling. A worktable in the middle was roughened with knife marks and stains, littered with tubes, brushes in coffee cans, supermarket meat trays piled with chunks of dusty chalk, lozenge tins full of pen nibs. The stink of solvent was tinged with a clay smell of pigment, the corner sink with an odor of summer pond.

Elsa was working at a canvas propped on an easel. She laid the brush carefully on the paint-spattered ledge so the brush hairs didn't touch the wood.

"Come in," she said in a dead voice.

She wore paint-lashed jeans and a man's flannel shirt safety-pinned in front over a missing button. A plastic bag, the kind vegetables came in, was wrapped around her hair and clamped with a clothespin.

"I'll have to start locking the door," she said.

"I'm sorry," he said.

There was a coffeepot plugged into an outlet, the coffee in it burned to a crust. The room was pungent with a slaughterhouse sweetness, with sharp metallic stinks that stabbed through the cigarette smoke and dense sulfuric and solder smells. The whitewash was dingy, the floor covered with burlap stiff with paint spills. Paintings, drawings and sketches covered the walls and chairs, as if she had propped and strewn and pinned them around to blind herself to a future without painting.

"Did you know," said Elsa, "that I was the mistress of an artist while I was at the Slade? He taught there and was quite well known. I was supposed to be staying with cousins in London, but I moved into his loft. He got in dreadful trouble, but it was worth it to him. I met absolutely everybody in the art world." She added deliberately, "Of course, my son lived with us."

He pitied her, but that didn't mean he was giving up, no way. He roamed admiring while she sloshed brushes in a can of water at the sink. Her paintings were beautiful, harsh and unexpected the way things were in nature. A color photo of rock cliffs was thumbtacked to the easel. The photo was dull and static; the painting, blocked in with pencil and swabs of color, was a jumble of heat and climbing ambition. The light, falling on a canvas that took on for a breath the lime glow of the trees outside, filled him with a sudden languor.

"I'm good, aren't I?" She looked around the room. "Someday I will be. This is what I won't give up. Painting. London, Paris, New York, Toronto. People who understand what I want to do. Ideas. Adventures that I'll look back on when I'm old and wonder at their strangeness."

She turned to him with that queenly look. This was her lair. He was trapped in here with the dungeon smell. Her finger pads were scarred with yellow whorls. The place between her breasts looked chapped and cold. She was in command, even with circles like bruises under her eyes and that thing on her head. She pulled it off. Her hair stayed the shape of the bag, squashed into a particolored mat. She shook her head and snakes of coiled hair unpressed.

"Nothing about you means freedom," she said. "Nothing about you ever has."

"What is this?" He looked into a tray of sour-smelling black water.

"Acid, don't touch it. I was getting interested in lithography," she said bitterly, wiping her hands on a rag. "Printmaking. It's enormously time-consuming. Now this." Meaning him.

He didn't miss a beat. "Don't stop saying whatever you feel on my account. It would turn you into a stranger."

He left the studio.

In the discorded living room was a portrait of Grey, propped on a stack of magazines. He was with his stallion, who was looking alertly away at something outside the range of the canvas. But the sleek indifferent male power of the horse did not diminish the man. Big for an Englishman, taller than most horsemen, he had learned to make himself light in the saddle. His hair was ruffled. The vivid eyes took the viewer's measure, found it fell short and forgave it, all in one look. And Harris wondered at not having seen the true mettle of his friend until the brightness was gone.

Early evening of the next day, he was tidying up the front room when the phone rang.

He had been thinking about whiskey, feeling guarded about not caring it was gone, not daring to hope for the peace of choice. For the dizzying grace of release. When whiskey crossed his mind he had no trouble replacing it with this new sense of purpose, which was, he saw, old—as old as that day at the train station when he had first seen her as a woman. She was supposed to be in his life and so was the boy and his intention was to make her see it. In the small hours he was consoled by the memory of those frantic banners of paint and scrawled crayon like a liquidation sale display.

Harris had nearly forgotten the phone's existence. He crossed the front room swiftly and picked it up on the third ring.

"Harris, it's me."

He put distance in his voice. "What do you want?"

"I must see you."

The handset was a hunk of lead under his chin. "Then come," he said, and cradled it.

He sat in the armchair under the Woolworth lamp, his heart thumping, and reached for a book, any book, from the stack by the chair. Bulfinch's *Mythology*. He flipped through it and lighted on Proserpine. *One of the greater goddesses . . . daughter of Ceres and wife of Pluto, who carried her off to the under-world where she became queen of the realms of the dead . . .*

He read, smoking a cigarette. After forty minutes a tap came at the screen door. He glanced up, saw Elsa screened and hatched, with her hair in flames.

"Come in," he said curtly.

She let herself in and perched on the arm of the chair. He kept reading with a slight frown. *Previously, however, he found means to plead his cause to Medea, daughter of the king. He promised her marriage, and as they stood before the altar of Hecate called the goddess to witness his oath.*

"Harris, I will marry you," she said.

"That's good," he said, and reached for her hand.

"Don't touch me," she said. "That's not what we're about now."

The book slid off his leg and hit the floor. "What the fuck are we about then? I'm tired of you, girl. Don't come here talking some shit about what you'll do, then push me off."

She was gazing around the room. The pansy-colored eyes were washy with exhaustion, the sunburst of hair dark-rooted like the seedbed of a large coarse flower. She wore a calico sundress in browns and pinks with a cardigan over it. The long white legs were bare and scratched.

"Can you leave me alone?" she said.

"I can leave you alone for life," he growled.

She went to the window.

"He used to give us tea and store-bought biscuits on the porch," she said in a trailing voice, looking out at the hemlocks languishing in dry heaps on the ground. "Wilf Humphries. He was so hearty and effusive; he was afraid of us because we were children. I don't think he'd been near one since he was a child himself. This room always smelled of fireplace ash and pekoe. That amber scent; remember it? Pym's Tea in the green box. They all have their relations send it from home. 'That's all I want, dear, a box of Pym's Irish Green if it isn't too much trouble.' Iseult's parlor smells like this with the windows closed. Did you know he used to raise whippets?"

"I just tore down the runs," he said in a frosty voice.

She turned, slowly like a little drifting boat, and floated down the hall.

Harris waited. Maybe she had gone to use the bathroom. When ten minutes had passed, he rose and went after her.

Elsa was in the bedroom, taking off her clothes. The long northern day was closing and the sky through the window was red-gold behind the black branches of the trees. She must have lingered, watching it darken, before she started to undress. The cardigan was weeping over a chair. She lifted the sundress over her head. Her breasts were bare. He leaned against the door frame and watched. Her feet made a little slapping sound when she stepped out of her underpants. It was the only sound in the room. She left the small two-ringed pool on the floor, faced him momentarily with a blind look, and sat on the bed.

He came in and opened the window. She sat watching him with her hands in her lap. The summer night flowed into the room, full of the plant fragrance of water willows and alfalfa. He dropped his pants on a chair and came to her. He could smell the sharp scent coming off her, the scent of her shoulders and the spice of the hair between her legs; he smelled his own smell of good mineral earth. He took her hand and held it against him. She let it stay. The weight of his prick curled heavily in her palm, slowly straightening until it stood like a thick plant growing from a root and nudged along her wrist.

"I can't," she said. "Let me alone, goddamn you."

"Forget the marriage thing then," he said, furious.

She fell across the bed on her stomach and went to sleep.

He dressed again and went into the front room. There he paced, excited and restless, for a quarter hour. He went back in the bedroom and stood at the foot of the bed. She lay with her arms limply cast down, her body velvety with the sheen of down that captured the early moon. The small of her back was a dusky pool. Below the cropped hair curling damp and dark at the roots the nape of her neck was fragile, a necklace of bones under the skin. Harris could have galloped Bluebell through the room without waking her.

He felt a sharp sorrow for her that was close to mourning.

When he woke it was the dead of night, and he felt better. He lay in front of the fireplace and looked out the newly naked front window at a warm sky full of stars. After a while he got out of the sleeping bag and put on a pot of coffee.

He had covered Elsa with a blanket and tucked it in, turning her awkwardly on her back first, while her head dragged on the mattress. By the stroke of light from the hall he saw her studying the outline of her tented feet and breasts. She seemed to be mustering her thoughts.

He switched the lamp on.

"I was exhausted," she said. "When I saw the bed I knew I would sleep."

"You were fending me off," he said.

"All right. I lost my courage. It wasn't what I was here for."

He closed his hand on her wrist. "Look, you can leave if you want to. I won't hold you to anything."

She stared at the faint tail of a scar that crossed his abdomen like a comet and disappeared into the waistband of his pants.

"Why did you say that?" she said bitterly, pulling her hand away. She got out of bed and went in the bathroom, shaking his eyes off her body.

He waited by the bed while she made peeing sounds, then washing sounds, then toothbrushing sounds. With his toothbrush and paste.

"You have to put something on," he said when she came out. "You're not going around me like that." He tossed her a T-shirt.

"It smells like you." She scowled, pulling it over her head.

"It's clean," he said.

The lamp was on in the kitchen, the percolator sighing and blubbing on one of the burners. Harris fired up the stove, got a bowl of eggs and a coffee can of bacon fat out of the icebox.

"You look very well when you cook," she said, watching him break eggs into a skillet. "Absorbed and slightly annoyed. I hope you'll like it, because I don't cook."

He gave a twitch of a smile. "So we're back together, according to you. What *do* you do?"

"Paint. Ride horses. Play checkers with my son. Worry about money."

"What about your students? You teach, right?"

She looked surprised. "I don't mind them," she said warily.

He spooned bacon fat into another skillet and turned up the fire, then dropped slices of bread from a wrinkled packet into the fat, turning them gently with a fork as they crisped. When they were golden brown he lifted the slices onto a paper towel.

"Now we can settle to pitched blows over a number of things," she said at his shoulder. "Are you ready?"

"Oh yes," he said calmly.

He gave her a plate of food first, then fixed himself a plate. He found an orange in the icebox and divided it into sections. They ate with gusto at the counter, swallowing noisily, scrubbing their plates with the crusts until they squeaked.

Chapter Sixty

HE GOT HIS WRISTWATCH from the bedroom and laid it neatly beside the lamp. It was one-thirty in the morning. He had, she said, watching this, always been a tidy man.

"I want to see how long this takes you," he said without smiling.

"You mean how long it takes me to tell you how deceitful and conniving you are, which you'll listen to for hours so you can get back in my life? You didn't say that."

"No, and I'm not going to either."

"Not much at groveling, are you? Not even for what you think you want."

"I don't mind saying what I want. I've already said it. But I'm not going to shuck and jive for you or anyone."

"Why don't you speak the King's English?" she snapped. "You're not a stupid man or uneducated either."

"I stick to my speaking style because it suits me," he said.

She marched to his chair and took possession of it. This was fine with him. He sat on the hearth. She cast him a profoundly indifferent glance, sitting with her knees drawn up, naked under his shirt, the hair on her head and between her legs fluffed out as if electrified. She had insight, she had power. He felt a sudden rush of humility before that insight, and the contrary humor, like a fairy's or wizard's, that had made her play dead so he couldn't get at her.

Her skin was pale under the lamp, pale as the nymphaea that floated on the flooded meadows near Salthill. The face was medieval. It could give him hatred, sensuality, intelligence, cruelty, mother love. It could give him anything but cheap sentiment. It wasn't a face you looked at the way you buried

your nose in a gardenia, until its sweet perfection cloyed. A bitter afterscent
was what it gave.

They stared at each other.

"What is your name?" she asked.

"Are you accepting a proposal or buying a mule?" he said, after a silence.
"Jesus, why did I pick you? I want someone who cooks the food I like to
eat and talks the way I do. Someone who wants me in her bed. That
wouldn't hurt either."

"That's tough," she said. "You're stuck with me, Southern man."

"I am not," said Harris. He flung his cigarette in the fireplace. "I don't
want the trouble you stand for."

"This was your idea, not mine. Don't whine to me about it."

"It wasn't anybody's idea. This is some joke God laid on me just when
things were going good."

"They were going rather well for me, too," said Elsa.

She left the chair and prowled barefoot over the carpet, to the fireplace
and back. "When I heard your voice, when I saw you at the restaurant it
returned, though I had worked so diligently to turn it to ash—the terrible,
terrible binding! I have always loved you, Harris. My love for you makes
my life desperate. My love is so unreflective and blind I feel half dead with
it—like a cast horse trying to get back on its legs, and in the end too exhausted to do anything but succumb. That it's not your way to preen yourself
on it makes you the more worthy of my passion, though it would burn even
if you did. How I love your majestic ordinariness!

"I've come here knowing that loving you means being turned over to
Salthill. No art, no career, no travel. No London, Paris, Toronto. No Vancouver even, much. I'll be trapped in that bloody castle with a pack of
children and nothing to paint, because I can't get rid of my love."

"What are you trying to say?" he asked. "I have this place. There'll be
Vancouver."

She turned to him, her face wild and woeful. "Harris, no. You came to
that valley because it was yours in some dream you don't even remember
having. You tried to fit in, hoping no one would notice your passion and
greed and your bloody industrious groveling. You knew you'd get what you
wanted at Salthill. And like fools we took you in."

"That isn't what *he* thought," he said quickly, stung. "Grey knew me."

"He knows you much better now." She sat down again, her hands folded
tightly, her eyes feverish. "The question in all our minds is, did you mean

to do what you did? Did you intend to reach Salthill through me, Harris? Or directly through my father?"

"You're mistaken," he said. "I've never cared for anyone the way I did for him."

"He loved what he thought you were: someone whose shining deeds would grace us. He's a proud, warlike man, Harris. He intended nothing less for you than he offered."

"He could afford to be noble."

"It's why Gordon hated you. He knew the night you came what you were going to be to Grey."

"All your brother saw was a hungry nigger," said Harris.

"I hate that word," she said automatically.

"Get used to it," he sneered. "We use it all the time."

"What a lie. It's not my *privilege* to use it. If you say it again, I'll throw something at your head."

"Nigger," he said dryly. She flung the ashtray at him. He ducked and it struck the fireplace and bounced, being plastic. He crossed the room and pinned her in the chair in a long kiss. She arched under his hand, then bit his tongue. He gasped.

"You broke his heart," she said.

He felt his mouth. "What broke it? What we did or what he thinks I did?"

"The latter, I think. Grey is complicated. He has his own interior, and few enter." She straightened and tidied the shirt over her hips. "Do you know he's lived with Sno-Bird on and off for years? My father and the high witch of the Skillihawk. When her old husband died last year, she moved into the house. Salthill is theirs until you come back to claim it."

He leaped up and roamed the room. "I'm not claiming anything. I have my own land."

"You left a token against your return."

He went to the window and stood looking out, as if the dark could tell him things. "You act like you're turning yourself in, talking about being tired as a cast horse and stuck up there in the wilderness. I'm staying here and if you're with me you'll be here too."

"Will I?" she said to his back. "I pray it won't matter where I am, as long as you're there! I've heard that women dream of faceless lovers as men dream of gods. You remember the old song Flavia used to sing, and that she taught me: 'He came in so sweetly his feet made no din/ He came close beside me and this he did say/ It will not be long dear, till our wedding day.' Never have I dreamed such a dream. Your face has always been the face of the husband of an arranged marriage."

"You mean you don't feel romantic about me?" he asked. "Now ain't that some shit."

She laughed. "You don't like that. Don't worry. You've still picked a wonderful consort. I'm strong, and I've got your token. And my dowry? You know what it is. Salthill. You should have seen Bron Georgewood's face when she met us on the street in Penticton. There you were in infant form, laced to my back in the little pouch Charley's mother made for me, guarding your legacy with those eyes! The woman nearly fainted with relief. What a lucky escape for her dear Trinity!"

She laughed again merrily.

He couldn't help smiling. He left the window and came toward her, wolfish with desire.

"I thought you'd come for me, but it was too soon. Fi knew it was; she knew. He threw the decanter through the window and the snow was laced with orange whiskey, and cold air came through the glass." She put her hands to her face, knocking the mug off the arm of the chair. It rolled away, leaving a trail of tan liquid on the carpet.

He sat on the arm of the chair and stroked her hair. He wanted to dive into those blue shadows for the pleasure of feeling himself glide blindly from world to world. He felt dread in the electric ends of her hair and in her hand, which seemed to get cool and lose flesh in his.

"I've come here to show you my wounds. Our wounds—mine and my father's. How you invaded our fastness and tore Salthill apart." She looked heavy-lidded and drained, her breasts loose points under the shirt. A dry hair fell on her forehead and she swept it away with a hand.

"I'll listen," he said, and touched his lips to the back of her hand.

There was a knock on the door.

Neither of them moved. Then Elsa put her legs down, rose and walked out of the room.

A man was standing on the other side of the screen, his head and shoulders blocking out a chunk of night sky. A discreet oval of torchlight played down his boots.

"Evening, sir. Police here."

Every emotion seemed to pool into a complete attention. Harris became as calm as he had been roiled moments ago. He stepped outside. The crickets had stopped singing in the grass.

The man was his age, blond and heavy, in an RCMP uniform. The face was a bland teutonic mask. Harris wondered what he had seen before he rang the bell.

"Do you own a big red horse?" asked the Mountie.

This was what happened when you came back. Coming back uprooted the dead and transported them to the present. He didn't think of the Russel fence and the gully by the Klaxta reserve. He thought of the horse stalking on long legs across his property, stopping to feed and test the wind, moving closer.

"Why?"

"There's a horse in the road at the end of your drive. Dead. It got out through a fence somewhere and wandered onto the highway. A tractor-trailer truck hit it and went into the ditch. You might have seen the lights."

They looked toward the road simultaneously. Harris saw a foggy glow, either the headlamps of a tow truck or the lights of the ditched trailer.

"Perhaps you can have a look at it," said the Mountie.

Harris followed him on foot. The idea of riding anywhere in a police car gave him a thrill of horror. He ducked inside for his tennis shoes and walked down the drive to the highway, passing the Caddy parked in the grass near the bridge. The night sky was the color of a river under moonlight, the mountains black and sharp against it. Flares threw scratchy light around a mound straddling the centerline. Another cop stood on the shoulder, looking down the road for traffic. There may have been other people around, trucks and equipment. There may have been, but he didn't notice. A circle of torchlight played briefly over his face and chest, then dropped down his legs. He stood patiently until it swung away. The tractor-trailer lay in the ditch like a foundered mastodon, its wheels elevated.

He stared down at the dead horse. It was big but not big enough, a rangy, good-sized chestnut with more gold than red in the blood-spattered coat.

"It's not mine," he said. "I don't have anything to move it with either. You'll have to try next door."

He waited, counting: one, two, three, four.

"You're the owner here?" asked the MP.

"Yes."

"Sorry to have troubled you at this hour."

Harris raised one brow. "My wife and I were up anyway. Talking."

Elsa was sitting in the armchair with her legs crossed.

"What was't?"

"Police," he said. "Accident."

"What sort of accident?"

"Horse got run over."

She seemed to consider. "Big red horse," she said distantly.

"You heard."

"I didn't." She swept the loose hair off her forehead again. "I've thought as much as I can think about all this," she said. "When the knock came I was going to leave. Actually I was going to walk to the road and lie down at the beginning of your drive and go to sleep, because I'm so tired. But I can't now. There are gaffs and winches and men, and I can't. I'm trapped by that thing on the road." She closed her eyes.

"But you'd made up your mind before," he said.

"True. After you left my studio the other day." She felt on the side table for his cigarettes. Harris lit one and passed it to her, trying not to touch her fingers. "I started cleaning up very slowly. It took a long time to wash the brushes and put things away. I saw that it was all no use, that I was going to go on loving you." She opened her eyes. "I'm going to fight to paint, Harris, even though I'll lose. I don't like children. I don't want to be any-one's wife. I was made for adventure and wandering. You won't be happy with me."

"You like our son," he stated.

"He is a nice child," she drawled, and he felt that he would never get to the bottom of that. "He felt good in my belly. When he was suckling the milk was so much it ran down my ribs. I wanted to scream with sensuality and lust—for everything in life. . . . Flavia was shocked. She uses bottles, they all do. Boiling glass in pots at one in the morning. I hid in my room.

"Yes, Harris, I must define the boundaries within which I can accept this—life—I'm choosing. And that you must accept, too. You must know us in a different way. Ah, how unhappy I shall be, how trapped, how des-perately in love!" she said. "I'll have to get in bed with you next, I'll have to let you in. Loving you will kill me."

He withdrew from the lamp silently, leaving her striped white and gold beneath it, and sat down on the hearth to listen.

"I stayed in Winnipeg as long as I could, after I found out," said Elsa. "It took a lot of cleverness to manage. I had no idea I was so resourceful at thinking up reasons to stay on, nonexistent friends and the like. I won't go into it.

"It was mid-March when I came home. I don't know whether you re-member that comment Iseult makes every spring, about the lion going in and the lamb coming out. It's a ritual with her and we would repeat it in a joking way after reading one of her letters. Well, the lion stayed in that year. It was so cold, that March. I remember coming over the pass—no one in the car was speaking, we were all speechless—and seeing the jagged outcroppings of rock appear, still covered with snow, and the ocher and peach-colored granite soaring into the shadowless light.

"Tom Pushkin had come with my father to meet me at the station. It was frightful. I was seven months gone, sticking out to there and pink in the face. A whole autumn had passed without you, and a Christmas; the first foals had arrived without you. Do you know what it was like, Harris, because you were gone? Every day was a torment; I would wake in the morning heavy and sick with your not being there, in a strange city that I hated because you had never seen it.

"Tom had been going to spend the night at Salthill at least—I think they were planning to go over some business things—but of course he couldn't after that. He didn't even stay for dinner. How could he? It isn't what's done. He said good-bye and drove away and left me alone with my father. Grey told me to put my things away and meet him in the study."

Chapter Sixty-one

HER LUGGAGE HAD BEEN DROPPED hastily inside the door. Grey must have brought everything up while she was looking for Sno-Bird. She had to see Sno-Bird. But the kitchen had been empty except for the dogs sleeping around the range.

Elsa removed scarf, coat, sweaters. Under everything was the one dress that still fit, bought when she could no longer get her other things closed at the waist, when the insidious, betraying body had suddenly flared like a balloon after months of being nearly flat: a gingham dress with a plain collar and cuffs and an expandable panel in front, the sort of thing a respectable housewife would wear. She pulled off her boots but kept on the black tights, which she had been able to pull up around her abdomen because the elastic was flabby. She went down to the study where her father waited beside his desk.

"Close the door," he said.

She stood for the interview, in the silence of the house that neither breathed nor settled, because it was made of stone. The whiskey decanter stood among the books and papers, and she was often drawn to the orange glow trapped in ladders of thick, greenish glass. It was a lodestone, something to fix on.

"I won't ask what happened," said Grey bitterly. "That is perfectly clear." He looked at her again in disbelief, as though the dress that swelled at the waist and was too tight in the breasts might suddenly dissolve, and she would be thin and a child again. "I can't believe this. Not that you're at fault; you can't be. But that you could hide it for so long, Elsa! That— Never mind. How many months have you been . . . in this state?"

"Five," said Elsa.

"Five months," he repeated. "You're beyond that."

"Just five months looking like this."

He was too absorbed in the whirl of his thoughts to hear. "I left you in Winnipeg too long, with Gordon gone. You were too much by yourself. All I do is make mistakes with you." He took a turn around the room and came back. "Why on earth didn't you write me?" he asked. "Or Flavia?"

She looked away, toward the window. "I didn't want you to know."

"Nonsense, there was nothing to be frightened of. I'd never punish you for doing such a stupid thing. My god, why didn't I send you to the nuns like your sister. You'll have to marry the boy."

"He's not available," she said sadly.

"Not available," he said. "Elsa, I know you like to keep things to your-self—you *have* kept this to yourself—but you must speak now. You must tell me who is responsible for this. Unless—" He frowned. "Not young George-wood?"

She shook her head.

His chest rose and fell, in relief or regret. "Very well . . . we'll know in a moment. I've been thinking what's to be done. I'm going to call Daisy. She's a sensible woman, she'll be able to help. What a pity the phone lines aren't in yet. They're putting them through the valley at the end of spring. I'll drive to Four Queens in the morning."

"I want to keep the baby," said Elsa.

He stared at her as though the duck decoy on the shelf had come to life and begun quacking. "Don't be a silly girl. Daisy will find out where to send you. There are homes for girls in your situation. You can't keep an illegiti-mate child."

"I'm going to. I won't put it up for adoption."

"You've no choice. You're underage and I won't allow it," said Grey. "I need the facts first, then we can make arrangements. The boy's parents must be spoken with. Do you—you do know the father?" He made a sound of self-contempt. "I'm sorry. Forgive me. Of course you do. You've been taken advantage of. Tell me who he is and we'll go on from there. I have to know, you know."

"I suppose you do," she said. "It was Harris."

"Harris?" he said, as though he had never heard the name. His brows lifted, wrinkling his forehead and opening the network of small lines that fronded his eyes. It was the expression of a man being told a highly distasteful joke who is too polite to protest.

"Harris is the father," she said calmly.

A rush of blood darkened his cheeks. "No."

"I'm sorry," said Elsa. "It is."

He slapped her. She put her hand to her face, blinking.

"Don't lie to me!" he said. He was white around the mouth. He grasped her by the shoulders. She reeled backward, catching the desk clumsily with her hands.

"I'm not lying," she quavered.

"Oh my god," he said. "Oh my god. No." He flung himself away and roamed the room in a kind of frenzy, pacing to the window and back with his fists clenched. She waited, backed against the desk, sick to her stomach. His eyes were bright with tears, she saw. He dashed them away with his hand.

"Get out of here," he groaned. "Get away from me. Oh my god."

"I'm going to keep it," said Elsa faintly.

"Get out!" he shouted.

It was vital that she see Sno-Bird. Elsa sat in the bedroom with the lamp off and picked out her braid. It was impossible to sleep or read. She could do nothing but wait, trapped like a field under a squall.

Her room was furnished as it had always been, with a four-poster covered with a spread, India in winter, dotted Swiss in summer; a wool carpet, a chiffonier with a looking glass, a walnut dresser. It was very large like all the rooms at Salthill, so that one was always conscious of one's small size in it, like Alice in the Eat Me Drink Me Room, the contrasting length and gloomy height of the walls, papered in an optimistic pattern of leaves and tumbling olives, the ceiling with its moldings of colonnades and Roman victory wreaths. There was a basin and ewer of water in the absence of upstairs plumbing. Elsa had pulled the largest suitcase onto the bed and undone the straps. Like the furniture it was the cast-off of some relation, an uncle or cousin who had used it to cross from Dover to Calais or Bristol to East India, as some spinster aunt had slept in the bed. There had never been money for new furnishings at Salthill. Everything went on the horses.

At the close of day, when the moon had risen and hung like a Christmas ornament in the window, in a deeply blue sky in which the stars were almost too bright for the naked gaze, Sno-Bird came.

Elsa unlocked the door. They had found the key in the pantry years ago, in a drawer of loose ends, and she had left it in the keyhole.

The housekeeper held a tray of dishes with saucepan lids over them. There was a smoking teapot properly covered with a cloth. She wore outdoor clothing. Her deerskin boots were damp in patches, as though she had just come into the house, but her hair was loose, as if she were ready for bed.

"Welcome home," said Sno-Bird.

"Take that away," said Elsa.

"I don't care if you starve, but he said to bring you food. He's down there sick, drinking whiskey."

Elsa took the tray and set it outside the door. "He's lucky."

Sno-Bird gave her the once-over she had grown accustomed to. Her eyes were like raisins. "What do you want?" she asked. "I know you want something."

"The baby," said Elsa grimly. "I'm not going to eat or come out of this room until he says I can keep the baby. I want you to tell him that."

Sno-Bird wagged her head. "To have a child without the proper ceremony in your tradition is very bad. And with this one, much worse. You'll ruin yourself and the shame will kill him."

"I don't care what anyone thinks!" she shouted. "He shouldn't either! I'm not giving it up! You can bloody tell him—"

"I don't have to," said Sno-Bird. "You never change your mind once it's set on anything, do you?"

Elsa shut the door in her face and turned the key in the lock. After a quarter hour during which she heard no sound from the hall, she opened the door and took the teapot from the tray. Light from the ground floor filled the stairwell. He was down there, sick and drinking whiskey.

Elsa sat heavily on the mattress and opened the suitcase. Beneath the bloomers and undershirts was a collection of packets wrapped in Christmas paper—gold foil stars and grenadiers, holly sprigs on a mint-green field. Each had been neatly sealed with tape. She unstuck one, revealing a Cadbury bar, a bag of peanuts, a Seville orange and a packet of jerky. These she arranged neatly on the paper, and felt in the suitcase for the mug she had packed. She poured tea and took a long draught, shivering with pleasure as the hot drink went down.

Then she settled down to munch her way glumly through the contents of the packet.

Sno-Bird returned the next morning.

"Your father wants to see you," she said when Elsa opened the door. She wore a housedress over long underwear. Elsa could see the snaps of her woolens through the bodice.

"What about?" Elsa asked guardedly.

"You can't do this," said Sno-Bird, lively with exasperation. "He wants to help you. He needs more information. Go to him, and you may get what you want."

"You machiavellian old bat," said Elsa. But she went downstairs.

They met in the dining room. The room was silver with cold, like the ice on the fingers of the lake near Four Queens. His face, newly old and ravaged with misery, had the same evanescence. His eyes were sunk in their sockets, blue-hollowed underneath, like hers.

"Sno-Bird says you're not eating," said Grey, sinking into a chair.

"No."

"You're trying to starve yourself. You've barricaded yourself in your room without food, because you want to keep . . . that."

"Yes."

"Would it help you do the right thing," he said, "if I said I couldn't live with such a memento . . . such a shameful reminder of a painful betrayal?"

She swallowed. "It wasn't betrayal."

"You poor child." He regarded her compassionately for the first time. "You've always been a troublesome spirit, haven't you? Tell me how long this terrible thing went on."

"Only the summer," she answered.

"Thank god," he said quietly.

"I want to keep it," said Elsa. She was beginning to feel like the cuckoo that thrusts its head out of a clock every hour and says the same thing any number of times.

He gave her a look that made her shiver. "You can't, of course. Aside from your own reputation, d'you think I'm going to be made a figure of fun everywhere within a hundred-mile radius?" He rose. "I've spoken with Daisy. You'll go to her in a few days when everything's been arranged."

"I will not!"

"Don't cross me," he said coldly. "You've done enough, the two of you. Even granted your innocence, *he* surely must have known what jeopardy he was putting you in. As long as you go quietly and get rid of it without anyone knowing, we may yet circumvent this. And that's precisely what will happen."

"I'll run away," she cried. "I'll kill myself."

"Get to your room. I'll come for you when it's time to leave."

She labored up the stairs. There was another tray in front of the door, on it a sandwich wrapped in waxed paper, an apple and a glass of milk. Elsa hesitated at sight of the milk, then pushed the tray away hard with her foot. The glass rolled over and milk puddled on the runner.

She slammed the door and locked herself in.

Harris wanted to leave. He wanted to walk down the drive under the river of sky and watch the dead horse being winched up by headlight and torch to the shouts of exasperated men and meshing of gears. He didn't move.

"You're telling me everything, aren't you?" he said. "Everything, remember."

"I am. Otherwise it wouldn't work, would it? Just be sure you watch me tell you. Don't cross the room, don't look away."

"I'm not going anywhere," Harris said.

She was under siege. She spent hours at the window, staring at the garden and grounds with their networking of pathways. The room smelled of raw earth with the window open. The ruffled sky settled over elevations veneered with snow, to an atmospheric vanishing point of dull land and dull sky.

In the afternoon of the third endless day, Elsa saw a horse come down the drive at a stately walk.

It was a great creature as tall as a draft horse, with a curving neck and enormous iron-shod feet which it lifted and set down with ponderous grace. It was caparisoned in red cloth swagged and trimmed with gold. Over its head was a red hood, bejeweled and winking; a blaze of cloth of gold ran down the face and around the eyeholes. The swagged covering lifted from its body as though stirred by a breeze, and she saw a glimpse of red coat beneath.

A man sat astride him. Though the air was still, the same breeze lifted his shirt gently away from his body. She couldn't see his face from above, only the crown of his head and his shoulders as they skirted the truck parked at the gate.

She pressed her forehead against the icy glass of the half-raised window and closed her eyes. When she looked again, the drive was empty.

She withdrew and sat on the bed to wait.

There was a crashing sound below. Between the two turrets the front of the veranda collapsed inward like a stormed barrier. Snow erupted in a titanic cloud, rose billowing to the ceilings and twisted along the passage, sending polar air rushing through the ground floor.

She screwed her hands into fists and pressed them against each other.

The great horse stood in the lower hallway, filling it from wall to wall with its animal bulk. There was no sound but the rasp of breath through its nostrils, the howl of the wind down the broken cave of the hall, the ring of an iron shoe on the floorboards. It stepped forward slowly. The tasseled fringes of the cloth swung below its belly, the rider's legs hung by the swags. She could see the warp of the cloth, the roundness of the weight beneath it, as they moved toward her in and out of the shadows.

Elsa jumped from the bed and stood rooted to the carpet.

There was a loud knock on the door.

She screamed with excitement and triumph and fear, stumbled forward and threw the door wide.

Flavia stared back at her.

Chapter Sixty-two

ELSA SHOWED FLAVIA THE BALLS of rolled-up Christmas paper. "I've eaten three every day," she said proudly. "For the baby. Except once it was four. One gets frightfully hungry with nothing to do."

"I believe you have," said Flavia with wonder.

She had become a handsome matron, plump and brown as a hazelnut in a suit of peacock blue that matched the highlights in the bangs showing under her scarf. Her boots trailed slush into the room, for in her consternation she had forgotten to remove them. She had brought a pot of tea and two cups and saucers. She set the tray on the chiffonier and took off the scarf, revealing a glossy page boy. The two sisters embraced.

"You look so white and rather mad," said Flavia, holding her at arm's length. "My poor darling."

Elsa scowled. "Only you could say that and get away with it." But her voice trembled with relief. She poked in the suitcase and produced a bar of chocolate. "Look, Cadbury." She broke the bar in two pieces. "For our tea."

"Thank you." Flavia bit into the nutty thing, looking bemused.

They sat on the bed and drank tea.

"You're thinking, aren't you?" said Elsa. "I can tell. All St. Oeggers are good at thinking furiously behind a facade of calm."

"Of course I am. I've come to help you decide," said Flavia. "You can't decide alone, darling. But what made you do it? Hiding, I mean. Not telling us. Did you think we wouldn't help?"

"I was afraid you *would*. Hiding seemed best once I knew what I wanted."

"Elsa, Grey told me . . . who the father is. Who you said it is."

"It is who I said it is."

"It's really true then!" cried Flavia. "H-he was our *family*. He was one of *ours*. He *seduced* you. This is dreadful!" Her lips trembled; she studied Elsa with eyes shining with tears. "O dear, this is because of Galway isn't it? This is a desperate attempt to right great wrongs."

Elsa pushed the lank hair nervously from her face. "I loved him, Flavia. Always, you know, since we began here. That's why I have to keep it. Whenever I think of going through all this and having it, then never seeing it again, or him . . . and the baby going to live with strangers someplace— *my* baby . . . and *his*. It belongs here, Fi. This is its home."

"I don't think Salthill will ever be this child's home," said Flavia.

She rose distractedly and crossed to the window. Elsa hesitated, then followed her. They gazed down on the yard below. A man bundled in a coat and scarf was crossing the drive toward the stable. It was Grey. He swayed listlessly, as though something had broken inside and destroyed his equilibrium.

"He's terribly sad," said Flavia in a doleful voice.

"Please don't misunderstand," said Elsa, still looking out. "It wasn't his idea. I wouldn't let him alone. I made sure after a while it would be all he'd want. Sure of it, Fi. He wanted it over and over again. I could make him do that."

"Stop. *Please*."

"I just want you to understand," said Elsa.

"I do understand! I do." Grey had disappeared into the stable. One of the dogs followed, wagging its tail slowly.

"I'm glad, Fi."

Flavia moved away and stood facing the room with her fingers pressed to her mouth.

"Adoption is the only thing," she said finally, dropping her hands. "The baby will have a good home and your reputation will be saved. That's important, Elsa, whatever you may think. You can't imagine what it means to have a child out of wedlock."

"It might not have a good home," said Elsa, watching her intently. "It'll be the wrong color."

"Him or her," said Flavia automatically. "Not it. Elsa, someday you'll be married and have a husband of your own and children, and then you'll know you did the right thing for this child. You'll be able to forget this . . . thing that has happened."

"I don't want all that. I want what I have!"

"Elsa, the *stigma*—"

"It's my baby," cried Elsa. "I told him I'd die before I gave it up! Fi, you can't be on his side!" She began to fling herself about, wringing her hands and moaning. She paced the room, knocked something off the vanity, stumbled over a chair and straightened it with hands that trembled.

"I'm the one who's right!" she shouted. "If I'd a way to make him do as he should, I'd be keeping it then, wouldn't I? The baby's not at fault for me laying with a man, is't? 'Tis a dreadful thing ye're making me do, and if God knew the wickedness *that one* was planning He'd strike me dead and put me out of this misery!"

"Don't talk Irish, El—" Flavia stopped and let loose a hysterical titter. "What a thing to say!" she muttered.

Elsa dug into the closet and brought out the chamber pot, opened the sash and tossed a cupful of urine out the window.

"I hope it lands on one of 'em," she said. "Him, or the auld woman."

Flavia laughed, in a gust of relief. "I have to get out of here for a few minutes," she said. "I can't think. Let me put my things away."

"I'm not leaving the room. Of that you may be sure."

"Fine. Put that thing down."

"You won't be far?"

"Just across the way, love. Wait for me."

Flavia was back in half an hour.

"I had to change the bed," she said thoughtfully. She had put on a pair of house slippers, which looked odd with the blue suit. "The linen was actually dusty. Have you bathed since you came?"

"No. Why?"

"Someone's been in the bath. I mean, not father. It smells of almonds, rather a nice smell, and there's a dish of hairpins on the washstand."

"Sno-Bird no doubt. She's taken over the house. The woman's on *his* side. All sympathy, she is."

Flavia sat on the bed. She pushed the heavy bang off her forehead with both hands and let her head fall back.

"You look like Nefertiti under her gold miter," murmured Elsa.

Her sister sighed. "It's damp, as if she's bathed in there. Elsa, when I look at you I think of the way you were that day in Ireland, on the beach. D'you remember? Nana was trying to take you back to the house and you wouldn't go."

"I should think. We were having a tearing row."

"It was a rout, I'm afraid," said Flavia, eyes shining. "I remember your face. Forgive me, darling. It was wild, almost idiotic, really more a smudge than a face. There was such despair in it, such friendlessness. I don't think

I've ever seen a lonelier human being, and you were only a child. I'm sorry, I probably sound incoherent, but my ideas all seem like dreams this afternoon. Sometimes I think I'll never make another sensible decision."

She meditated. Elsa watched from the window, the thick rope of hair tarnished and ablaze down her back. There was a crafty look on her face.

"I'm going to have another baby in seven months," said Flavia abruptly. "A brother or sister for little Dean. That's probably why I'm going to tell you what I will. But first, a bath. You'll feel much better after a bath and some milk."

"I'm not bloody going down there."

"It will all be right, I promise. You smell like a goat. He's not downstairs at any rate, he's in the stable. He'll stay clear of us. Let's go now."

After bathing Elsa changed into wool pants and a sweater from Flavia's suitcase. There was even a maternity bra with an oversized plaque of hooks.

"You need this," murmured Flavia, doing her up. "You've got frightfully big."

At the vanity Flavia stood with the hairbrush raised. She looked as though she were about to begin an aria, but she only spoke out loud. "Blessed Mother, help me do the right thing. A child is a child, and this one is one as well."

She had taken off her jacket to help Elsa bathe and step out of the tub. Underneath was a blouse patterned with flowers. The colors were gay and springlike, and the red in the flowers matched the red of her mouth.

"Does that mean you still love me?" asked Elsa in jerks as her head was being yanked back and forth.

"We don't get to choose who we love," said Flavia briskly, working the bristles through.

"Ouch."

"Or the way we do either. That's the mystery we struggle with all our lives. *I* think it boils down to accepting you're choiceless about love. You're bound to who you're given, even when they seem to be turning themselves inside out to show you someone you never thought they were, or could bear them to be."

"And if you don't stick, you're lazy," pronounced Elsa.

Flavia laughed. "No, you're guilty. You're a nothing."

She leaned forward a little, over the bright head, and rested her hand on Elsa's cheek. Elsa heard her draw in her breath. "We aren't sisters, my love. And Gordon is not your brother."

Elsa pulled her head away. "What?"

"Oh my dear, I'm so sorry. I could have said it better. I've thought and thought how to say it."

"But I'm his daughter. We *look* alike." Her voice rose, beseeching, in panic.

"You're Grey's daughter, it's true. But we have different mothers. So we're half-sisters, you see."

Elsa stared round-eyed into the mirror. At blond and raven, at hazel eyes and lapis eyes, freckles and olive smoothness. At Flavia's face, with the bone structure, refined and classically regular, of the woman in the portrait in her grandmother's house, with the pearls and dark hair. At Flavia's dramatic coloring, and her own dull ivory sheen.

"Who was mine, then?" she whispered.

"The daughter of the tenants on Grandfather's largest farm," said Flavia. "At Cudagh, seven miles east of us. D'you remember that farm? They're gone, the tenants; the Nortons have had it for years now.

"She was about twenty-five. I saw her at a musical event in the village one Christmas. I knew who she was by then. I mean, I knew what had happened, that my father had had a child with her. Everybody knew. She was blond and tall, like an Icelander or a Swede, but she was Irish. Her people were Protestants from Leitrim and kept to themselves."

"Go on," said Elsa ominously.

"My mother was Grey's wife, Alice Sheridan. And Gordon's too, of course," said Flavia. "She was in a hunting accident about the time you were born. She was an avid horsewoman, she rode with hunts all over Ireland, and a horse ran under a tree with her at Meadford. It cracked her skull and did something to her spine, and she had to stay in a chair or in bed. We all lived in one wing of Carrollton Lodge and my grandparents lived in the other. Grey's mother and my mother were close."

"You mean they were two cold, mean women who enjoyed each other's company," snapped Elsa, scarlet in the face.

"I don't know whether she was cold, my mother," said Flavia. "Just a certain type of woman. I see that now, though she *felt* distant, when I was a child.

"At any rate my mother finally died, of kidney failure and other problems. The day after the funeral, Grey drove to Cudagh and brought you home. Just like that. You were about two years old."

Chapter Sixty-three

"JESUS, WHAT A MAN," said Harris.

"It was outrageous," said Elsa with a smile. "He came for me in a pony cart, possibly so I wouldn't be frightened, as I might have been in a car. For years I remembered the pony walking ahead of us, white with a mousy tail, and passing a man on the blind road behind a donkey burdened with hay, and the man tipping his cap. I used to think it happened later, before he left for Canada, but now I'm sure it was that day. It's my earliest memory. The St. Oeggers please themselves, don't they?"

"The St. Oeggers are something else," said Harris.

He had lit the kindling in the fireplace and was feeding it dried pine cones. They had been staring into the blaze for a while, watching sparks fly against the stones.

"What happened to your mother?" he asked, squatting back on his heels.

"My mother moved to Liverpool before the war, I suppose to find work," said Elsa. "Probably she was glad to see the last of me and begin a new life. She was gone before I was old enough to remember her.

"Fi and Gordie knew, of course. Everybody knew, but no one mentioned it ever. Not the servants at the house, or the fishermen's children in cut-down trousers who took me out in their boats, or the lads in our stables. There are no secrets in Irish country towns, and seven miles is no great length for gossip to travel. Yet I never heard or knew anything. It was miraculous.

"I think no one informed me of it because I was a girl. If I'd been a boy I feel I'd have heard of it somehow. And my father was popular with the people of the district; that also may have been why they said nothing. And of course, we were Catholic."

"I was six when he left for Canada, abandoning me to my grandmother.

She probably hoped I'd tumble unsupervised into a bog hole or drown in one of the canals. I can still understand Irish, and speak it a little, because the kitchen and the laundry room were where I lived. I remember quite well sleeping with the dogs under the big washbasin bolted to the wall."

He was staring at her. He wiped his mouth with the back of his hand to take the grin off.

"You think you've found an ally, don't you?" she said coldly. "It makes you feel damned good to have another foundling to cozy up with."

"Go on."

"Anyway I was dumbfounded the day Flavia told me," said Elsa. "D'you know that phrase, 'the scales fell from his eyes'? When I was a child I used to think they meant fish scales. That day I stared at myself in the mirror, and the scales fell from my eyes."

They were to meet with Grey that evening. Flavia had arranged what she called a sensible discussion, to keep emotions out of it as much as possible.

"You've got a tongue: go in and speak for the child," she said to Elsa before they went in. "Just don't make ultimatums. It'll push him the other way."

"You'd have made a grand lawyer."

Flavia had tea with him and brought Elsa up a plate of food after. She gulped it like one of the ranch dogs, with tears in her throat. They went down together to the study.

In the hallway Elsa heard Sno-Bird at the kitchen range, cooking up potions, whistling incantations under her breath. The Indian woman never left the house while they were there. They did not know where she slept, only that she quelled and soothed, somewhere. At times Elsa was certain they were laboring under a spell Sno-Bird had cast upon them; but of course there was no spell, no force at work for good or evil. They were a family wandering lost in the corridors of their own history, looking for the way out.

Grey was waiting in his big chair that looked like a piece of medieval saddlery. People had traveled in such chairs, swaying on thoroughbraced oak. You could open any book about those times and see the drawings, distempered and spidery, of the powerful horses with the dogs running underneath and the flags overhead, thin against a linotype sky.

In that room of browns, the decanter of whiskey and the lamp with its yellow-threaded shade gave the only color. It was snowing again, a soft wet fall. Globs of white splashed like sea froth on the windows, slid down the glass and dissolved. The weather changed every day in March in the Skillihawk. One day you thought spring was coming, the next it seemed winter would never end.

"Sit," said her father. But they stood the entire time.

The air was heavy with his grief. He watched them enter as though he had forgotten who they were, and why they were to stand before him. A distant world seemed to absorb him, filled with passions and travails and lost expeditions that had never been their concern.

"I've found out I'm your bastard," said Elsa. This sounded so melodramatic that she regretted it instantly.

He was perfectly still. Then he said bitterly to Flavia, "I thought you were going to help."

Flavia, flanking Elsa in the blue suit, flinched but looked resolute.

He studied Elsa. They had not met since the interview in the dining room. "For god's sake, what did he see in you?" he asked.

"I loved him," she answered.

The remaining color drained from his face. He leaped to his feet, seized the decanter and hurled it at the window. It struck the leaded glass; they heard tinkling as the shattered pane fell in pieces on the stone walk outside. Cold air rushed in greedily to devour the heat. The decanter hit one of the leads and dropped to the floor, and whiskey throbbed out of the open stopper onto the carpet.

Grey stared at the spreading puddle, then sank into the chair and dropped his face in his hands.

It's Harris; Harris, thought Elsa in a daze. At her shoulder Flavia had begun to weep quietly. They both would have gone to him if they dared but there was something about him, as though he were finally being bled of a poison that had sickened him for days, that made them know not to touch him. And in the midst of this anguish Elsa stood struck with thunder. She saw how completely he had been betrayed, how she had been nothing but the instrument through which betrayal was accomplished. She saw how complicated human beings really were, how love was not the simple thing that songs made of it but a vast, messy stewpot with everything thrown in, from the purest and most disinterested spirit to the meanest and most vengeful. Even Flavia had plotted against him, striking him a blow in the name of her own morality, which was as essential to her as Gordon's racial hatred was to him.

He regained command of himself. His power returned before their eyes; he was like the old Norse god being reborn in the fairy tale. He used a cotton handerchief, folded and return it to his pocket, then said calmly, "All right, go on. What are you here for?"

"The baby," said Elsa. "I want to keep it. The way you kept me."

"Impossible," he said. "I did what a man should do, acknowledge his child. To a degree that's accepted in this society. You're a girl, you can't flaunt an illegitimate baby."

"Then acknowledge it for *him*."

His face went like granite. "You're mad," he said coldly. "If he were here now I'd kill him."

Flavia had moved forward and was watching them worriedly, like a referee anxious to call a play squarely.

"You brought me to your house to live with that dreadful bitch," said Elsa. "Don't think I don't remember. I bit her hand."

"I took care of it. You've no complaint to make."

"She hated me because of what I was."

"It was unfortunate," Grey said haughtily.

"Unfortunate?" shouted Elsa. "You wanted to do what you did with my mother, didn't you? What was the difference between you and *him*? There *is* no difference. You both got what you wanted."

Flavia gasped. The room was perfectly still. Even the broken window let in no sound. It was always so quiet when it snowed.

"Fi," he said, "this is your doing and I won't thank you for it soon."

"She's done nothing. This is my idea," said Elsa.

"I'm not going to look at his bastard," said Grey, rising. "Not once will I. The fornicating, murdering thief. I won't have all the world knowing what he's done to you."

There was a dumb pause while Elsa gathered herself. "She hated me." Her voice quavered wildly. "That bloody skinny beast-woman."

"Hold your tongue now, girl!"

"You left me with her. You knew what she was. I'll forget everything that happened, how you got me and tossed me away, if you give me what you claimed for yourself."

"You've nothing to claim," he said. "You'll find that out soon enough if you keep your mistake. Nothing will indemnify you. Rights come with a piece of paper and a ceremony and a decent husband."

She began to wheedle. "I won't be here. I'll go away and you'll never see me again. You won't have to ever see it."

"Good! Because if I did . . ." He stopped. "Please leave, both of you. I've got to think. And Flavia, get the dustpan. I'll have to clean up this spill."

. . .

"One of the happy days of my marriage was the day of my wedding," Grey said to Elsa, on a later visit to Salthill. "We drove in a horse and carriage to the hotel in town where we were to spend our wedding night. All along the road bonfires had been lighted for us. It's an old Irish custom. It was a fine summer evening, the hills and road were under the moon, and the fires burned on either side for a mile out of the village." He held the child on his lap under the Jonagold tree and touched his lips to the darling curls. "Love lies thin on the ground, doesn't it?"

"It's all right," she said.

Elsa learned later that it was Sno-Bird, not her father, who had sent for Flavia. It was Sno-Bird who had driven to Dee's in the old Chevy, over the treacherous mucked pass, and summoned Flavia to Salthill. And Flavia had put the tool in her hands.

He let Elsa keep the baby, after more harsh interviews and rounds of silence and gloom. Elsa locked herself in her room and lay like a stone on the bed. At night he sat up drinking too much before the study window where snow piled on the ledges in the dark. Flavia, out for a drive to calm herself, ran the sedan into a ditch. It took Piwonka's men hours to get it out, and she had a terrible weeping bout.

Sno-Bird cooked a soup so good, they had never tasted anything of its like. They avoided the kitchen those days: It was off limits, to prevent the benign spirits that dwelled there from being extinguished by their confusion. Only Sno-Bird moved freely in and out, lithe in blue jeans, with a grace they had once seen only in themselves.

She made the soup on the third morning. At one o'clock, the dinner hour, she brought the tureen into the dining room and set it on the table. There was a plate of sliced bread and butter to go with, but nothing more. Then she left, perhaps to have her own meal in the bunkhouse with Dai.

Although they hadn't sat together in three days, they gathered at the table as obediently as though they had been summoned, and muttered grace, and drank. The soup had a thick, scented, tranquilizing broth. They sat letting it warm their stomachs and moisten their faces with its rising steam. They sighed with relief; they could have wept.

Gradually and warily, then in broken, rushing, hesitant, overconsidered phrases, Flavia and Grey began to speak. Whether the child would remain in the family was then and afterward unmentioned. Flavia treaded with enormous caution, and stuck to practicalities. He watched her with exhausted eyes. He was a little drunk, having begun earlier in the morning on the whiskey in the sideboard.

He said once, "I don't give a damn if I never see her again, Fi. Tell me I won't have to see her again."

"Never," she said.

"She did this. She drove him away. I believe her now."

"Father." Flavia cast an uneasy glance at Elsa, huge and dreamy at the end of the table, as far from her father as she could get.

"I know I'm not being fair," he said. "I'm not being fair to you, am I, girl? But I know what you are now. And what you're getting you'll always regret, because whenever you look at it you'll remember. Pfaugh! The thought makes me sick. How you'll stomach it I can't think."

Gradually he and Flavia began to speak of time and doctors, where Elsa would stay, what must be said to everyone, how devout Iseult was to be dealt with. Elsa was left out of the discussion entirely. She didn't mind. She was getting what she wanted, a miracle.

The soup's fragrance filled the room. They stirred beneath it like flowers in thawing ground, growing hardy, gaining strength enough for anything. Its own, old warmth replaced Grey's bloodshot pallor; his hair glinted gold and red as it had in his youth. Flavia's tremulous expression gave way to serenity, like a woman waking from sleep in a happy mood. At the end of the table, Elsa drowsed. They meditated in unison, not upon resolution but upon a furtive hope.

Flavia helped her pack a few things. Everything was done in a rush, as though they couldn't leave the grief-stricken house fast enough. Elsa was driven away, leaving what she had behind, clothes and art things, boots and books; everything she had collected in six years at Salthill. When you're fleeing a burning house you don't stop for mementos. She was leaving for the unknown, and the third beginning of her life.

Grey drove. Elsa stared at her father's back as he sat at the wheel, in a bomber jacket with a fur nape. She loathed the winter-burned back of his neck. Beside her sat Flavia in tweeds, squeezing her own cold hand with gloved fingers. Outside the fields fell away, crowned with black bramble. Inside the baby, in motion because she was still, swam like a fish in its aqueous portion. Everywhere, silence.

Chapter Sixty-four

"I HAD THE BABY AT A NURSING HOME in Vancouver, and took him to stay with Flavia and Charley," said Elsa. "That winter was the last time I lived at Salthill. The last time I saw Gordon was at his engagement dinner. Flavia wrote and told him what had happened, and he won't allow my name to be spoken in his presence. There has always been something so Victorian about Gordon! He won't come to Canada to see Grey. He told Flavia that Grey and I conspired to rob him of his inheritance. What inheritance? He'll come into my father's fortune in due time. But I know what he means, poor Gordon. We robbed him for our own ends, we left him lying in the road. He lost his place in the family to a traveler. Even after I went back to Salthill to visit, and Grey began to be attached to Sherry, and everyone had got used to seeing the little mulatto boy of the St. Oeggers in Four Queens, shopping with me or eating lunch with his grandfather at the Plaza like the other ranchers' children, he couldn't forgive."

She leaned forward sharply. "Is it painful, hearing this?" He was sitting with his head in his hands. "His grief was so monumental," she said deliberately. "All the while, I knew he would have traded me for you gladly. Isn't love a dreadful, hammering thing?"

He felt a sharp tumult of pity. "You won't be alone anymore," he said.

She ignored this. "Harris, why did you leave?"

"It wasn't going to get any easier," he said.

Her eyes widened. "You won't talk about it."

"No, goddamn it, I won't," he said lightly.

He went out on the porch, wiggling his shoulders. This stuff was work.

She followed him. They leaned on the rail under the sagging arbor, whose blossoms clouded the air with their faint astringency. The sky had cleared and the stars were a flotilla of lights clustered on the sea of night.

"We went to Atlanta, Georgia," said Elsa, "for an exhibition of North American artists. Sherry and I. We had just come from London and I was invited with some other artists. It was a great honor, my first really. People stared. Or looked confused, as though he and I together fit no recognizable pattern, no order. . . . When they heard my accent their faces would clear. . . . I wasn't American, just some foreigner, and god knew what misbegotten cultural freak I was indulging, taking a small Negro child about with me. The rest rooms were marked WHITES ONLY. I took him to a restaurant and we were asked to leave. After that I bought food at a shop and made sandwiches in our room, and found a black maid to look after him when I had to go to the exhibit. She was confused too, even though I explained that it wasn't this way everywhere, that there were entire countries not like this. . . . She looked right through me politely and giggled. We were allowed to stay at our hotel only after the exhibition people threatened to withdraw if we left. Every time I walked through the lobby I could feel eyes burning into my back."

"That's the South," said Harris grimly.

"There was rioting in another part of the city. I saw lurid photos in the newspapers of cars on fire, buildings on fire, people looting shops. Everywhere I sensed a nightmarish desperation. Even though we were far from the troubles, our sleep at night was broken by police sirens and fire trucks rushing past."

"Did you think of me?" asked Harris.

"I couldn't help it. Your image was stamped on every dark face. Once I saw a man with light eyes, a *transformation* into something unbearably powerful, a genesis. Other than that he didn't look like you, he was fair with a buttery fairness and he was freckled. I wondered what roiled his thoughts, carrying that history around inside. . . . Or did he even think of it? He was selling newspapers. . . . Perhaps he was mindless as so many people are, carrying on with his life, ignoring the terrestrial presence glancing back at him in the mirror, no more interested than an Arab horse in its centuries of lineage. . . . Carrying a Founding Father or some Scottish tobacco farmer around in his genes, and a woman of Mali. It was painful for me, seeing it from the perspective of family, from *inside*, our lives shared, without the ideas that had rooted so long in the minds around me. I never *knew*. They were given no quarter at Salthill, those ideas. That was my father's gift."

"Yes, it was."

"And in exchange for it," she said, smiling, "you moved in on us. Relentless, restless man of the diaspora. Always hustling. I believe you call it that?"

"We call it that," he said.

"You had to, to live, I suppose."

"Your viewpoint is myopic," said Harris. "You talk about being *inside,* but you don't know any more about being black in America than I do about the religious wars in Ireland."

"They're not religious," she pointed out gently. "They're land wars."

"So are these," he said.

They stayed on the porch, watching the stars fade, until they were cold and tired of standing.

"Are you ready to let me love you?" asked Harris.

She shivered. "Am I ready to let you love me. What a funny expression 'make love' is. So different from 'fucking.' What *is* the difference?"

"I said love you, not fuck or make love. 'Make love' is make-believe anyway."

"When a man says 'make love' it's heartbreaking somehow," she said. "It makes me feel I *must* be generous. Not with my body but from my heart, as though nothing less could count beside your saying that. Why, why is it so hard for you to say love and do love? We—women—must be satisfied with so little! We weave spells around the word, light candles to it, hope that by gesture or word you'll let us know you've given up and admitted that loving is human. It takes so little time or effort. Yet you act as though love is some intolerable burden, the one that will finally make you crack beneath your load of other burdens."

He leaned on the rail and looked out at the fields, smiling. By this she knew he was angry.

"Don't act confused," she said. "That's another ploy men use, pretending not to understand what women want. They want what anyone else would want, an acknowledgment of love. Not to be on the outside looking in, at a self-sufficiency so dreadful."

He took her in his arms. Her body felt thin and hot under the shirt.

"It was what you were really saying, wasn't it?" she said with her head back. "That summer. That you couldn't do it, you couldn't bear this burden. You'd rather let the romance of puritanism take you down twenty roads than look at the one clear way you have to go."

"Yes," he said. "It was what I was saying. I know that now."

"Are you humoring me?"

"No."

"You drew a firm line between your desire and what I wanted from you. You were not going to commit love."

"But I'm committing love right here," said Harris.

"None of us cared enough to wrench your name out of you and use it. It was a test of *our* love, and we failed it."

"We all fail at times," he said.

"When you said you didn't know whether you loved me because you didn't know what love is, you really meant you don't think anyone does." Her voice rose in panic. "I don't know whether I can stand carrying it all on my back like a donkey, Harris. With no help from you or anyone, just Sophronia and Flavia, who have their own candles to light and their own loads to carry."

"You said it didn't take much time or effort," he pointed out, pressing close.

"Not when I'm alone with it, Harris. I don't think I'm the type. It's too much for me. I've never been afraid of painting or mothering or death, but I'm afraid of this . . . this settling down with what's left after everything else has been burned away."

"Do you think I can't give you what you need?" he asked.

"I'm afraid you won't," said Elsa. "You'll just go back to your horses. You and Grey are alike."

"Stop talking about Grey. I'm not going back to Salthill."

"You'll have to see him sometime. Oh god, don't *do* that."

"I'll see him. Are you ready to be loved? We're going 'round in circles."

"I don't know how we're going to work this out," she murmured under his lips.

"Let's work it out in here," he said firmly, walking her inside with his arm around her shoulders.

They were sitting on the porch steps. The sun sifted through the wisteria onto their necks.

"It's Garnet," he said suddenly, in a formal, dignified voice.

She looked startled. "Like the gem?"

"Yeah." He worked a cigarette butt to shreds with his shoe.

"Garnet Harris?"

"That's right."

"What a splendid name," she said in wonderment. "Garnet! Like the inside of a pomegranate when you open it. Those pearly red seeds."

He was suddenly filled with a swooping panic, as if he had pushed off down a steep slope without even a rudimentary knowledge of skiing, and with no skis. The decision to return to Grey already made long skid marks in his mind. The decision to have Elsa. To be had by Elsa. The decision already taken from him and put in force, to have children. To reclaim a family, the cockeyed, wily and sly St. Oeggers, stepping back into the trap they had unwittingly set for him. Face Grey St. Oegger with his humanity in his hands, admitting that he'd wanted to do what he did over and over, and that if he could, he'd do it again. To say love and do love.

One day, skirting the city limits, Harris passed her old school, with tiled roofs and a campanile over the main entrance. He slowed to look, because it was coeducational now and they—she, her father—had planned for his son to go there. The newer-looking buildings were painted bright colors to get rid of the monastery look; an acre of lawn was taken up by a sheet-cake gymnasium iced in orange and chocolate. The courts and fields were fallow, the nets down for the summer. She had been good at games, swift and with a dead keen eye, fearless in inflicting or receiving injury. There had been no early indoctrination in female decorum to discourage the aggression, patient and cold-blooded as a barn cat stalking a rat, that had made her an alarming presence on the playing field.

He had picked up too, without effort, the aunts' disapproval, muffled and ominous, directed not at the child she was but at life, for allowing wrong to happen. In these people's lives, bad things were not supposed to happen. Yet she had been abandoned. Something always went wrong, no matter how careful, respectable or religious you were. Loaves fell, rain fell, adults practiced their secret desires, tiptoeing off to do what they knew damned well was forbidden and unkind. Their eye rolled past the eye of some priest, himself a flawed creature, and they all marched in a processional toward what they wanted. The trick was making yourself want the right thing, the thing for the common good, because God knew that whatever you wanted, you were going to do.

They were on their way to Salthill in the red truck.

"Elsa. You said Grey loved me as he thought he knew me."

"Yes."

"Could he love what he knows now?"

"I can't tell you that," she said gently. "It would be dangerous and unfair."

She wore a blouse and skirt from Simpson-Sears that had seen better days. Her hair was tied in a scarf with pictures of Lake Louise and Banff painted on it. You're stylish as a motherfucker, he said admiringly when she came out. Stop putting me on, she said. It didn't matter what she wore; she would have looked fine as a duchess in a paper bag. The shapely legs were stockinged and shod in low heels. Since reaching the Skillihawk Trail she had at times crossed and quickly uncrossed them in an exasperated gesture.

"Where were you, Harris, for so long?" she asked.

He lifted her hand out of her lap and sniffed the inside of her wrist. "On a jackladder in Ontario."

She scowled, arm extended. "You just dredged that up."

"Okay. In Newfoundland, curing cod."

"Loading trucks with iron ore in Atikokan," she countered.

"Roughnecking on an oil drill," he said, grinning.

"Raising shorthorn cattle and Marquis wheat."

"Teeming an open-hearth furnace in a steel plant."

"Sourdoughing in the Klondike."

"Yeah. That's how I made my fortune."

She pulled her wrist away. "Oh, dry up."

They passed the library at Main and Leaf where Harris had checked out books. *Bluebeard and Seven Marvellous Tales* came to mind when he saw the building through the trees, with the grated basement and the lawn burned brown. There was a new Indian totem with bird-dragon eyes in the park, looking ancient among the evergreens. It was the tail end of the tourist season, the start of harvest and fall shipping, and the streets were busy. They passed a souvenir shop with sidewalk racks of postcards of Mounties and Parliament buildings in Ottawa. No one paid them any mind. They were just two more strangers, unmatched, and it was hard to see in the cab.

As Harris was congratulating himself on slipping unnoticed through town, he heard a shout from the sidewalk:

"Hey, Miz Elsa!"

"Hullo, Clem!" called Elsa out the window.

Harris glanced at the red light and swore under his breath.

Clem Lemuels swung his double canes across the intersection. His wife came too, a big Yorkshire woman who listed from side to side in opposing rhythm to her husband's forward grab and swing. Clem owned the local hauling service. He had lost his leg the summer Harris got the Red, when his truck went off a bridge and into the Enid. He had stayed pinned between two boulders, in rolling water up to his chest, until someone came over the bridge and saw the broken rail.

Traffic flowed around the truck, slow foot and motor under the mountains in their haze. Clem stuck his grizzled head in the passenger window. "Now what are you doing up here, little girl?" Then he saw Harris.

"We're on our way home," said Elsa.

Their faces stiffened. Mrs. Lemuels raked him with her eyes. Elsa held out her hand to show the band on her finger. There was a fleck of red paint under one nail.

"You're *married*?" boomed Mrs. Lemuels.

"Well, well," said Clem. "Welcome back, young fellow."

"Thanks," said Harris.

Two Klaxta passed in front of the truck. One of them glanced in the window, then said something to his companion. They stepped onto the curb and were gone.

"Glad to see you taking advantage of opportunity," said Clem. "You got your work cut out for you. I guess you know that."

"Yes," said Harris.

They had to sit through another red light. The town had lost its air of untouchable distance and seemed to fit around him in a new way. Harris saw legions of armed men strung across the top of a hill, lances sharp, him in a draw, waiting grinning with a slingshot.

"Well, that does it for Four Queens," said Elsa as they turned onto Seventeen. "It's going around the Plaza as we speak, being dinnertime. I'm dying for a cigarette." She had given up smoking.

"He was hostile," said Harris.

"I think he was just startled."

"He fucking disapproved."

"He'll get over it."

He saw the Klaxta coming in two days or three, bearing salmon jerky, to sit with him in the oven heat of the truck. He saw Four Queens buzzing like a knocked-over beehive. He saw himself being cold-shouldered, welcomed, grilled, socked in the mouth.

"Let's throw a barbecue," he said suddenly. It sounded good, a barbecue. How long since he'd been to one? Years, under shaggy trees in the back field at Taylorsville, smoke rising over the grass and everybody dark, his people, cousins, uncles, aunts, the languid women and men he would never see again.

Back ribs and potato salad, uhm. He'd have to make sure Sno-Bird put enough brown sugar in the beans.

"What a good idea," said Elsa. "The Skillihawk will come and inspect you. Get it over in one day."

"Maybe he won't want to. It may be all he can tolerate to see me by himself."

"Are we going to do this, for god's sake?" she said. "Just *be,* without any commitment but the one you made when I shot that man? That will have to do, won't it?

"*I* made a commitment?"

"You gave me asylum. You let me know it was all right to be slightly mad as long as we were just: eye for eye, tooth for tooth. As long as we admitted it and knew the shadows that roamed beside us."

"I recognized you, that's all."

She gave him her fierce hawk face, then laughed, in one of those freshets of humor that were growing familiar to him. She always seemed most dangerous then, because he was never fooled by her merriment into mistaking it for goodwill.

He pulled onto a shoulder at the foot of the pass.

"Yeah. That was the commitment," he said. "It's good for all time."

"You are an austere man," she muttered. "When I was young it anchored me. Now I don't know."

"Don't think," he said.

"It's too much." Their hands fumbled. Hers were cold. "I can't stand being filled and emptied like this."

"Hush. I'm giving up, too. Remember?"

They exchanged shining looks.

There had been no Indian summer for years, she said, just the ending of the hot days and the start of autumn. When Harris rolled the window down, the air that pushed against his hand was warm and heavy. The benchland stretched ahead, solid gold with coniferous woods, the dark green and bronze stippled with aspens starting to turn. Spills of white and yellow sego lily blanketed the steep upper slopes. They passed cattle, a few Brahma and a sprinkling of buffalo with bearded faces.

"Marv's gotten interested in what he calls 'alternative' breeds," Elsa explained. "The buffalo are for the American market and he crosses the Brahma with shorthorns. They're tick and drought resistant."

He listened. It kept him from thinking about what lay ahead.

The row of birches appeared beside the road, dry fields the color of oatmeal swelling gently above the branches. Harris shifted into second to cross the ditch. As they wound through the dense wood toward the crown of the hill, waiting for the house roofs to appear above the grass moving like a nap beneath the heavy air, he felt a rush of emotion. It grew with each turn of the wheels, the past singing to him, like an eagle turning in its flight. Grey and him on horseback, riding beneath Mount Endeavour. The tamaracks rising in dark green spears before the mountains. The knife skidding and flashing in the snow. The Red soaring over a fence, his tail held up with life. Images carved in stone, springing out of the daytime shadows—wolves, bears, birds, all eerie and fierce-looking, with fruit vines and strange flowers woven in between. The saloon in Four Queens. The Klaxta dance hall. Beautiful brides, stone-faced chieftains and wild, piped reels. Lake Lavender shaking out its crests in the sun of noon.

At the top of the path still planted on either side with lobelia and dog-wood, beside the weathered bell on its hanger, were two figures nearly comic in their lopsidedness: one tiny, one towering. He could detect no sign of movement or separation between them. They were waiting, the boy standing still, the way he had noticed children did when their attention was com-pletely taken up, the man beside him seated and intent. As his foot felt automatically for the brake Harris saw the still-powerful arms shoot out, brace the wheels and spin them around. He stared at rubber-lined chrome, legs twigging under a tartan blanket.

He parked in front of the gate with the flowering vine and sat behind the wheel.

"I would have had to come back this winter, to take care of him," mused Elsa.

"He was walking," he said stupidly.

"Sometimes he does. We've built a ramp in front," said Elsa. "He has the whole ground floor and the garden."

"He'll never ride again, will he."

"No," she said.

They climbed the steps. The white face watched, grim, gaunt and fleshless against the dark stone, as he climbed. Harris stepped on a loose flag and stumbled forward, just when he was hoping to look good. Then he was swept with pity; the face above him seemed to break into ugly shards, the pieces struggling, like emotions, against themselves, the eyes flaring with rancor but the rims damp. The child darted forward as if after a bird, with the same impulse as flight. Harris saw Grey squeeze the small hand to bring him back, saw the child fuse himself to Grey's side, so that man and boy faced them together as one. His heart turned over with jealousy. All this, before he had reached the old bell on its hanger.

"This is Sherry," said his mother, with a hand on the boy's shoulder.

The boy looked small for his age, even to him who was unused to children. He was diminutive, even elfin. He wore a little polo shirt, a pair of shorts and sandals. His hair was soft, not nappy but full of loose spronging urchin curls, nutmeg streaked with blond from the sun, or from his St. Oegger blood. He was staring at Harris the way his mother had stared at Harris the day he came to Salthill. Harris realized that this might be the first time the boy had seen a man of his color. Women were different to children; you knew their hands, their bellies, the backs of their legs, their smell. The parts represented so much that the whole was a long time being put together, and even then you saw the whole through a haze of old remembered needs. A man was an iconic figure; you saw him all at once; he appeared to you the same when you were five as when you were fifty, like a horse standing on a hill.

"Hello, son," he said, and offered his hand.

The boy touched it reluctantly with a little paw. "Hullo." In that word Harris could hear the St. Oegger inflection. His eyes looked pale as spit, lighter than in the painting, water-green threaded with a minute, tigerish gold.

"We saw Clem and Kate Lemuels in Four Queens," said Elsa, kissing her father's forehead. He moved his head away slightly.

"Wonderful," he said in a dry voice, watching Harris. "The place is on its end by now."

"Where's Scottie?"

"Inside. Helping Sno-Bird with luncheon. Are you hungry, young man?"

"No," said Harris. "Are you?"

Grey laughed. "You haven't changed, have you? Remember how hard you worked to get a job here? You jumped one of my horses over a six-foot fence in the dark."

"I remember," said Harris.

"I don't want any nonsense out of you two," said Elsa sharply. "I'm not interested in your bloody feelings about each other. Sherry, will you please ask Sno-Bird if we can have lunch in the garden?" The boy gave Harris a last spit-pale look and ran into the house.

Chapter Sixty-five

IT WAS MIDDAY. Harris let himself into the kitchen from the side porch. The women were working at the sink. When they stood side by side, before one of them moved away to get something, you could tell they were sisters. Flavia was more hourglassy than Elsa, but their shapes were the same. Their legs were long, and the same rear end flared out neatly from under each apron. The kids had come in from the yard. Grey was sitting at the table waiting, his wheelchair folded against the wall.

Harris saw them from a distance, as a stranger. A stranger once known, living among people slowly recovering from amnesia. He had misused them, had set a cat among the pigeons, to borrow one of their own idle references. Now Flavia, passing him with a stack of plates, smiled brilliantly, her eyes and lips not matching. The eyes said, *Please don't mind our taking so long with this. We're trying to learn you again.* She looked cool as always, with her hair pulled back and not a drop of sweat on her radiant brown skin.

He went to wash his hands.

He had spent the morning cutting hay. They were having a heat wave, in October. The valley lay panting under it. Men were coming tomorrow to reap and bind the hay; in this heat it would be cured by noon. When he turned the tractor around in the field the sky had been the color of a spectacular peach in bloom, a fuzzy hot pinkish gold. There wasn't a single cloud, just the sky burning over the tamaracks. The drone of an airplane matched the grizzling of the tractor as it bumped over the dry clods. One of his nephews ran out in the middle of the field and waved at him to get washed up for dinner, and he finished the section and shut off the engine. The airplane had vanished. There was no sound anywhere. Even the birds had gone off to sleep in the cooler glades. On the porch, he peeled off his socks and left them draped beside his boots like the skins of small animals.

The three boys were running underfoot, filling the kitchen with noise. The windows had been left open to confound the heat, but even though a little air stirred the curtains it hadn't cooled down much.

"Everybody sit," said Flavia.

Her children, Dean and the other boy, the one only a few months younger than Sherry, rustled around grabbing chairs. Both boys were dark, being a quarter Haida, with dark blue merry eyes. Sherry was the solemn one with ash-leaf stare, the one who smiled slowly when he understood something.

Harris took the chair next to Grey. Walter the hired man came in, hung his high-crowned hat on a nail on the porch and sat on Grey's other side. The two men instinctively did this every day. Sometimes, seeing the older man's head turn toward him when he came in, tired and dusty from the work, Harris knew why. Sherry sat next to his father, probably because he had been told to, the women across the table. Sun poured through the screens onto their heads and set their hair on fire.

There was a clink of silver hitting the floor. "Jared," said Flavia in an undertone. "Get another fork. You're going to get a talking-to if you can't behave."

The men said nothing. It wasn't their job to keep children quiet.

Elsa brought a pan of rolls to the table. Her face was flushed and her hair frizzing; she didn't take the heat as well as Flavia. As she set the pan down, reaching between two heads, their eyes met. They stared at each other for seconds. Even with their eyes locked, Harris could see the tops of her breasts inside the sort of low neck of her housedress. He saw them the way you did when a woman wearing a dress like that leaned forward a little. The breasts thinned out and drooped soft and loose, so you thought of gathering them in your hands.

But it was so goddamned hot.

She dropped her eyes and moved away, but not before he saw a little smile soften her face. He watched her blow sideways at the hair falling over one eye, and sit down slowly next to her nephew.

Harris woke, dazed, to his son intoning grace with the requisite swiftness. His voice with its Irish inflection rose and fell like deer bounding liquidly through undergrowth. "Bless us, O Lord, and these Thy gifts which through Thy bounty we are about to receive through Christ Our Lord Amen."

The food started around, coleslaw and beans one way, meat and potato salad the other. Harris forked up cold ham for Sherry, looking down at the curly head as he laid a slice on his plate. He and his son didn't talk much yet. They were still strangers to each other. He didn't know what to say to the boy. He was too formal. He wasn't used to kids. He held the platter for Grey to help himself. Across the table the women were buttering bread and pouring lemonade, their faces composed, their arms flowing away from their bodies and back like sailors rowing to the tinkle of ice cubes.

Grey moved the fork slowly toward his mouth, the fork wavering. It was one of his bad days. Elsa had said once that her father looked like a grandee. He was a negative of himself now, ghostly and dehydrated, colorless except for a mottling of veins on his cheeks and a pink crust on one ear. He had kept his thick hair, now dry and haylike, and although the skin around his knuckles was loose, the blond hair still grew plentifully on the backs of his hands.

Harris dug into his potato salad. Grey's arm and his brushed in their sleeves, faintly signaling the muscle and sinew beneath. He darted a glance at Elsa. She was watching him. She reached for a roll and broke it open without taking her eyes off his mouth. Steam burst out of the roll. She patted blindly around for the butter knife. A bead of perspiration glided down her neck and vanished into the opening of her dress. Another drop appeared in the hollow of her throat, where the moisture collected in a mist. He felt a shudder, then the stinging fire, and thought how simple it was. He made the look on his face shut up and common, his eyes blank as if he hunched over his food. He ate slowly, tearing off pieces of the bread balanced like an oar on his plate, hearing his swallowing crackle in his ears.

"Mummy, can we let the dogs in?" asked Sherry.

"I'm sorry," she said calmly. "Not today."

The boy hung his head in disappointment. Flavia didn't like the dogs under the table. When she was visiting they were shut up on the veranda. Her mystery was a fragrance, no more to be named than you could step outside one spring day and identify the soft air that stirred the ghosts of past springs in your heart. He did not know her. Of all the ones at the table, she was the one he had known the least.

"Did you have to prime that engine?" Grey asked. "It sounds like a machine gun."

"Yeah, with about two cups of gas," said Harris, fighting his way to the edge of the spell. "The carburetor's going."

"The whole job's going, but I can't afford another machine. You'll have to keep feeding it."

"Remember the steam-driven Harvester?" said Flavia. "You had to build a fire under it, literally. I was always afraid it was going to turn over and burn up the field."

"You're wasted on cutting hay," said Grey to him. "Who's working the two-year-olds?"

They all looked at each other. "I am," said Elsa. Her voice sounded thick.

"I thought you were painting." They were turning Grey's room upstairs into a studio, with burlap on the floor. When the snow fell they were going back down to pick up her art equipment—the canvases, paint tubes, the crusts and stains and evidential colors and stinks of her world.

"Walter could run the tractor," said Grey.

"I'm nearly done," Harris answered.

"There are yearlings down there waiting to be trained."

"I'll train them. Don't worry."

"I thought I'd take the finished ones," said Flavia. "Before I leave. I don't ride enough at home, there's so much to do."

"Take that red colt out," said Harris. "Put him over some natural barriers. He's a shy jumper."

"All right," said Flavia.

Silence fell over the table.

The kitchen and family and eating sounds flowed around them; the clink of utensils, the rustling murmurs, the squirming of bodies and small legs stuck like dry leaves to hot chairs. Flavia made a remark about the heat. Then Walter said something. Once in a while he would put down his fork and just sit there in wonder at the power flowing between them, the way the faint breeze from the windows wafted their desire back and forth, lightly kissing their skins. And then her eyes would almost close and her irises gleam like a wolf's between the drooping lids, a pale, sorrowing gaze that meant he knew what. He wanted to stand up and kick the chair over behind him and grasp her by the arms.

Finally the meal was over. Everybody scattered, the boys to the yard, their son too, running along hard behind his cousins, afraid of missing something. Flavia and Elsa started clearing up. Harris went outside and called to the boys, hollering down the hill.

"Hey! Get up here and help your mothers with the dishes."

They came plodding back, looking surprised. He never told them to do anything.

Harris let the dogs out and took Grey to the veranda. They sat together and smoked a cigarette, not saying much. Since his return to Salthill, Harris had kept a waiting brief on Grey. Through the screen door he saw the boys running back down the path. Walter followed, headed for the bunkhouse in the flat white glare for the nap any sensible man would want to take in this heat.

"I'd better lie down," said Grey finally.

Harris rolled him back to his room. Grey was capable of handling the wheelchair alone, he could even use the crutches to get around, but not today. He had silently allowed Flavia to help him up that morning.

The turret room was dark.

"Open the window," said Grey roughly. "I'm a cripple, I'm not blind."

Harris drew back the heavy curtains that bad sleepers had in their rooms and threw the windows wide. Heat from outside blasted into the room. It felt fine to stretch, release some of that tension. He felt springy and good. The grass in the garden was jewel green because Sno-Bird kept it wet. Deer still came in over the wall in front and sometimes ate the flowers right off the bushes.

"You think you're going to get this place, don't you," said the man behind him. "Just come in here and sweep everything clean."

"No," he said.

"Sweep me out of here too. I'm gone already."

"I'm here to work, not get you out."

"What a fool I must have looked, offering you a partnership that evening, ignorant of what was going on in my house." The voice was harsh and depressed. "Do you know what I've wondered? Not that I let it keep me awake at night."

"What."

"Although it did at first. Not the outrage to my daughter. You saw your chance there and took it. Who but she could have brought you back? God help you if she had been a day under sixteen when it happened; I would have put an end to you with a smile."

He faced Grey. "It wasn't like that. It was between me and her. You never entered into it at all. If you think I had other plans, you're mistaken."

"I've wondered since then what you really wanted from us," said Grey as though he hadn't spoken. "Whether you've left your heart buried in some long-ago field or whether it's available."

"It's available," said Harris.

"I hope getting what you want doesn't break it. Help me into this damned bed."

He helped Grey lie on the bed in his clothes and put the chair against the wall. Back here where the bed had been moved, it was dark even with the curtains open. Grey lay in the dimness, his legs that weren't really useful anymore stretched on the maroon spread like two pieces of wood. He could see Grey clearly, but he couldn't read the expression in the blue grandee eyes.

"What are you going to do on *my place* now, I wonder?" said Grey bitterly.

"I'm going to take my wife upstairs," he said after a silence.

Grey got up on his elbows. "I had my day," he said. "By god, I had my day."

"You still do," said Harris. "It's just a different day."

"You don't know what I mean."

"I think I know," said Harris, sitting on the bed, no longer angry. "Look, I'm here, okay? It doesn't matter why. I've always tried not to burn too bright. Maybe I was afraid my feelings would get in the way of my intentions. Now I know I can't afford not to feel them, no matter what the price. I learned that from you."

Grey looked away toward the window, a glance of bitter longing. There was a thread of broken capillary in the white of one eye.

"I won't let you down," said Harris. "I promise it."

"Your small son Sherry means a great deal to me," said Grey, studying him. He extended a rail-thin hand. "I suppose you'll work yourself to death as a way of making amends."

"I might could do that," said Harris. His warm dark hand lay briefly over the dry white one, which did not reject it.

"I'll feel better later." The eyes whose icy and warm blues had one day rearranged themselves for him completely and forever closed. The lids were translucent, like onionskin. "Forgive me, I'd better rest. Leave me be."

He let himself out the door quietly. Down the hall she was waiting. He could hear her breath inside his heart place. *This was what you didn't want to know,* he said to the man on the bed. And the thought was gone.

The dishes were drying in the rack, her apron hanging on the hook by the sink with the other household aprons. When she heard his step she turned, clutching a tea towel.

"They went to Piwonka's in the sedan," she breathed. "All of them." She said it as if she was having trouble moving her lips. Harris felt the same way standing there, as if everything was made of lead, slowly heating at the forge of the kitchen.

She dropped the towel and lifted her arms. He kissed her with his hand twisted in her hair. She was nearly as tall as he was. She groaned.

He said nothing. Men were silent, women got to groan.

She picked the shirttail out of his jeans and clasped his bare middle. His nipples stood up like gooseflesh. She slid her hands under his arms and felt the hair in his armpits. She touched his eyelids, beard, lips.

They stumbled up the stairs, searing each other with a deadly look at every third step. In the hall upstairs he pressed her against the wall, lifted her hair and buried his face in her neck. Their clothes stuck to their bodies; there were dark soaked circles under their arms and in the hollows of their backs. The floor under them seemed to vibrate with mirages the way the land did in summer.

Their room had been Gordon's room. It had fine big casement windows open to the sky, facing north above the veranda. Even unshaded, it was cooler than the kitchen. They fell fumbling onto the dotted Swiss spread. He undid the damp front of her dress.

"Darling," she whispered.

He got up to take off his shirt. The room faced the great sweep of the valley, and the peak called Skillihawk, glittering with granite and sharp wind gaps. He had wondered since his return why Grey had chosen the south-facing room to sleep in when he first came to Salthill. Was it because the view from here was too much, and a man had to get away from it to visualize conquering it? He began to close the curtains. He wanted them drawn now, to dampen the sun's strength and wrap the room in a gauze. He moved from one window to the next. The valley appeared briefly in each, framed in muslin folds, yellow under the fruity sky, the mountains sand castles in various stages of mutilation or destruction by sea. To his right appeared a mirror in which he saw accidentally, because he seldom looked in mirrors, himself, a blaze of copper and bronze like an ancient wood, the arms burned dark, the eyes alive and intent.

"I wanted to destroy your composure, and all you did was duck your head to evade me and stare at your plate," came her voice. "I wanted you to show your lust at the table; I wanted to shame you and bring you to the flame of battle. I wanted to taste the food on your plate and fork it into my mouth because your mouth had tasted it. I wanted to drown in your saliva."

He stood before Mount Endeavour, the red drift of ridges in their autumnal velvet. A few clouds were beginning to smudge the lustrous plain of the sky.

"Look," he said gently. "I'm running this place now. I'm the boss. I won't hurt you but you have to understand." He stopped.

"I do understand," she said.

"All I'm saying is, it's just me here," he said.

He glanced at her lying on the bed. Her hair spilled over the bedspread, honey streaked with brown, dark at the roots as if the heat between them had gathered in a thunder in the long thick hair. She had her waiting look on, the look that said nothing was going to stop them.

"Yes," she said in that drowned voice. "Come, my darling. Please."

He drew in his breath and turned away from the window, feeling without looking for the studs on his jeans.